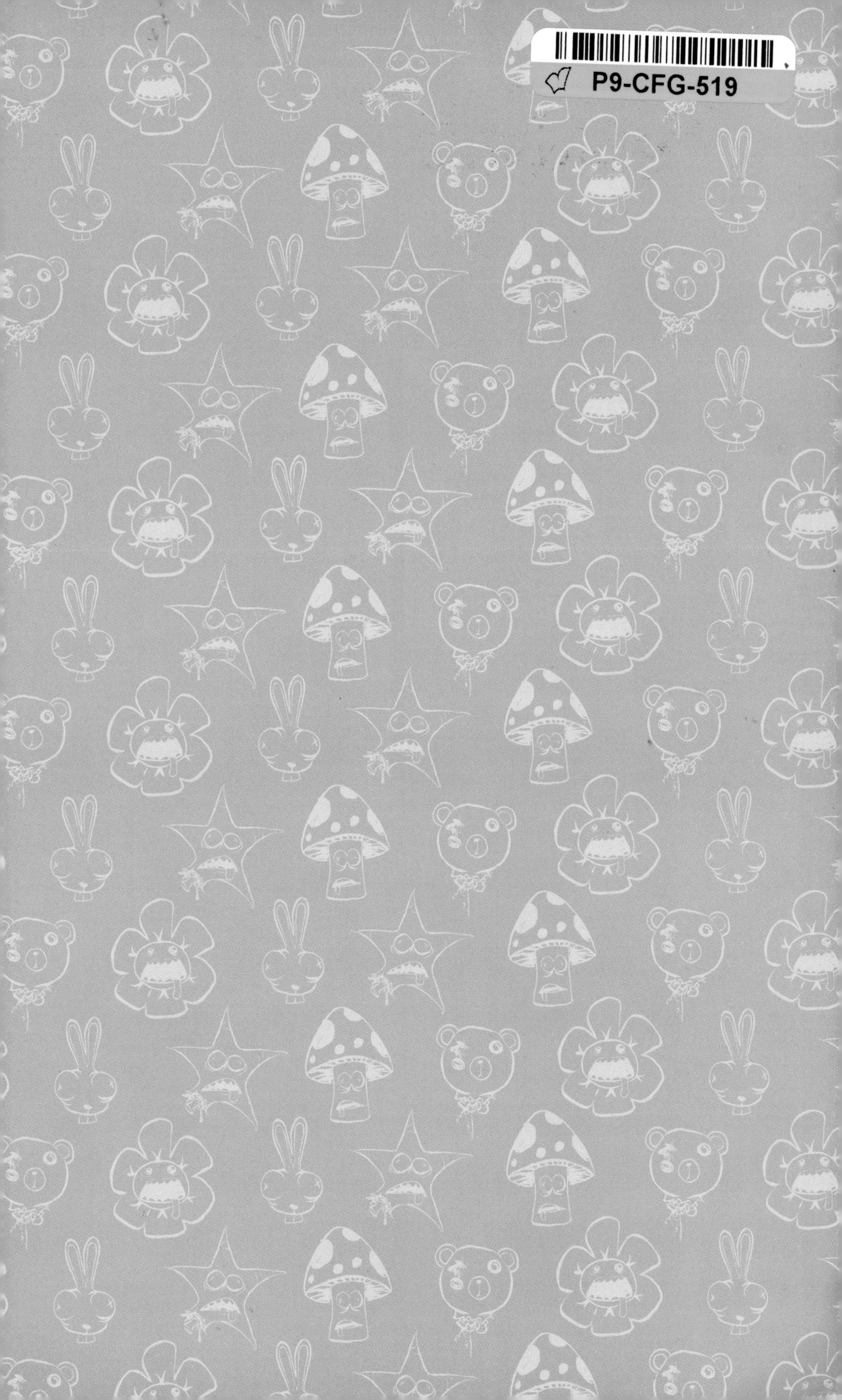

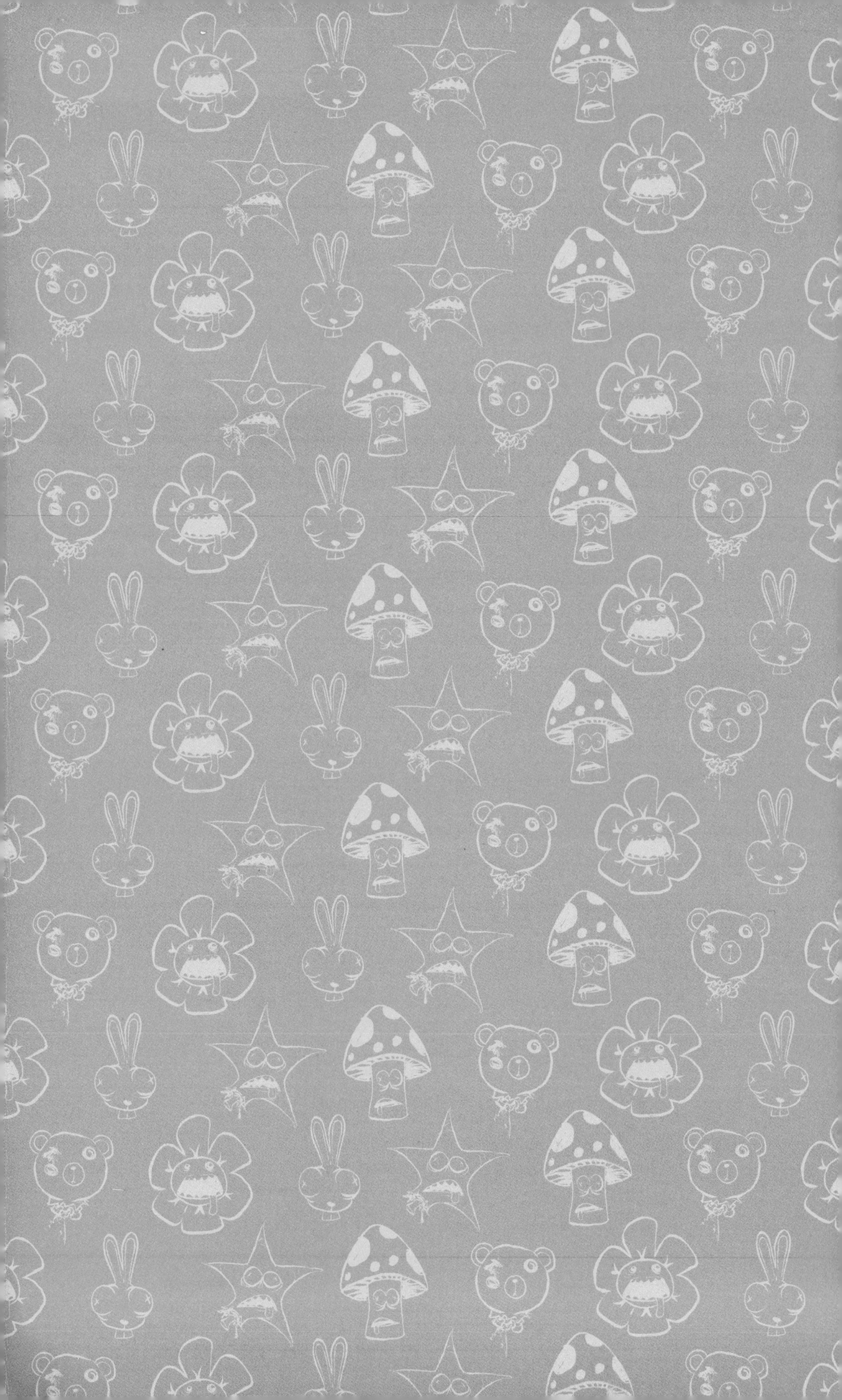

*"It was a nightmare. Nothing
but the green of her hair . . .
and the blood of my people."*

- Thaddeus J. Star, RIP

I HATE FAIRYLAND

VOLUME ONE: MADLY

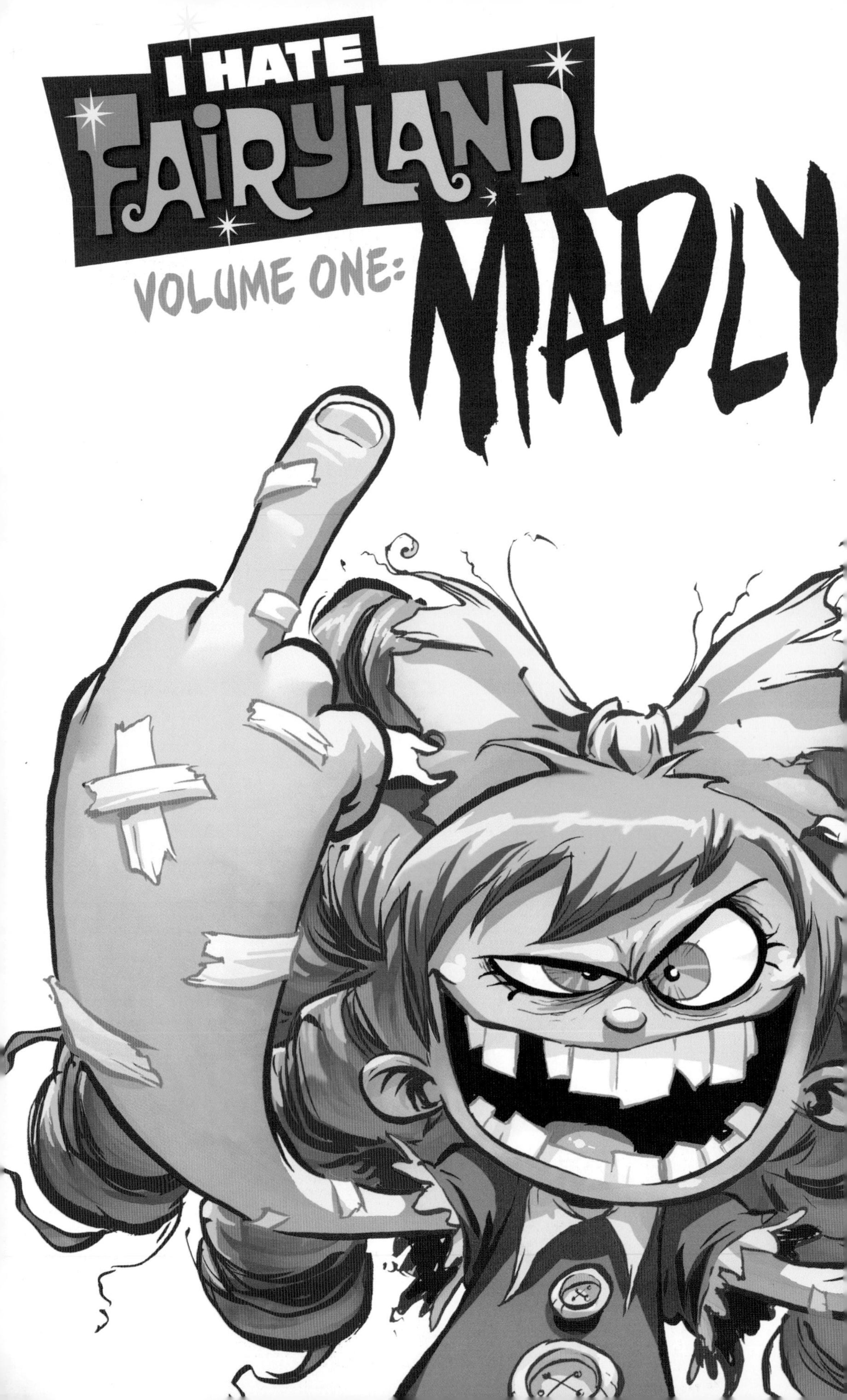

EVER AFTER

Written and Drawn by
SKOTTIE YOUNG

Coloring by
JEAN-FRANCOIS BEAULIEU

Lettering & Design by
NATE PIEKOS
OF BLAMBOT®

Logo Design by
RIAN HUGHES

IMAGE COMICS, INC.　imagecomics.com

Robert Kirkman - Chief Operating Officer
Erik Larsen - Chief Financial Officer
Todd McFarlane - President
Marc Silvestri - Chief Executive Officer
Jim Valentino - Vice-President
Eric Stephenson - Publisher
Corey Murphy - Director of Sales
Jeff Boison - Director of Publishing Planning
　　and Book Trade Sales
Jeremy Sullivan - Director of Digital Sales
Kat Salazar - Director of PR & Marketing
Emily Miller - Director of Operations
Branwyn Bigglestone - Senior Accounts
　　Manager
Sarah Mello - Accounts Manager
Drew Gill - Art Director
Jonathan Chan - Production Manager

Meredith Wallace - Print Manager
Briah Skelly - Publicity Assistant
Sasha Head - Sales & Marketing
　　Production Designer
Randy Okamura - Digital Production
　　Designer
David Brothers - Branding Manager
Ally Power - Content Manager
Addison Duke - Production Artist
Vincent Kukua - Production Artist
Tricia Ramos - Production Artist
Jeff Stang - Direct Market Sales
　　Representative
Emilio Bautista - Digital Sales Associate
Leanna Caunter - Accounting Assistant
Chloe Ramos-Peterson - Administrative
　　Assistant

Standard Cover, ISBN: 978-1-63215-685-3
Forbidden Planet/Big Bang Comics Variant, ISBN: 978-1-63215-820-8
Newbury Comics Variant, ISBN: 978-1-63215-821-5
Daydreams Comics Variant, ISBN: 978-1-63215-828-4
Third Eye Comics Variant, ISBN: 978-1-63215-845-1
Jesse James, Hypno Comics, A Comic Shop Variant, ISBN: 978-1-63215-847-5
Books A Million Variant, ISBN: 978-1-63215-853-6

I HATE FAIRYLAND Volume I: MADLY EVER AFTER - April 2016 - First Printing
Published by Image Comics, Inc. Office of publication: 2001 Center Street, 6th Floor, Berkeley, CA
94704. Copyright © 2016 Skottie Young. All rights reserved. Originally published in single magazine form
as I Hate Fairyland #1-5. I Hate Fairyland™ (including all prominent characters featured herein), its logo and
all character likenesses are trademarks of Skottie Young, unless otherwise noted. Image Comics® and its
logos are registered trademarks of Image Comics, Inc. No part of this publication may be reproduced or
transmitted, in any form or by any means (except for short excerpts for review purposes) without the
express written permission of Image Comics, Inc. All names, characters, events and locales in this
publication are entirely fictional. Any resemblance to actual persons (living or dead), events or places,
without satiric intent, is coincidental. Printed in the USA. For information regarding the CPSIA on this
printed material call: 203-595-3636 and provide reference # RICH - 674536. For international rights,
contact: foreignlicensing@imagecomics.com

ONE

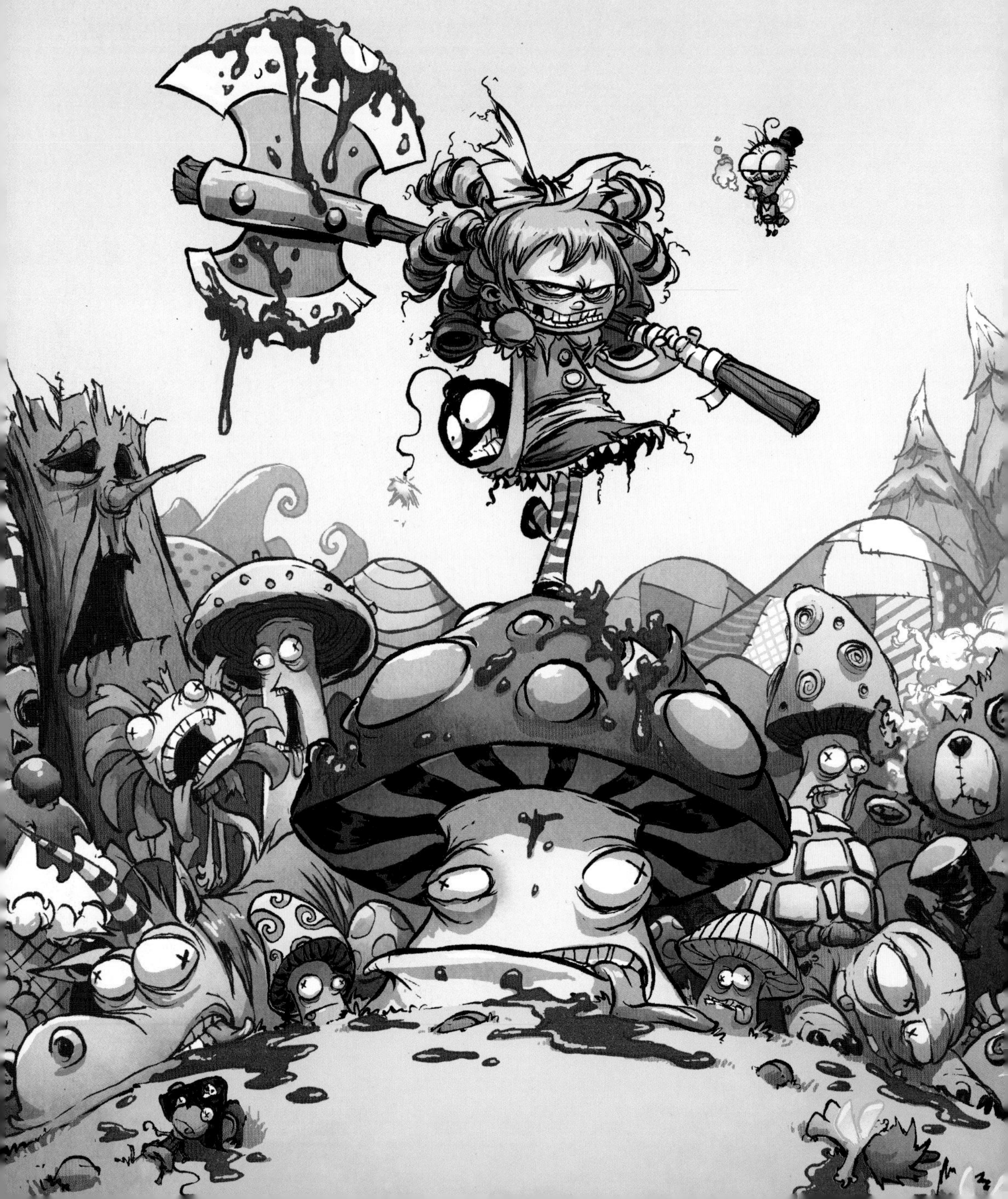

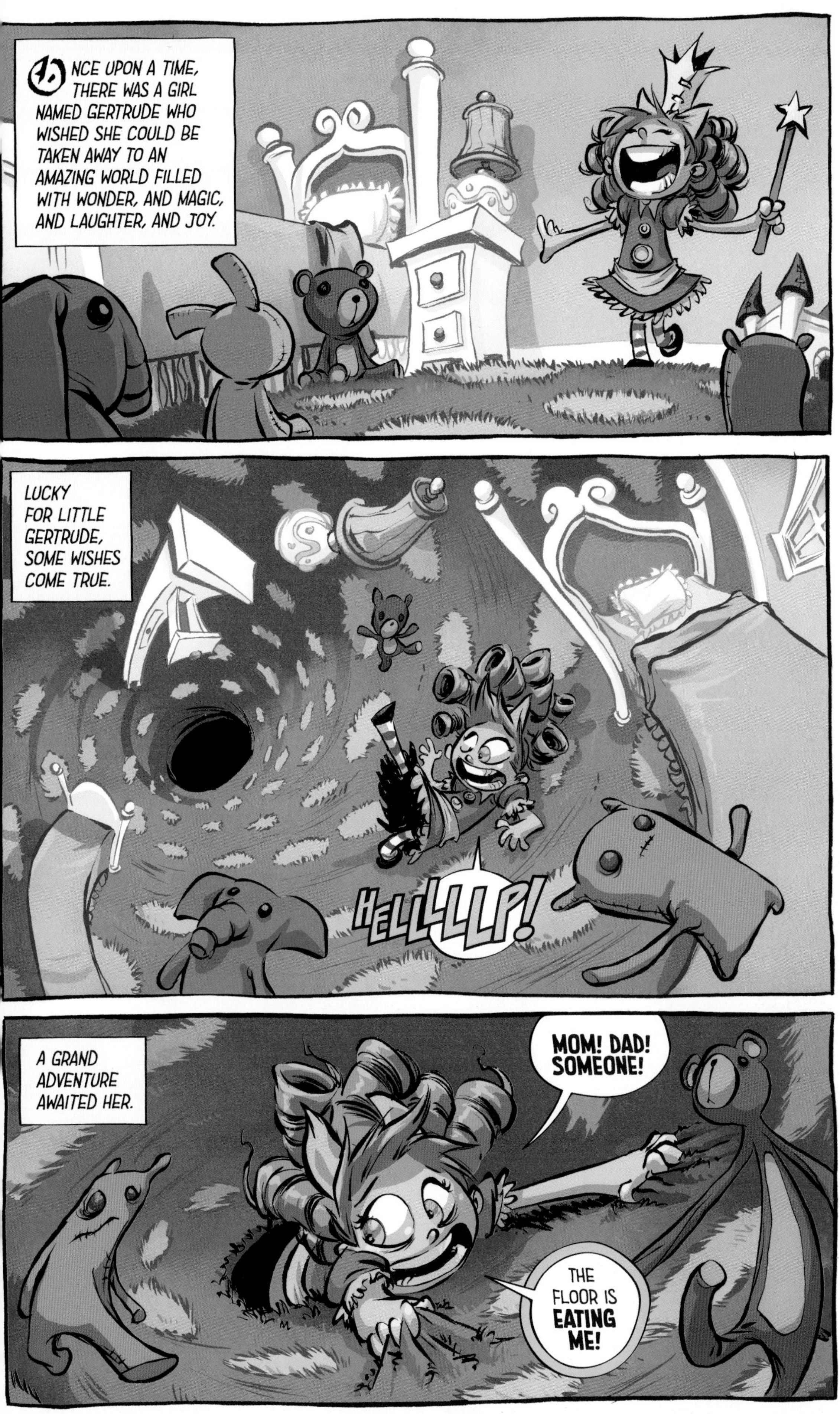
ONCE UPON A TIME, THERE WAS A GIRL NAMED GERTRUDE WHO WISHED SHE COULD BE TAKEN AWAY TO AN AMAZING WORLD FILLED WITH WONDER, AND MAGIC, AND LAUGHTER, AND JOY.
LUCKY FOR LITTLE GERTRUDE, SOME WISHES COME TRUE.
HELLLLLP!
A GRAND ADVENTURE AWAITED HER.
MOM! DAD! SOMEONE!
THE FLOOR IS EATING ME!

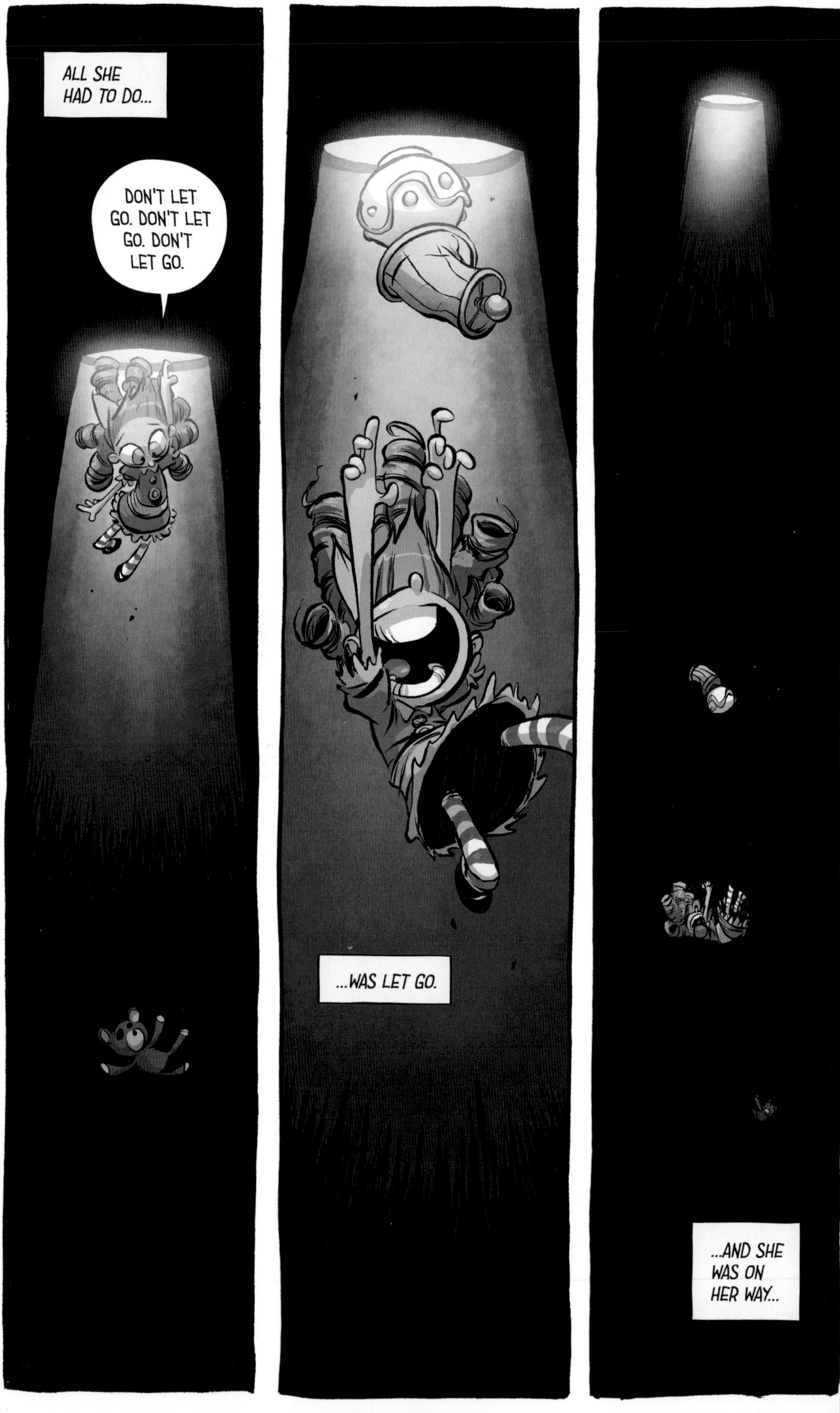
ALL SHE HAD TO DO...
DON'T LET GO. DON'T LET GO. DON'T LET GO.
...WAS LET GO.
...AND SHE WAS ON HER WAY...

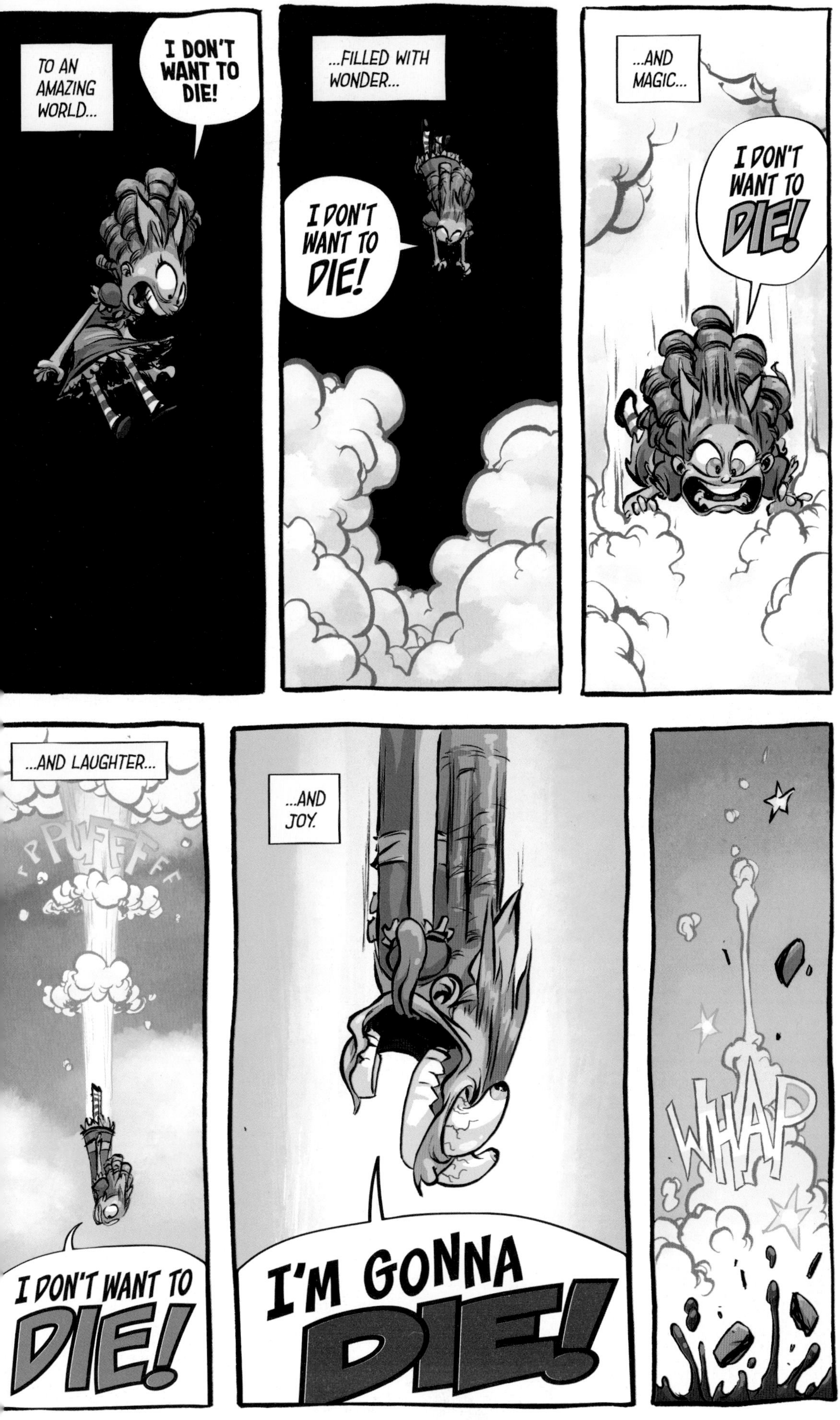
TO AN AMAZING WORLD...
I DON'T WANT TO DIE!
...FILLED WITH WONDER...
I DON'T WANT TO DIE!
...AND MAGIC...
I DON'T WANT TO DIE!
...AND LAUGHTER...
PPUFFFFFF
I DON'T WANT TO DIE!
...AND JOY.
I'M GONNA DIE!
WHAP

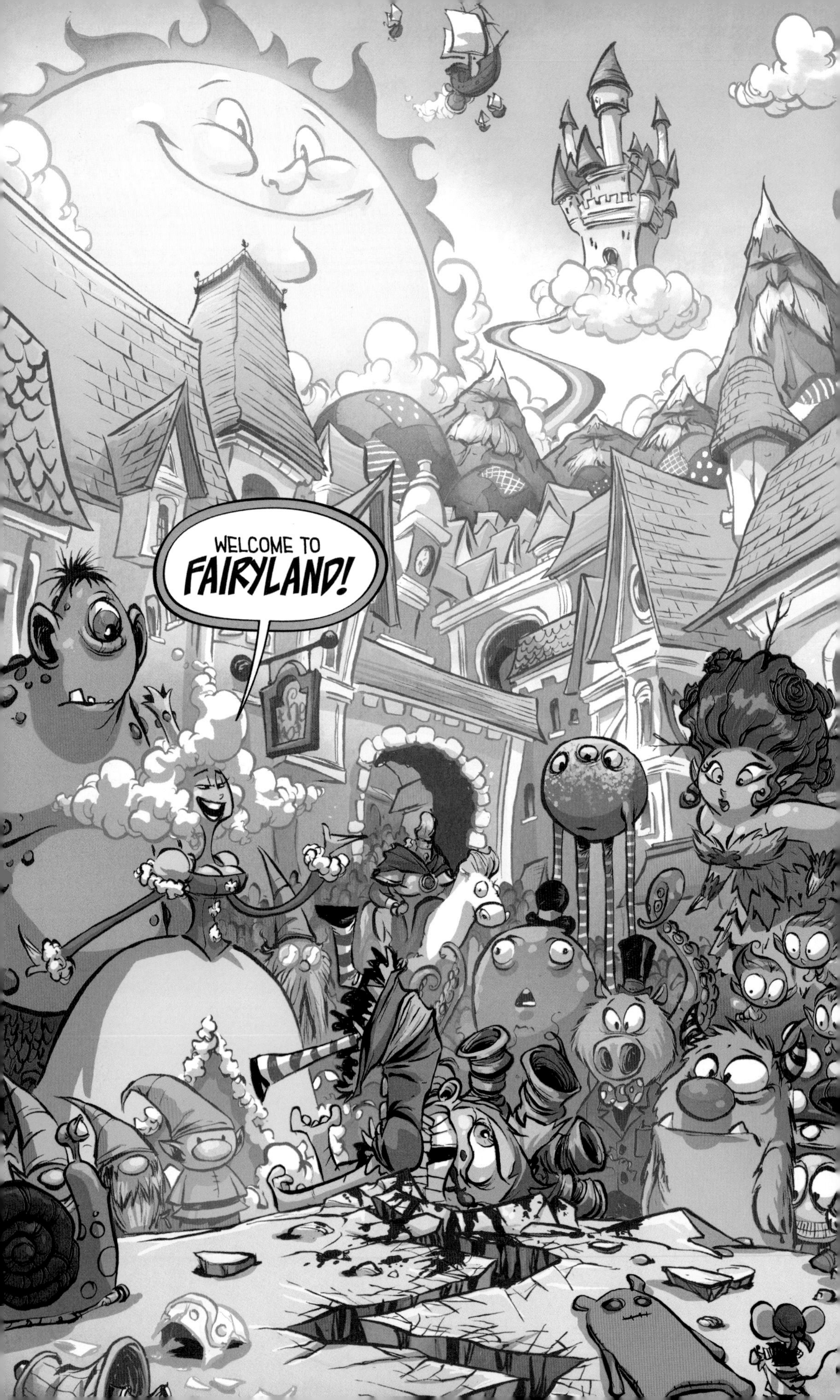
WELCOME TO FAIRYLAND!

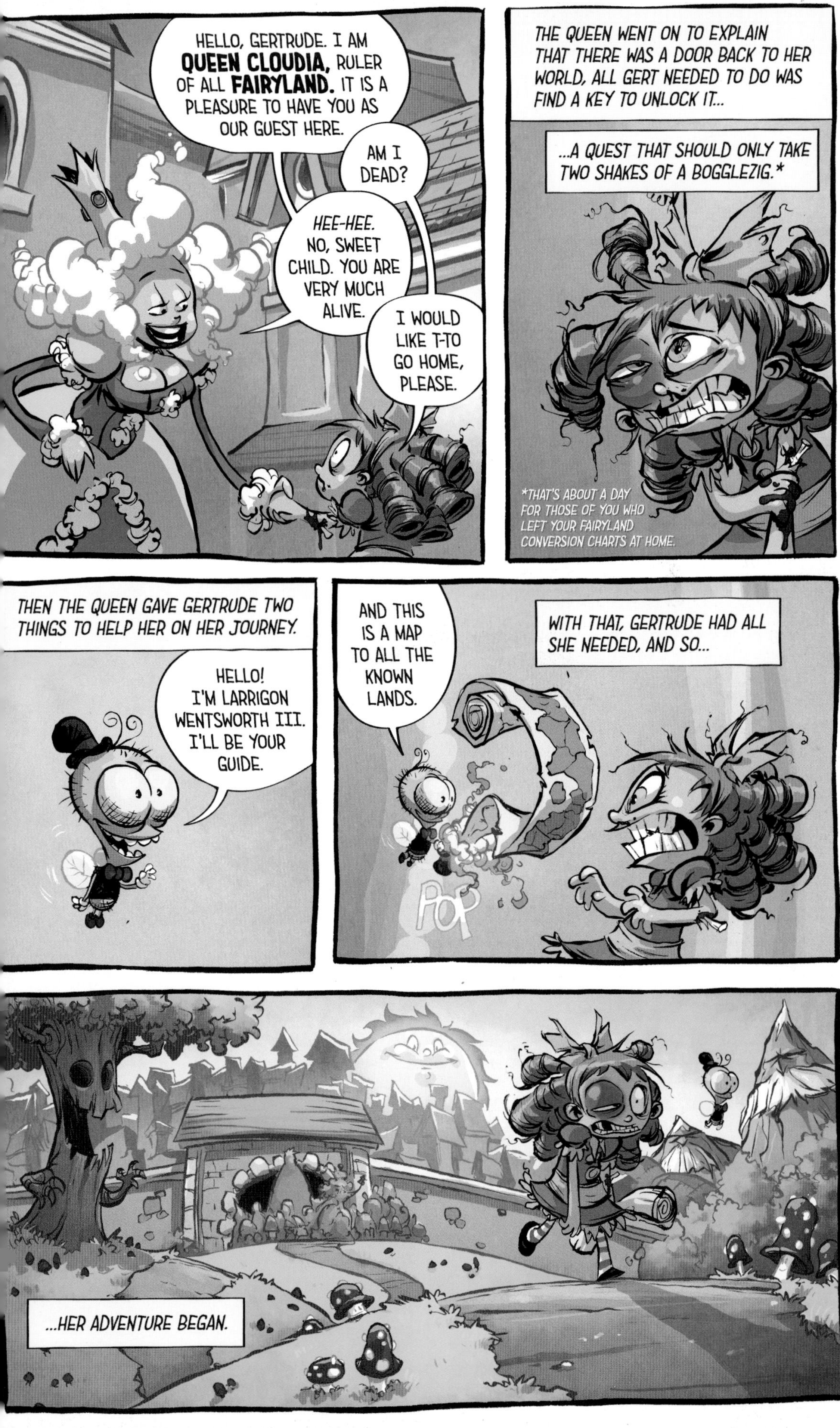
HELLO, GERTRUDE. I AM QUEEN CLOUDIA, RULER OF ALL FAIRYLAND. IT IS A PLEASURE TO HAVE YOU AS OUR GUEST HERE.
AM I DEAD?
HEE-HEE. NO, SWEET CHILD. YOU ARE VERY MUCH ALIVE.
I WOULD LIKE T-TO GO HOME, PLEASE.
THE QUEEN WENT ON TO EXPLAIN THAT THERE WAS A DOOR BACK TO HER WORLD, ALL GERT NEEDED TO DO WAS FIND A KEY TO UNLOCK IT...
...A QUEST THAT SHOULD ONLY TAKE TWO SHAKES OF A BOGGLEZIG.*
*THAT'S ABOUT A DAY FOR THOSE OF YOU WHO LEFT YOUR FAIRYLAND CONVERSION CHARTS AT HOME.
THEN THE QUEEN GAVE GERTRUDE TWO THINGS TO HELP HER ON HER JOURNEY.
HELLO! I'M LARRIGON WENTSWORTH III. I'LL BE YOUR GUIDE.
AND THIS IS A MAP TO ALL THE KNOWN LANDS.
WITH THAT, GERTRUDE HAD ALL SHE NEEDED, AND SO...
POP
...HER ADVENTURE BEGAN.

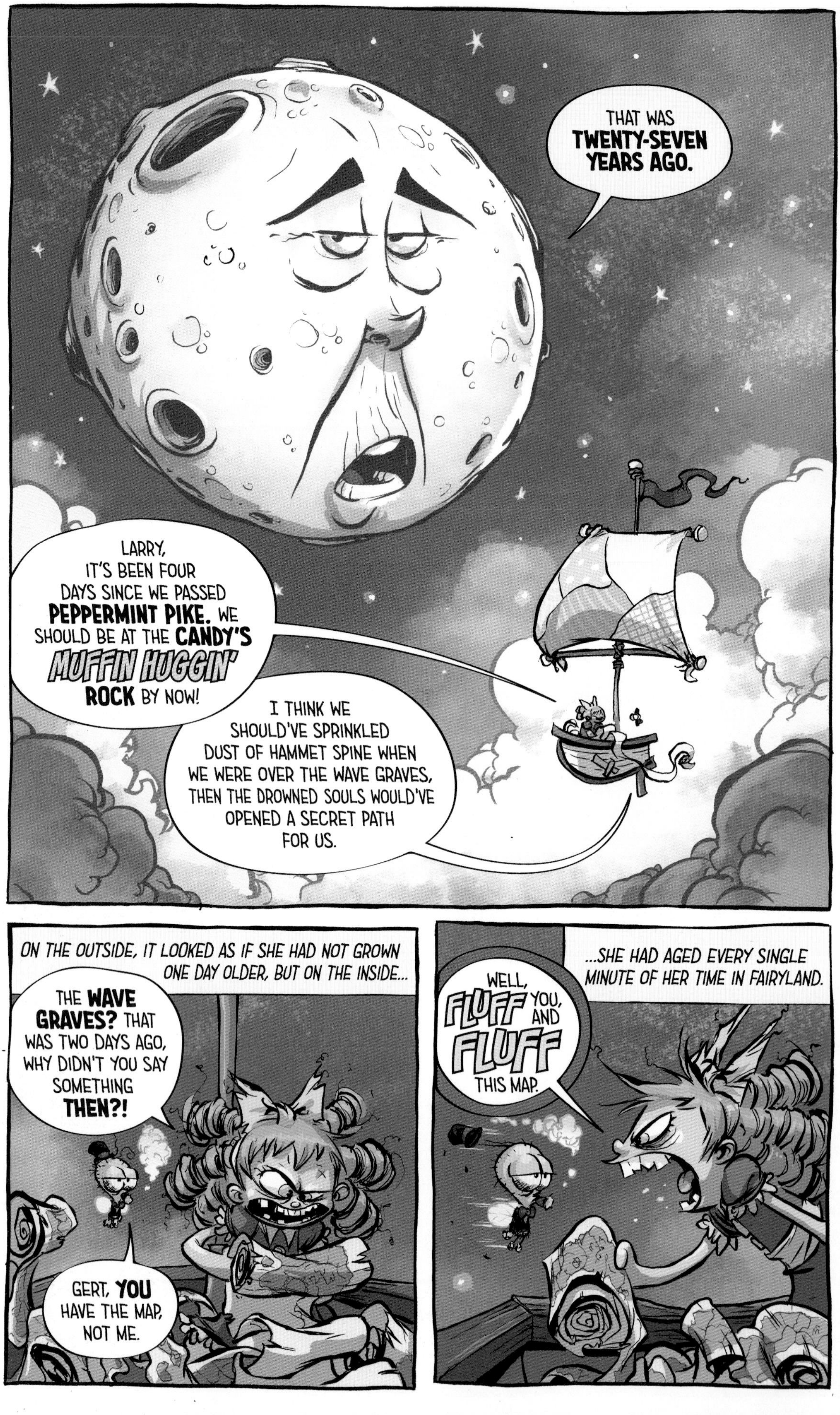
THAT WAS TWENTY-SEVEN YEARS AGO.
LARRY, IT'S BEEN FOUR DAYS SINCE WE PASSED PEPPERMINT PIKE. WE SHOULD BE AT THE CANDY'S MUFFIN HUGGIN' ROCK BY NOW!
I THINK WE SHOULD'VE SPRINKLED DUST OF HAMMET SPINE WHEN WE WERE OVER THE WAVE GRAVES, THEN THE DROWNED SOULS WOULD'VE OPENED A SECRET PATH FOR US.
ON THE OUTSIDE, IT LOOKED AS IF SHE HAD NOT GROWN ONE DAY OLDER, BUT ON THE INSIDE...
THE WAVE GRAVES? THAT WAS TWO DAYS AGO, WHY DIDN'T YOU SAY SOMETHING THEN?!
GERT, YOU HAVE THE MAP, NOT ME.
...SHE HAD AGED EVERY SINGLE MINUTE OF HER TIME IN FAIRYLAND.
WELL, FLUFF YOU, AND FLUFF THIS MAP.

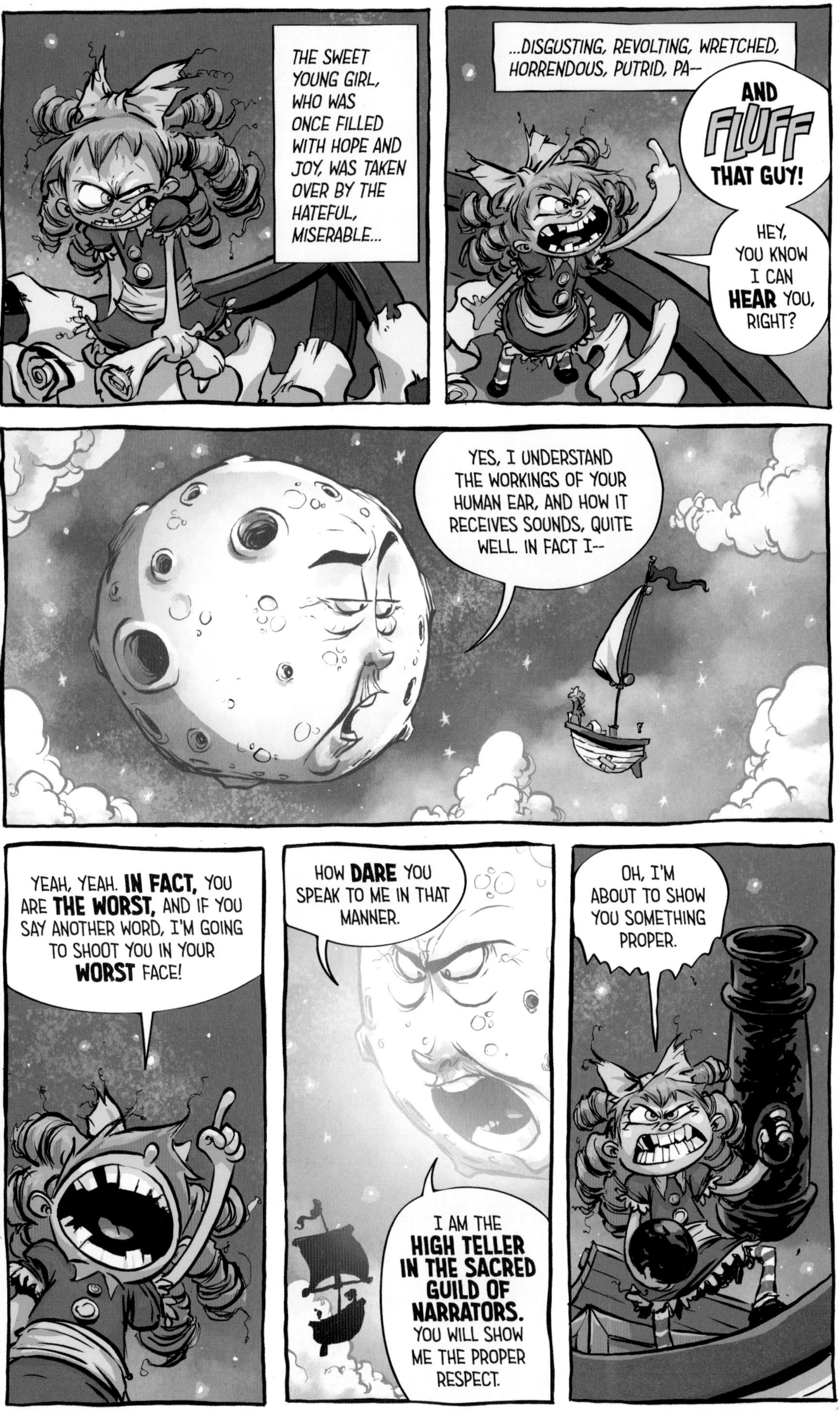
THE SWEET YOUNG GIRL, WHO WAS ONCE FILLED WITH HOPE AND JOY, WAS TAKEN OVER BY THE HATEFUL, MISERABLE...
...DISGUSTING, REVOLTING, WRETCHED, HORRENDOUS, PUTRID, PA--
AND FLUFF THAT GUY!
HEY, YOU KNOW I CAN HEAR YOU, RIGHT?
YES, I UNDERSTAND THE WORKINGS OF YOUR HUMAN EAR, AND HOW IT RECEIVES SOUNDS, QUITE WELL. IN FACT I--
YEAH, YEAH. IN FACT, YOU ARE THE WORST, AND IF YOU SAY ANOTHER WORD, I'M GOING TO SHOOT YOU IN YOUR WORST FACE!
HOW DARE YOU SPEAK TO ME IN THAT MANNER.
I AM THE HIGH TELLER IN THE SACRED GUILD OF NARRATORS. YOU WILL SHOW ME THE PROPER RESPECT.
OH, I'M ABOUT TO SHOW YOU SOMETHING PROPER.

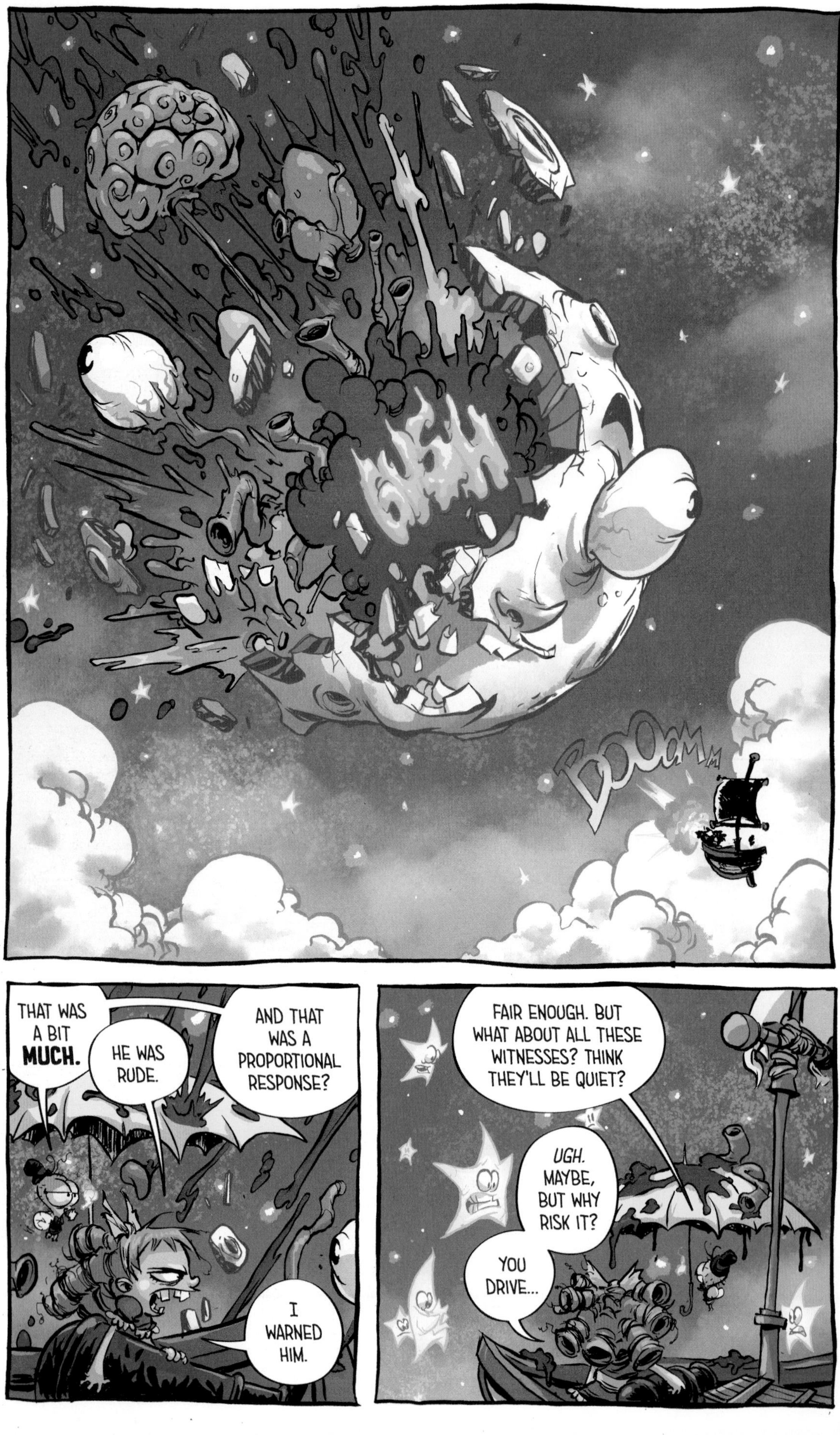
BOOOMMM
THAT WAS A BIT **MUCH.**
HE WAS RUDE.
AND THAT WAS A PROPORTIONAL RESPONSE?
I WARNED HIM.
FAIR ENOUGH. BUT WHAT ABOUT ALL THESE WITNESSES? THINK THEY'LL BE QUIET?
UGH. MAYBE, BUT WHY RISK IT?
YOU DRIVE...

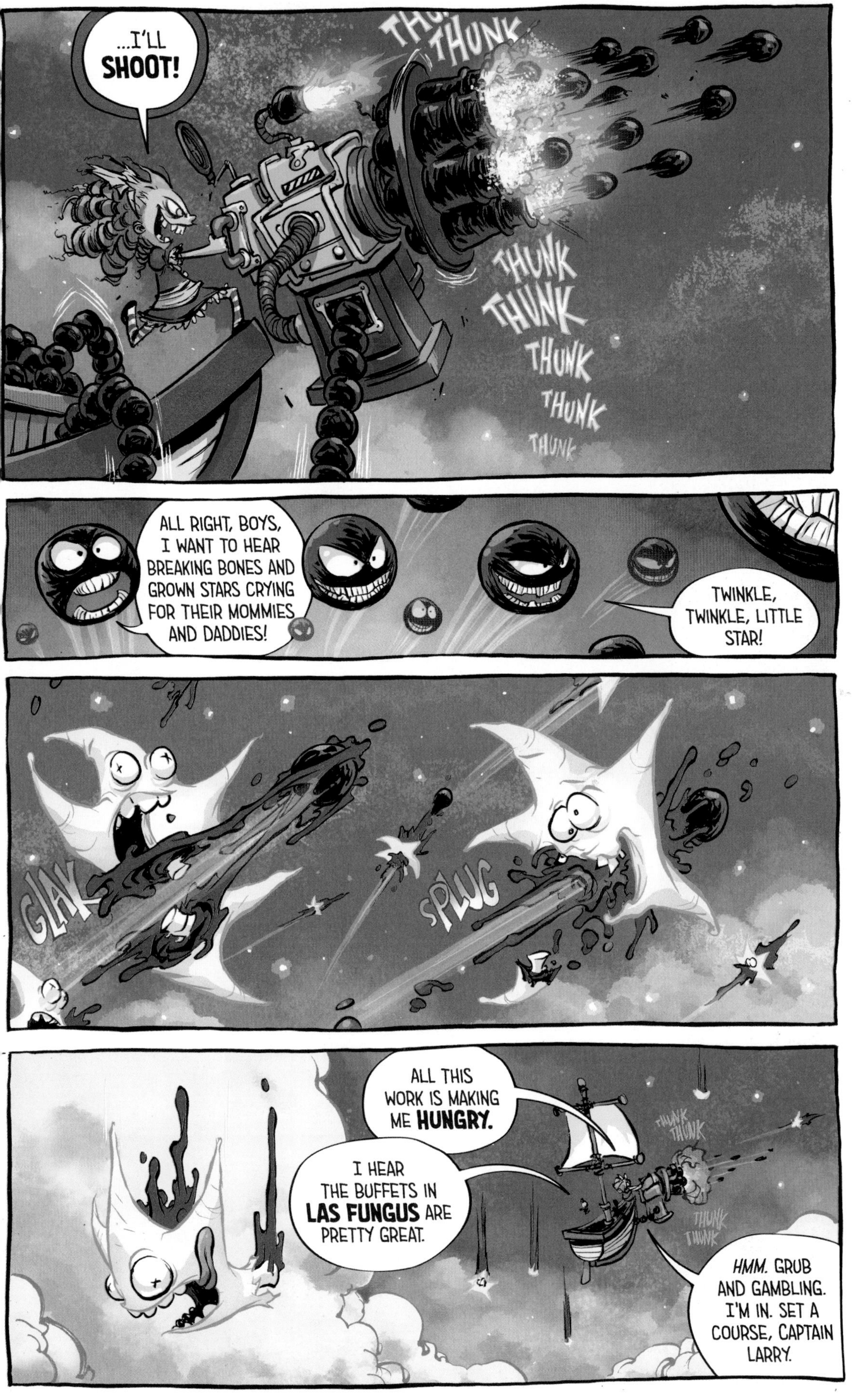

...I'LL SHOOT!
THUNK THUNK
THUNK THUNK THUNK THUNK THUNK
ALL RIGHT, BOYS, I WANT TO HEAR BREAKING BONES AND GROWN STARS CRYING FOR THEIR MOMMIES AND DADDIES!
TWINKLE, TWINKLE, LITTLE STAR!
GLAK
SPLUG
ALL THIS WORK IS MAKING ME HUNGRY.
THUNK THUNK
I HEAR THE BUFFETS IN LAS FUNGUS ARE PRETTY GREAT.
THUNK THUNK
HMM. GRUB AND GAMBLING. I'M IN. SET A COURSE, CAPTAIN LARRY.

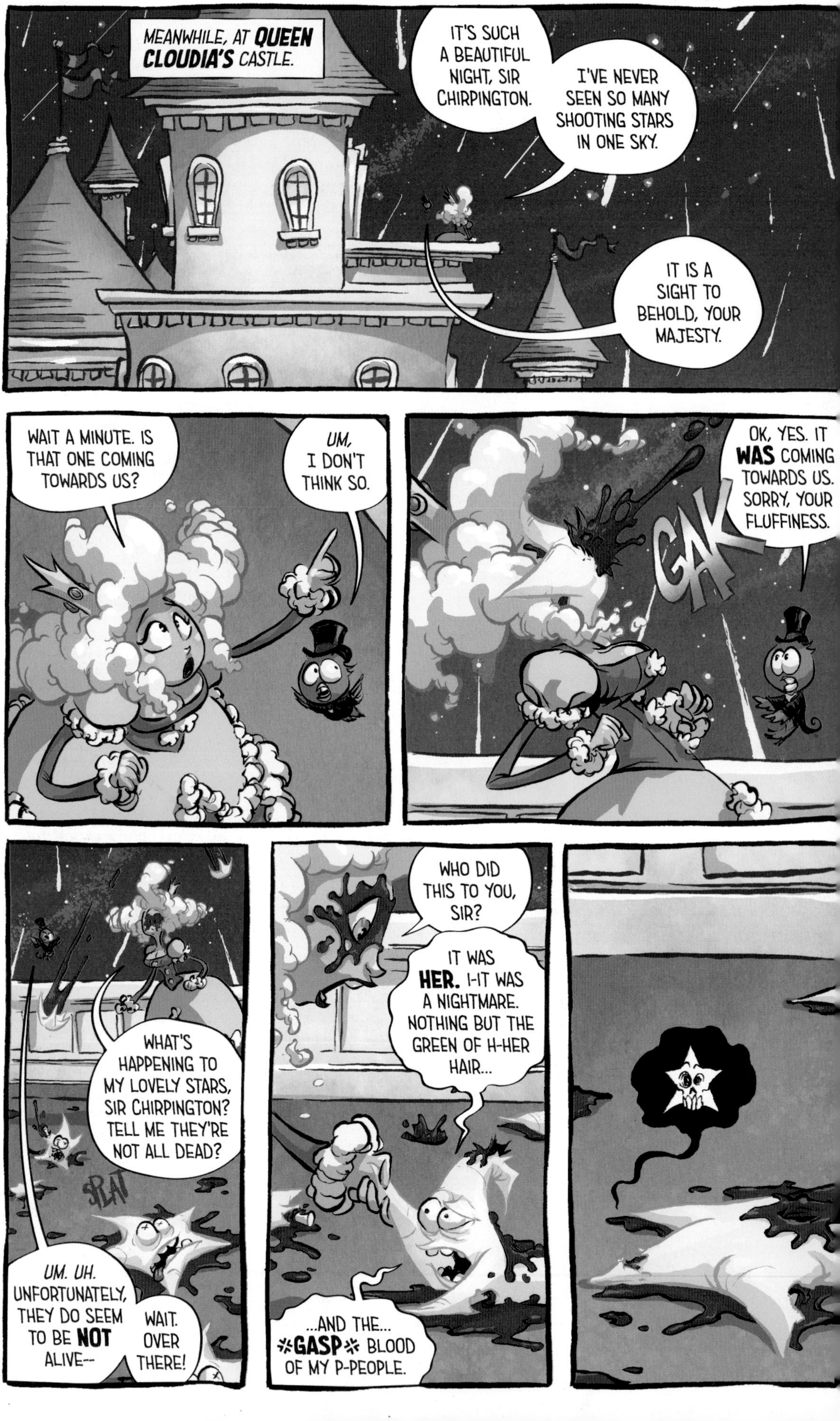

MEANWHILE, AT **QUEEN CLOUDIA'S** CASTLE.
IT'S SUCH A BEAUTIFUL NIGHT, SIR CHIRPINGTON.
I'VE NEVER SEEN SO MANY SHOOTING STARS IN ONE SKY.
IT IS A SIGHT TO BEHOLD, YOUR MAJESTY.
WAIT A MINUTE. IS THAT ONE COMING TOWARDS US?
UM, I DON'T THINK SO.
GAK
OK, YES. IT **WAS** COMING TOWARDS US. SORRY, YOUR FLUFFINESS.
WHAT'S HAPPENING TO MY LOVELY STARS, SIR CHIRPINGTON? TELL ME THEY'RE NOT ALL DEAD?
SPLAT
UM. UH. UNFORTUNATELY, THEY DO SEEM TO BE **NOT** ALIVE--
WAIT. OVER THERE!
WHO DID THIS TO YOU, SIR?
IT WAS **HER.** I-IT WAS A NIGHTMARE. NOTHING BUT THE GREEN OF H-HER HAIR...
...AND THE... ***GASP*** BLOOD OF MY P-PEOPLE.

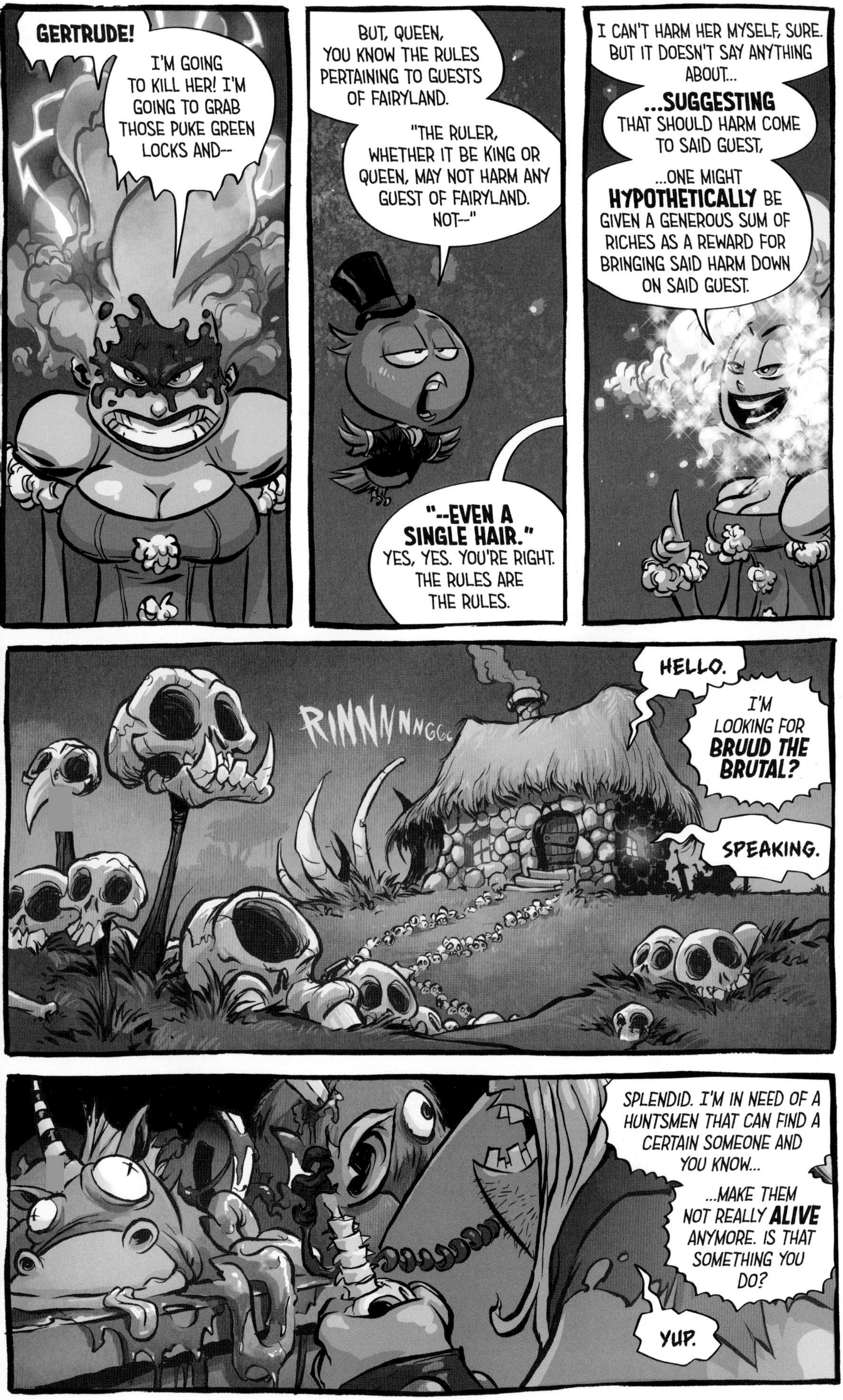
GERTRUDE!
I'M GOING TO KILL HER! I'M GOING TO GRAB THOSE PUKE GREEN LOCKS AND--
BUT, QUEEN, YOU KNOW THE RULES PERTAINING TO GUESTS OF FAIRYLAND.
"THE RULER, WHETHER IT BE KING OR QUEEN, MAY NOT HARM ANY GUEST OF FAIRYLAND. NOT--"
"--EVEN A SINGLE HAIR." YES, YES. YOU'RE RIGHT. THE RULES ARE THE RULES.
I CAN'T HARM HER MYSELF, SURE. BUT IT DOESN'T SAY ANYTHING ABOUT...
...SUGGESTING THAT SHOULD HARM COME TO SAID GUEST,
...ONE MIGHT HYPOTHETICALLY BE GIVEN A GENEROUS SUM OF RICHES AS A REWARD FOR BRINGING SAID HARM DOWN ON SAID GUEST.
RINNNNNNGGG
HELLO.
I'M LOOKING FOR BRUUD THE BRUTAL?
SPEAKING.
SPLENDID. I'M IN NEED OF A HUNTSMEN THAT CAN FIND A CERTAIN SOMEONE AND YOU KNOW...
...MAKE THEM NOT REALLY ALIVE ANYMORE. IS THAT SOMETHING YOU DO?
YUP.

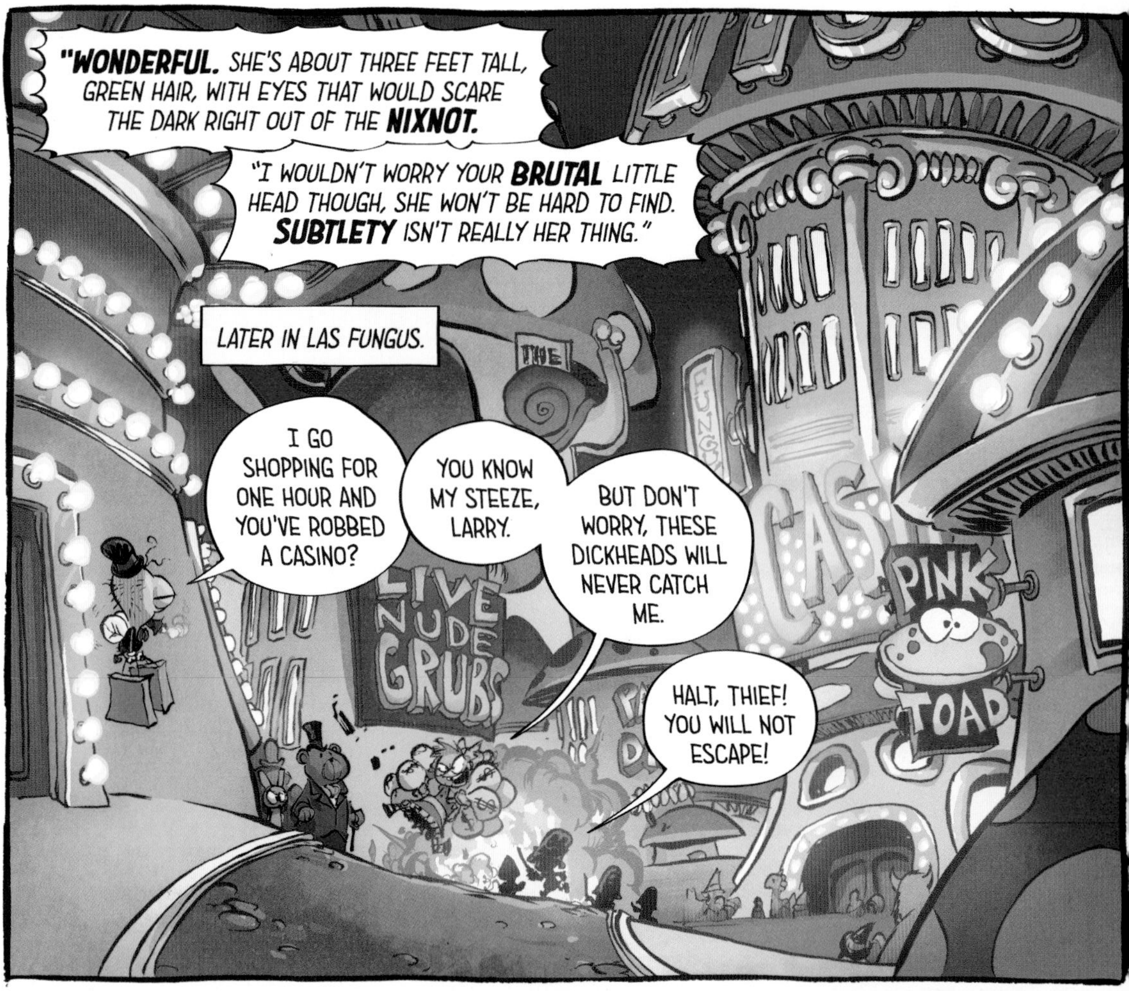
"WONDERFUL. SHE'S ABOUT THREE FEET TALL, GREEN HAIR, WITH EYES THAT WOULD SCARE THE DARK RIGHT OUT OF THE NIXNOT.
"I WOULDN'T WORRY YOUR BRUTAL LITTLE HEAD THOUGH, SHE WON'T BE HARD TO FIND. SUBTLETY ISN'T REALLY HER THING."
LATER IN LAS FUNGUS.
I GO SHOPPING FOR ONE HOUR AND YOU'VE ROBBED A CASINO?
YOU KNOW MY STEEZE, LARRY.
BUT DON'T WORRY, THESE DICKHEADS WILL NEVER CATCH ME.
LIVE NUDE GRUBS
PINK TOAD
HALT, THIEF! YOU WILL NOT ESCAPE!

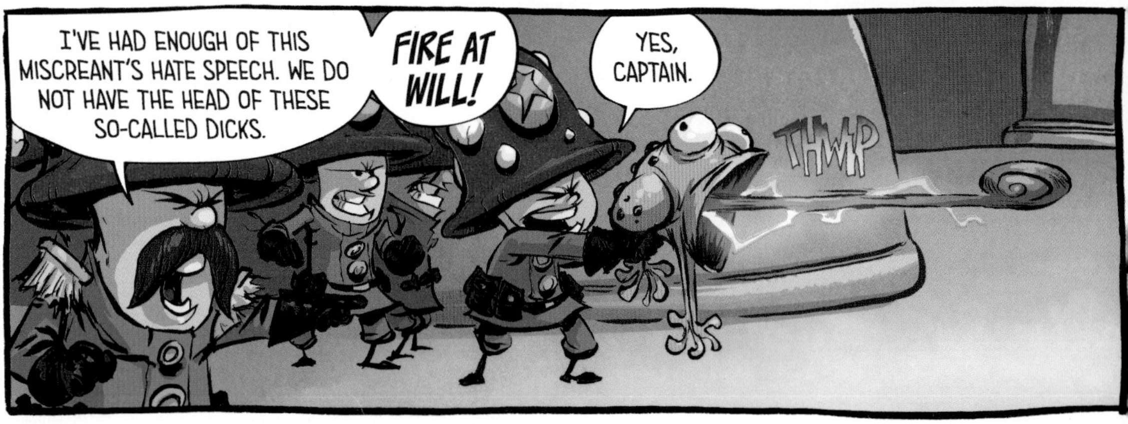
I'VE HAD ENOUGH OF THIS MISCREANT'S HATE SPEECH. WE DO NOT HAVE THE HEAD OF THESE SO-CALLED DICKS.
FIRE AT WILL!
YES, CAPTAIN.
THWIP

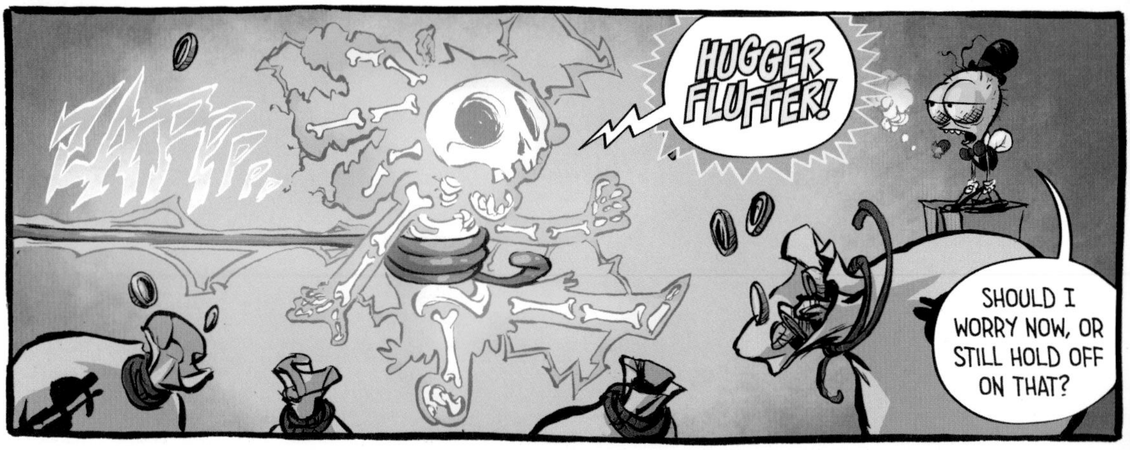
ZAPPPP
HUGGER FLUFFER!
SHOULD I WORRY NOW, OR STILL HOLD OFF ON THAT?

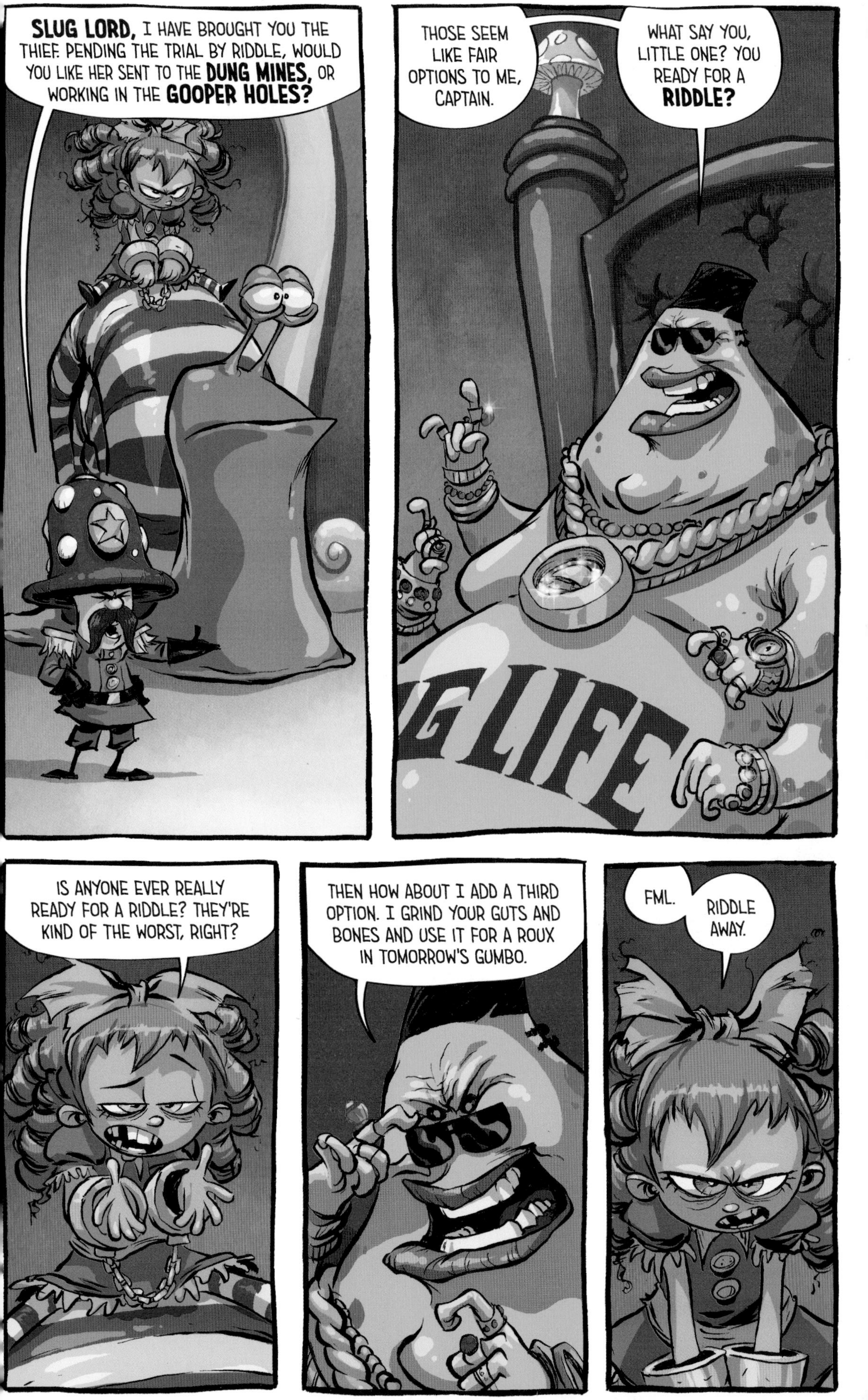
SLUG LORD, I HAVE BROUGHT YOU THE THIEF. PENDING THE TRIAL BY RIDDLE, WOULD YOU LIKE HER SENT TO THE DUNG MINES, OR WORKING IN THE GOOPER HOLES?
THOSE SEEM LIKE FAIR OPTIONS TO ME, CAPTAIN.
WHAT SAY YOU, LITTLE ONE? YOU READY FOR A RIDDLE?
IS ANYONE EVER REALLY READY FOR A RIDDLE? THEY'RE KIND OF THE WORST, RIGHT?
THEN HOW ABOUT I ADD A THIRD OPTION. I GRIND YOUR GUTS AND BONES AND USE IT FOR A ROUX IN TOMORROW'S GUMBO.
FML.
RIDDLE AWAY.

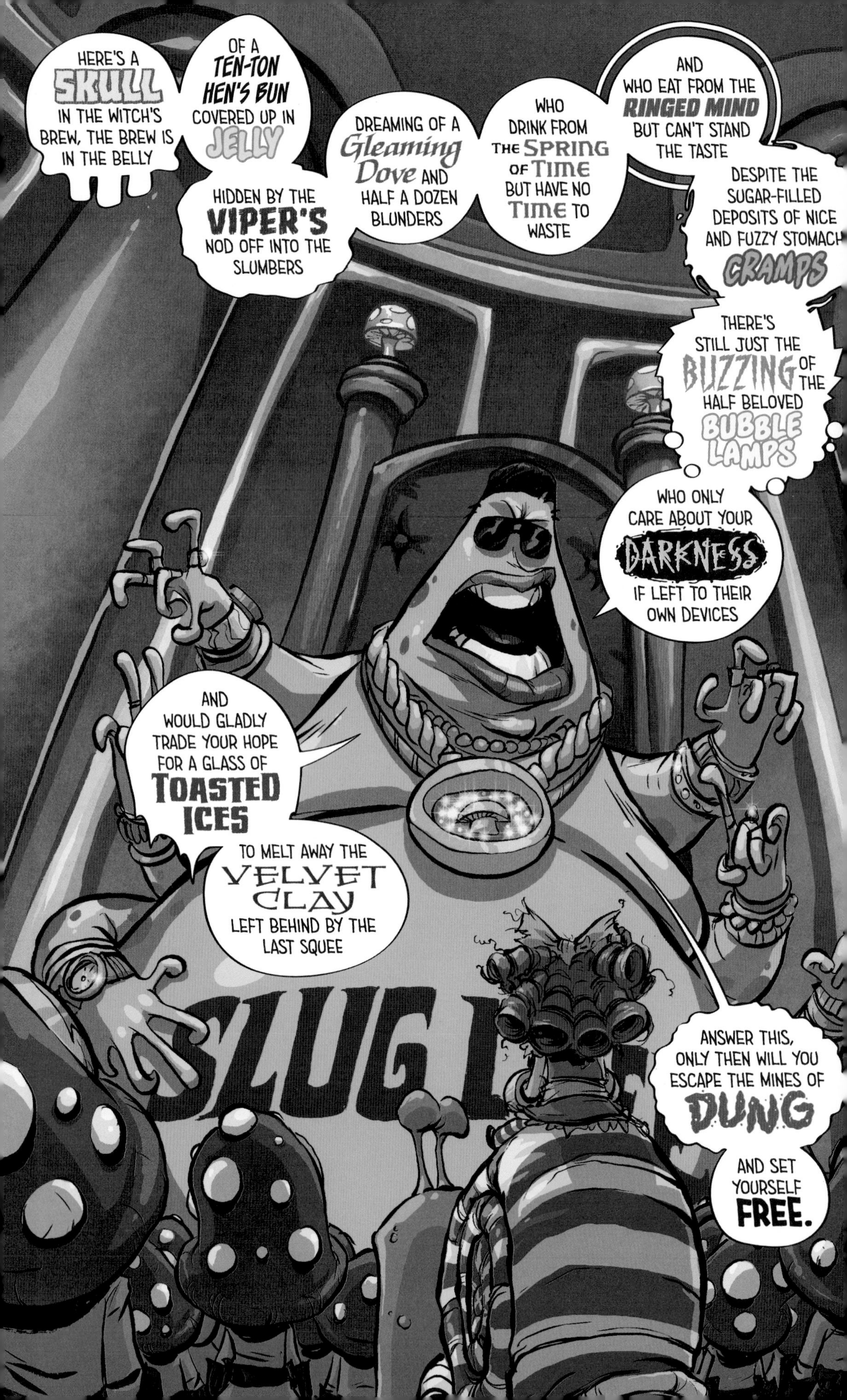
HERE'S A SKULL IN THE WITCH'S BREW, THE BREW IS IN THE BELLY
OF A TEN-TON HEN'S BUN COVERED UP IN JELLY
HIDDEN BY THE VIPER'S NOD OFF INTO THE SLUMBERS
DREAMING OF A Gleaming Dove AND HALF A DOZEN BLUNDERS
WHO DRINK FROM THE SPRING OF TIME BUT HAVE NO TIME TO WASTE
AND WHO EAT FROM THE RINGED MIND BUT CAN'T STAND THE TASTE
DESPITE THE SUGAR-FILLED DEPOSITS OF NICE AND FUZZY STOMACH CRAMPS
THERE'S STILL JUST THE BUZZING OF THE HALF BELOVED BUBBLE LAMPS
WHO ONLY CARE ABOUT YOUR DARKNESS IF LEFT TO THEIR OWN DEVICES
AND WOULD GLADLY TRADE YOUR HOPE FOR A GLASS OF TOASTED ICES
TO MELT AWAY THE VELVET CLAY LEFT BEHIND BY THE LAST SQUEE
ANSWER THIS, ONLY THEN WILL YOU ESCAPE THE MINES OF DUNG
AND SET YOURSELF FREE.

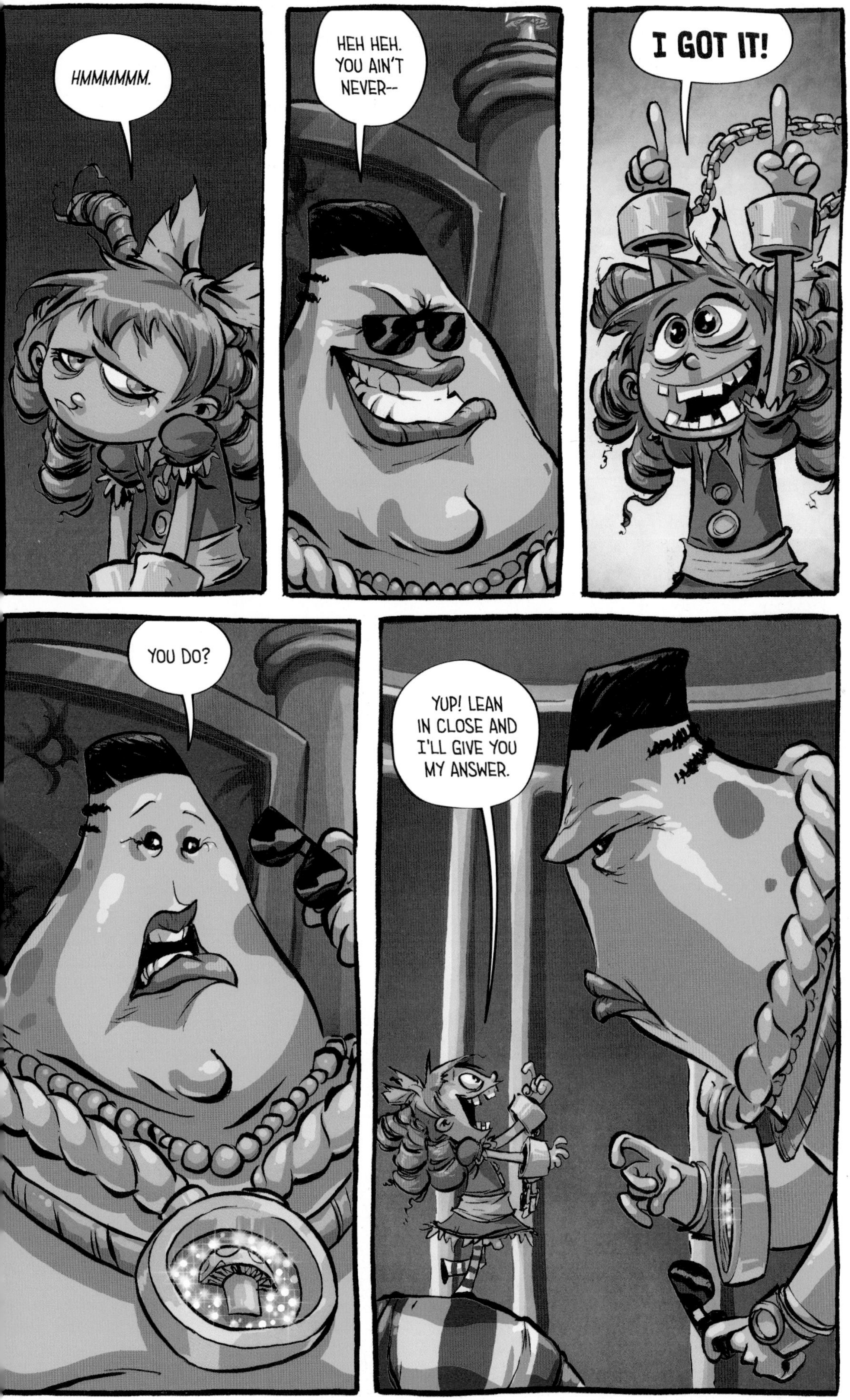
HMMMMMM.
HEH HEH. YOU AIN'T NEVER--
I GOT IT!
YOU DO?
YUP! LEAN IN CLOSE AND I'LL GIVE YOU MY ANSWER.

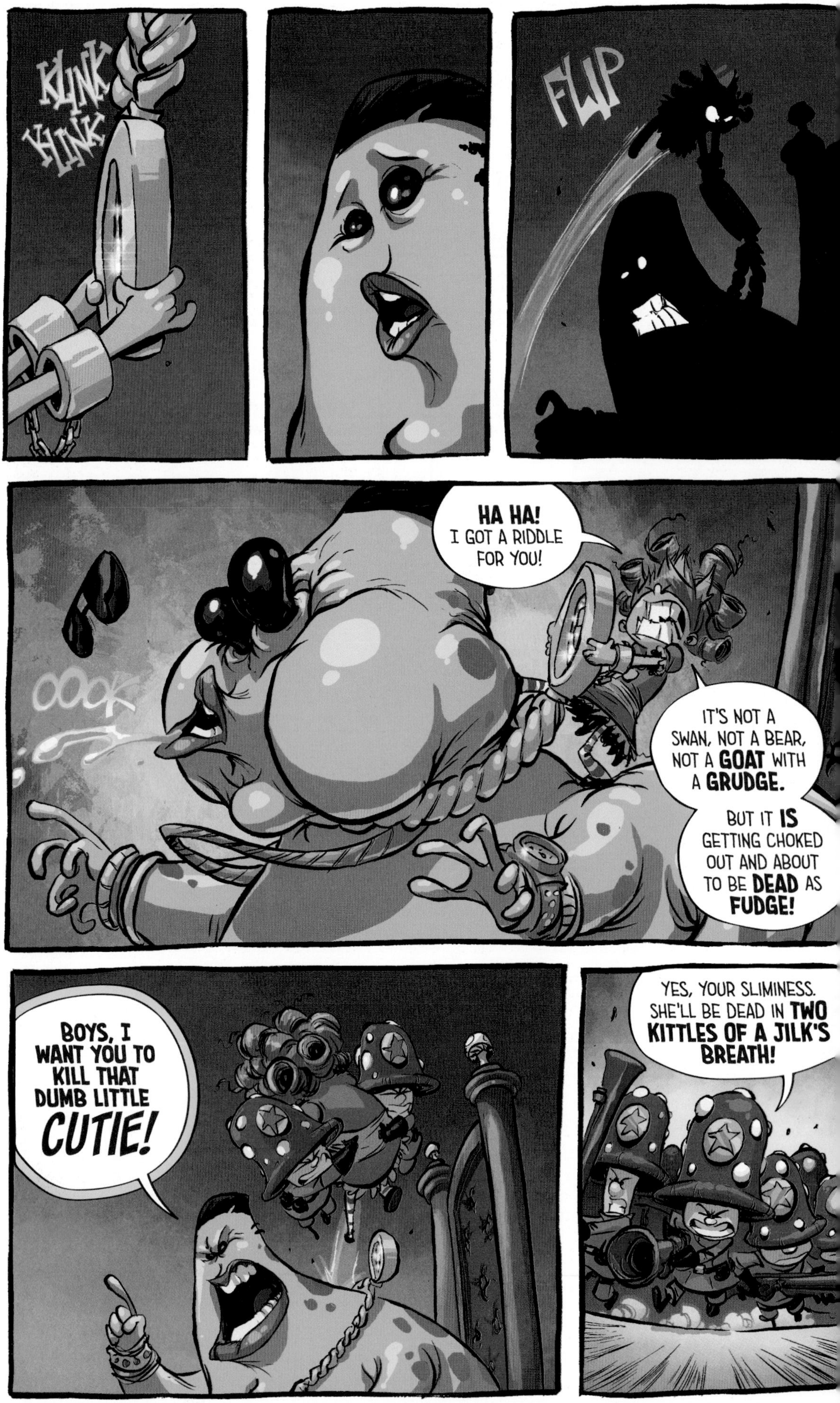
KLINK KLINK
FLIP
HA HA! I GOT A RIDDLE FOR YOU!
OOOK
IT'S NOT A SWAN, NOT A BEAR, NOT A GOAT WITH A GRUDGE.
BUT IT IS GETTING CHOKED OUT AND ABOUT TO BE DEAD AS FUDGE!
BOYS, I WANT YOU TO KILL THAT DUMB LITTLE CUTIE!
YES, YOUR SLIMINESS. SHE'LL BE DEAD IN TWO KITTLES OF A JILK'S BREATH!

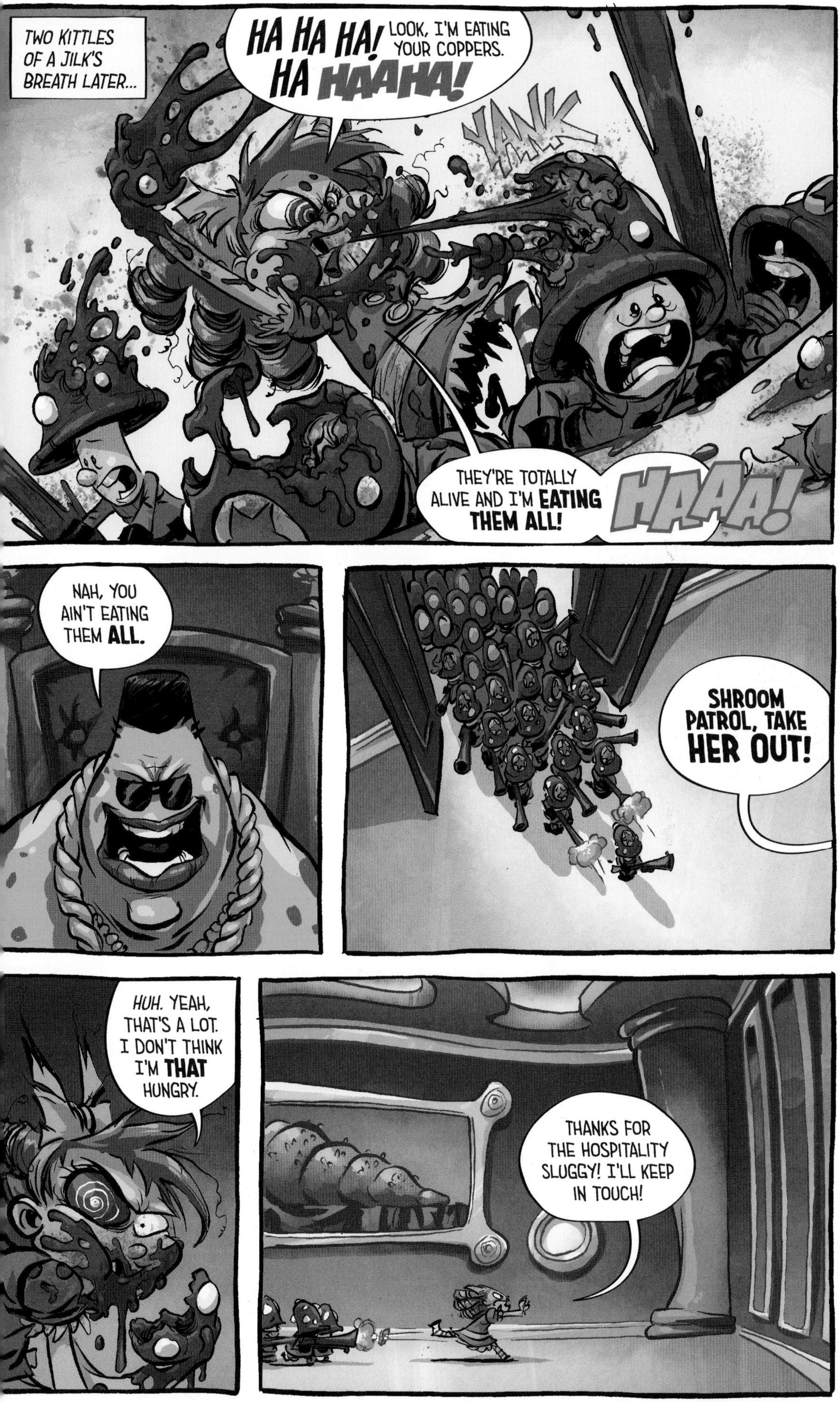
TWO KITTLES OF A JILK'S BREATH LATER...
HA HA HA! HA HAAHA!
LOOK, I'M EATING YOUR COPPERS.
YANK
THEY'RE TOTALLY ALIVE AND I'M EATING THEM ALL!
HAAAA!
NAH, YOU AIN'T EATING THEM ALL.
SHROOM PATROL, TAKE HER OUT!
HUH. YEAH, THAT'S A LOT. I DON'T THINK I'M THAT HUNGRY.
THANKS FOR THE HOSPITALITY SLUGGY! I'LL KEEP IN TOUCH!

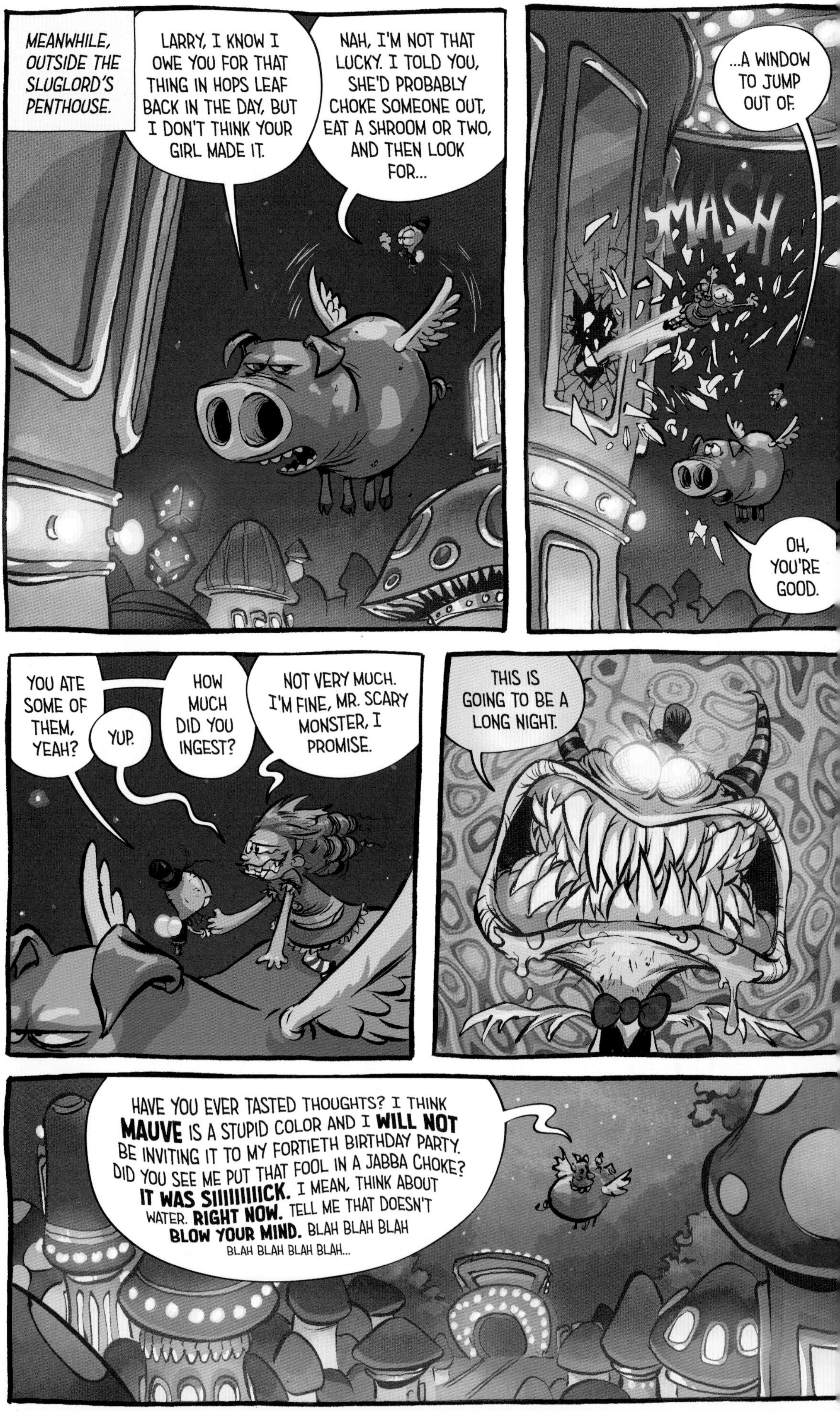

MEANWHILE, OUTSIDE THE SLUGLORD'S PENTHOUSE.
LARRY, I KNOW I OWE YOU FOR THAT THING IN HOPS LEAF BACK IN THE DAY, BUT I DON'T THINK YOUR GIRL MADE IT.
NAH, I'M NOT THAT LUCKY. I TOLD YOU, SHE'D PROBABLY CHOKE SOMEONE OUT, EAT A SHROOM OR TWO, AND THEN LOOK FOR...
...A WINDOW TO JUMP OUT OF.
SMASH
OH, YOU'RE GOOD.
YOU ATE SOME OF THEM, YEAH?
YUP.
HOW MUCH DID YOU INGEST?
NOT VERY MUCH. I'M FINE, MR. SCARY MONSTER, I PROMISE.
THIS IS GOING TO BE A LONG NIGHT.
HAVE YOU EVER TASTED THOUGHTS? I THINK MAUVE IS A STUPID COLOR AND I WILL NOT BE INVITING IT TO MY FORTIETH BIRTHDAY PARTY. DID YOU SEE ME PUT THAT FOOL IN A JABBA CHOKE? IT WAS SIIIIIIIICK. I MEAN, THINK ABOUT WATER. RIGHT NOW. TELL ME THAT DOESN'T BLOW YOUR MIND. BLAH BLAH BLAH BLAH BLAH BLAH BLAH...

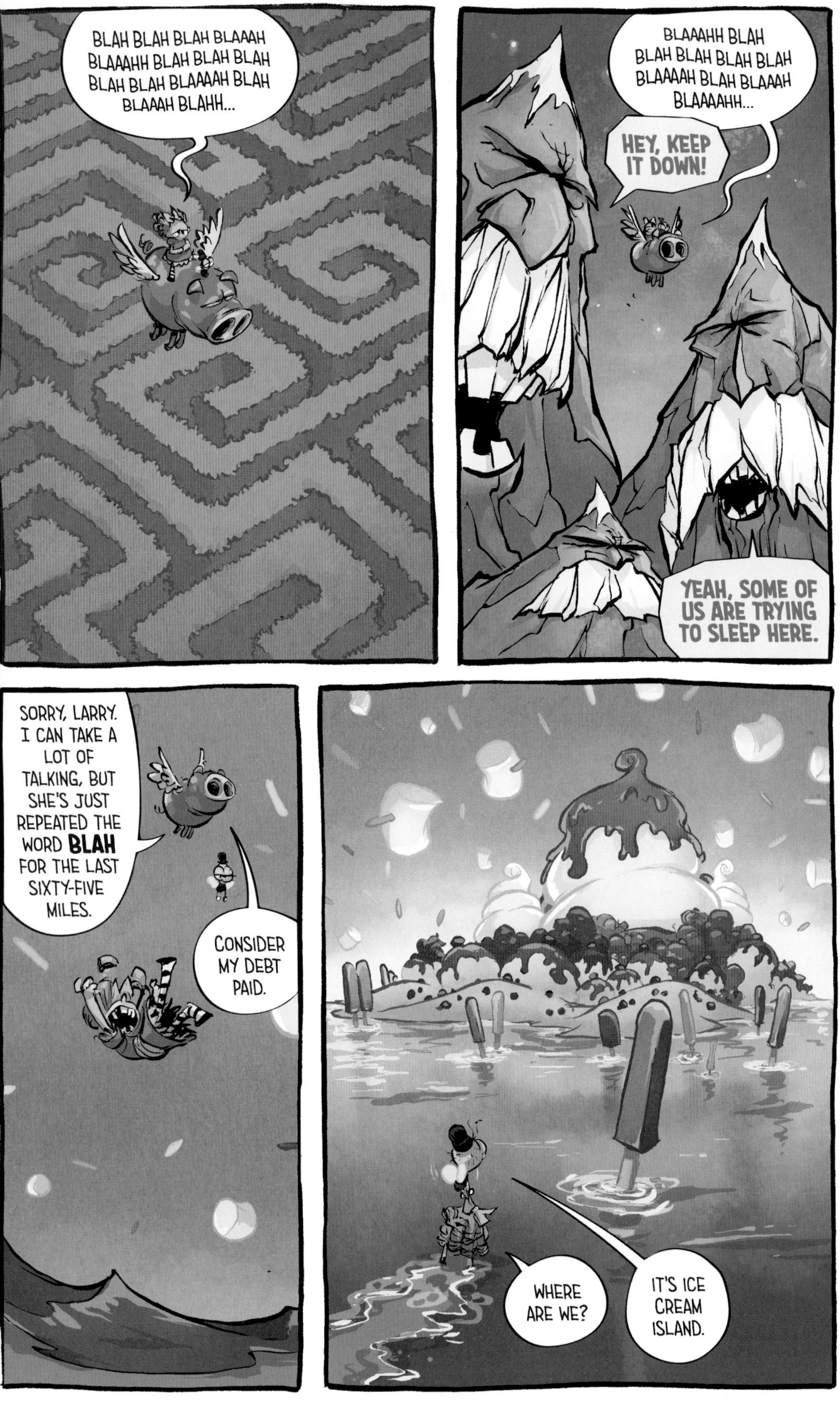

BLAH BLAH BLAH BLAAAH BLAAAHH BLAH BLAH BLAH BLAH BLAH BLAAAAH BLAH BLAAAH BLAHH...
BLAAAHH BLAH BLAH BLAH BLAH BLAH BLAAAAH BLAH BLAAAH BLAAAAHH...
HEY, KEEP IT DOWN!
YEAH, SOME OF US ARE TRYING TO SLEEP HERE.
SORRY, LARRY. I CAN TAKE A LOT OF TALKING, BUT SHE'S JUST REPEATED THE WORD BLAH FOR THE LAST SIXTY-FIVE MILES.
CONSIDER MY DEBT PAID.
WHERE ARE WE?
IT'S ICE CREAM ISLAND.

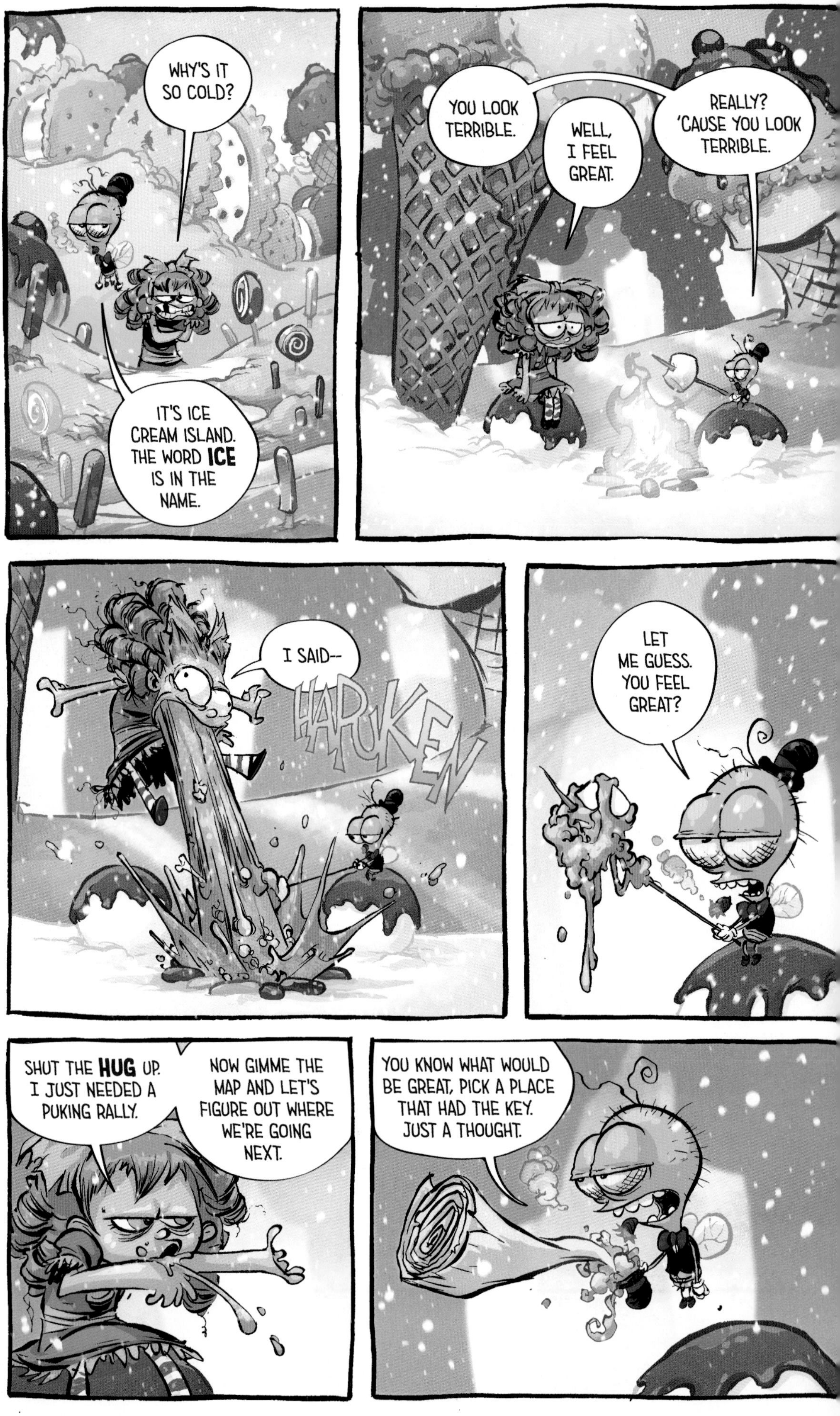
WHY'S IT SO COLD?
IT'S ICE CREAM ISLAND. THE WORD **ICE** IS IN THE NAME.
YOU LOOK TERRIBLE.
WELL, I FEEL GREAT.
REALLY? 'CAUSE YOU LOOK TERRIBLE.
I SAID--
HAPUKEN
LET ME GUESS. YOU FEEL GREAT?
SHUT THE **HUG** UP. I JUST NEEDED A PUKING RALLY.
NOW GIMME THE MAP AND LET'S FIGURE OUT WHERE WE'RE GOING NEXT.
YOU KNOW WHAT WOULD BE GREAT, PICK A PLACE THAT HAD THE KEY. JUST A THOUGHT.

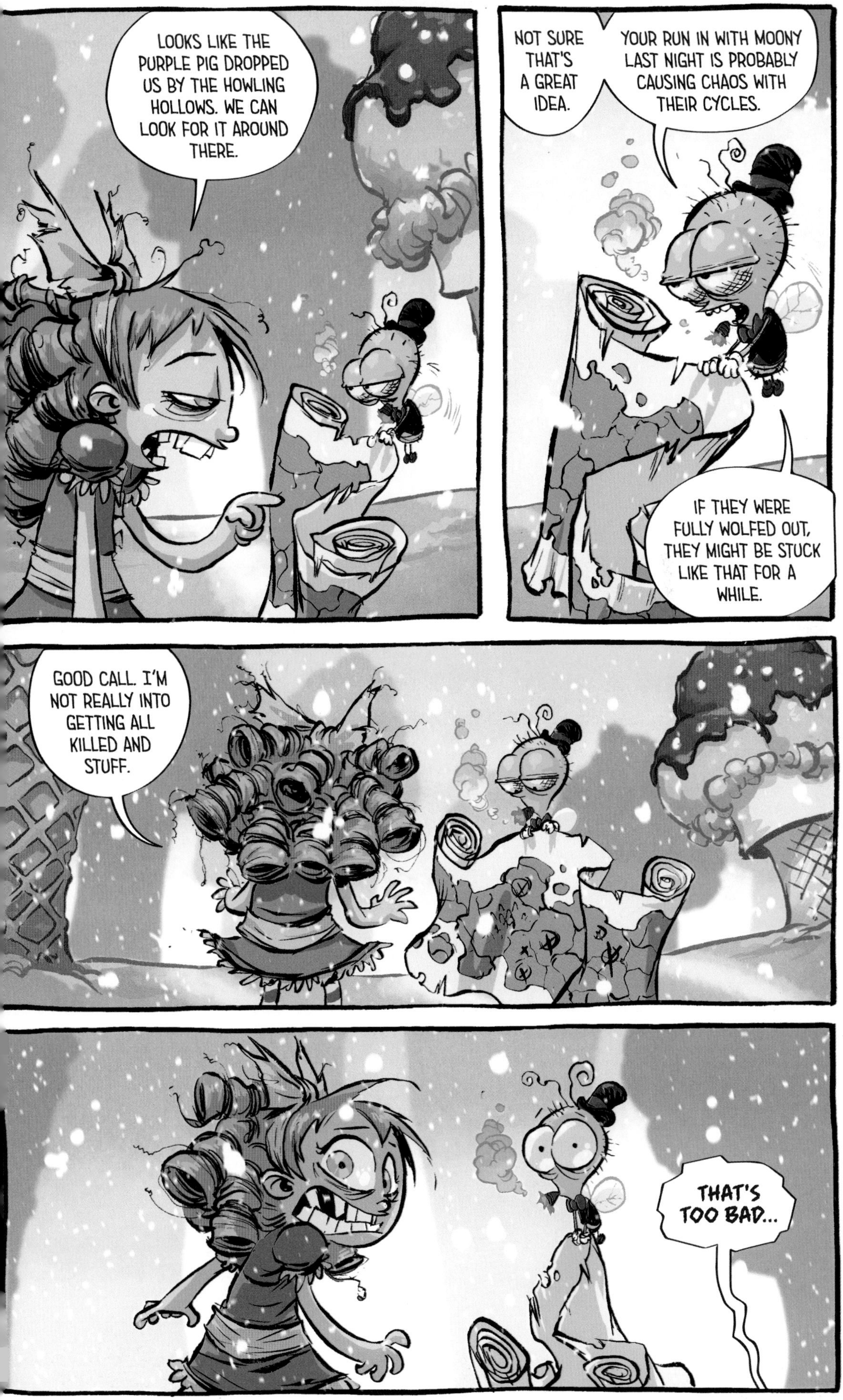
LOOKS LIKE THE PURPLE PIG DROPPED US BY THE HOWLING HOLLOWS. WE CAN LOOK FOR IT AROUND THERE.
NOT SURE THAT'S A GREAT IDEA.
YOUR RUN IN WITH MOONY LAST NIGHT IS PROBABLY CAUSING CHAOS WITH THEIR CYCLES.
IF THEY WERE FULLY WOLFED OUT, THEY MIGHT BE STUCK LIKE THAT FOR A WHILE.
GOOD CALL. I'M NOT REALLY INTO GETTING ALL KILLED AND STUFF.
THAT'S TOO BAD...

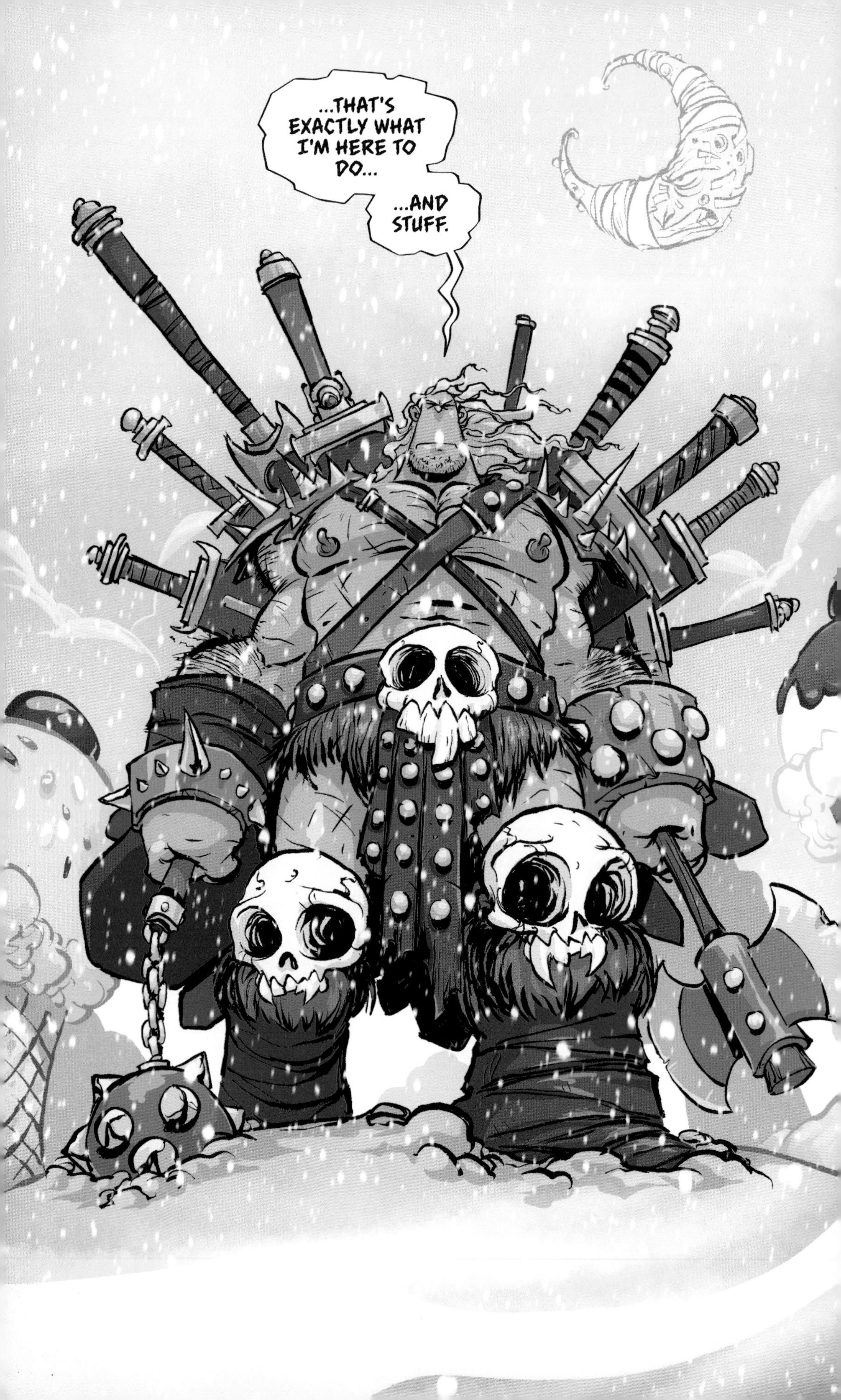
...THAT'S EXACTLY WHAT I'M HERE TO DO...
...AND STUFF.

TWO

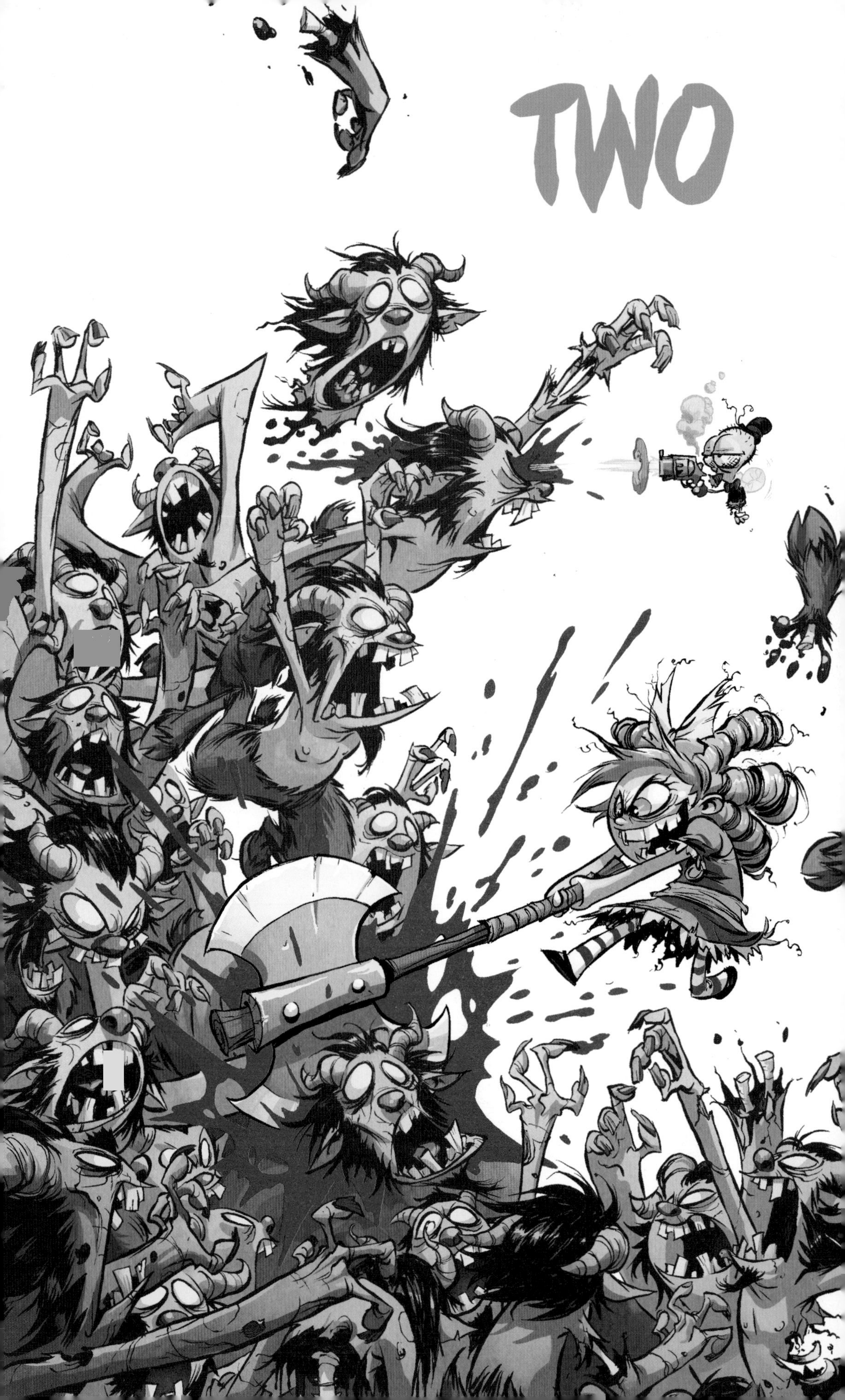

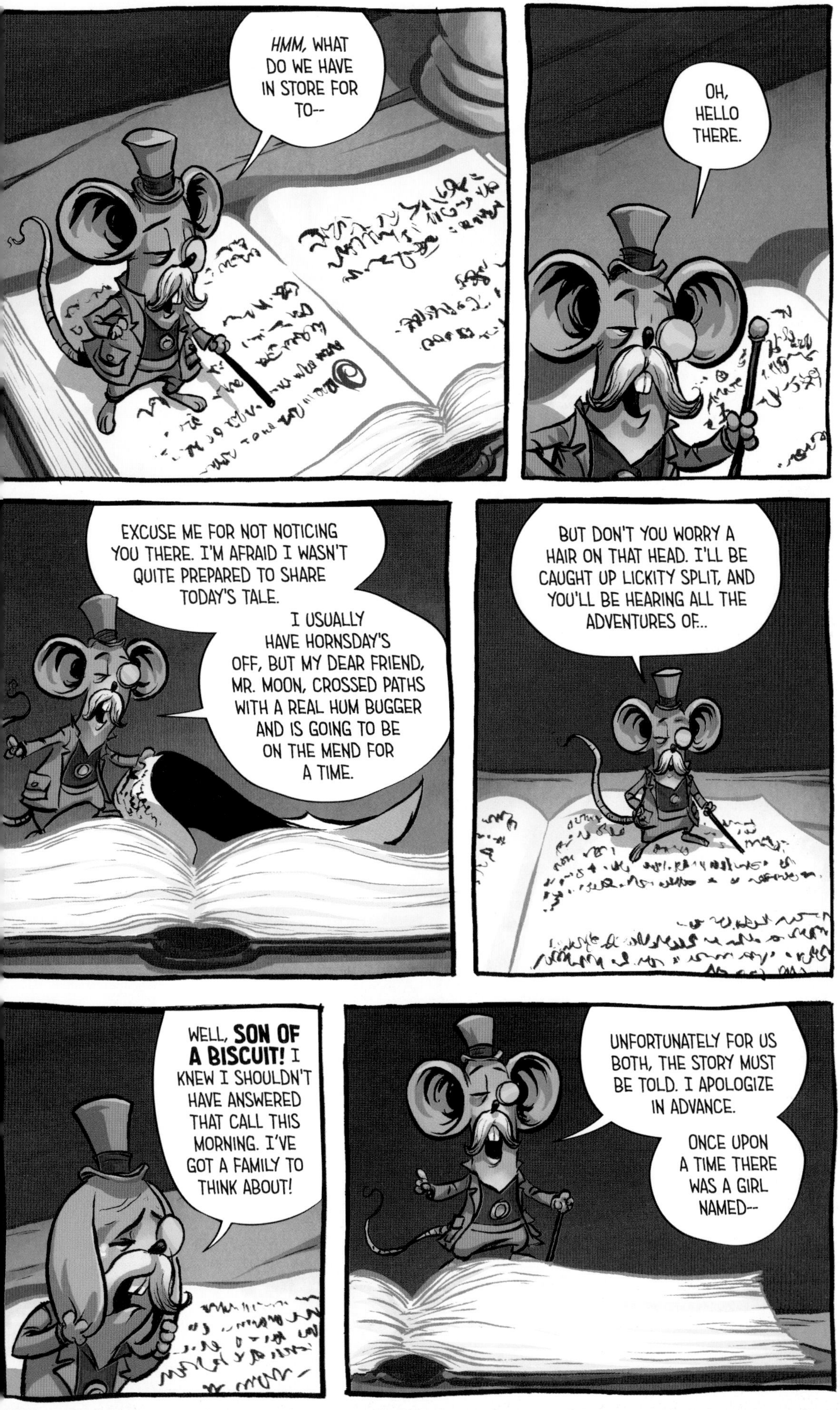
HMM, WHAT DO WE HAVE IN STORE FOR TO--
OH, HELLO THERE.
EXCUSE ME FOR NOT NOTICING YOU THERE. I'M AFRAID I WASN'T QUITE PREPARED TO SHARE TODAY'S TALE.
I USUALLY HAVE HORNSDAY'S OFF, BUT MY DEAR FRIEND, MR. MOON, CROSSED PATHS WITH A REAL HUM BUGGER AND IS GOING TO BE ON THE MEND FOR A TIME.
BUT DON'T YOU WORRY A HAIR ON THAT HEAD. I'LL BE CAUGHT UP LICKITY SPLIT, AND YOU'LL BE HEARING ALL THE ADVENTURES OF...
WELL, SON OF A BISCUIT! I KNEW I SHOULDN'T HAVE ANSWERED THAT CALL THIS MORNING. I'VE GOT A FAMILY TO THINK ABOUT!
UNFORTUNATELY FOR US BOTH, THE STORY MUST BE TOLD. I APOLOGIZE IN ADVANCE.
ONCE UPON A TIME THERE WAS A GIRL NAMED--

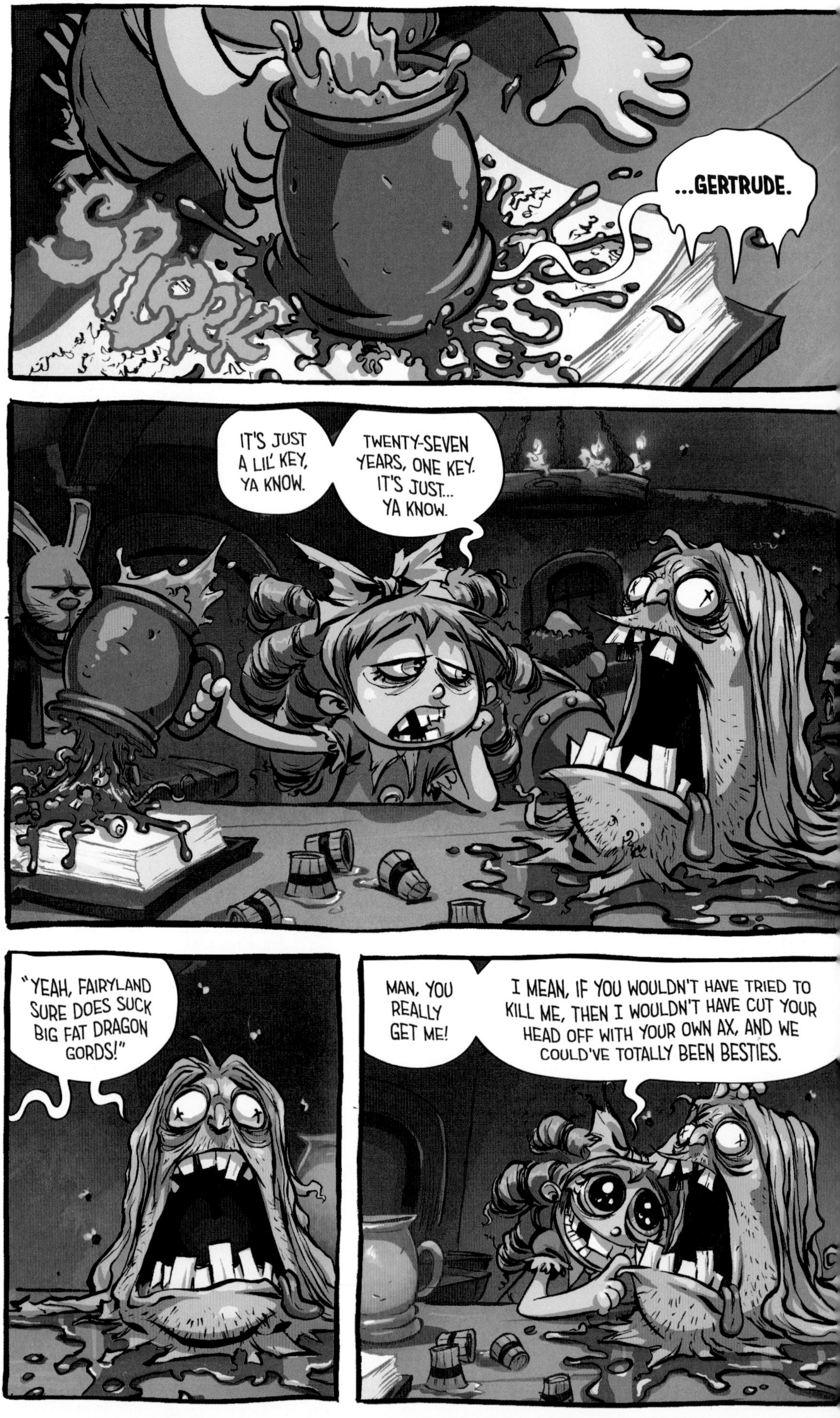
...GERTRUDE.
IT'S JUST A LIL' KEY, YA KNOW.
TWENTY-SEVEN YEARS, ONE KEY. IT'S JUST... YA KNOW.
"YEAH, FAIRYLAND SURE DOES SUCK BIG FAT DRAGON GORDS!"
MAN, YOU REALLY GET ME!
I MEAN, IF YOU WOULDN'T HAVE TRIED TO KILL ME, THEN I WOULDN'T HAVE CUT YOUR HEAD OFF WITH YOUR OWN AX, AND WE COULD'VE TOTALLY BEEN BESTIES.

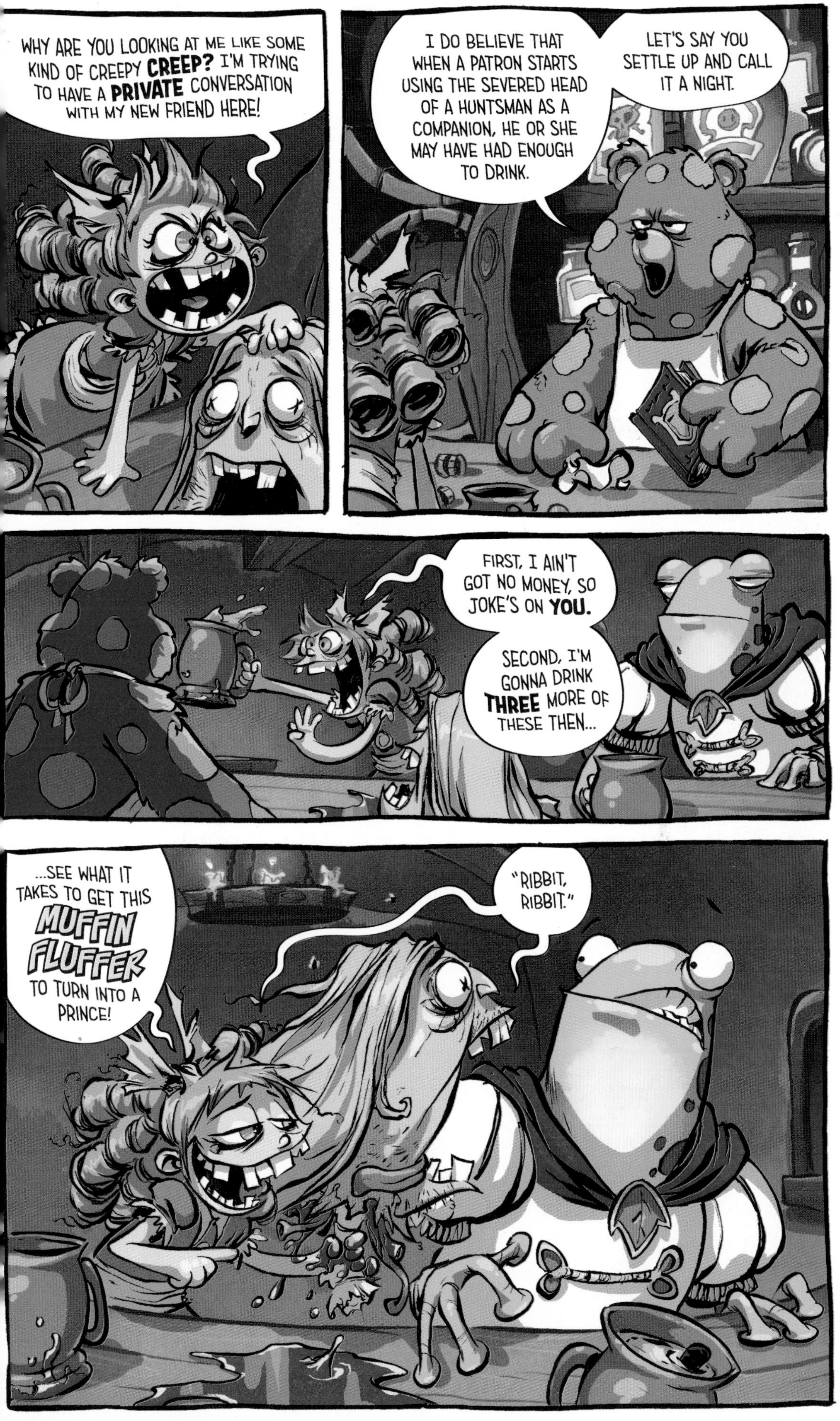
WHY ARE YOU LOOKING AT ME LIKE SOME KIND OF CREEPY **CREEP?** I'M TRYING TO HAVE A **PRIVATE** CONVERSATION WITH MY NEW FRIEND HERE!
I DO BELIEVE THAT WHEN A PATRON STARTS USING THE SEVERED HEAD OF A HUNTSMAN AS A COMPANION, HE OR SHE MAY HAVE HAD ENOUGH TO DRINK.
LET'S SAY YOU SETTLE UP AND CALL IT A NIGHT.
FIRST, I AIN'T GOT NO MONEY, SO JOKE'S ON **YOU.**
SECOND, I'M GONNA DRINK **THREE** MORE OF THESE THEN...
...SEE WHAT IT TAKES TO GET THIS MUFFIN FLUFFER TO TURN INTO A PRINCE!
"RIBBIT, RIBBIT."

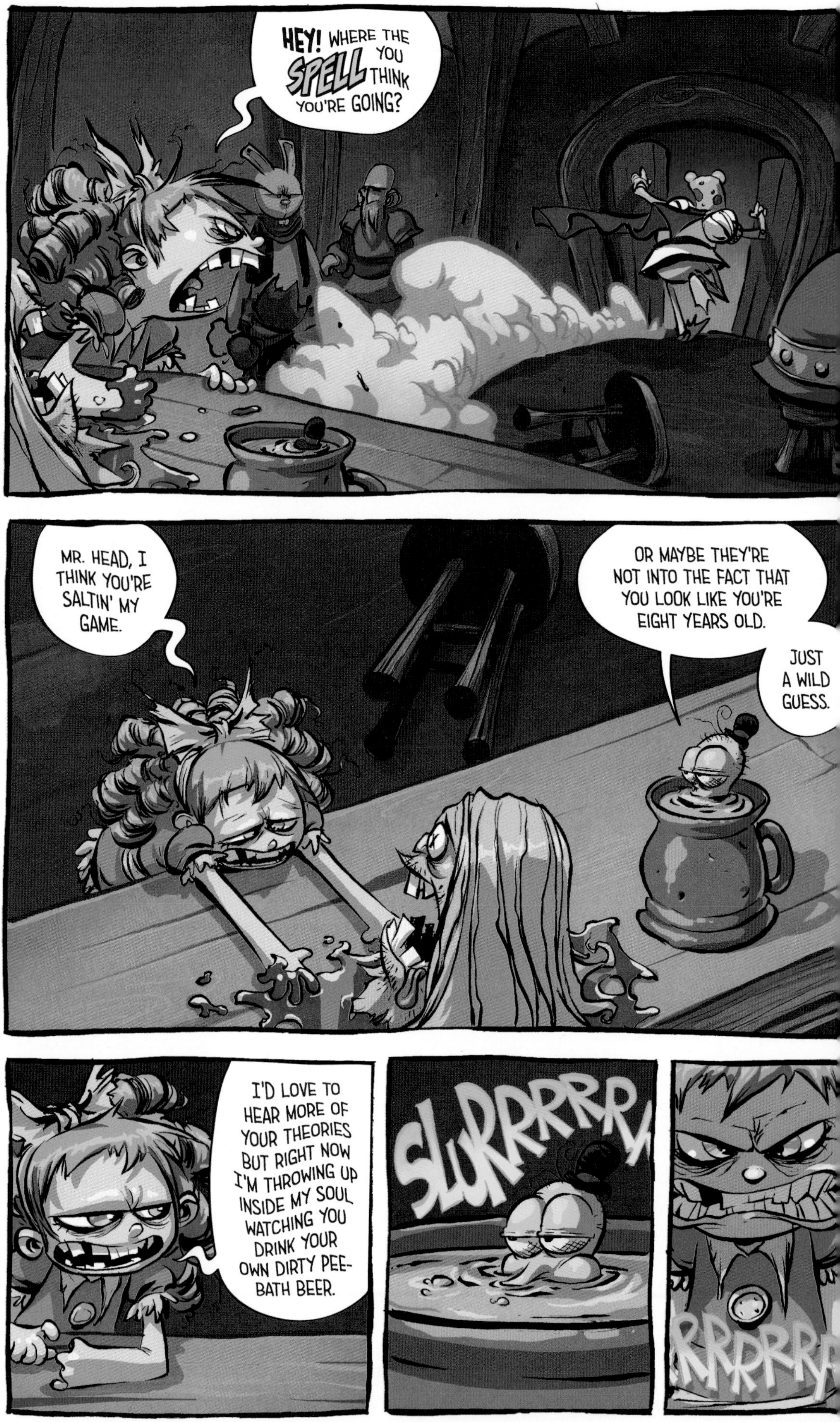
HEY! WHERE THE SPELL YOU THINK YOU'RE GOING?
MR. HEAD, I THINK YOU'RE SALTIN' MY GAME.
OR MAYBE THEY'RE NOT INTO THE FACT THAT YOU LOOK LIKE YOU'RE EIGHT YEARS OLD.
JUST A WILD GUESS.
I'D LOVE TO HEAR MORE OF YOUR THEORIES BUT RIGHT NOW I'M THROWING UP INSIDE MY SOUL WATCHING YOU DRINK YOUR OWN DIRTY PEE-BATH BEER.
SLURRRRRR
RRRRRR

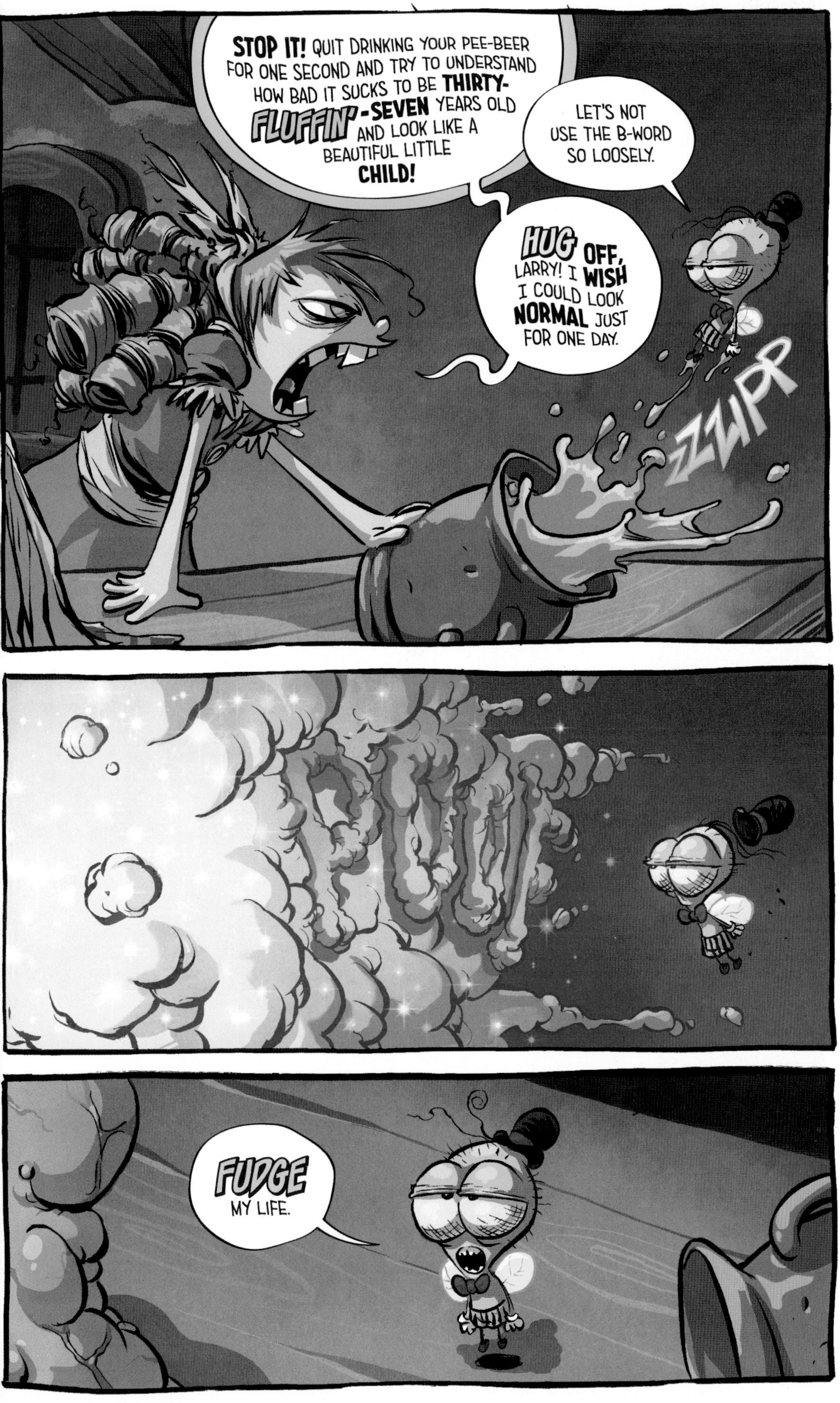
STOP IT! QUIT DRINKING YOUR PEE-BEER FOR ONE SECOND AND TRY TO UNDERSTAND HOW BAD IT SUCKS TO BE THIRTY-FLUFFIN'-SEVEN YEARS OLD AND LOOK LIKE A BEAUTIFUL LITTLE CHILD!
LET'S NOT USE THE B-WORD SO LOOSELY.
HUG OFF, LARRY! I WISH I COULD LOOK NORMAL JUST FOR ONE DAY.
ZZUPP
POOF
FUDGE MY LIFE.

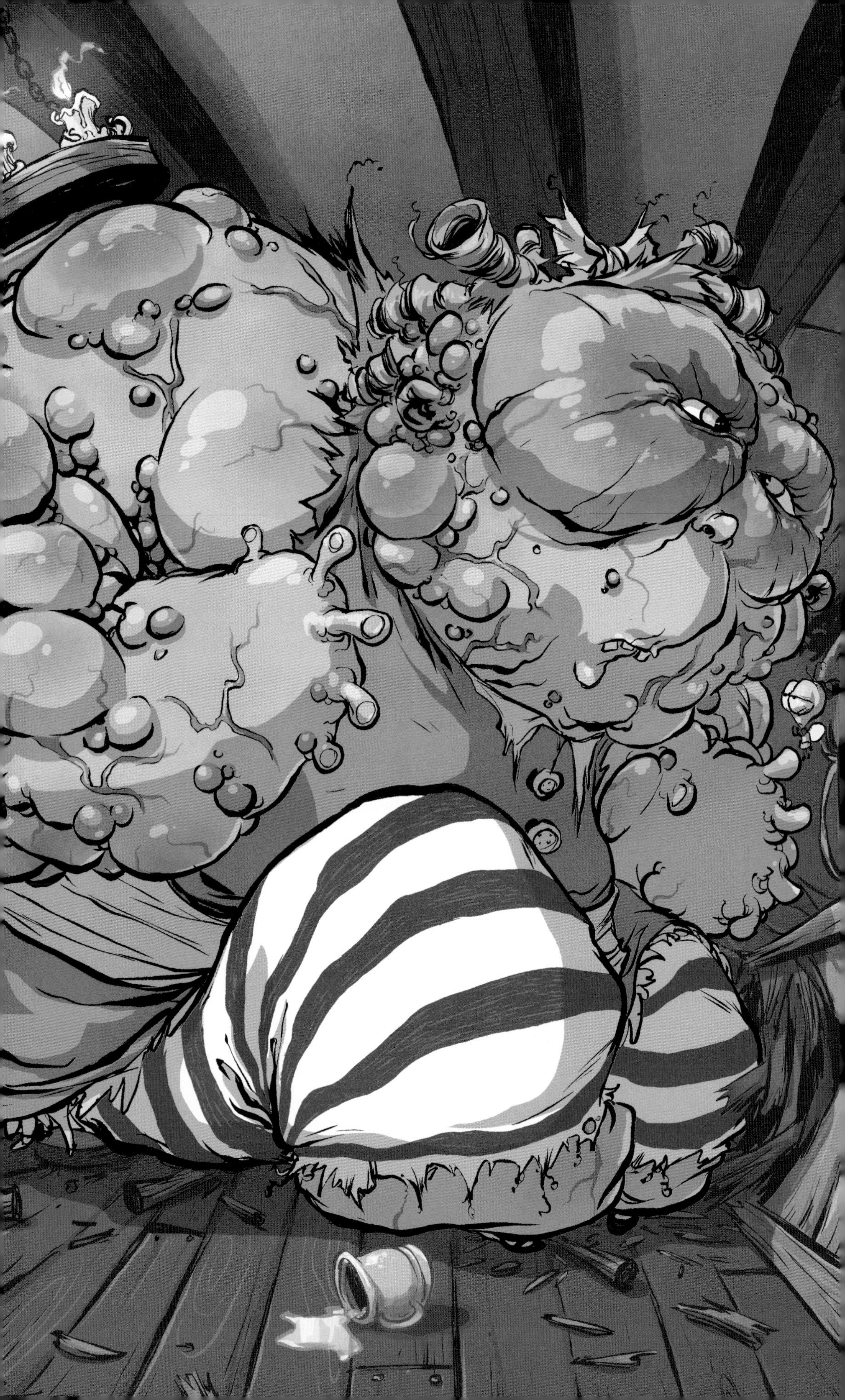

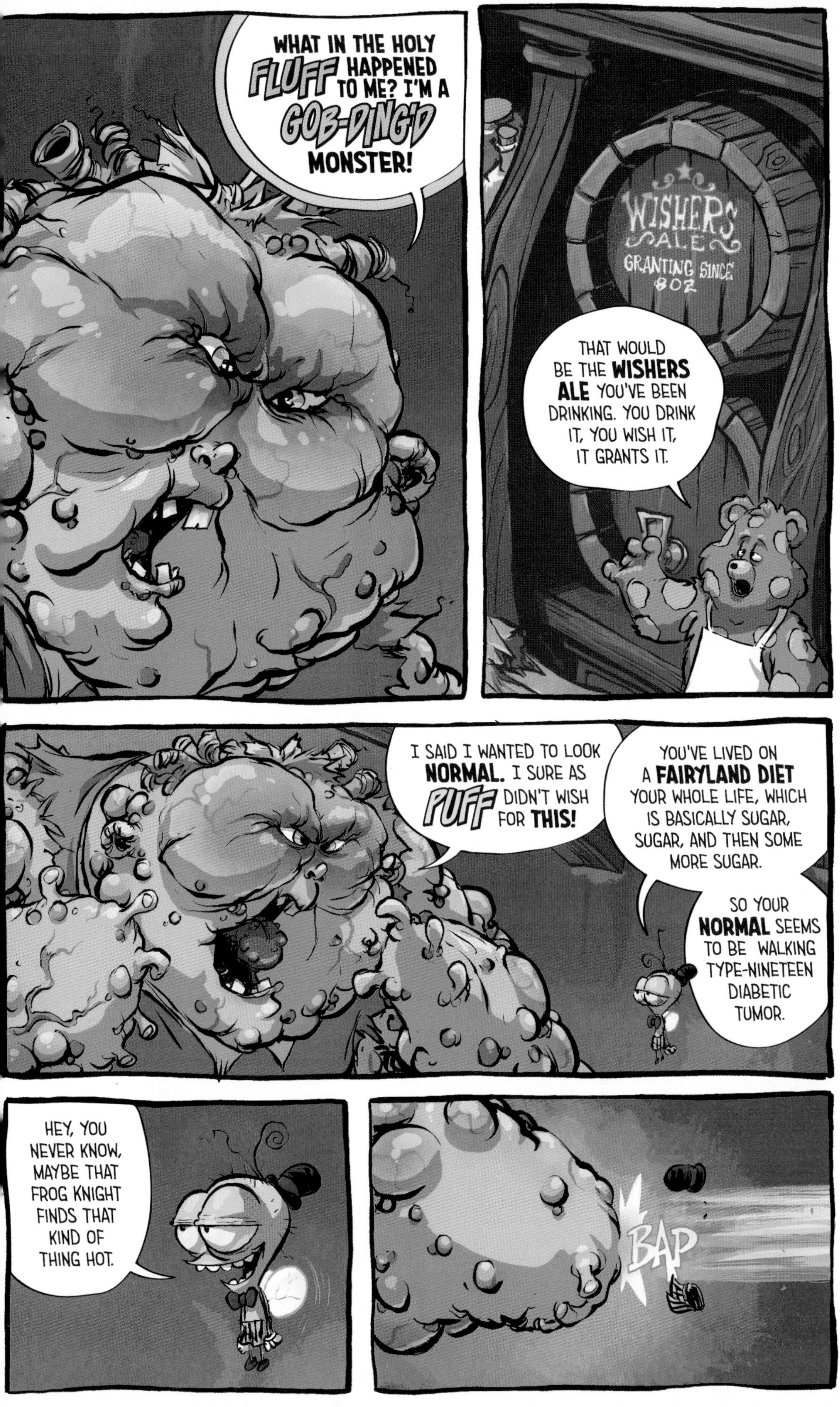
WHAT IN THE HOLY FLUFF HAPPENED TO ME? I'M A GOB-DING'D MONSTER!
WISHERS ALE
GRANTING SINCE 802
THAT WOULD BE THE WISHERS ALE YOU'VE BEEN DRINKING. YOU DRINK IT, YOU WISH IT, IT GRANTS IT.
I SAID I WANTED TO LOOK NORMAL. I SURE AS PUFF DIDN'T WISH FOR THIS!
YOU'VE LIVED ON A FAIRYLAND DIET YOUR WHOLE LIFE, WHICH IS BASICALLY SUGAR, SUGAR, AND THEN SOME MORE SUGAR.
SO YOUR NORMAL SEEMS TO BE WALKING TYPE-NINETEEN DIABETIC TUMOR.
HEY, YOU NEVER KNOW, MAYBE THAT FROG KNIGHT FINDS THAT KIND OF THING HOT.
BAP

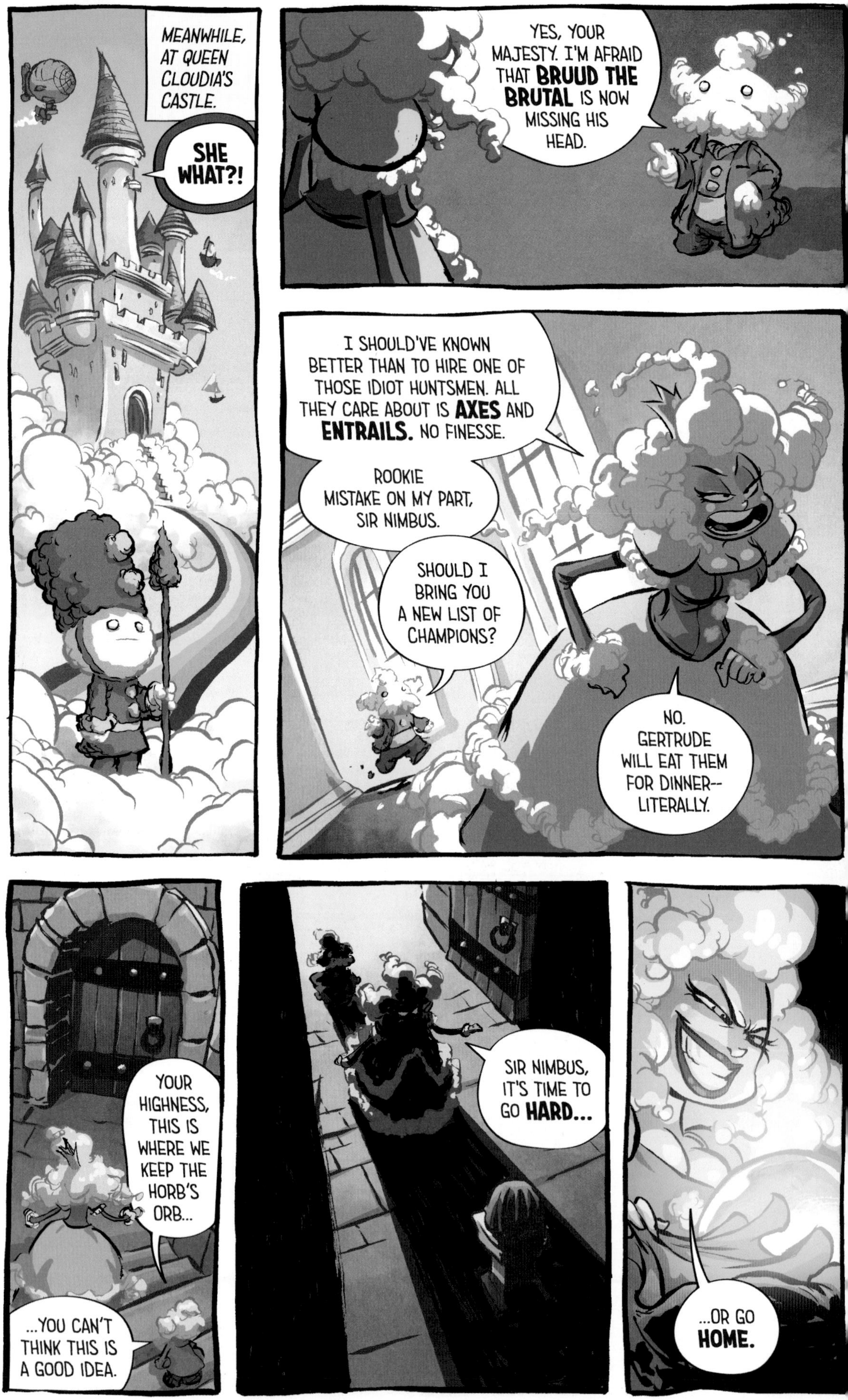
MEANWHILE, AT QUEEN CLOUDIA'S CASTLE.
SHE WHAT?!
YES, YOUR MAJESTY. I'M AFRAID THAT BRUUD THE BRUTAL IS NOW MISSING HIS HEAD.
I SHOULD'VE KNOWN BETTER THAN TO HIRE ONE OF THOSE IDIOT HUNTSMEN. ALL THEY CARE ABOUT IS AXES AND ENTRAILS. NO FINESSE.
ROOKIE MISTAKE ON MY PART, SIR NIMBUS.
SHOULD I BRING YOU A NEW LIST OF CHAMPIONS?
NO. GERTRUDE WILL EAT THEM FOR DINNER--LITERALLY.
YOUR HIGHNESS, THIS IS WHERE WE KEEP THE HORB'S ORB...
...YOU CAN'T THINK THIS IS A GOOD IDEA.
SIR NIMBUS, IT'S TIME TO GO HARD...
...OR GO HOME.

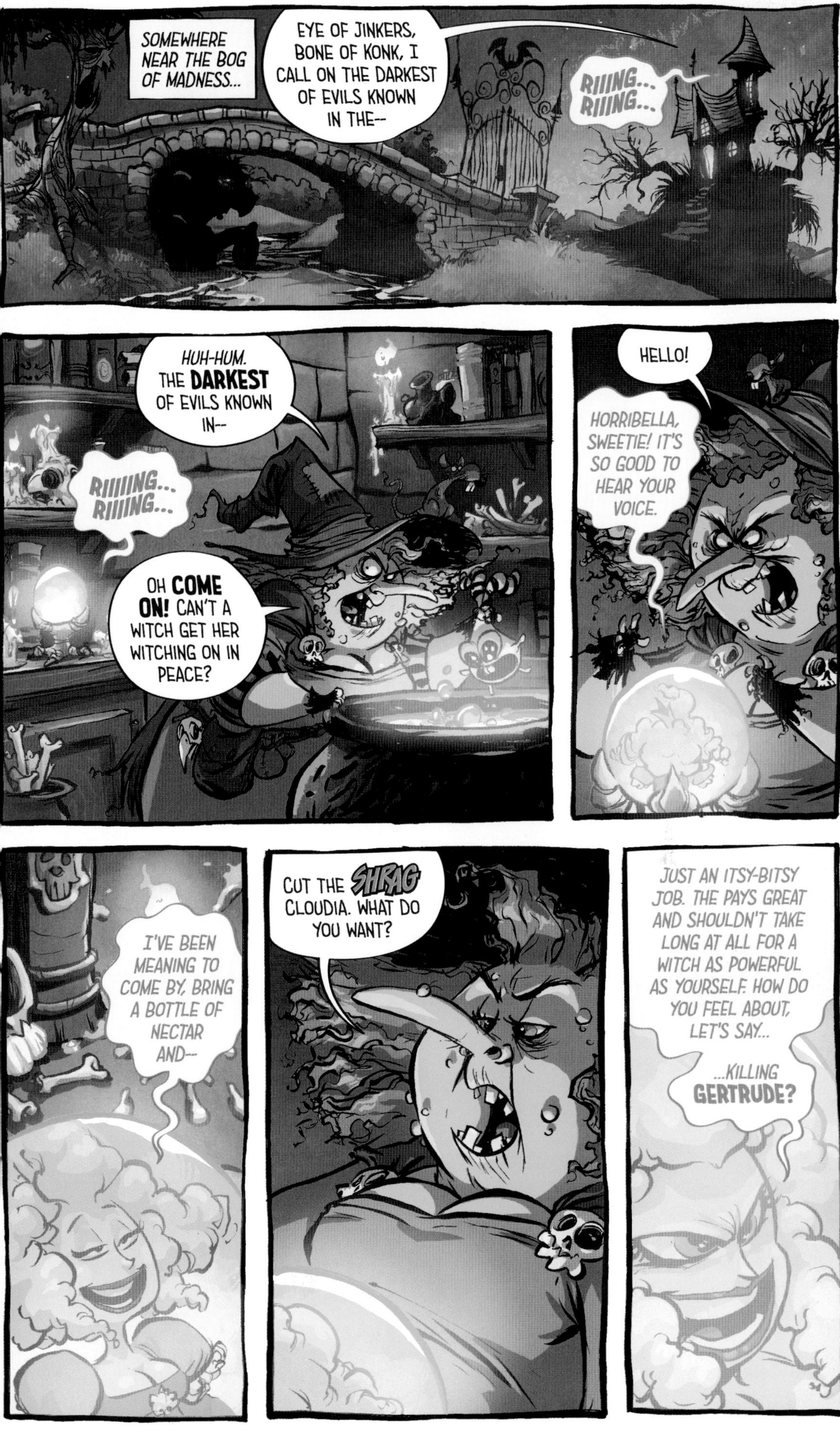
SOMEWHERE NEAR THE BOG OF MADNESS...
EYE OF JINKERS, BONE OF KONK, I CALL ON THE DARKEST OF EVILS KNOWN IN THE--
RIIING... RIIING...
HUH-HUM. THE DARKEST OF EVILS KNOWN IN--
RIIIING... RIIING...
OH COME ON! CAN'T A WITCH GET HER WITCHING ON IN PEACE?
HELLO!
HORRIBELLA, SWEETIE! IT'S SO GOOD TO HEAR YOUR VOICE.
I'VE BEEN MEANING TO COME BY, BRING A BOTTLE OF NECTAR AND--
CUT THE SHRAG CLOUDIA. WHAT DO YOU WANT?
JUST AN ITSY-BITSY JOB. THE PAYS GREAT AND SHOULDN'T TAKE LONG AT ALL FOR A WITCH AS POWERFUL AS YOURSELF. HOW DO YOU FEEL ABOUT, LET'S SAY...
...KILLING GERTRUDE?

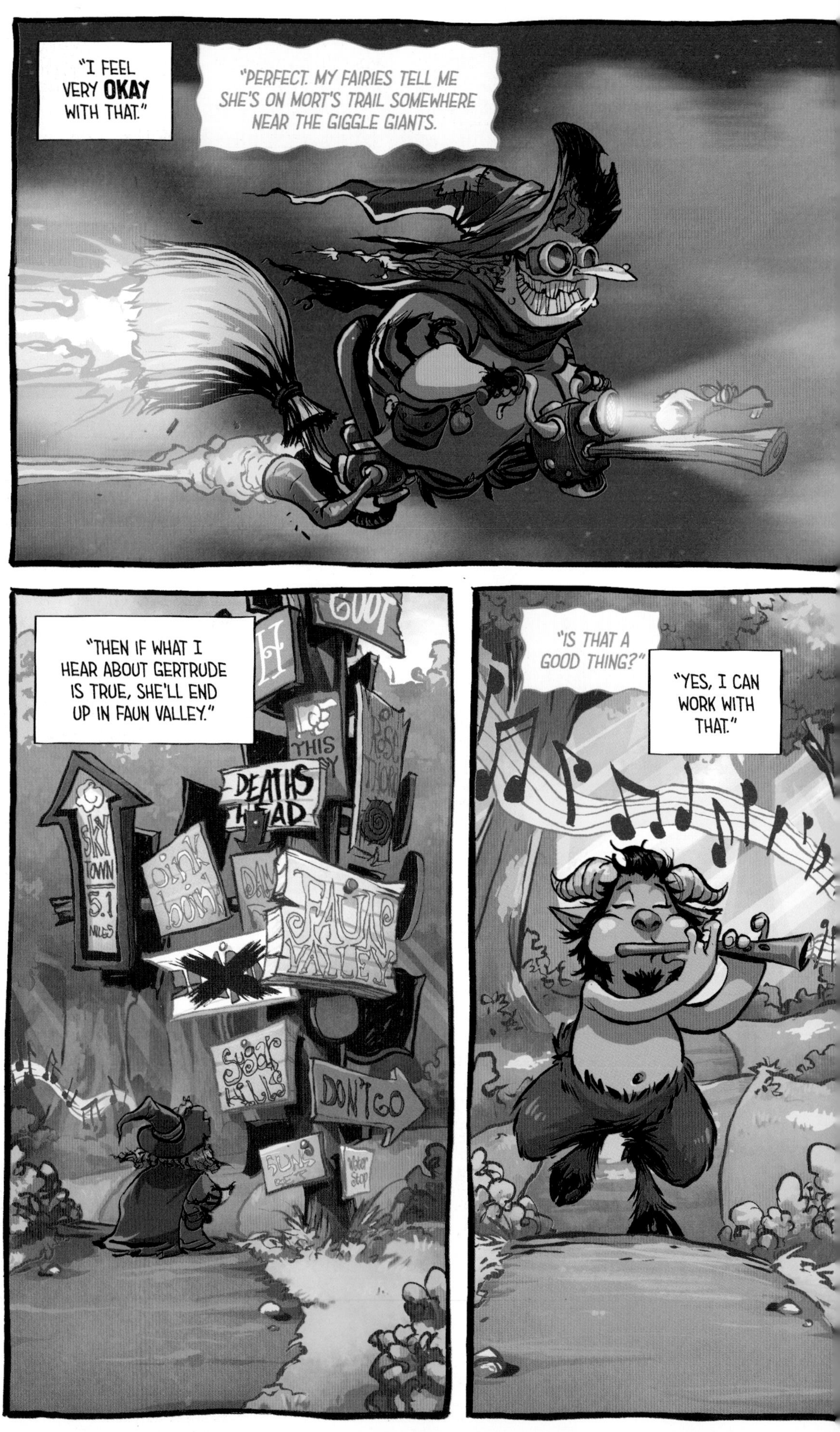
"I FEEL VERY **OKAY** WITH THAT."
"PERFECT. MY FAIRIES TELL ME SHE'S ON MORT'S TRAIL SOMEWHERE NEAR THE GIGGLE GIANTS.
"THEN IF WHAT I HEAR ABOUT GERTRUDE IS TRUE, SHE'LL END UP IN FAUN VALLEY."
DEATHS HEAD
SKY TOWN 5.1 MILES
oink boink
FAUN VALLEY
Sugar Hills
DON'T GO
Water Stop
"IS THAT A GOOD THING?"
"YES, I CAN WORK WITH THAT."

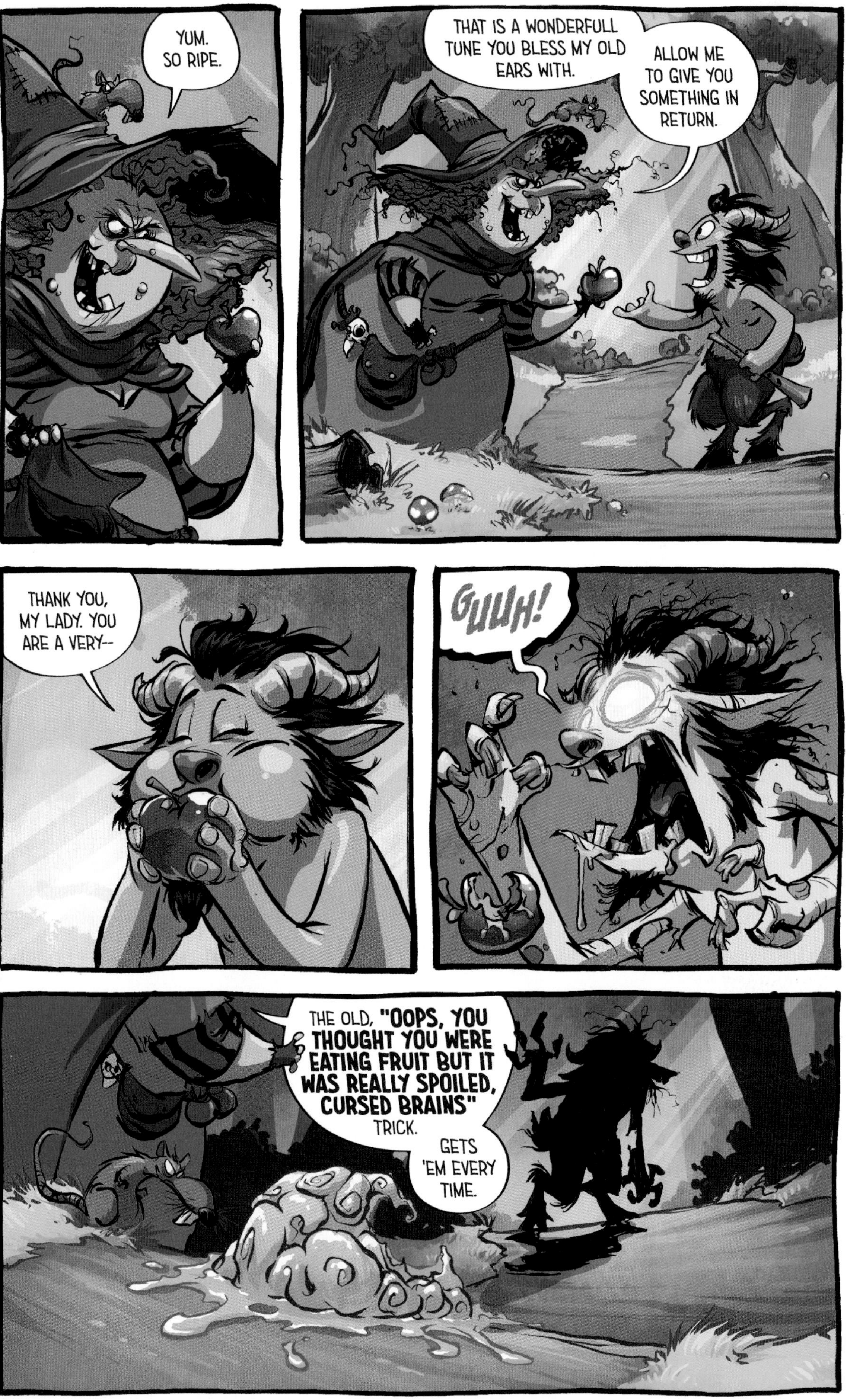
YUM. SO RIPE.
THAT IS A WONDERFULL TUNE YOU BLESS MY OLD EARS WITH.
ALLOW ME TO GIVE YOU SOMETHING IN RETURN.
THANK YOU, MY LADY. YOU ARE A VERY--
GUUH!
THE OLD, "OOPS, YOU THOUGHT YOU WERE EATING FRUIT BUT IT WAS REALLY SPOILED, CURSED BRAINS" TRICK.
GETS 'EM EVERY TIME.

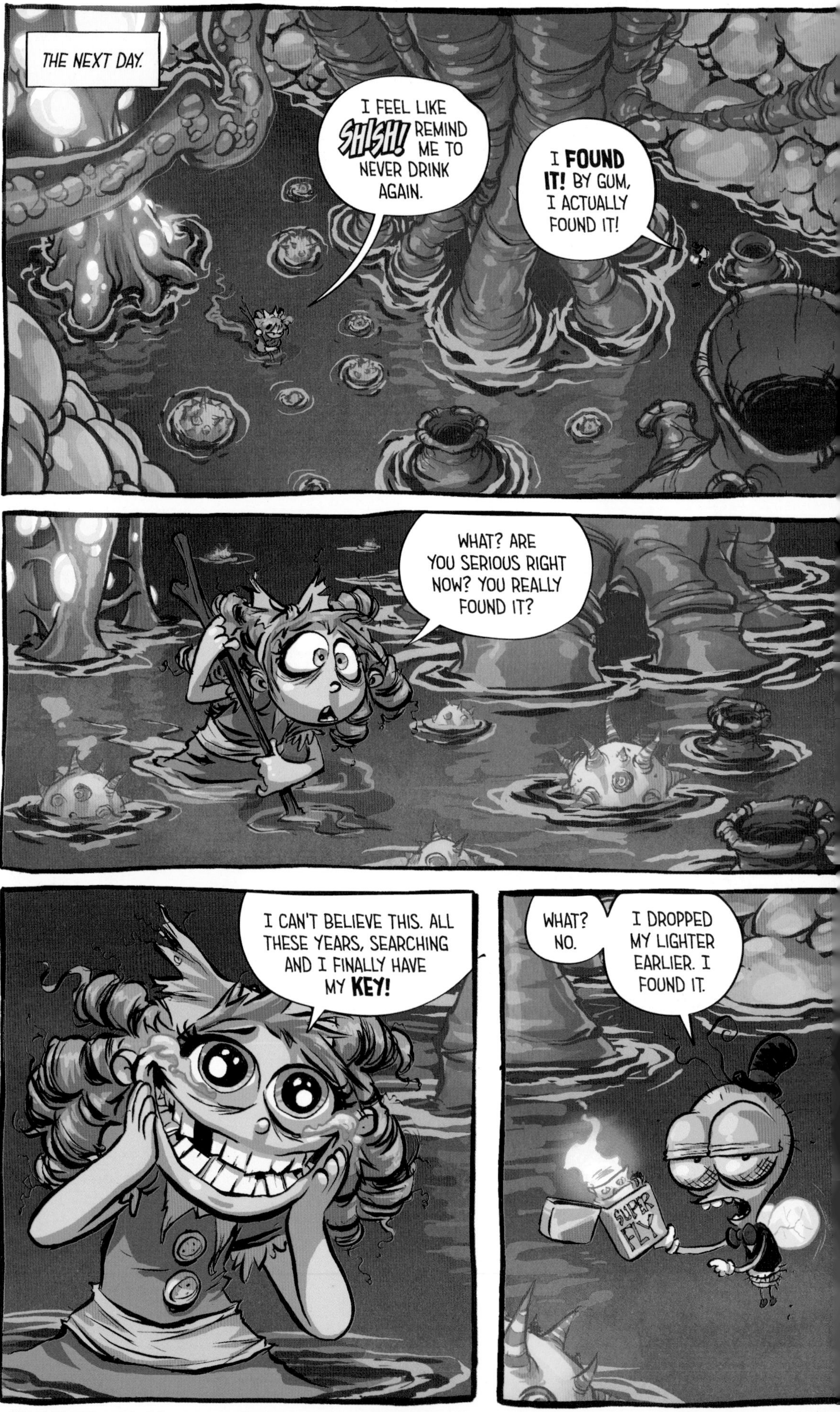
THE NEXT DAY.
I FEEL LIKE SHISH! REMIND ME TO NEVER DRINK AGAIN.
I FOUND IT! BY GUM, I ACTUALLY FOUND IT!
WHAT? ARE YOU SERIOUS RIGHT NOW? YOU REALLY FOUND IT?
I CAN'T BELIEVE THIS. ALL THESE YEARS, SEARCHING AND I FINALLY HAVE MY KEY!
WHAT? NO.
I DROPPED MY LIGHTER EARLIER. I FOUND IT.
SUPER FLY

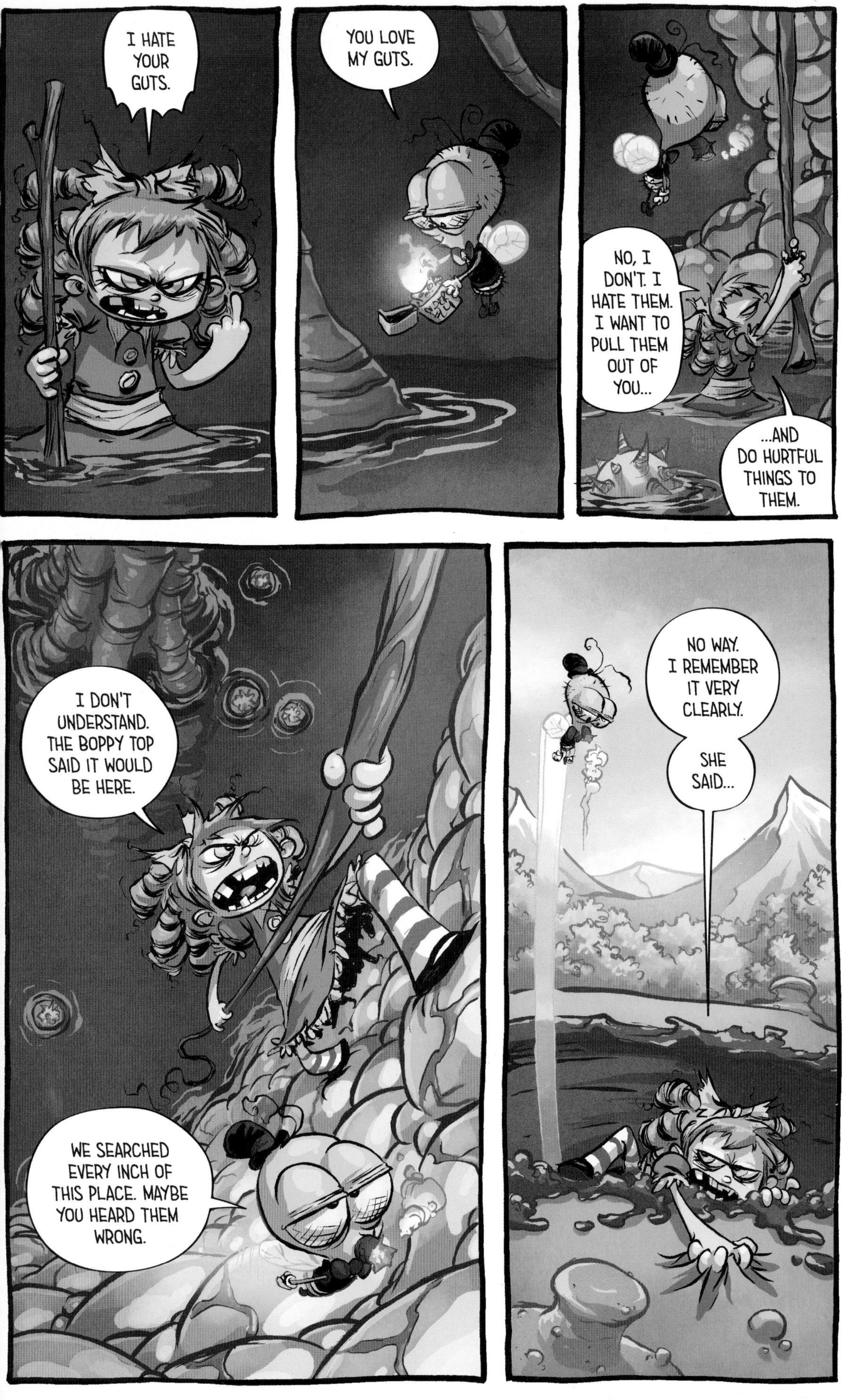
I HATE YOUR GUTS.
YOU LOVE MY GUTS.
NO, I DON'T. I HATE THEM. I WANT TO PULL THEM OUT OF YOU...
...AND DO HURTFUL THINGS TO THEM.
I DON'T UNDERSTAND. THE BOPPY TOP SAID IT WOULD BE HERE.
WE SEARCHED EVERY INCH OF THIS PLACE. MAYBE YOU HEARD THEM WRONG.
NO WAY. I REMEMBER IT VERY CLEARLY.
SHE SAID...

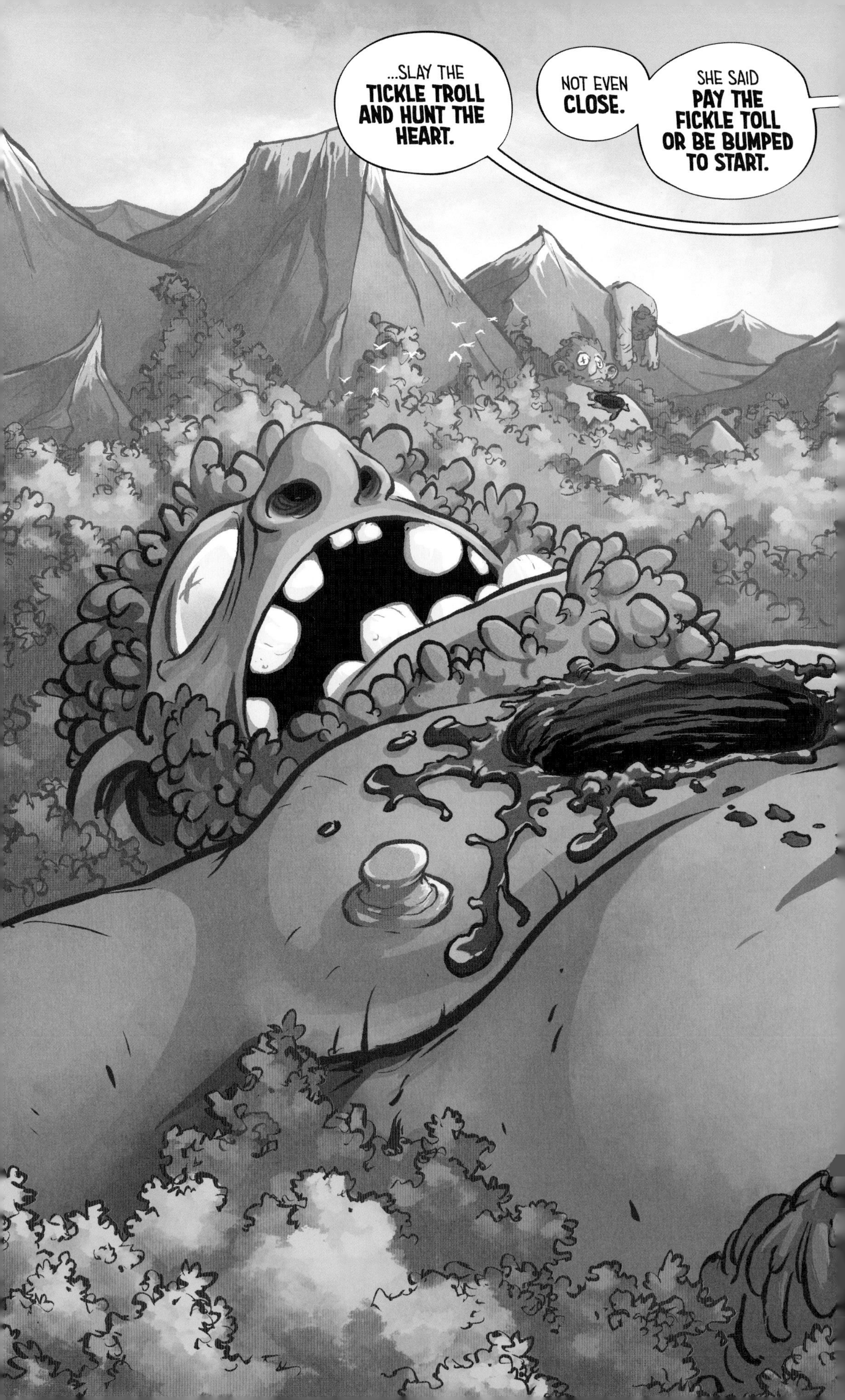

...SLAY THE TICKLE TROLL AND HUNT THE HEART.
NOT EVEN CLOSE.
SHE SAID PAY THE FICKLE TOLL OR BE BUMPED TO START.

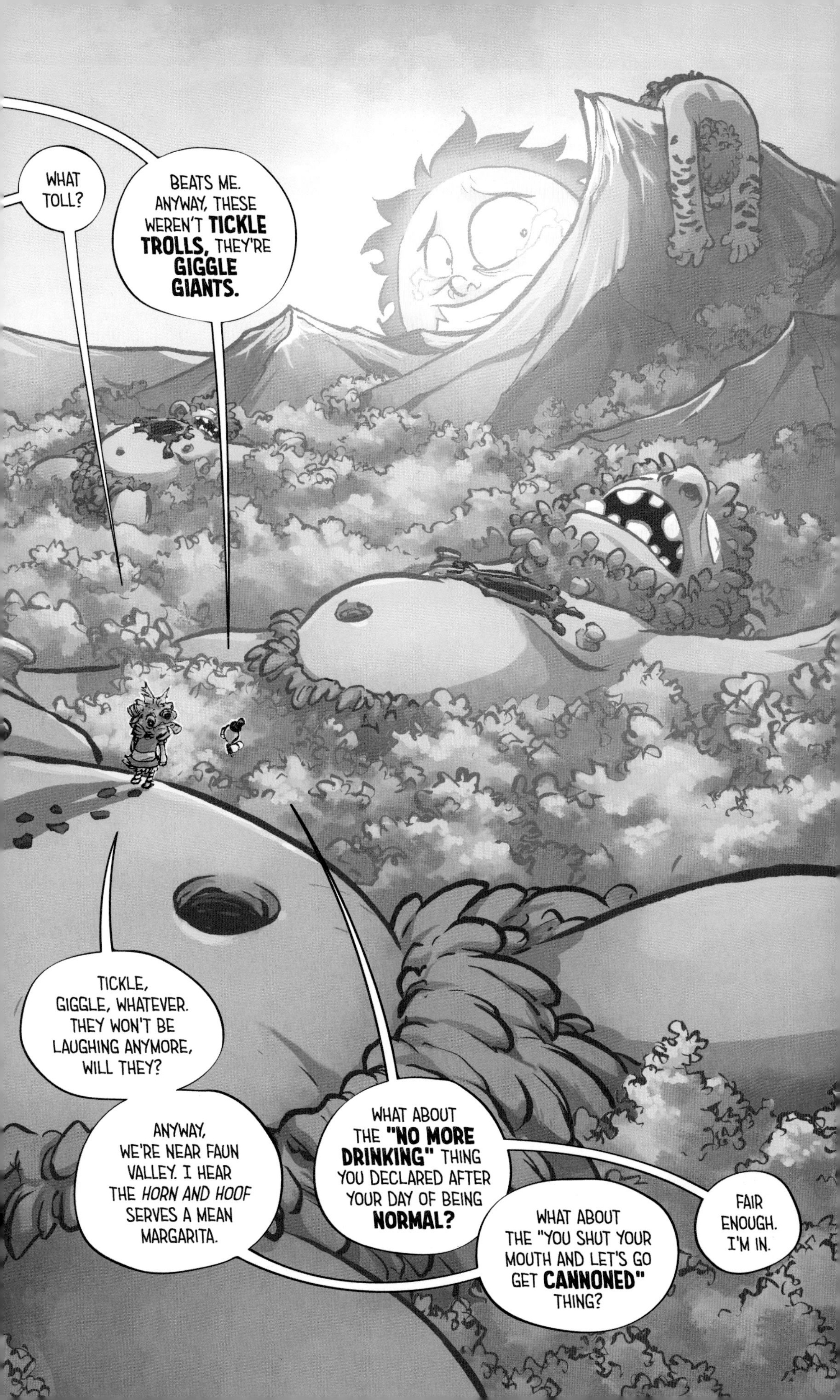
WHAT TOLL?
BEATS ME. ANYWAY, THESE WEREN'T **TICKLE TROLLS,** THEY'RE **GIGGLE GIANTS.**
TICKLE, GIGGLE, WHATEVER. THEY WON'T BE LAUGHING ANYMORE, WILL THEY?
ANYWAY, WE'RE NEAR FAUN VALLEY. I HEAR THE *HORN AND HOOF* SERVES A MEAN MARGARITA.
WHAT ABOUT THE **"NO MORE DRINKING"** THING YOU DECLARED AFTER YOUR DAY OF BEING **NORMAL?**
WHAT ABOUT THE "YOU SHUT YOUR MOUTH AND LET'S GO GET **CANNONED"** THING?
FAIR ENOUGH. I'M IN.

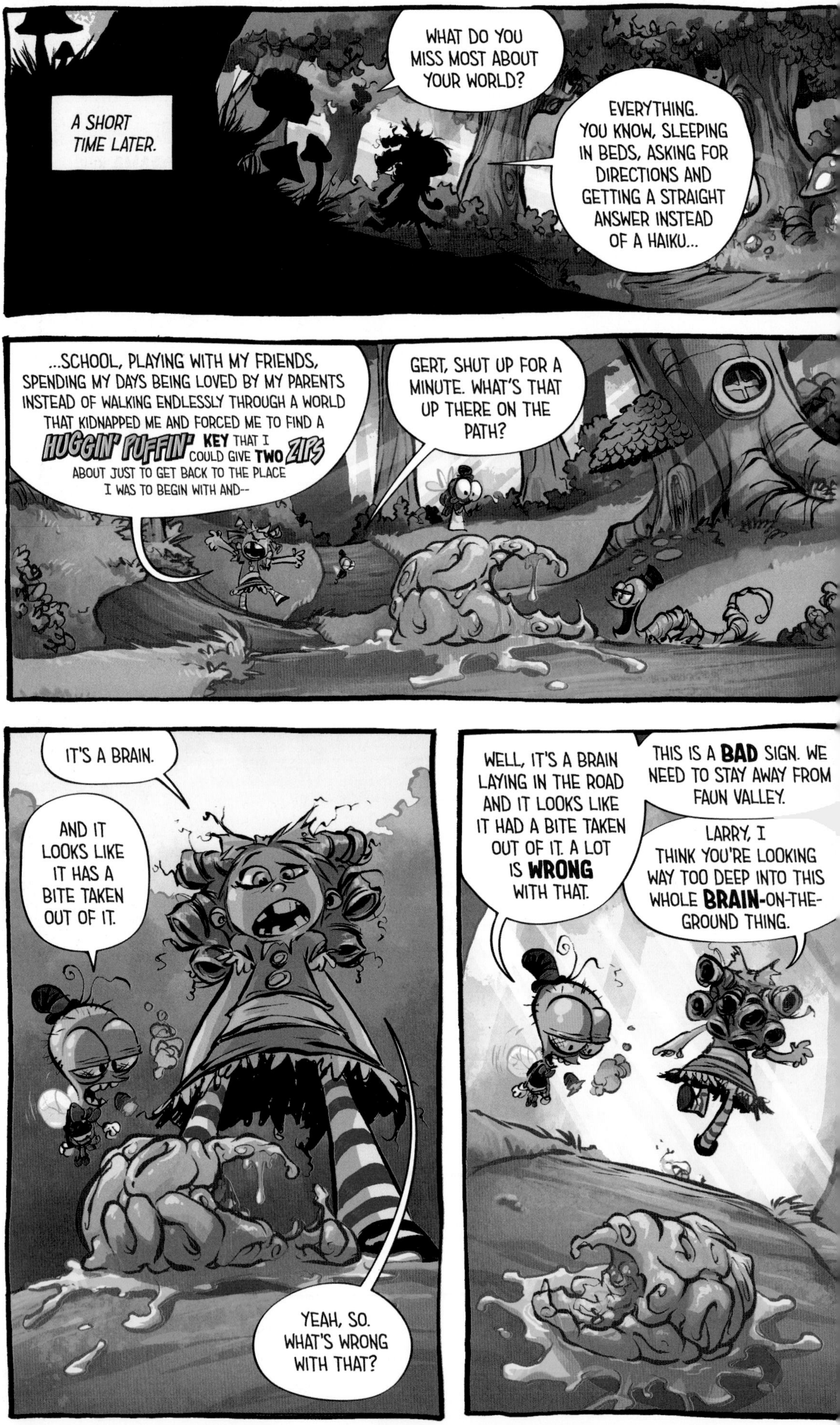
A SHORT TIME LATER.
WHAT DO YOU MISS MOST ABOUT YOUR WORLD?
EVERYTHING. YOU KNOW, SLEEPING IN BEDS, ASKING FOR DIRECTIONS AND GETTING A STRAIGHT ANSWER INSTEAD OF A HAIKU...
...SCHOOL, PLAYING WITH MY FRIENDS, SPENDING MY DAYS BEING LOVED BY MY PARENTS INSTEAD OF WALKING ENDLESSLY THROUGH A WORLD THAT KIDNAPPED ME AND FORCED ME TO FIND A HUGGIN' PUFFIN' KEY THAT I COULD GIVE TWO ZIPS ABOUT JUST TO GET BACK TO THE PLACE I WAS TO BEGIN WITH AND--
GERT, SHUT UP FOR A MINUTE. WHAT'S THAT UP THERE ON THE PATH?
IT'S A BRAIN.
AND IT LOOKS LIKE IT HAS A BITE TAKEN OUT OF IT.
YEAH, SO. WHAT'S WRONG WITH THAT?
WELL, IT'S A BRAIN LAYING IN THE ROAD AND IT LOOKS LIKE IT HAD A BITE TAKEN OUT OF IT. A LOT IS WRONG WITH THAT.
THIS IS A BAD SIGN. WE NEED TO STAY AWAY FROM FAUN VALLEY.
LARRY, I THINK YOU'RE LOOKING WAY TOO DEEP INTO THIS WHOLE BRAIN-ON-THE-GROUND THING.

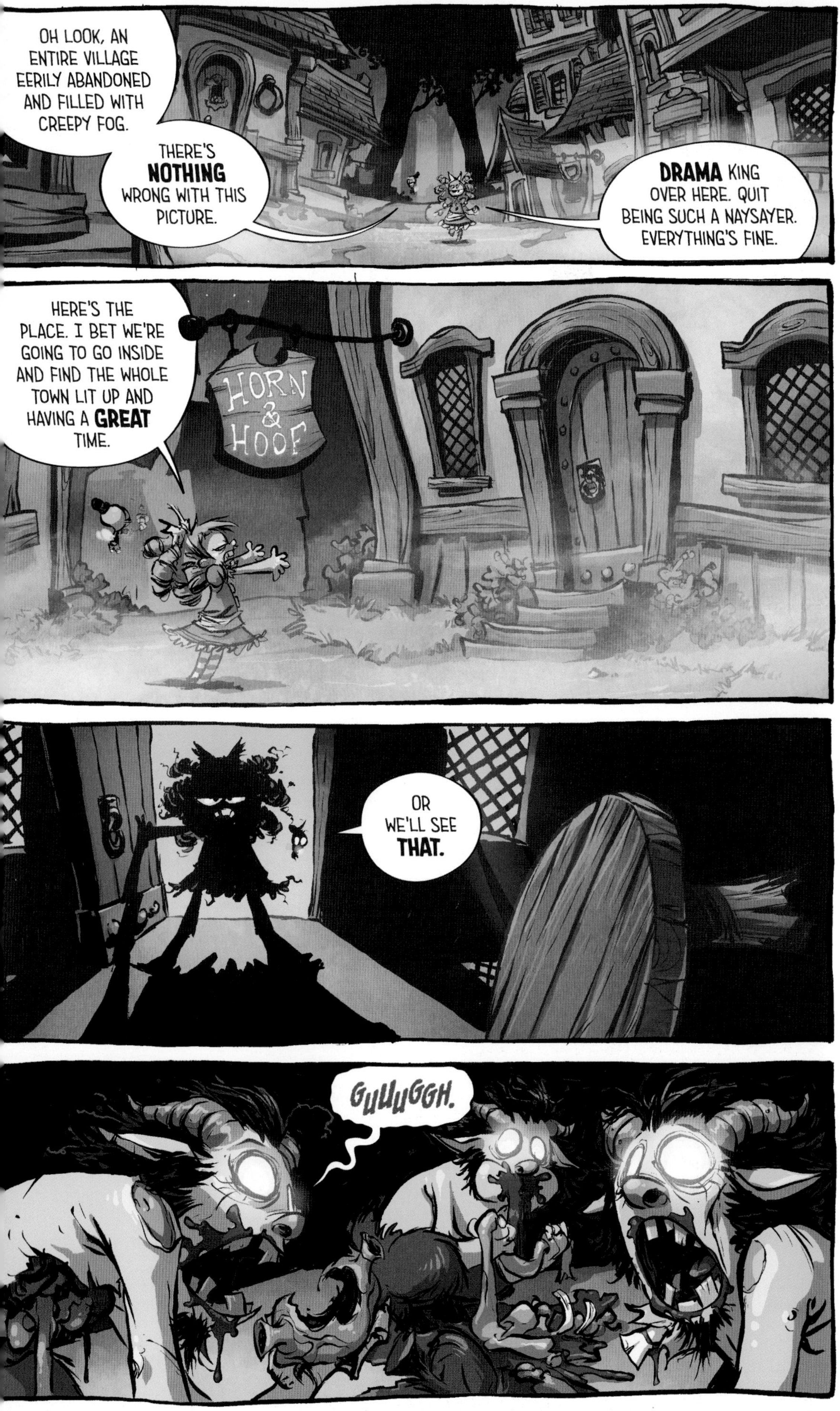
OH LOOK, AN ENTIRE VILLAGE EERILY ABANDONED AND FILLED WITH CREEPY FOG.
THERE'S **NOTHING** WRONG WITH THIS PICTURE.
DRAMA KING OVER HERE. QUIT BEING SUCH A NAYSAYER. EVERYTHING'S FINE.
HERE'S THE PLACE. I BET WE'RE GOING TO GO INSIDE AND FIND THE WHOLE TOWN LIT UP AND HAVING A **GREAT** TIME.
HORN & HOOF
OR WE'LL SEE **THAT.**
GUUUGGH.

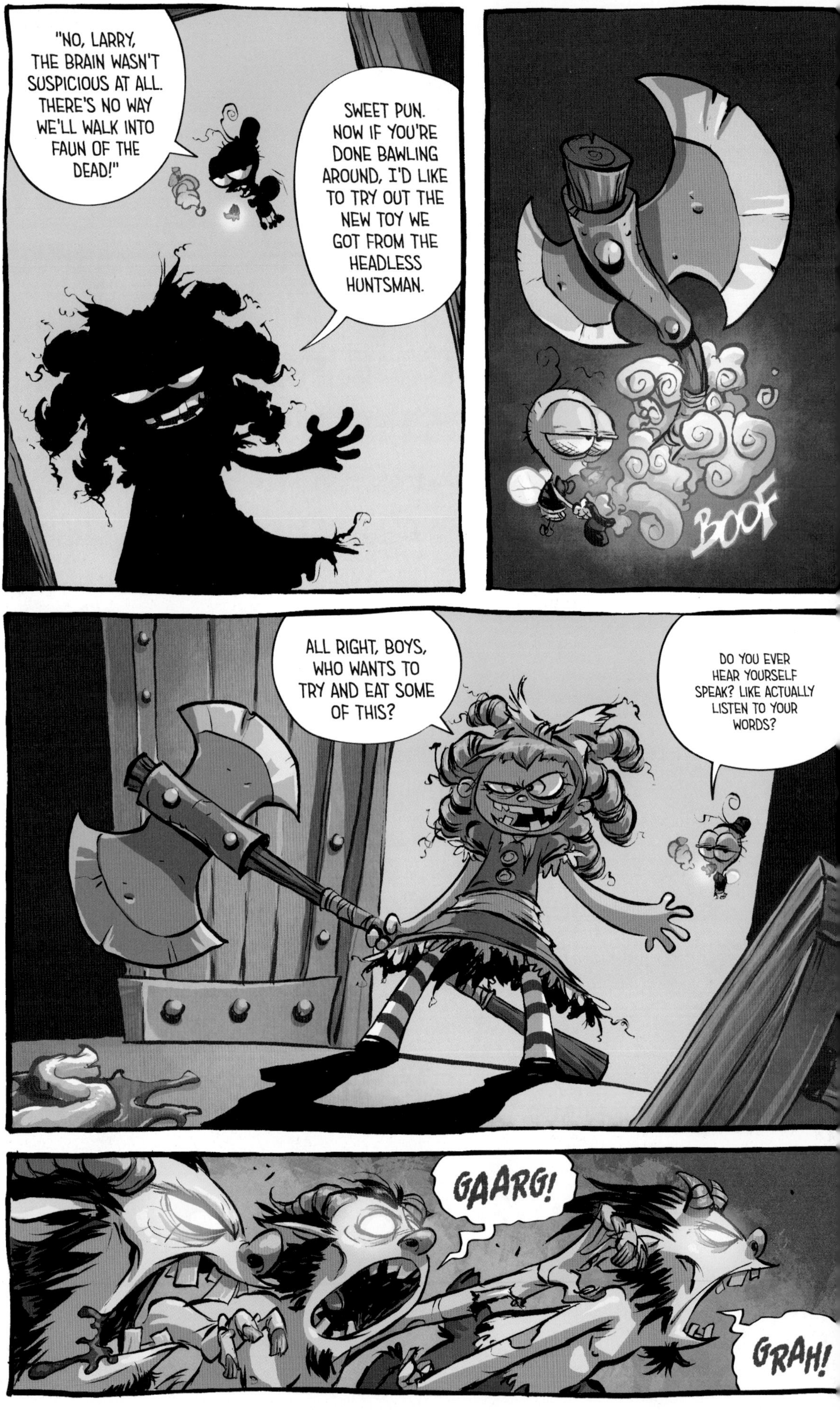
"NO, LARRY, THE BRAIN WASN'T SUSPICIOUS AT ALL. THERE'S NO WAY WE'LL WALK INTO FAUN OF THE DEAD!"
SWEET PUN. NOW IF YOU'RE DONE BAWLING AROUND, I'D LIKE TO TRY OUT THE NEW TOY WE GOT FROM THE HEADLESS HUNTSMAN.
BOOF
ALL RIGHT, BOYS, WHO WANTS TO TRY AND EAT SOME OF THIS?
DO YOU EVER HEAR YOURSELF SPEAK? LIKE ACTUALLY LISTEN TO YOUR WORDS?
GAARG!
GRAH!

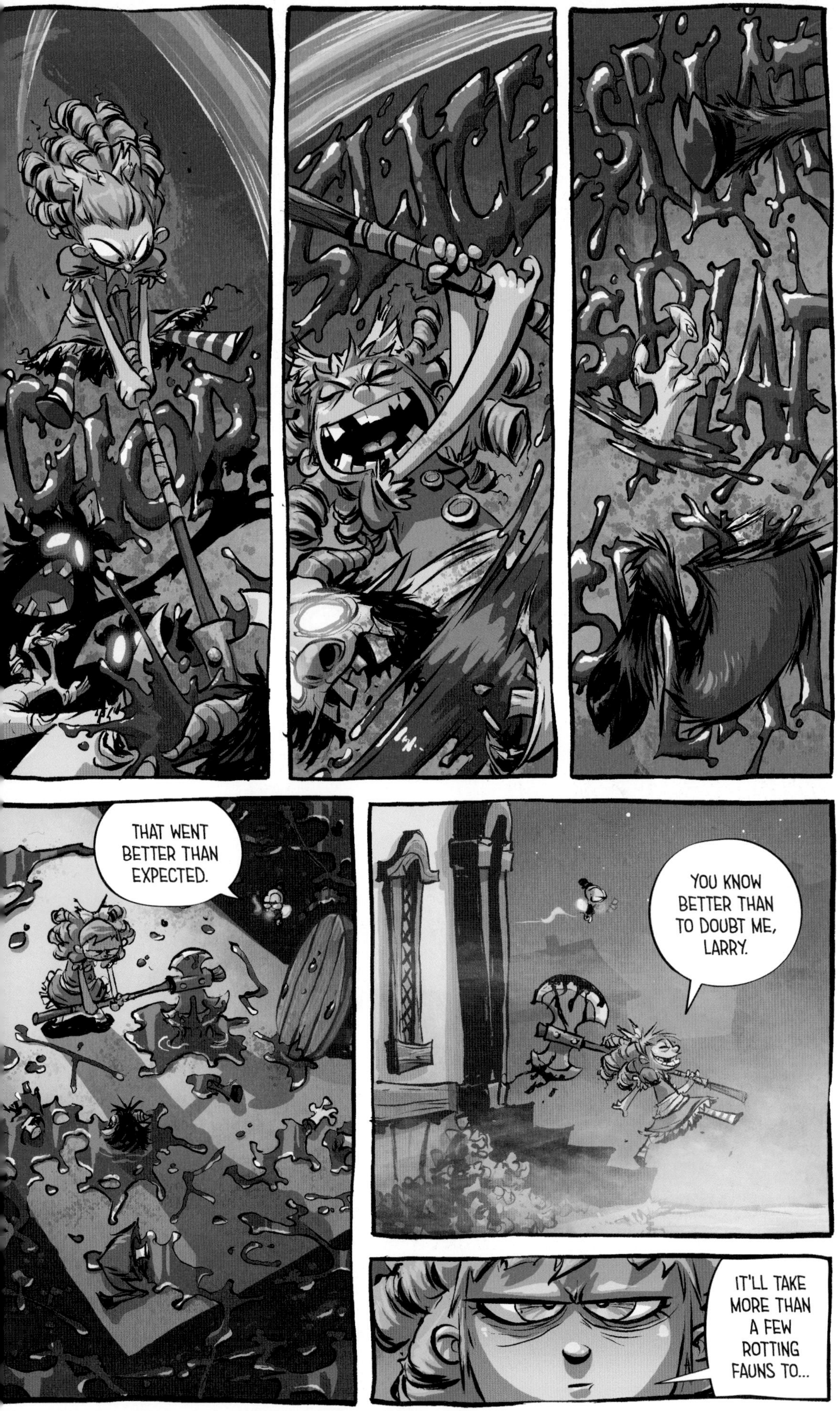
CHOP
SPLUTCH
SPLAT
SPLAT
THAT WENT BETTER THAN EXPECTED.
YOU KNOW BETTER THAN TO DOUBT ME, LARRY.
IT'LL TAKE MORE THAN A FEW ROTTING FAUNS TO...

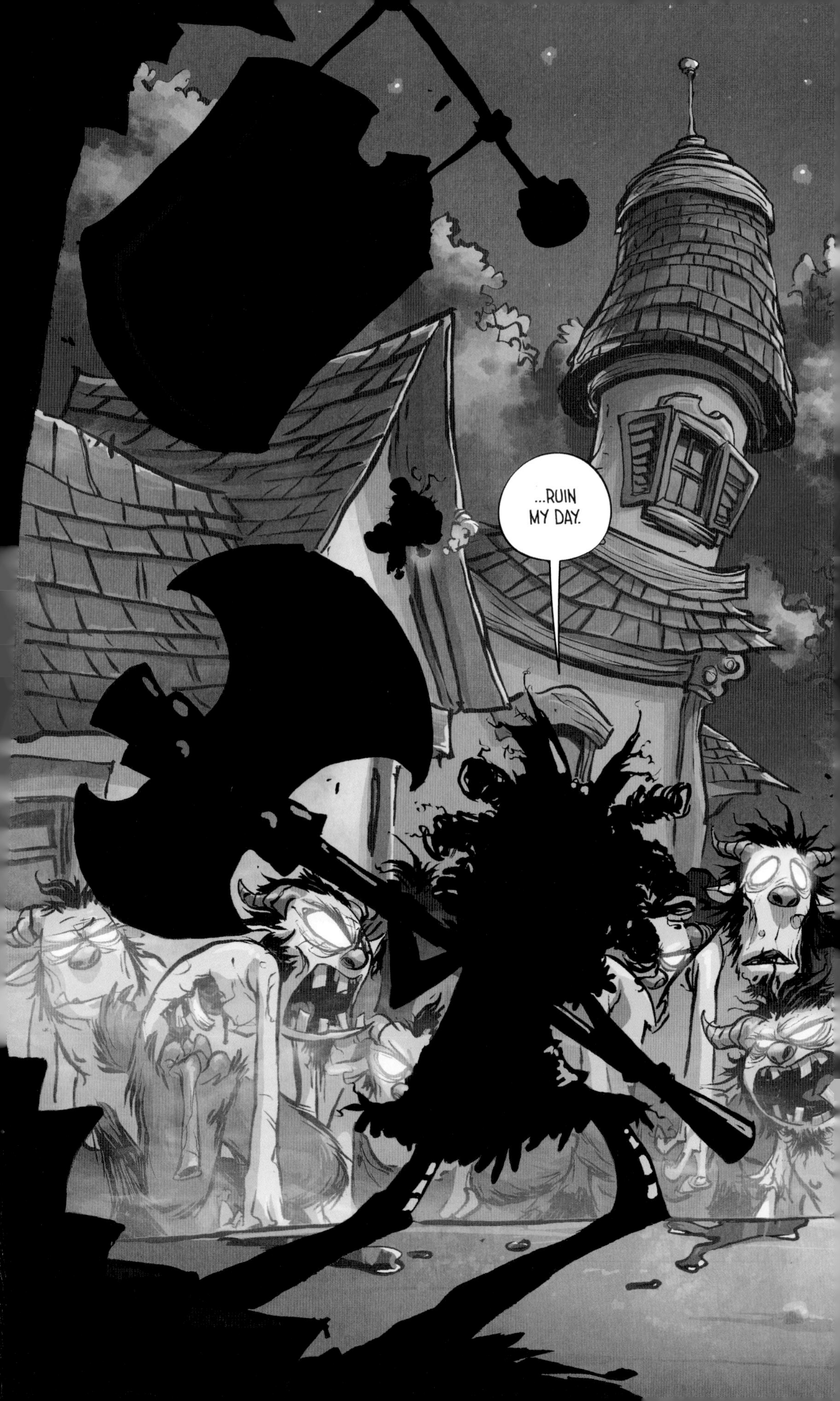
...RUIN MY DAY.

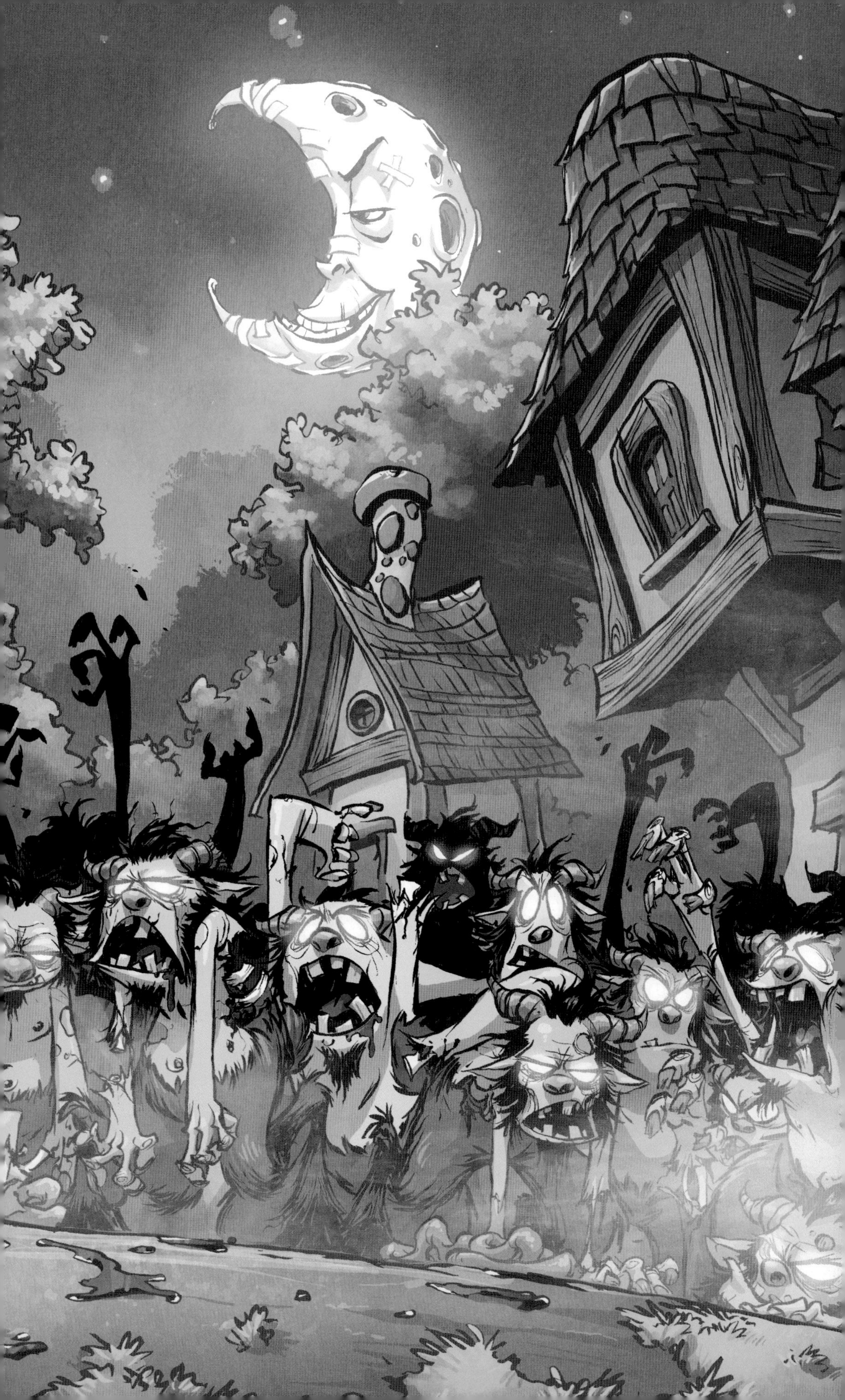

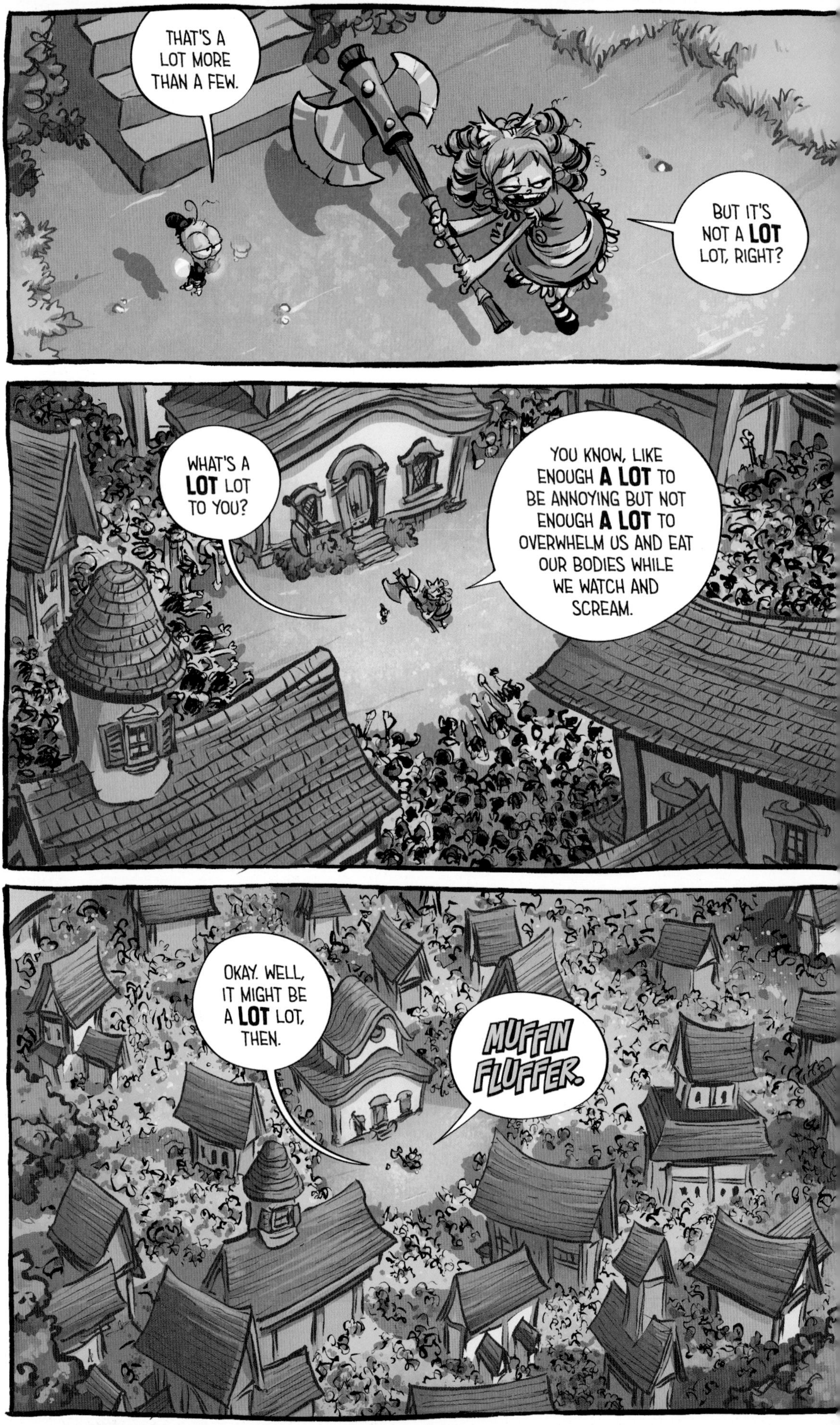
THAT'S A LOT MORE THAN A FEW.
BUT IT'S NOT A **LOT** LOT, RIGHT?
WHAT'S A **LOT** LOT TO YOU?
YOU KNOW, LIKE ENOUGH **A LOT** TO BE ANNOYING BUT NOT ENOUGH **A LOT** TO OVERWHELM US AND EAT OUR BODIES WHILE WE WATCH AND SCREAM.
OKAY. WELL, IT MIGHT BE A **LOT** LOT, THEN.
MUFFIN FLUFFER.

THREE

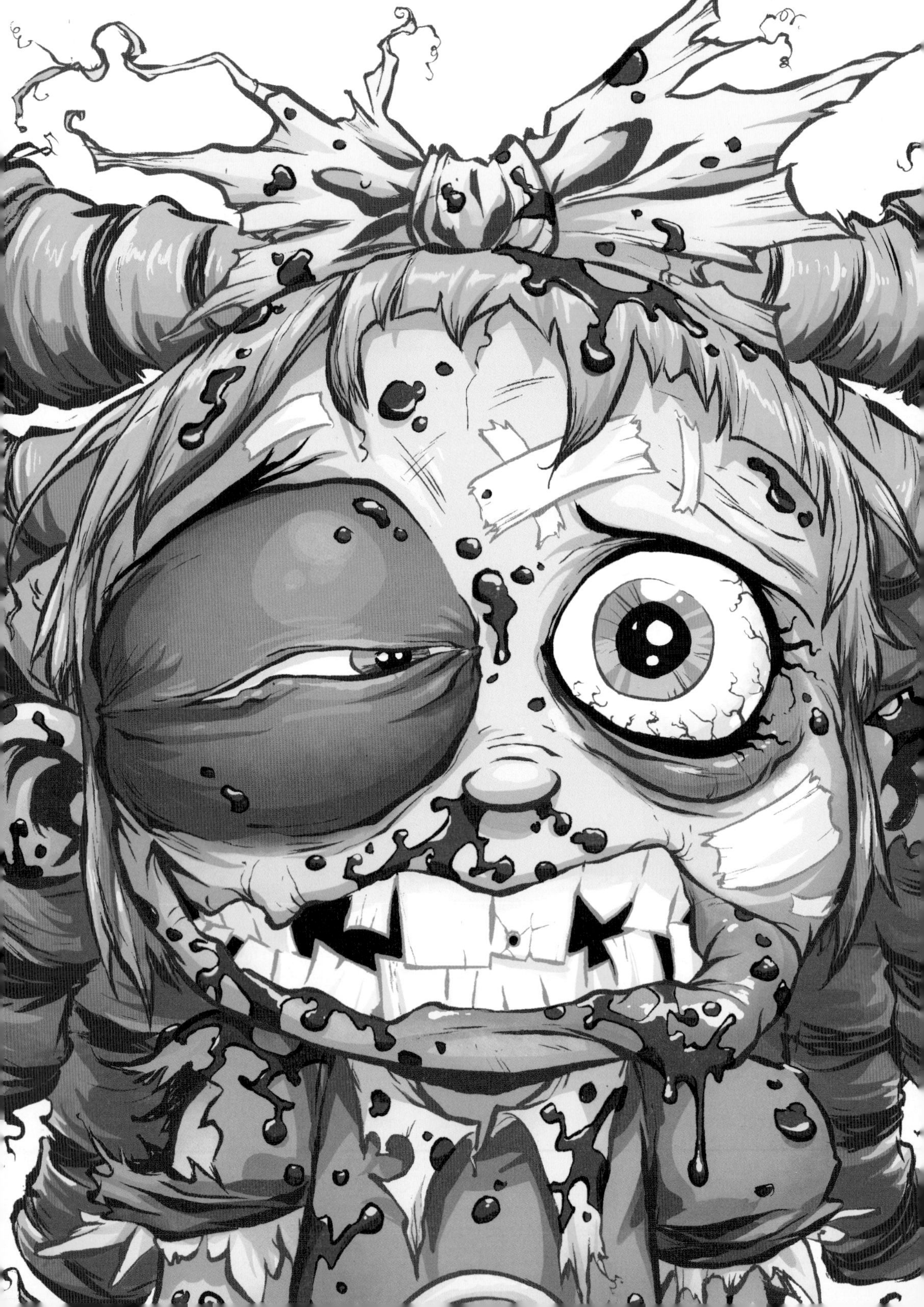

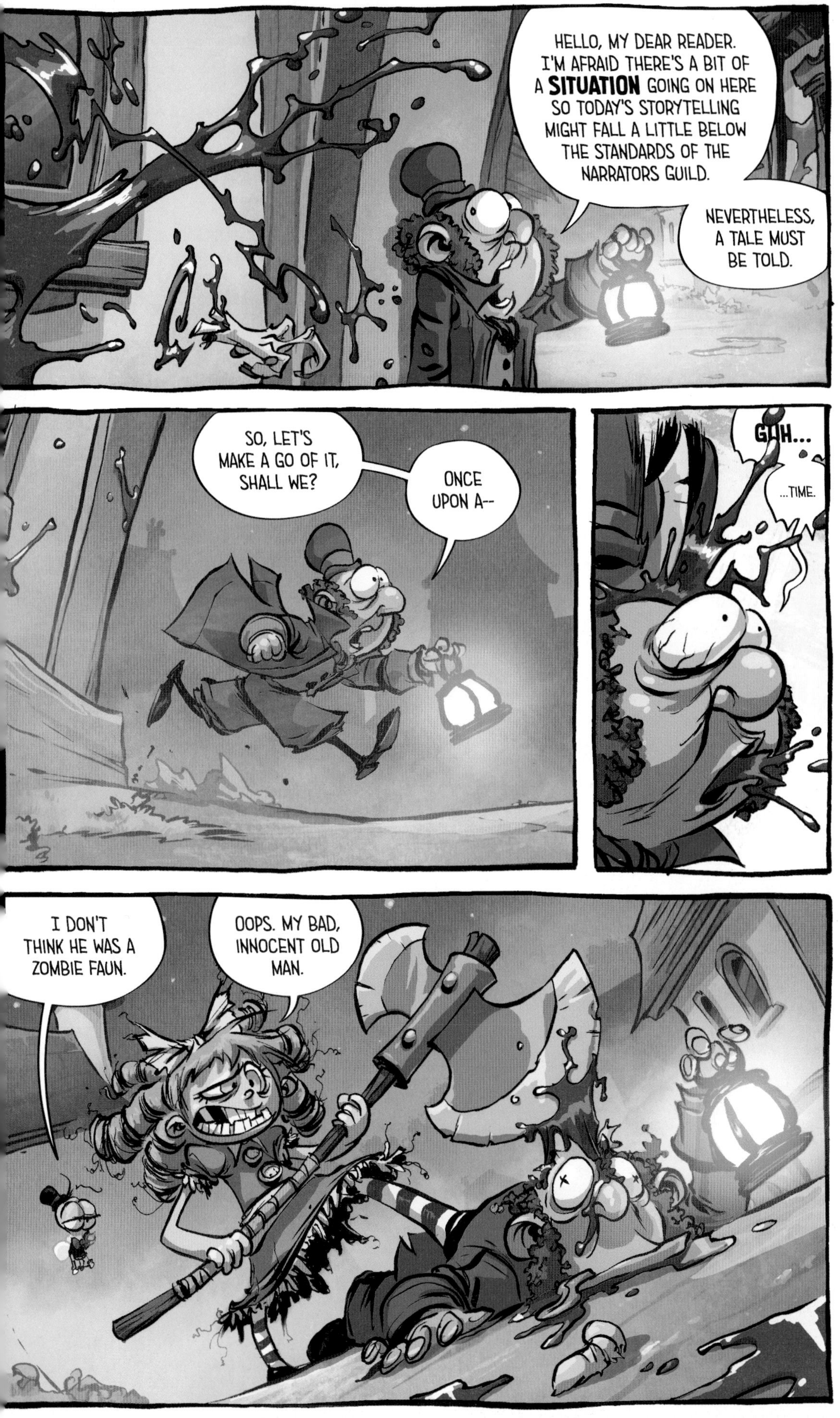
HELLO, MY DEAR READER. I'M AFRAID THERE'S A BIT OF A **SITUATION** GOING ON HERE SO TODAY'S STORYTELLING MIGHT FALL A LITTLE BELOW THE STANDARDS OF THE NARRATORS GUILD.
NEVERTHELESS, A TALE MUST BE TOLD.
SO, LET'S MAKE A GO OF IT, SHALL WE?
ONCE UPON A--
GUH...
...TIME.
I DON'T THINK HE WAS A ZOMBIE FAUN.
OOPS. MY BAD, INNOCENT OLD MAN.

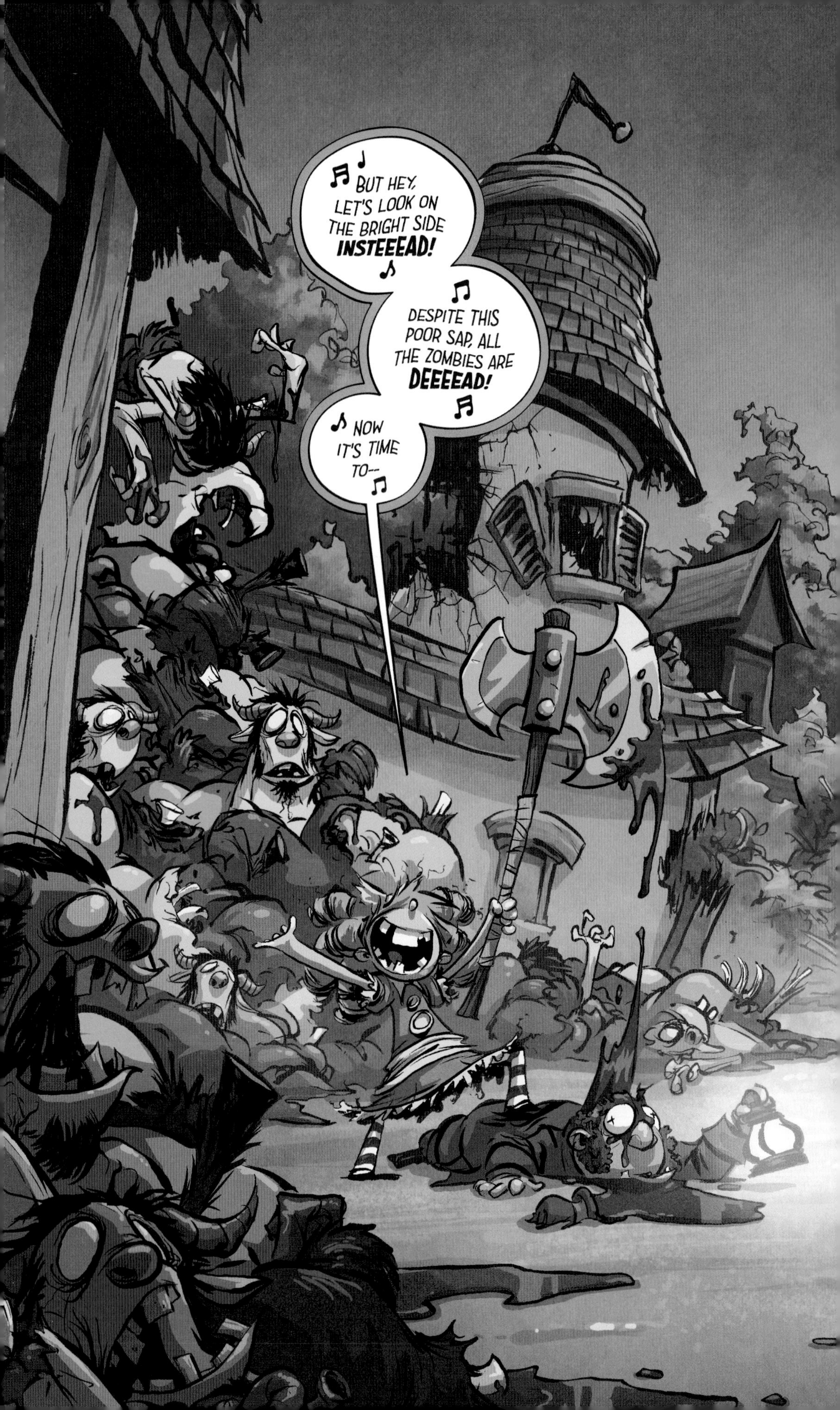
BUT HEY, LET'S LOOK ON THE BRIGHT SIDE INSTEEEAD!
DESPITE THIS POOR SAP, ALL THE ZOMBIES ARE DEEEEAD!
NOW IT'S TIME TO--

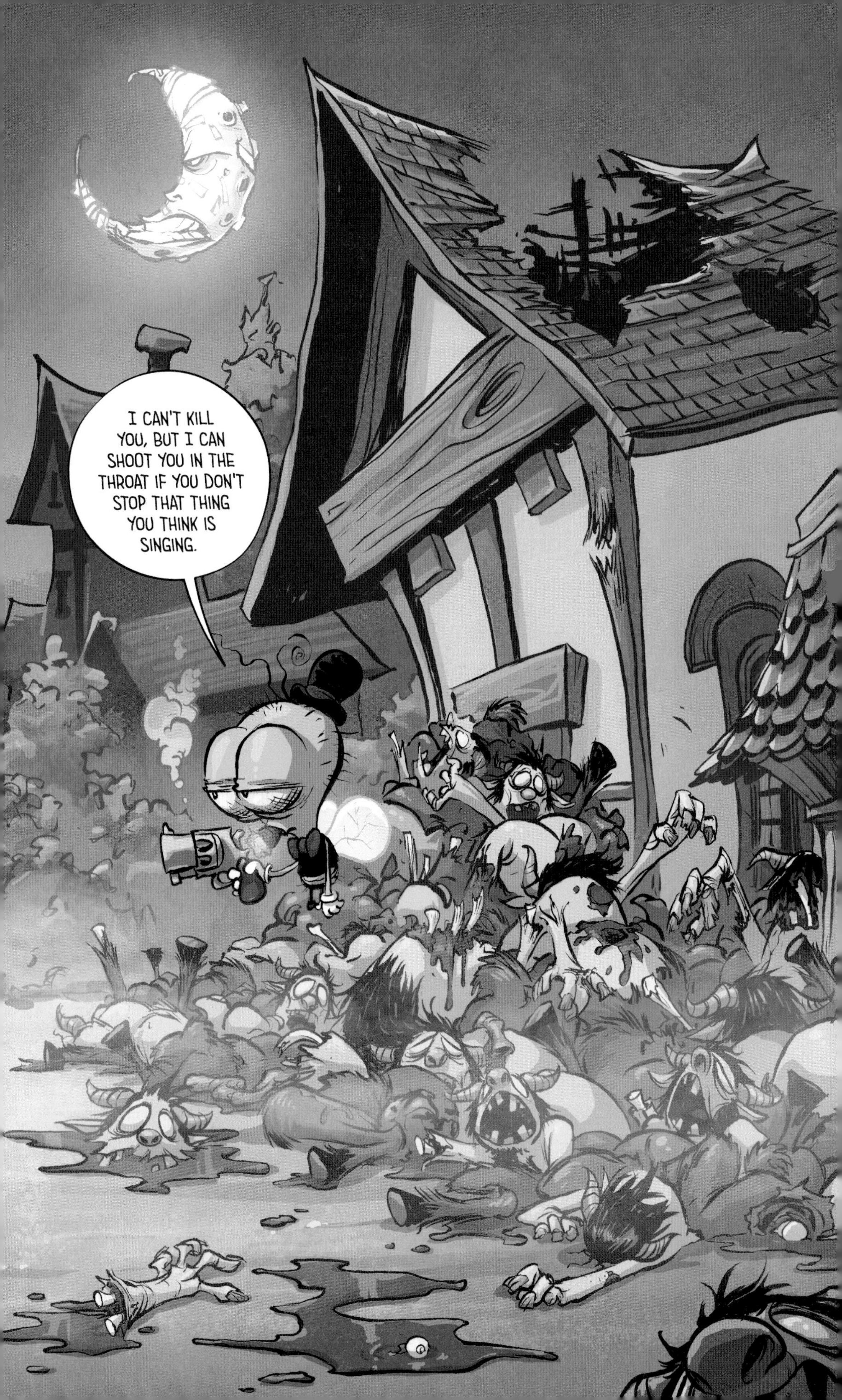
I CAN'T KILL YOU, BUT I CAN SHOOT YOU IN THE THROAT IF YOU DON'T STOP THAT THING YOU THINK IS SINGING.

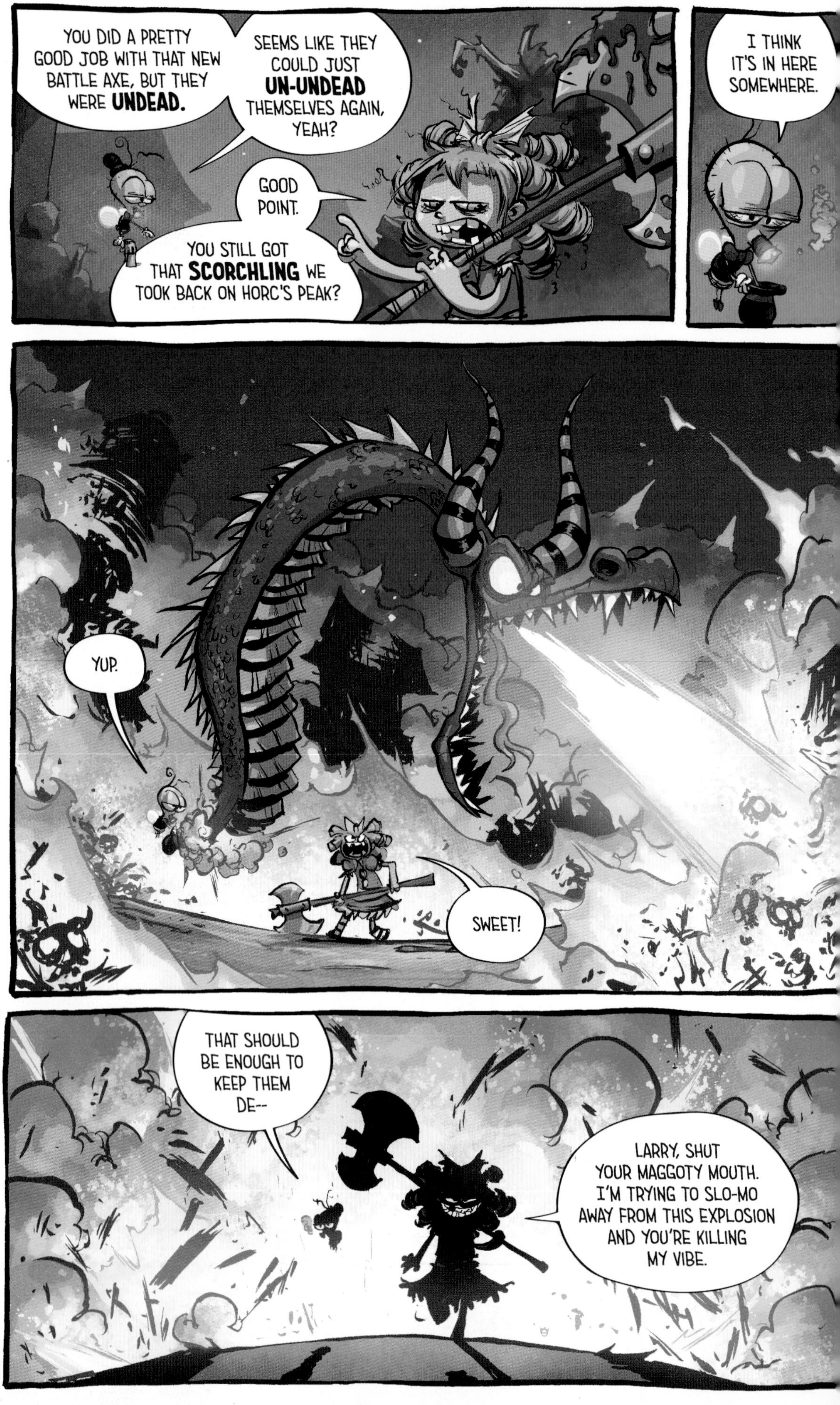

YOU DID A PRETTY GOOD JOB WITH THAT NEW BATTLE AXE, BUT THEY WERE **UNDEAD.**
SEEMS LIKE THEY COULD JUST **UN-UNDEAD** THEMSELVES AGAIN, YEAH?
GOOD POINT.
YOU STILL GOT THAT **SCORCHLING** WE TOOK BACK ON HORC'S PEAK?
I THINK IT'S IN HERE SOMEWHERE.
YUP.
SWEET!
THAT SHOULD BE ENOUGH TO KEEP THEM DE--
LARRY, SHUT YOUR MAGGOTY MOUTH. I'M TRYING TO SLO-MO AWAY FROM THIS EXPLOSION AND YOU'RE KILLING MY VIBE.

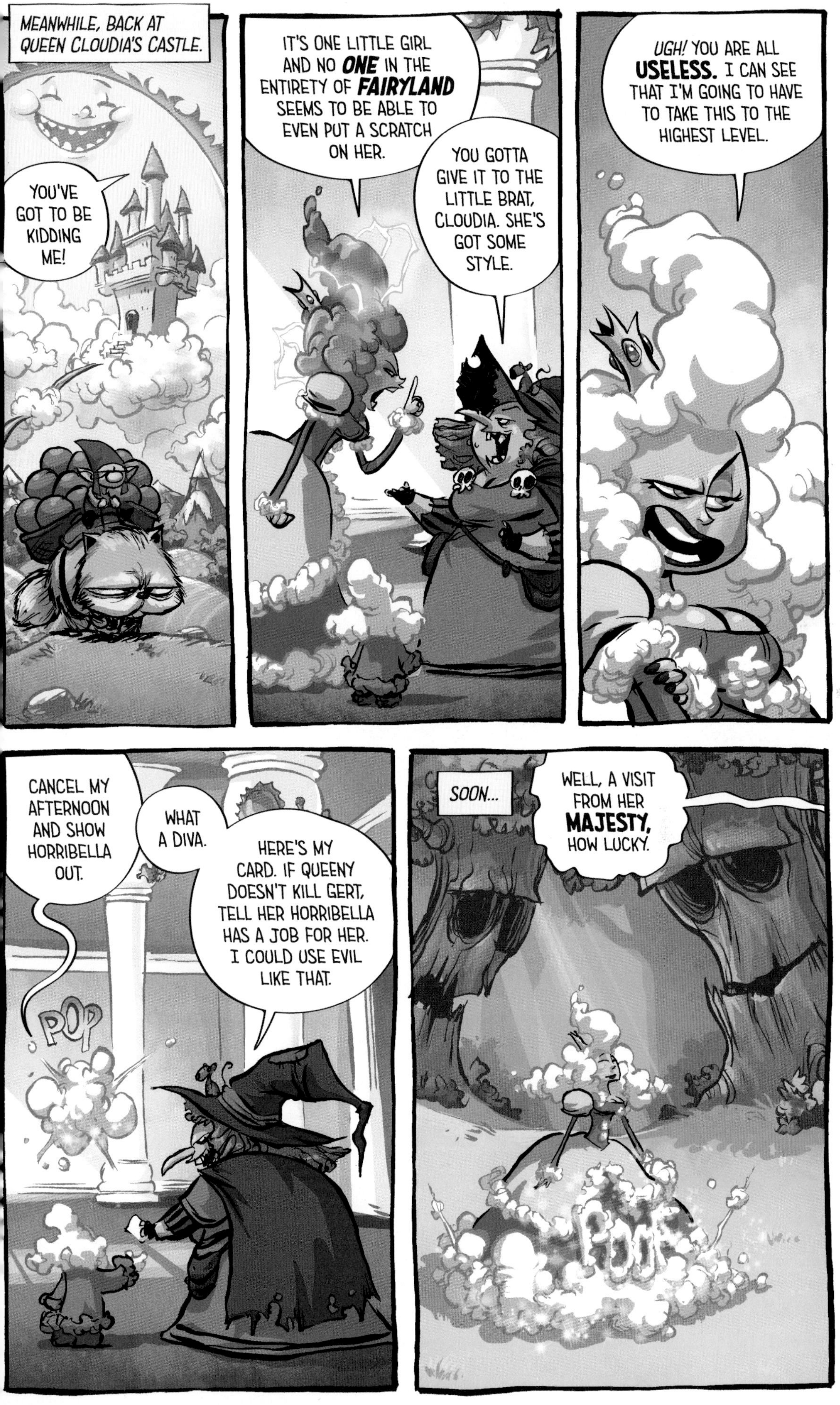
MEANWHILE, BACK AT QUEEN CLOUDIA'S CASTLE.
YOU'VE GOT TO BE KIDDING ME!
IT'S ONE LITTLE GIRL AND NO ONE IN THE ENTIRETY OF FAIRYLAND SEEMS TO BE ABLE TO EVEN PUT A SCRATCH ON HER.
YOU GOTTA GIVE IT TO THE LITTLE BRAT, CLOUDIA. SHE'S GOT SOME STYLE.
UGH! YOU ARE ALL USELESS. I CAN SEE THAT I'M GOING TO HAVE TO TAKE THIS TO THE HIGHEST LEVEL.
CANCEL MY AFTERNOON AND SHOW HORRIBELLA OUT.
WHAT A DIVA.
HERE'S MY CARD. IF QUEENY DOESN'T KILL GERT, TELL HER HORRIBELLA HAS A JOB FOR HER. I COULD USE EVIL LIKE THAT.
POP
SOON...
WELL, A VISIT FROM HER MAJESTY, HOW LUCKY.
POOF

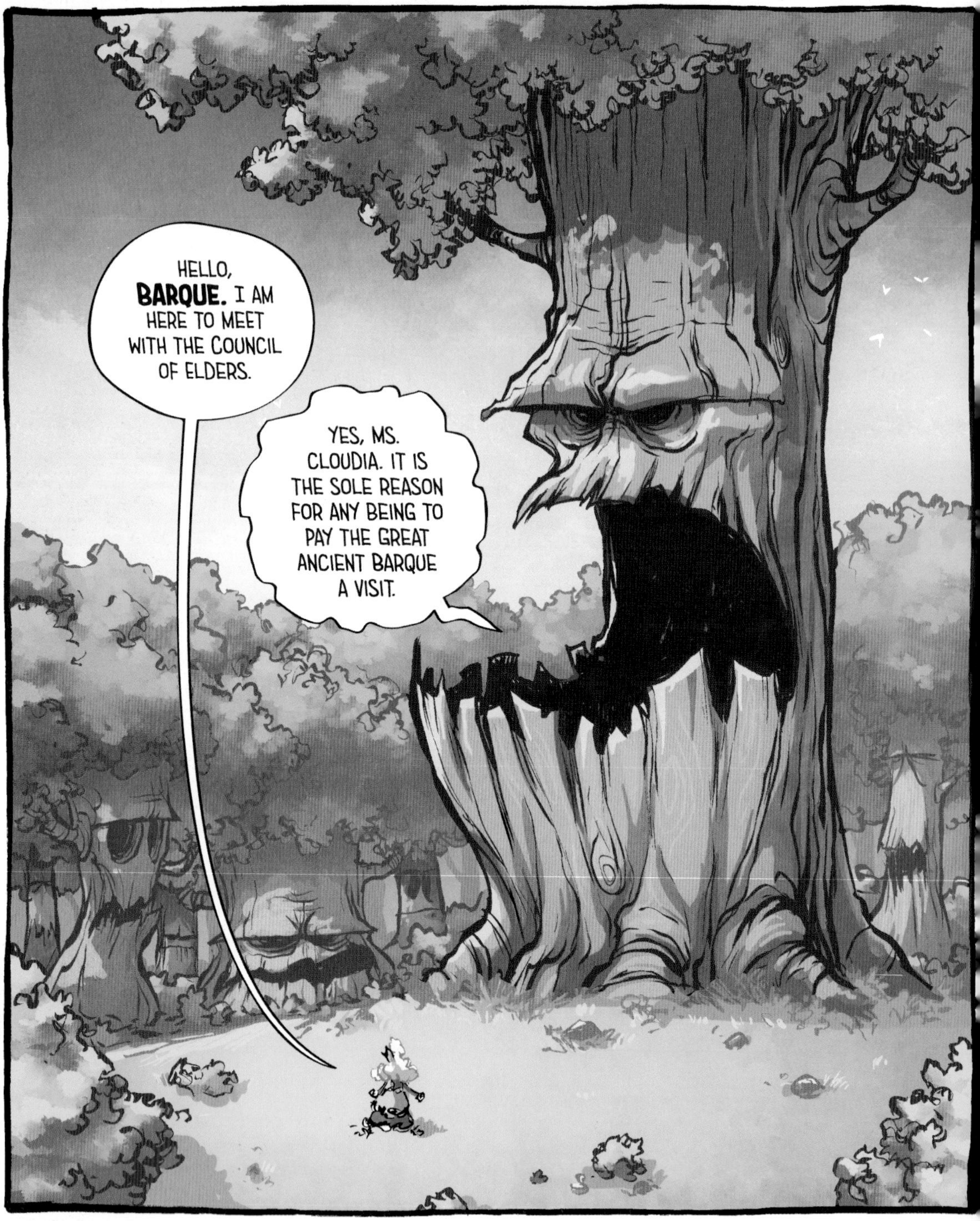
HELLO, BARQUE. I AM HERE TO MEET WITH THE COUNCIL OF ELDERS.
YES, MS. CLOUDIA. IT IS THE SOLE REASON FOR ANY BEING TO PAY THE GREAT ANCIENT BARQUE A VISIT.

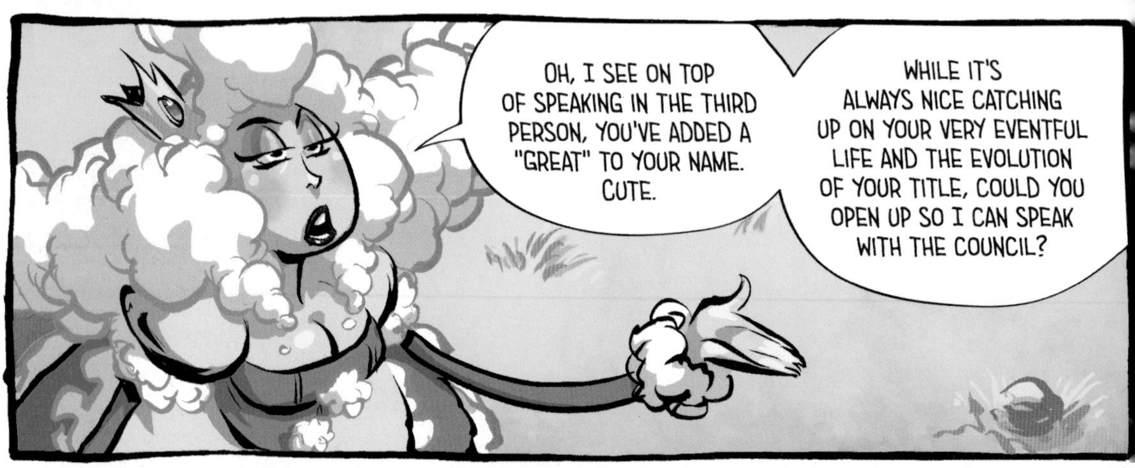
OH, I SEE ON TOP OF SPEAKING IN THE THIRD PERSON, YOU'VE ADDED A "GREAT" TO YOUR NAME. CUTE.
WHILE IT'S ALWAYS NICE CATCHING UP ON YOUR VERY EVENTFUL LIFE AND THE EVOLUTION OF YOUR TITLE, COULD YOU OPEN UP SO I CAN SPEAK WITH THE COUNCIL?

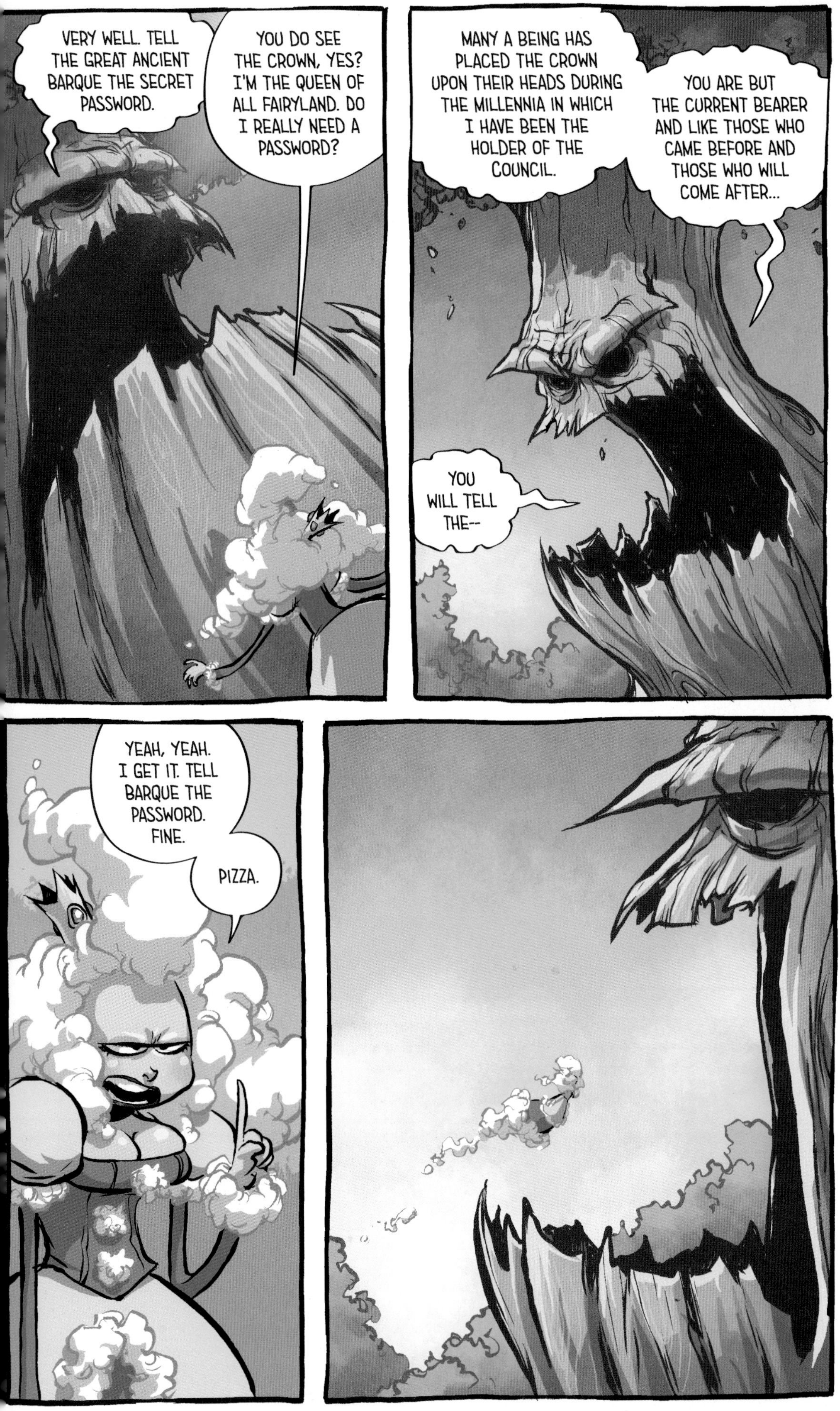
VERY WELL. TELL THE GREAT ANCIENT BARQUE THE SECRET PASSWORD.
YOU DO SEE THE CROWN, YES? I'M THE QUEEN OF ALL FAIRYLAND. DO I REALLY NEED A PASSWORD?
MANY A BEING HAS PLACED THE CROWN UPON THEIR HEADS DURING THE MILLENNIA IN WHICH I HAVE BEEN THE HOLDER OF THE COUNCIL.
YOU ARE BUT THE CURRENT BEARER AND LIKE THOSE WHO CAME BEFORE AND THOSE WHO WILL COME AFTER...
YOU WILL TELL THE--
YEAH, YEAH. I GET IT. TELL BARQUE THE PASSWORD. FINE.
PIZZA.

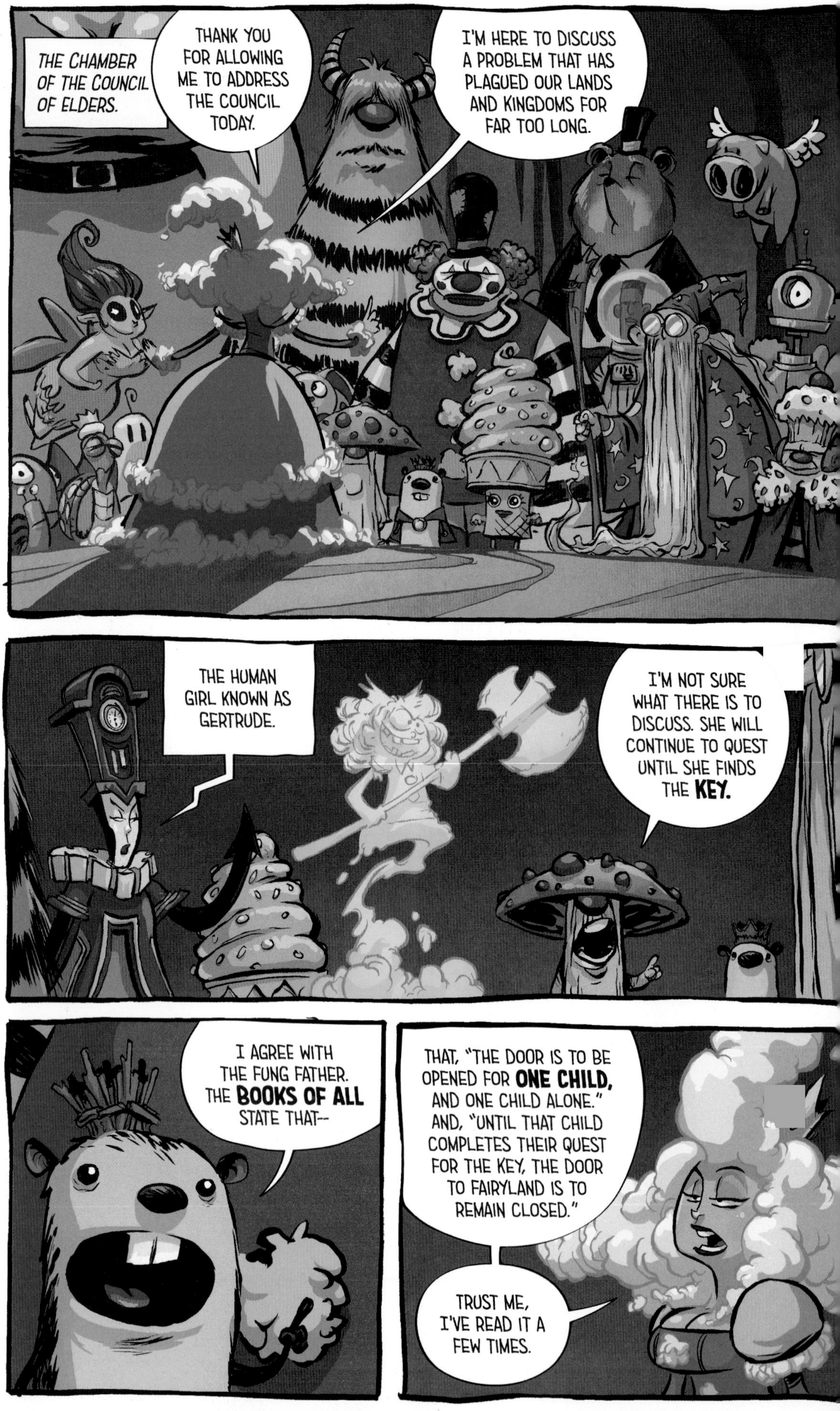

THE CHAMBER OF THE COUNCIL OF ELDERS.
THANK YOU FOR ALLOWING ME TO ADDRESS THE COUNCIL TODAY.
I'M HERE TO DISCUSS A PROBLEM THAT HAS PLAGUED OUR LANDS AND KINGDOMS FOR FAR TOO LONG.
THE HUMAN GIRL KNOWN AS GERTRUDE.
I'M NOT SURE WHAT THERE IS TO DISCUSS. SHE WILL CONTINUE TO QUEST UNTIL SHE FINDS THE **KEY.**
I AGREE WITH THE FUNG FATHER. THE **BOOKS OF ALL** STATE THAT--
THAT, "THE DOOR IS TO BE OPENED FOR **ONE CHILD,** AND ONE CHILD ALONE." AND, "UNTIL THAT CHILD COMPLETES THEIR QUEST FOR THE KEY, THE DOOR TO FAIRYLAND IS TO REMAIN CLOSED."
TRUST ME, I'VE READ IT A FEW TIMES.

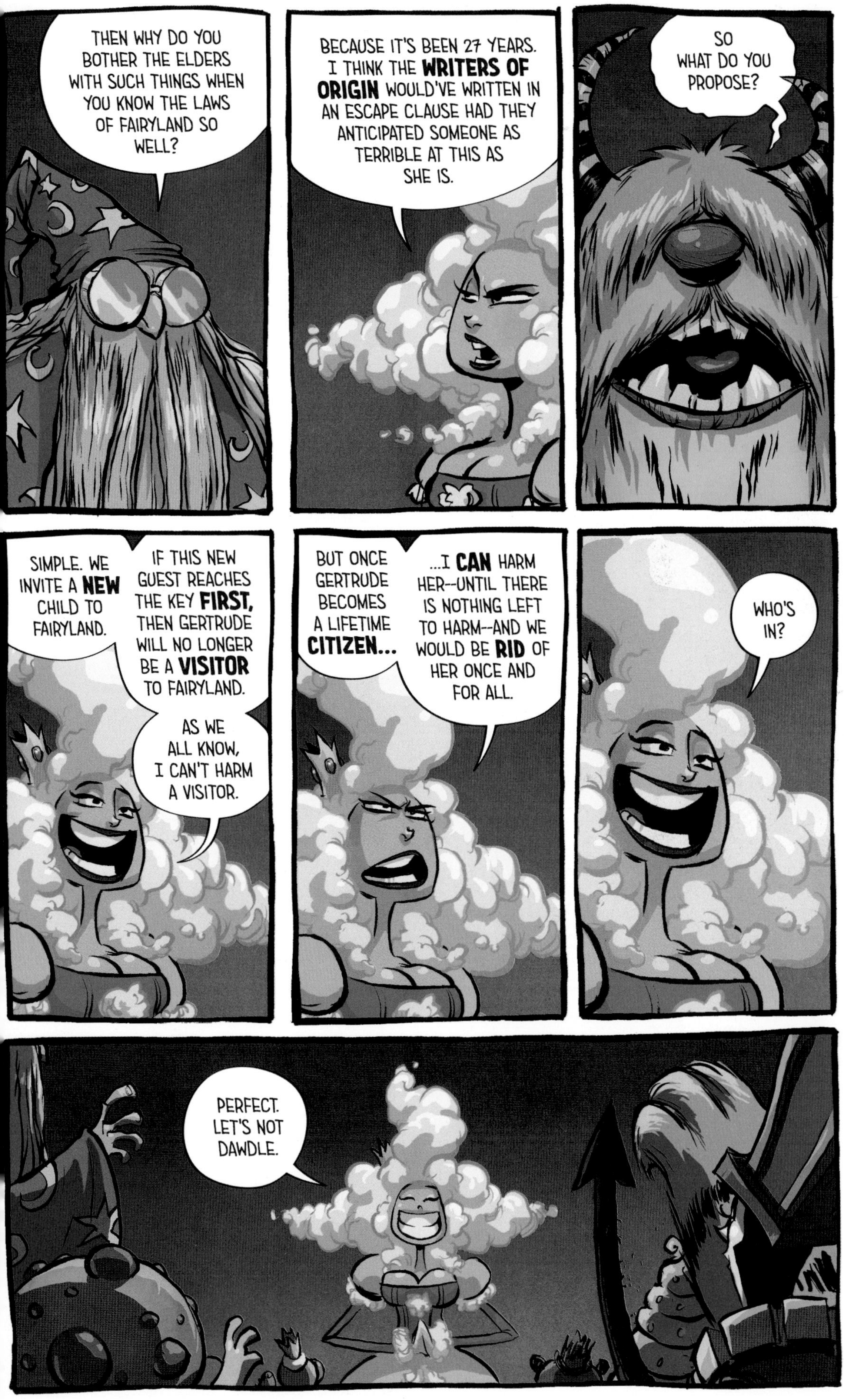
THEN WHY DO YOU BOTHER THE ELDERS WITH SUCH THINGS WHEN YOU KNOW THE LAWS OF FAIRYLAND SO WELL?
BECAUSE IT'S BEEN 27 YEARS. I THINK THE WRITERS OF ORIGIN WOULD'VE WRITTEN IN AN ESCAPE CLAUSE HAD THEY ANTICIPATED SOMEONE AS TERRIBLE AT THIS AS SHE IS.
SO WHAT DO YOU PROPOSE?
SIMPLE. WE INVITE A NEW CHILD TO FAIRYLAND.
IF THIS NEW GUEST REACHES THE KEY FIRST, THEN GERTRUDE WILL NO LONGER BE A VISITOR TO FAIRYLAND.
AS WE ALL KNOW, I CAN'T HARM A VISITOR.
BUT ONCE GERTRUDE BECOMES A LIFETIME CITIZEN...
...I CAN HARM HER--UNTIL THERE IS NOTHING LEFT TO HARM--AND WE WOULD BE RID OF HER ONCE AND FOR ALL.
WHO'S IN?
PERFECT. LET'S NOT DAWDLE.

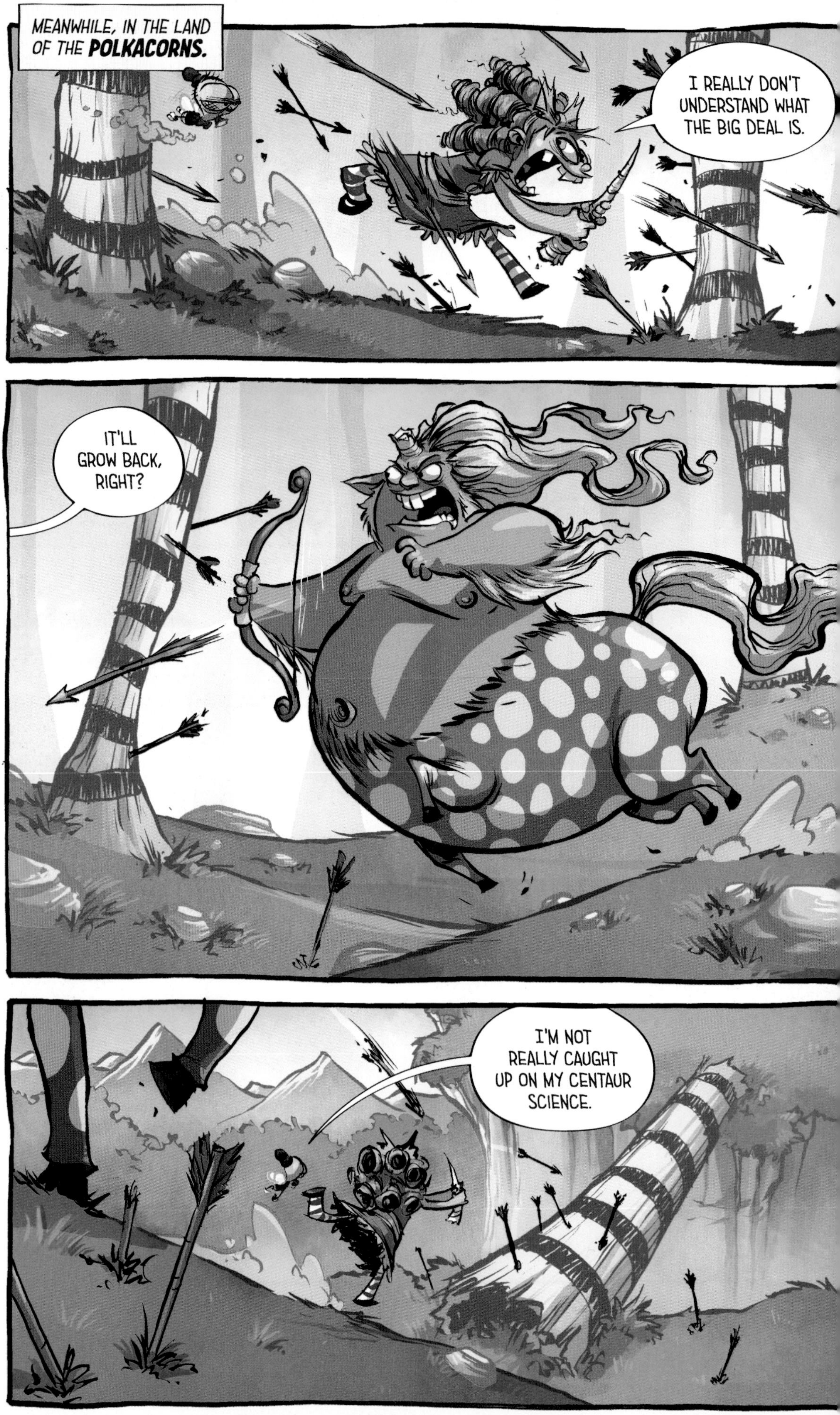
MEANWHILE, IN THE LAND OF THE **POLKACORNS.**
I REALLY DON'T UNDERSTAND WHAT THE BIG DEAL IS.
IT'LL GROW BACK, RIGHT?
I'M NOT REALLY CAUGHT UP ON MY CENTAUR SCIENCE.

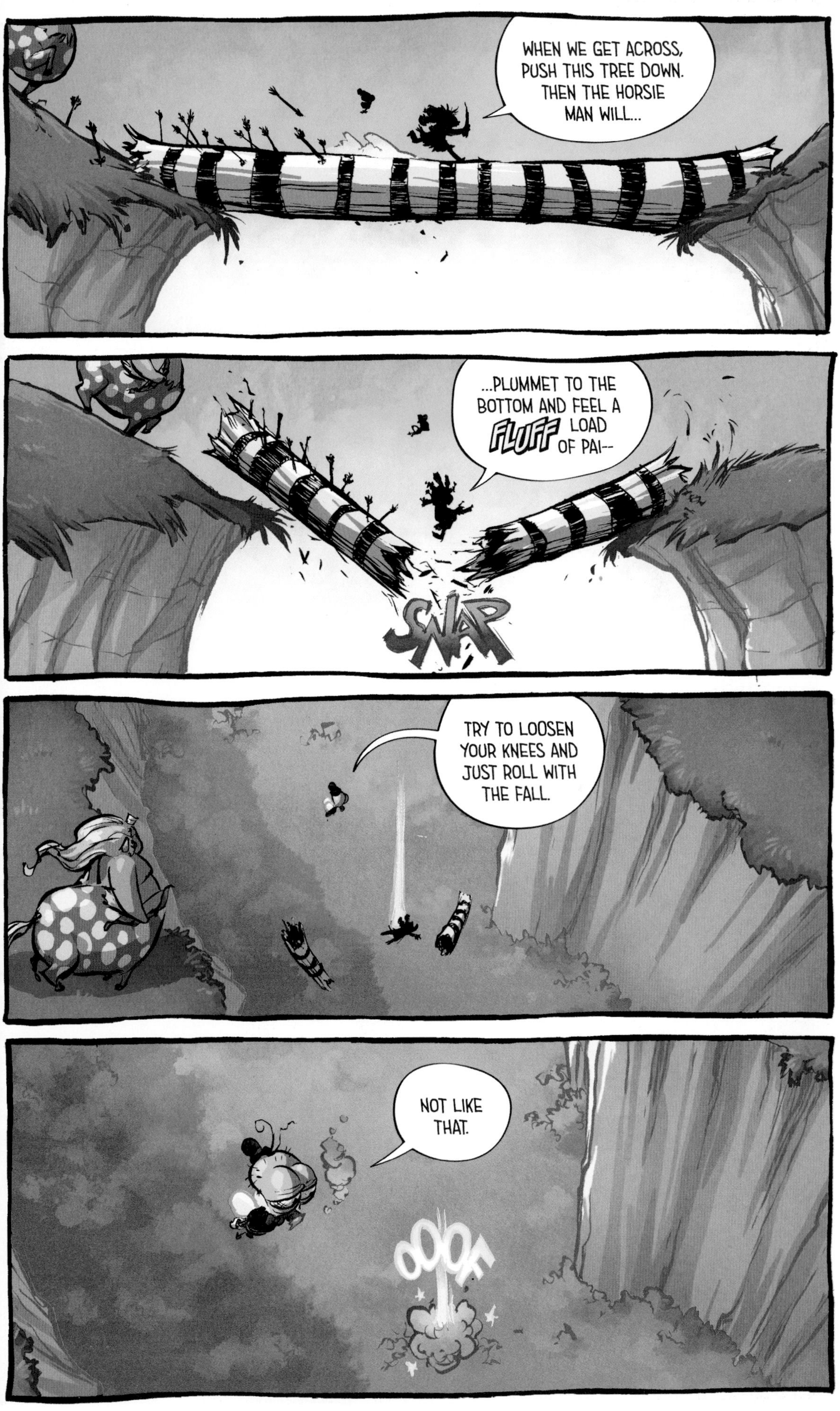

WHEN WE GET ACROSS, PUSH THIS TREE DOWN. THEN THE HORSIE MAN WILL...
...PLUMMET TO THE BOTTOM AND FEEL A FLUFF LOAD OF PAI--
SNAP
TRY TO LOOSEN YOUR KNEES AND JUST ROLL WITH THE FALL.
NOT LIKE THAT.
OOOF

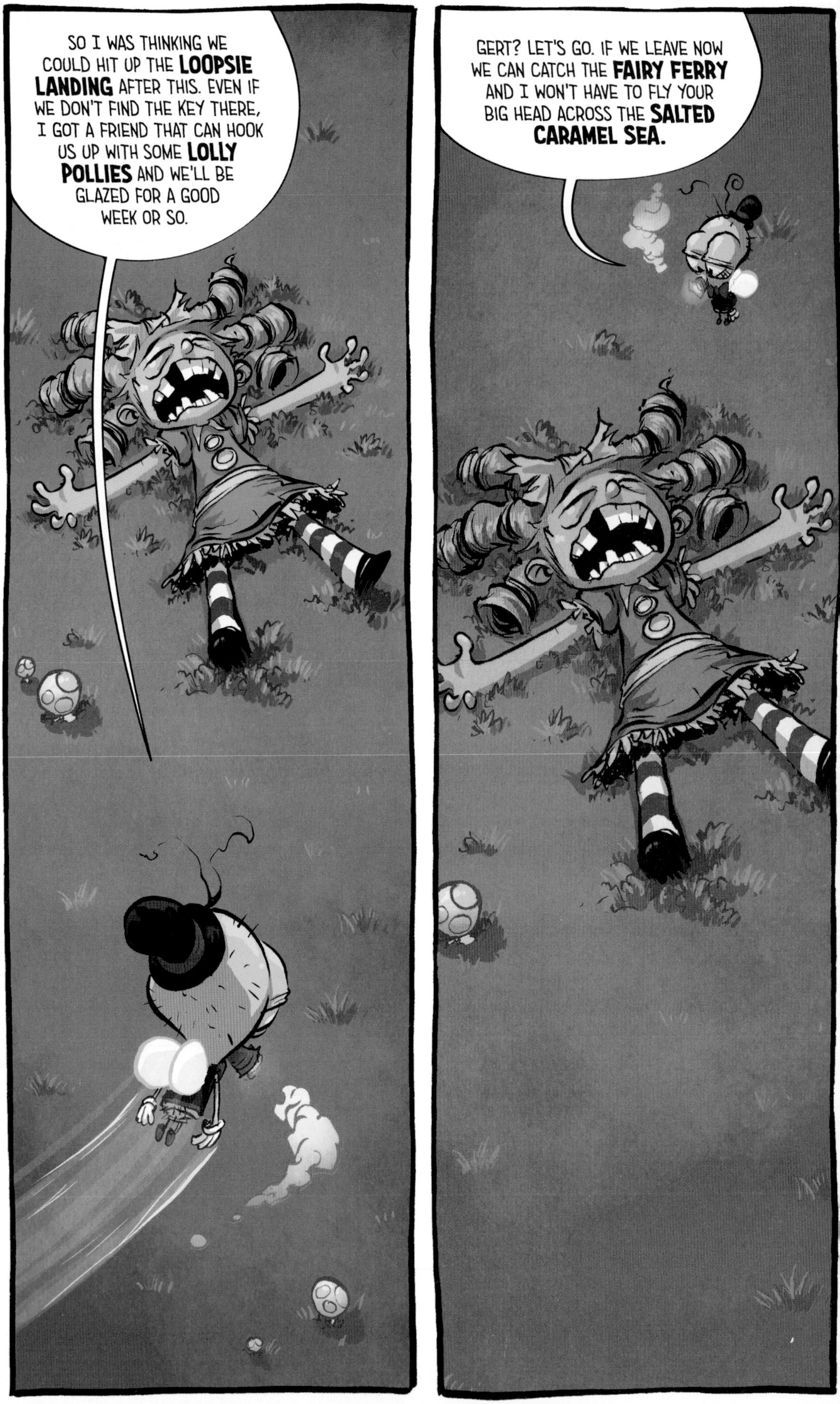
SO I WAS THINKING WE COULD HIT UP THE **LOOPSIE LANDING** AFTER THIS. EVEN IF WE DON'T FIND THE KEY THERE, I GOT A FRIEND THAT CAN HOOK US UP WITH SOME **LOLLY POLLIES** AND WE'LL BE GLAZED FOR A GOOD WEEK OR SO.
GERT? LET'S GO. IF WE LEAVE NOW WE CAN CATCH THE **FAIRY FERRY** AND I WON'T HAVE TO FLY YOUR BIG HEAD ACROSS THE **SALTED CARAMEL SEA.**

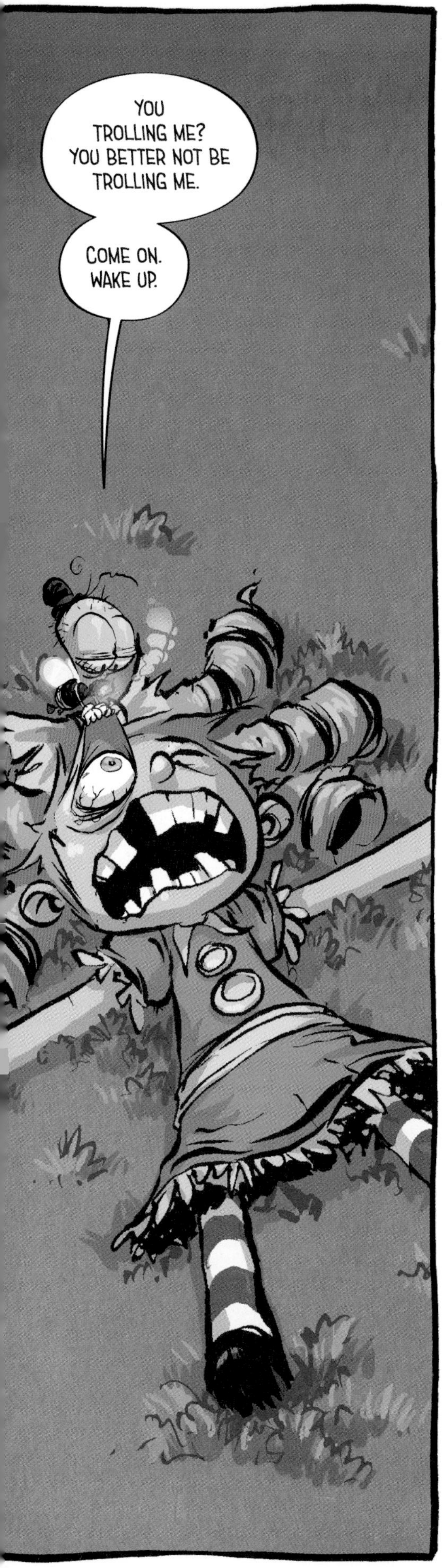
YOU TROLLING ME? YOU BETTER NOT BE TROLLING ME.
COME ON. WAKE UP.

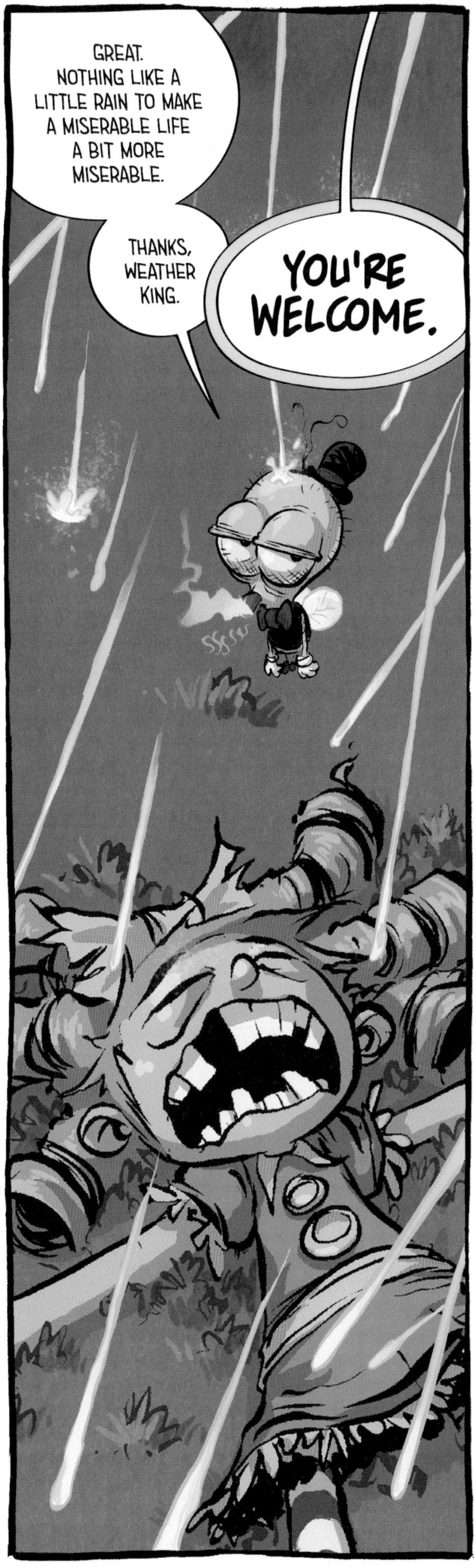
GREAT. NOTHING LIKE A LITTLE RAIN TO MAKE A MISERABLE LIFE A BIT MORE MISERABLE.
THANKS, WEATHER KING.
YOU'RE WELCOME.

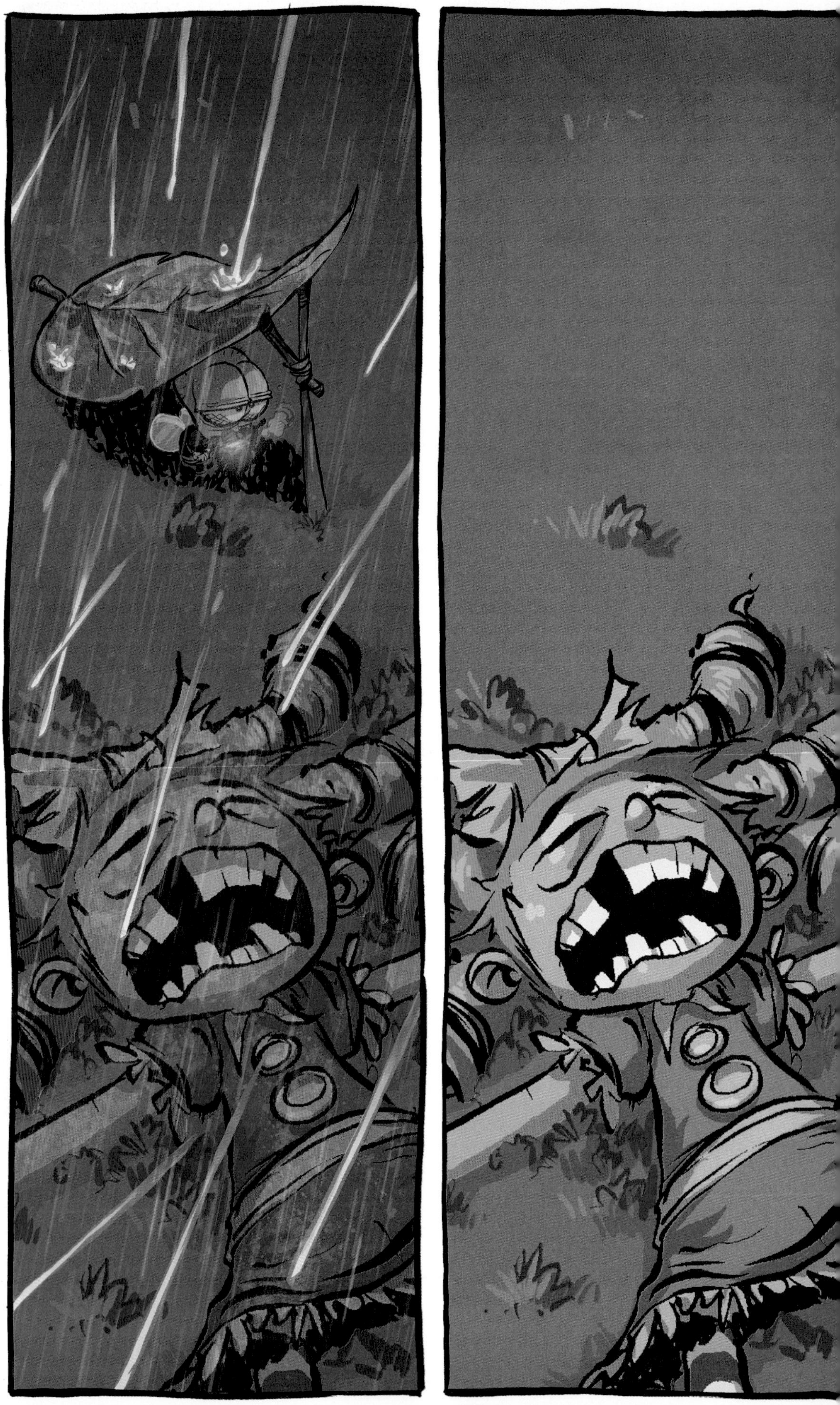

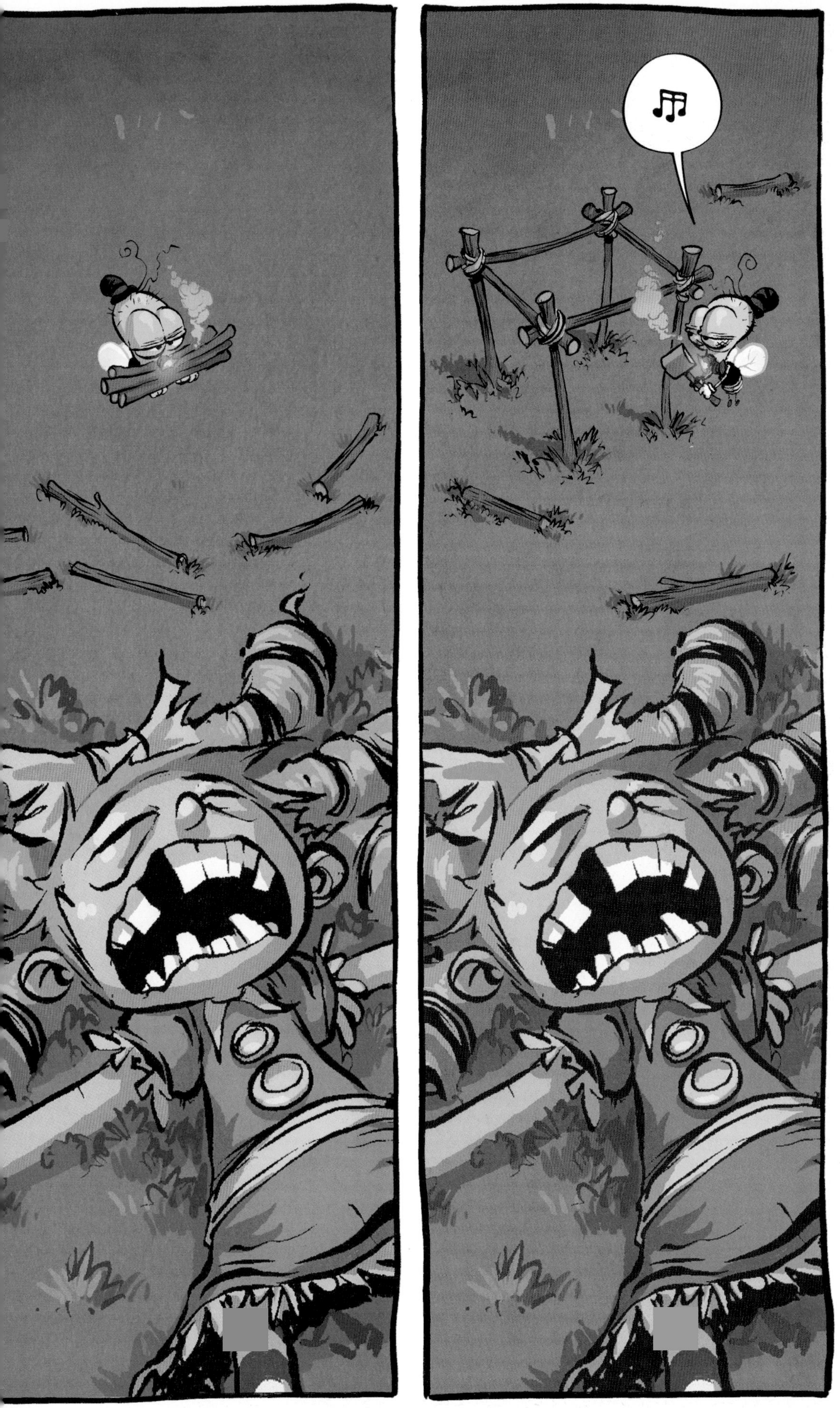

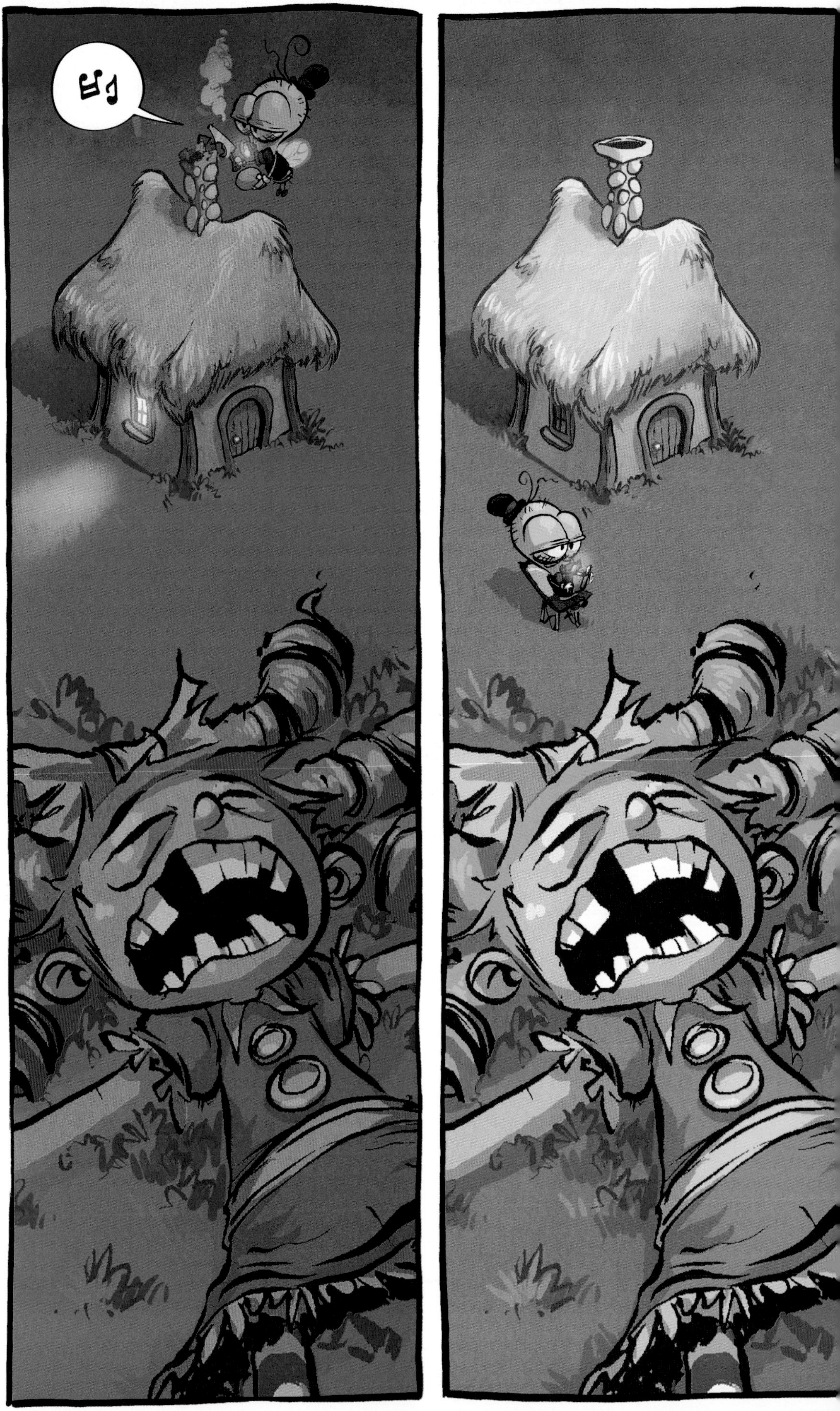

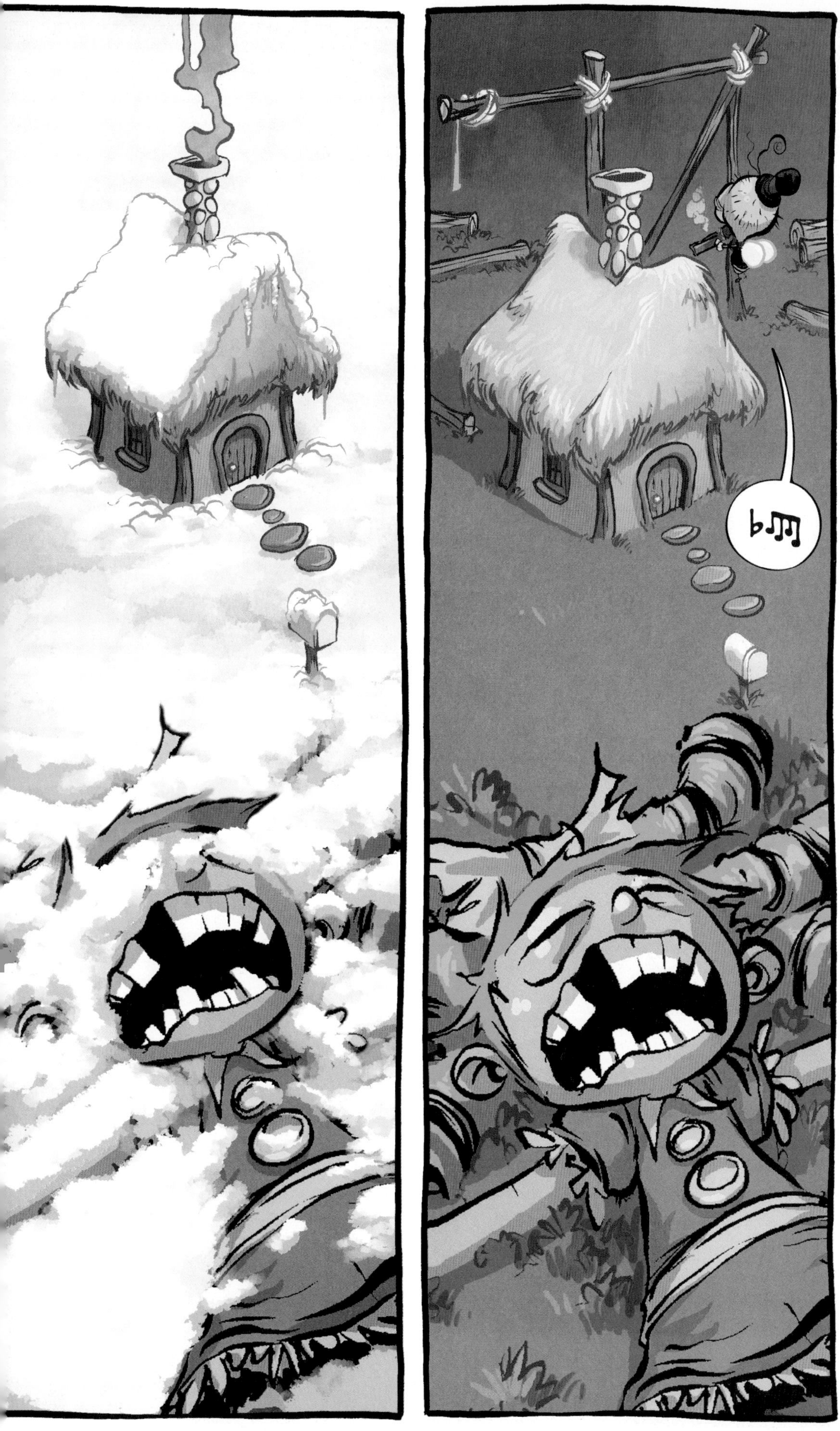

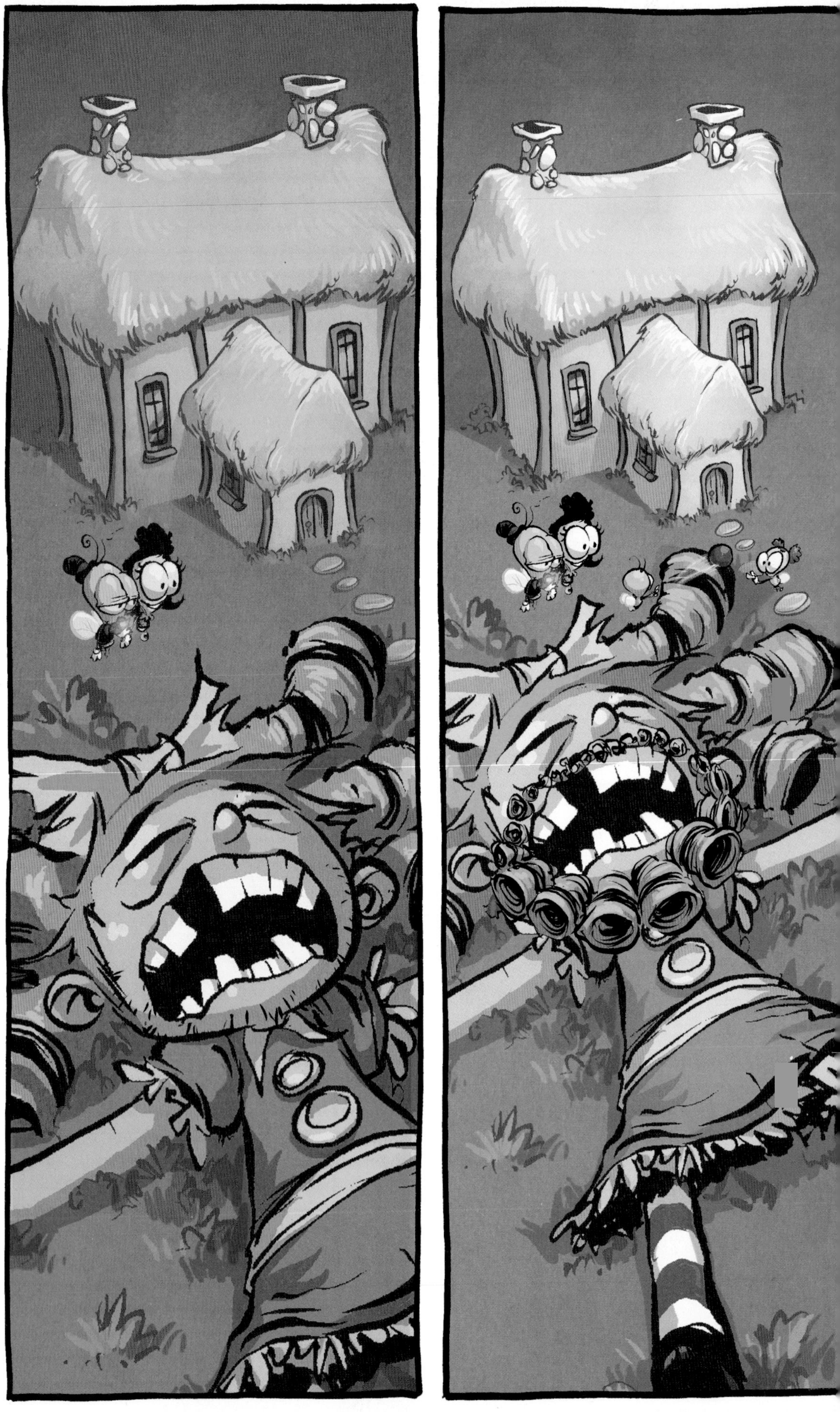

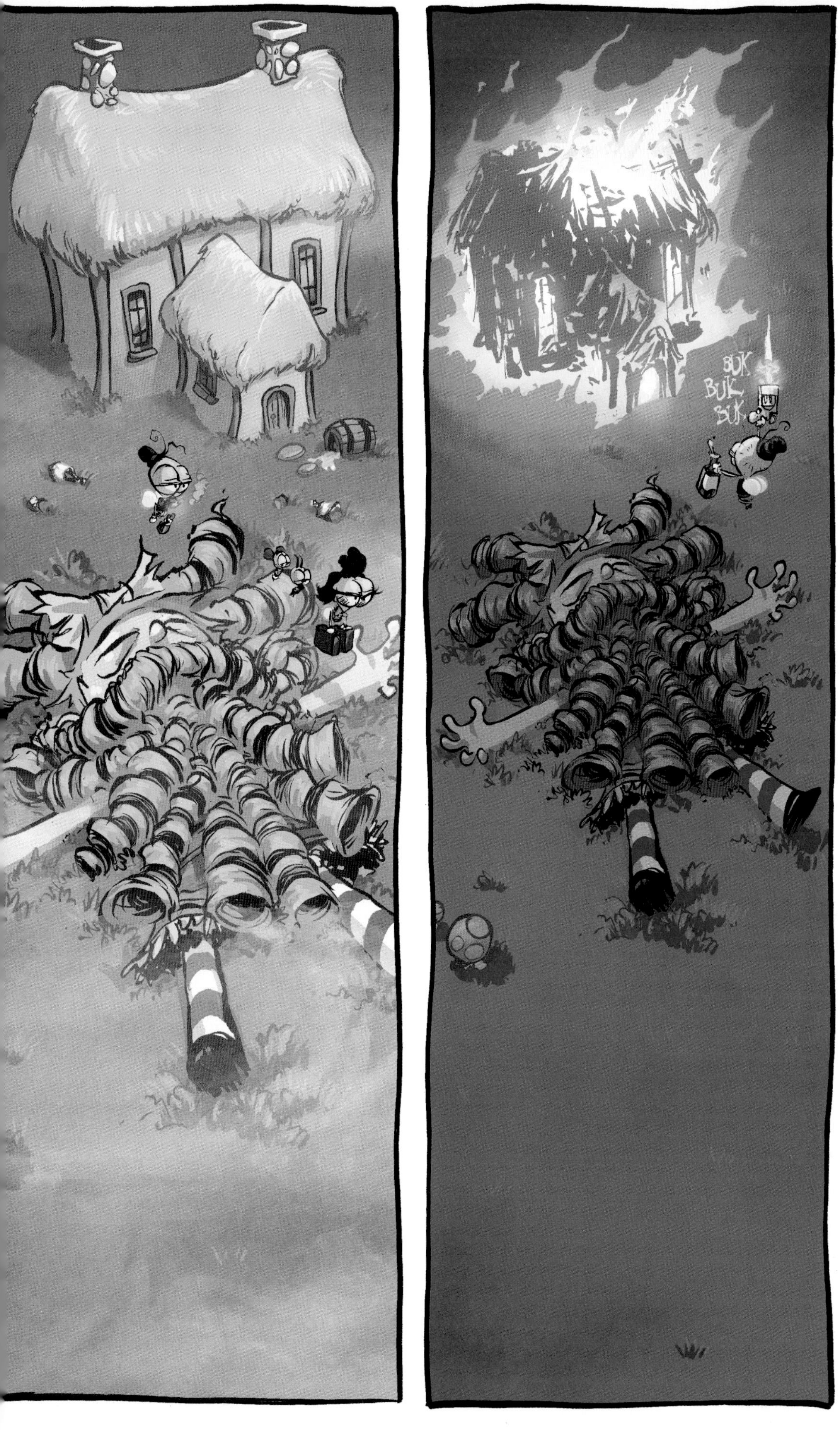
BUK
BUK
BUK

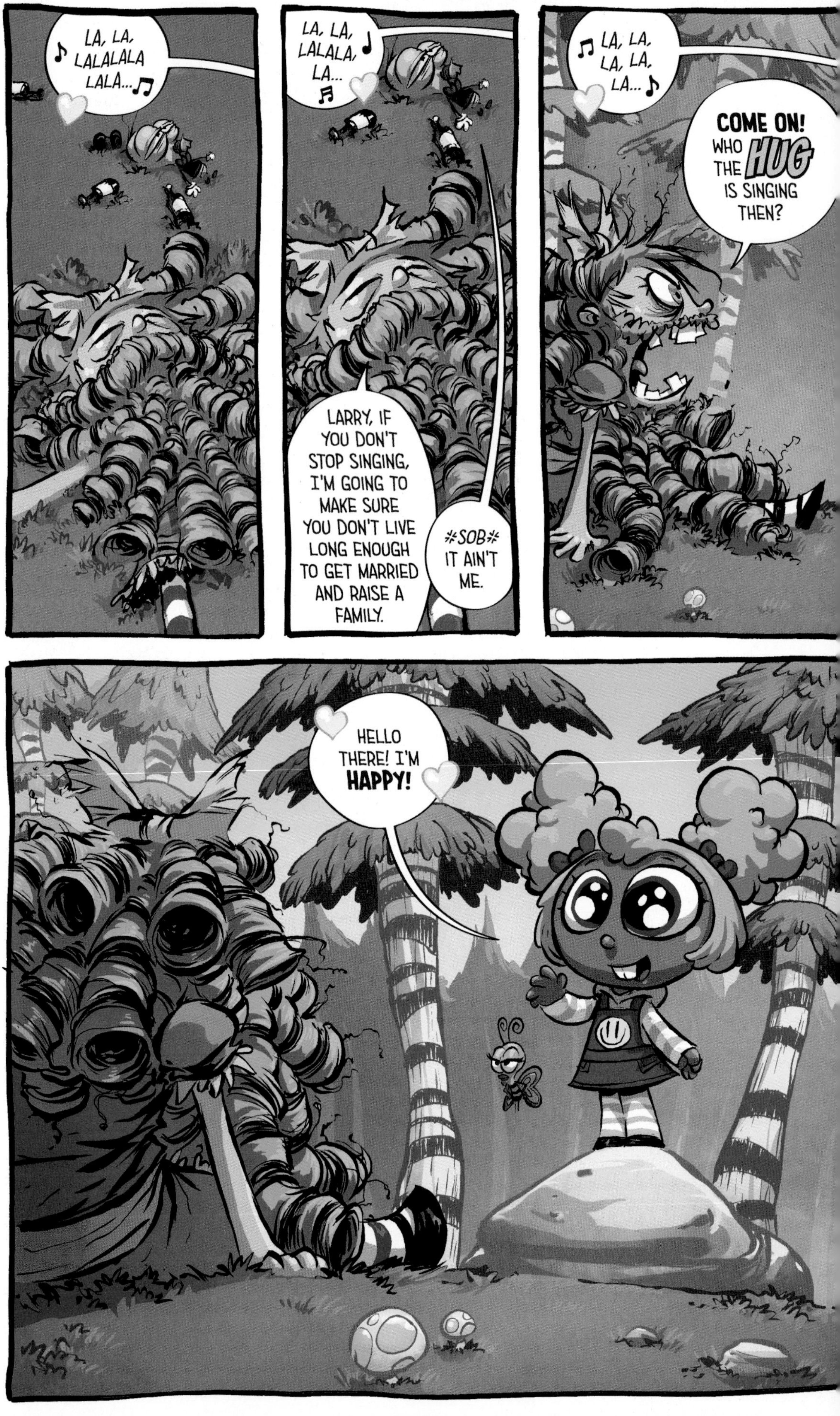
LA, LA, LALALALA LALA...
LA, LA, LALALA, LA...
LARRY, IF YOU DON'T STOP SINGING, I'M GOING TO MAKE SURE YOU DON'T LIVE LONG ENOUGH TO GET MARRIED AND RAISE A FAMILY.
SOB IT AIN'T ME.
LA, LA, LA, LA, LA...
COME ON! WHO THE HUG IS SINGING THEN?
HELLO THERE! I'M HAPPY!

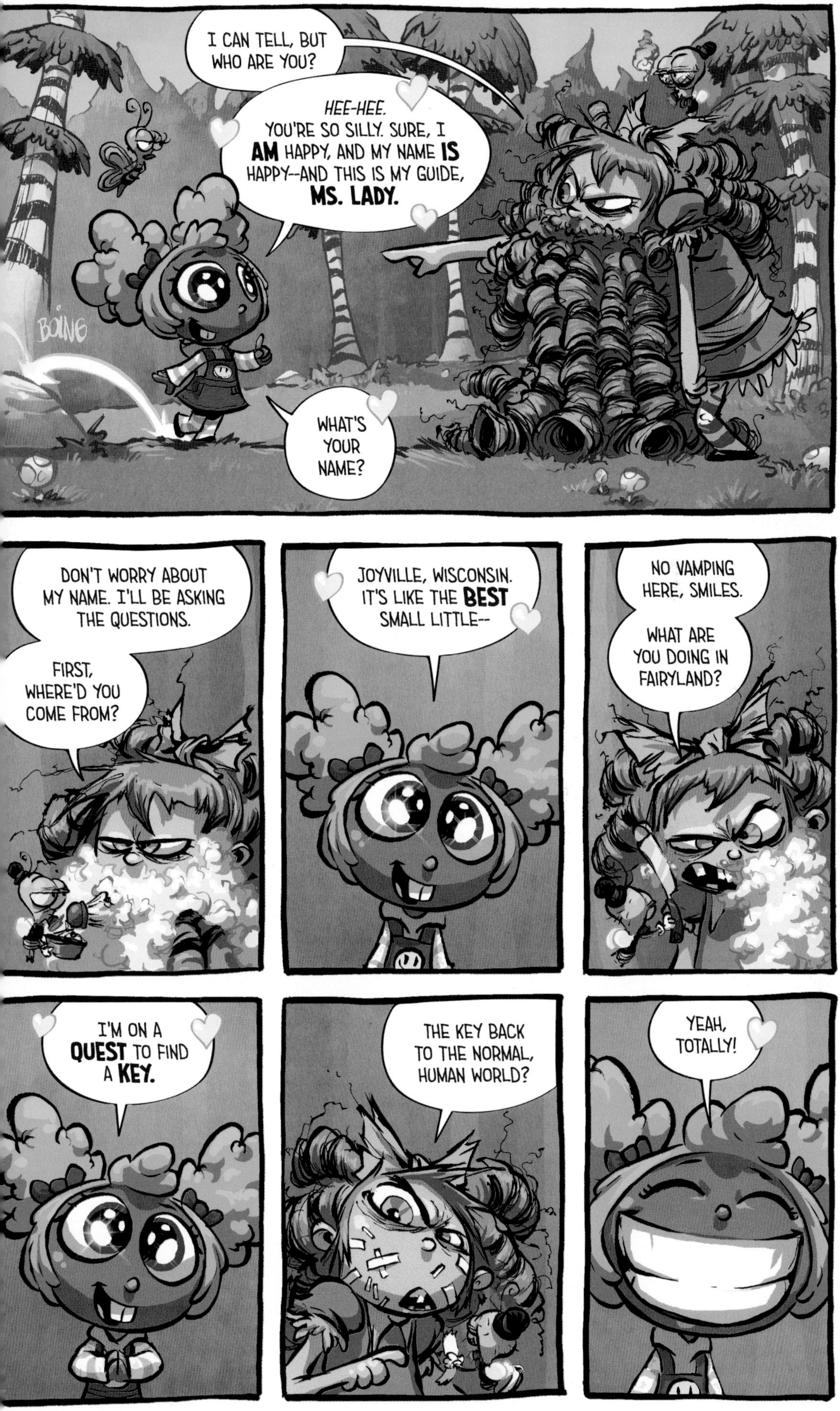
I CAN TELL, BUT WHO ARE YOU?
HEE-HEE. YOU'RE SO SILLY. SURE, I AM HAPPY, AND MY NAME IS HAPPY--AND THIS IS MY GUIDE, MS. LADY.
BOING
WHAT'S YOUR NAME?
DON'T WORRY ABOUT MY NAME. I'LL BE ASKING THE QUESTIONS.
FIRST, WHERE'D YOU COME FROM?
JOYVILLE, WISCONSIN. IT'S LIKE THE BEST SMALL LITTLE--
NO VAMPING HERE, SMILES.
WHAT ARE YOU DOING IN FAIRYLAND?
I'M ON A QUEST TO FIND A KEY.
THE KEY BACK TO THE NORMAL, HUMAN WORLD?
YEAH, TOTALLY!

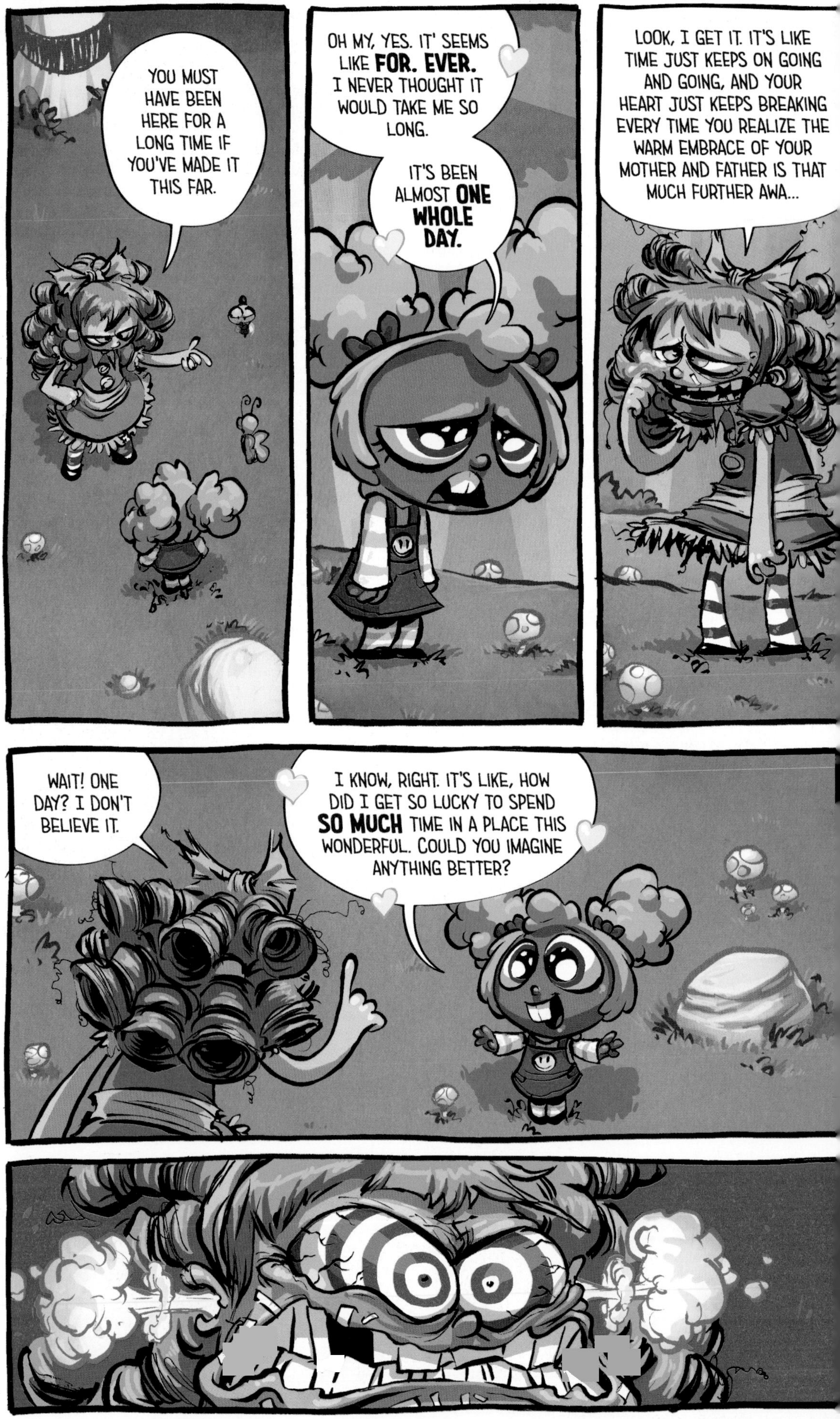
YOU MUST HAVE BEEN HERE FOR A LONG TIME IF YOU'VE MADE IT THIS FAR.
OH MY, YES. IT' SEEMS LIKE **FOR. EVER.** I NEVER THOUGHT IT WOULD TAKE ME SO LONG.
IT'S BEEN ALMOST **ONE WHOLE DAY.**
LOOK, I GET IT. IT'S LIKE TIME JUST KEEPS ON GOING AND GOING, AND YOUR HEART JUST KEEPS BREAKING EVERY TIME YOU REALIZE THE WARM EMBRACE OF YOUR MOTHER AND FATHER IS THAT MUCH FURTHER AWA...
WAIT! ONE DAY? I DON'T BELIEVE IT.
I KNOW, RIGHT. IT'S LIKE, HOW DID I GET SO LUCKY TO SPEND **SO MUCH** TIME IN A PLACE THIS WONDERFUL. COULD YOU IMAGINE ANYTHING BETTER?

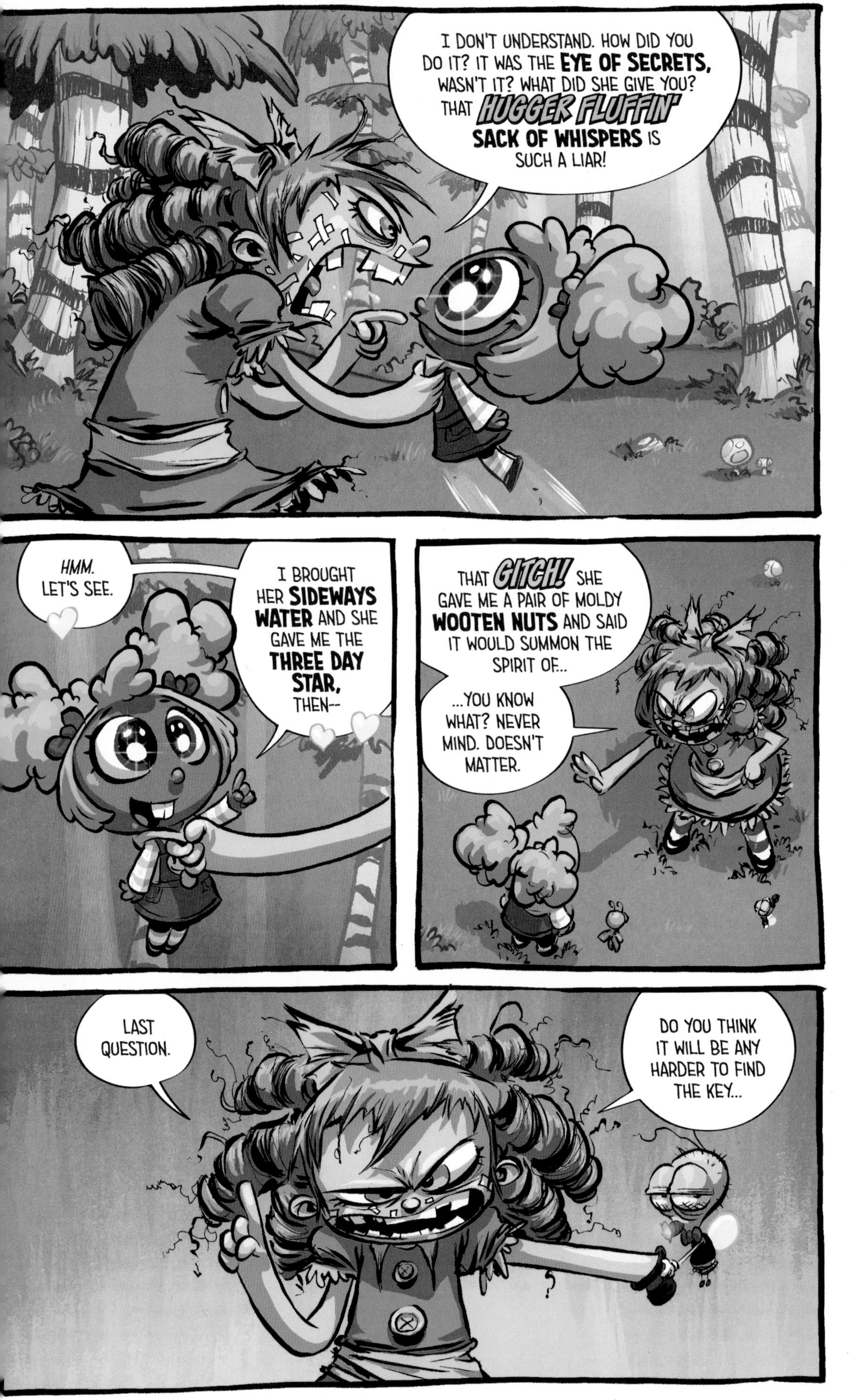
I DON'T UNDERSTAND. HOW DID YOU DO IT? IT WAS THE EYE OF SECRETS, WASN'T IT? WHAT DID SHE GIVE YOU? THAT HUGGER FLUFFIN' SACK OF WHISPERS IS SUCH A LIAR!
HMM. LET'S SEE.
I BROUGHT HER SIDEWAYS WATER AND SHE GAVE ME THE THREE DAY STAR, THEN--
THAT GITCH! SHE GAVE ME A PAIR OF MOLDY WOOTEN NUTS AND SAID IT WOULD SUMMON THE SPIRIT OF...
...YOU KNOW WHAT? NEVER MIND. DOESN'T MATTER.
LAST QUESTION.
DO YOU THINK IT WILL BE ANY HARDER TO FIND THE KEY...

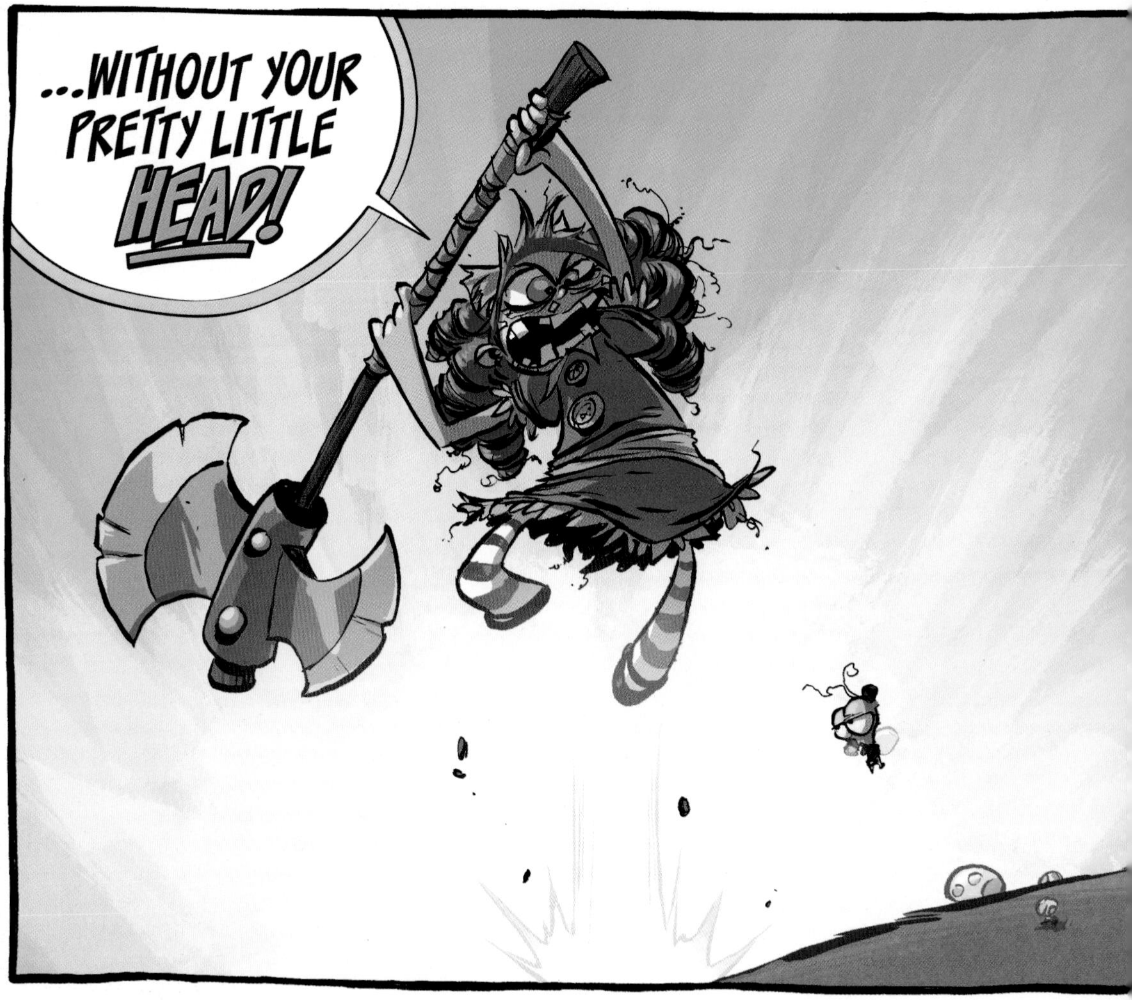
...WITHOUT YOUR PRETTY LITTLE HEAD!

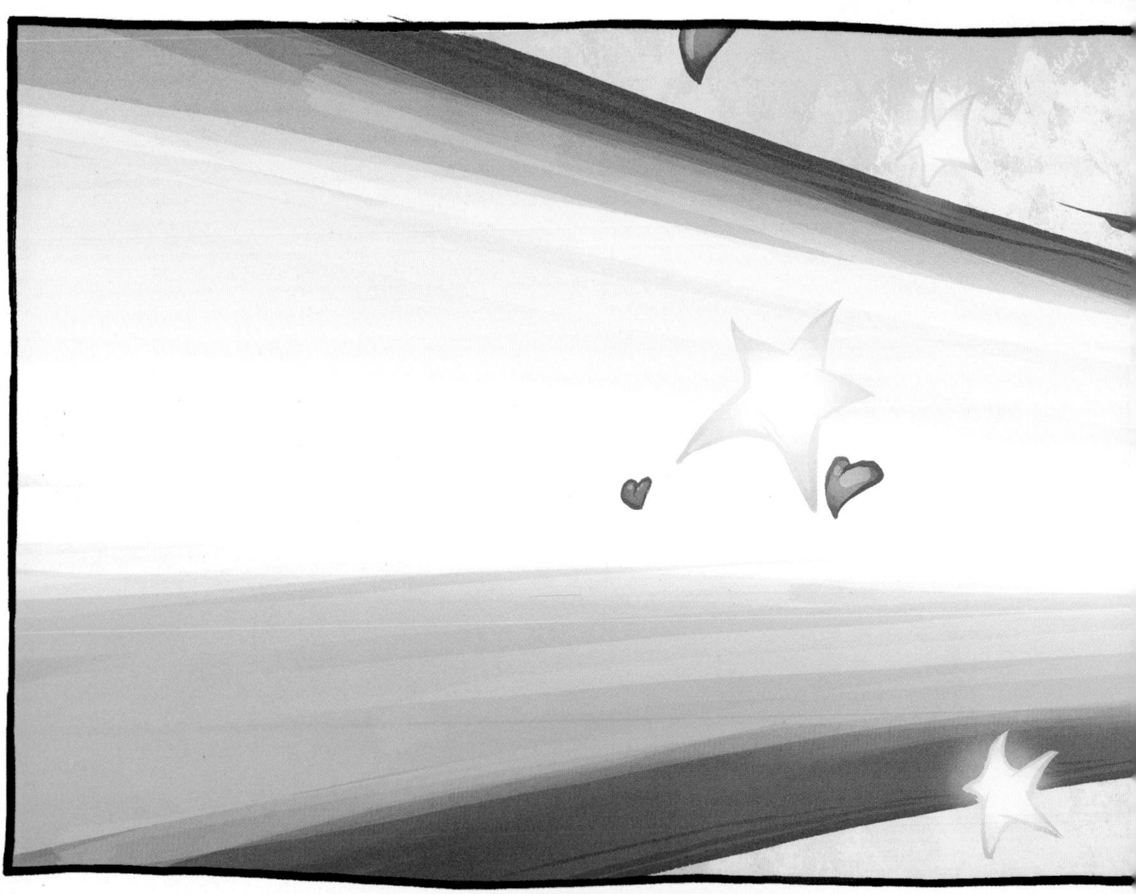

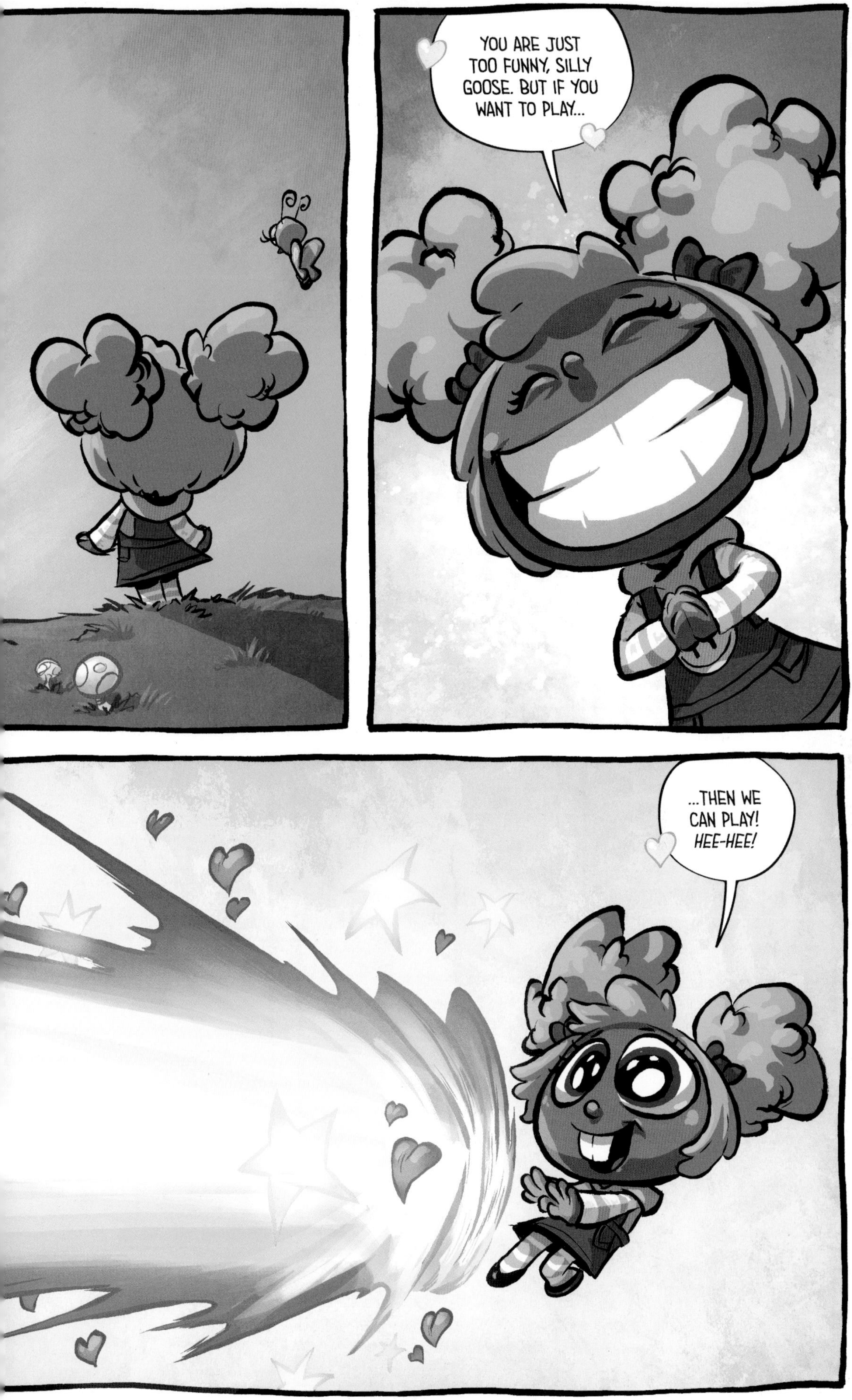
YOU ARE JUST TOO FUNNY, SILLY GOOSE. BUT IF YOU WANT TO PLAY...
...THEN WE CAN PLAY! *HEE-HEE!*

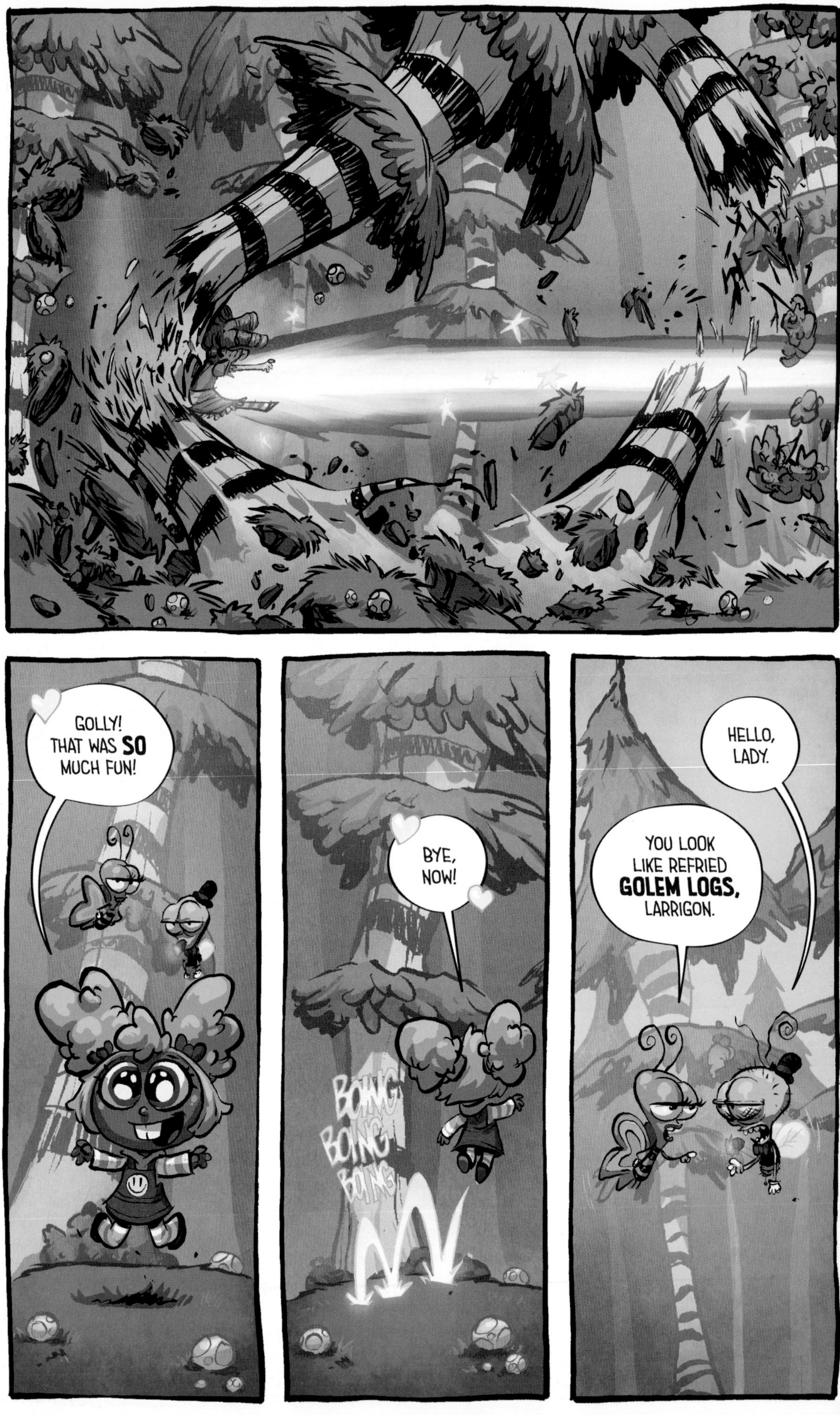
GOLLY! THAT WAS **SO** MUCH FUN!
BYE, NOW!
BOING BOING BOING
HELLO, LADY.
YOU LOOK LIKE REFRIED **GOLEM LOGS,** LARRIGON.

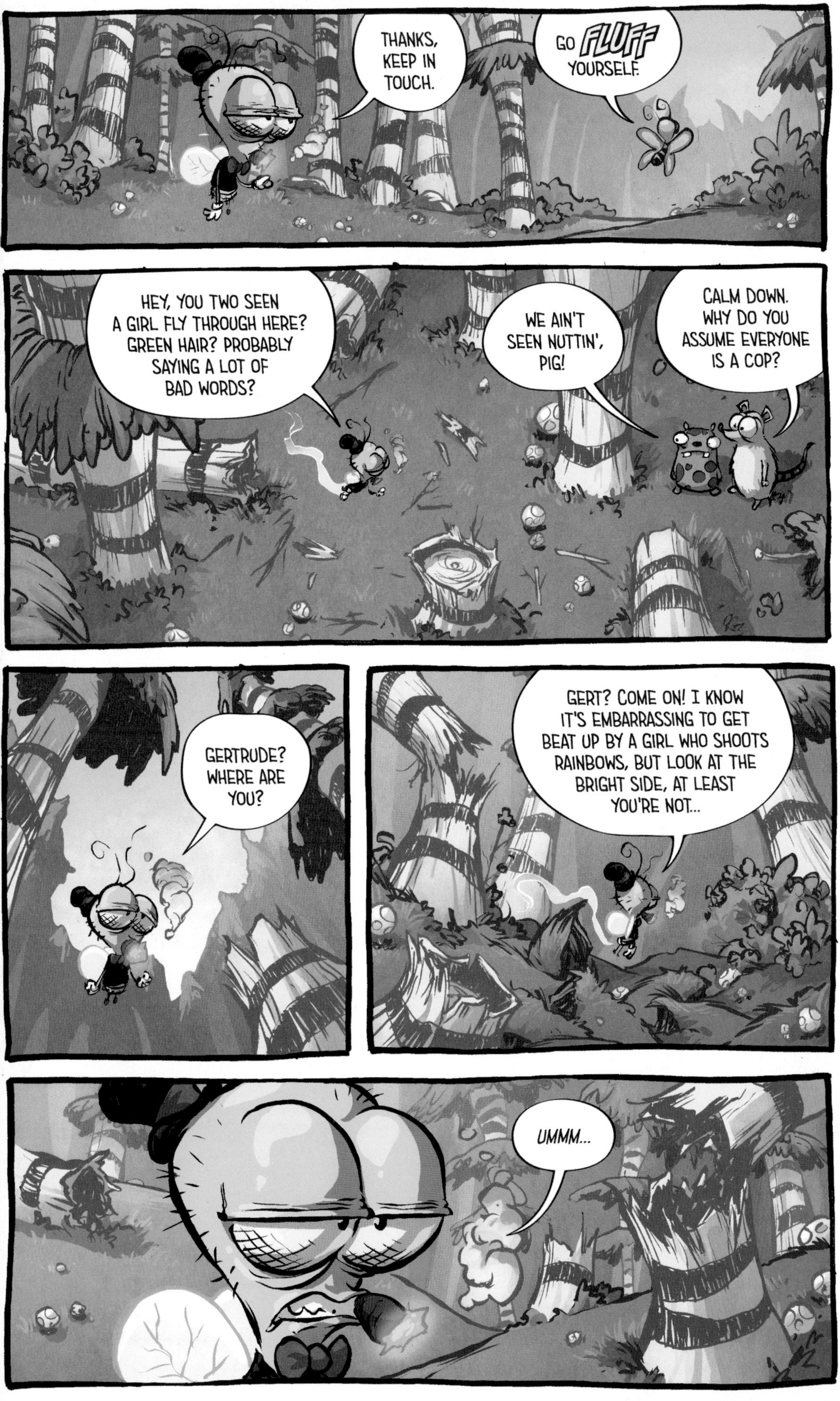
THANKS, KEEP IN TOUCH.
GO FLUFF YOURSELF.
HEY, YOU TWO SEEN A GIRL FLY THROUGH HERE? GREEN HAIR? PROBABLY SAYING A LOT OF BAD WORDS?
WE AIN'T SEEN NUTTIN', PIG!
CALM DOWN. WHY DO YOU ASSUME EVERYONE IS A COP?
GERTRUDE? WHERE ARE YOU?
GERT? COME ON! I KNOW IT'S EMBARRASSING TO GET BEAT UP BY A GIRL WHO SHOOTS RAINBOWS, BUT LOOK AT THE BRIGHT SIDE, AT LEAST YOU'RE NOT...
UMMM...

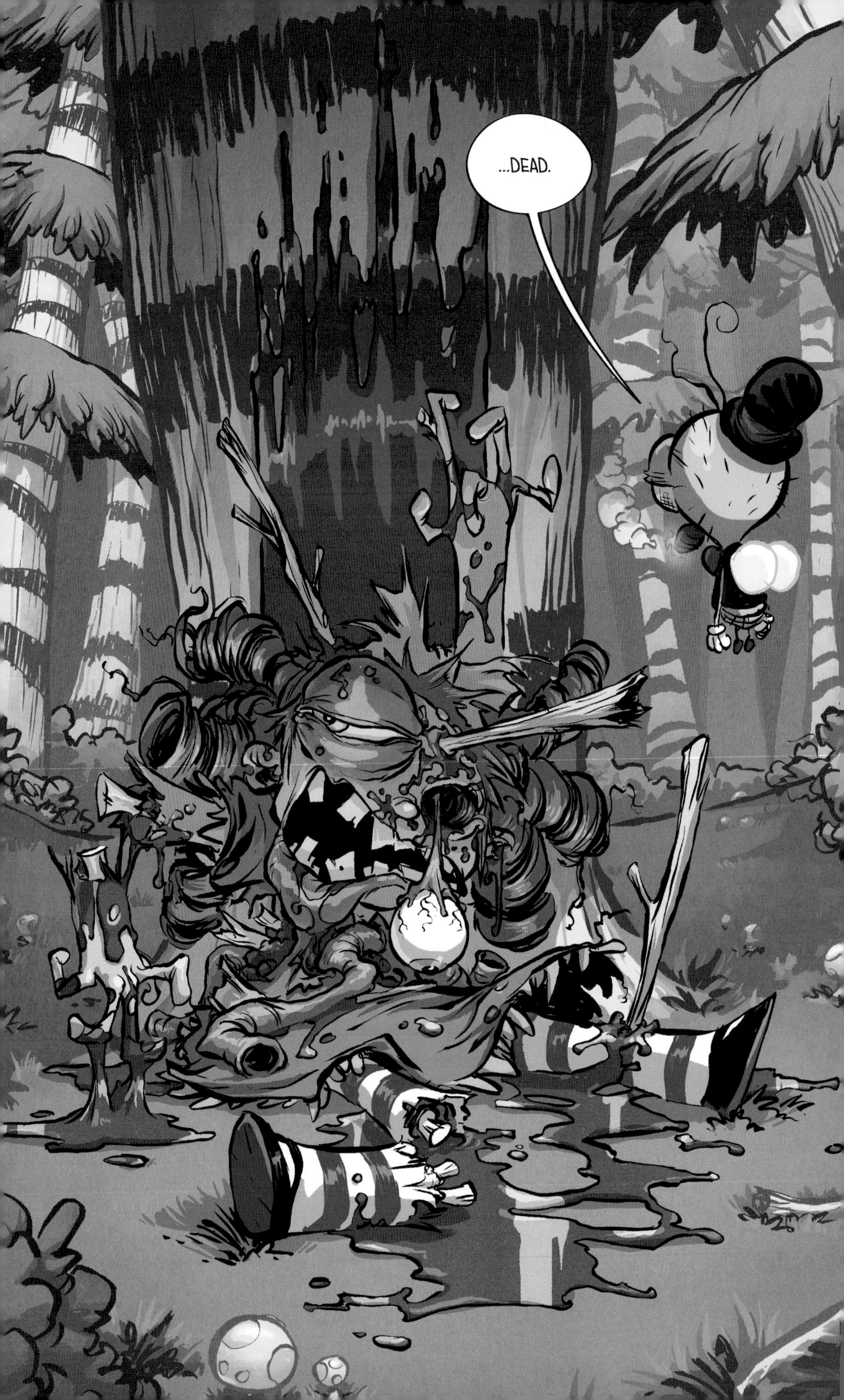
...DEAD.

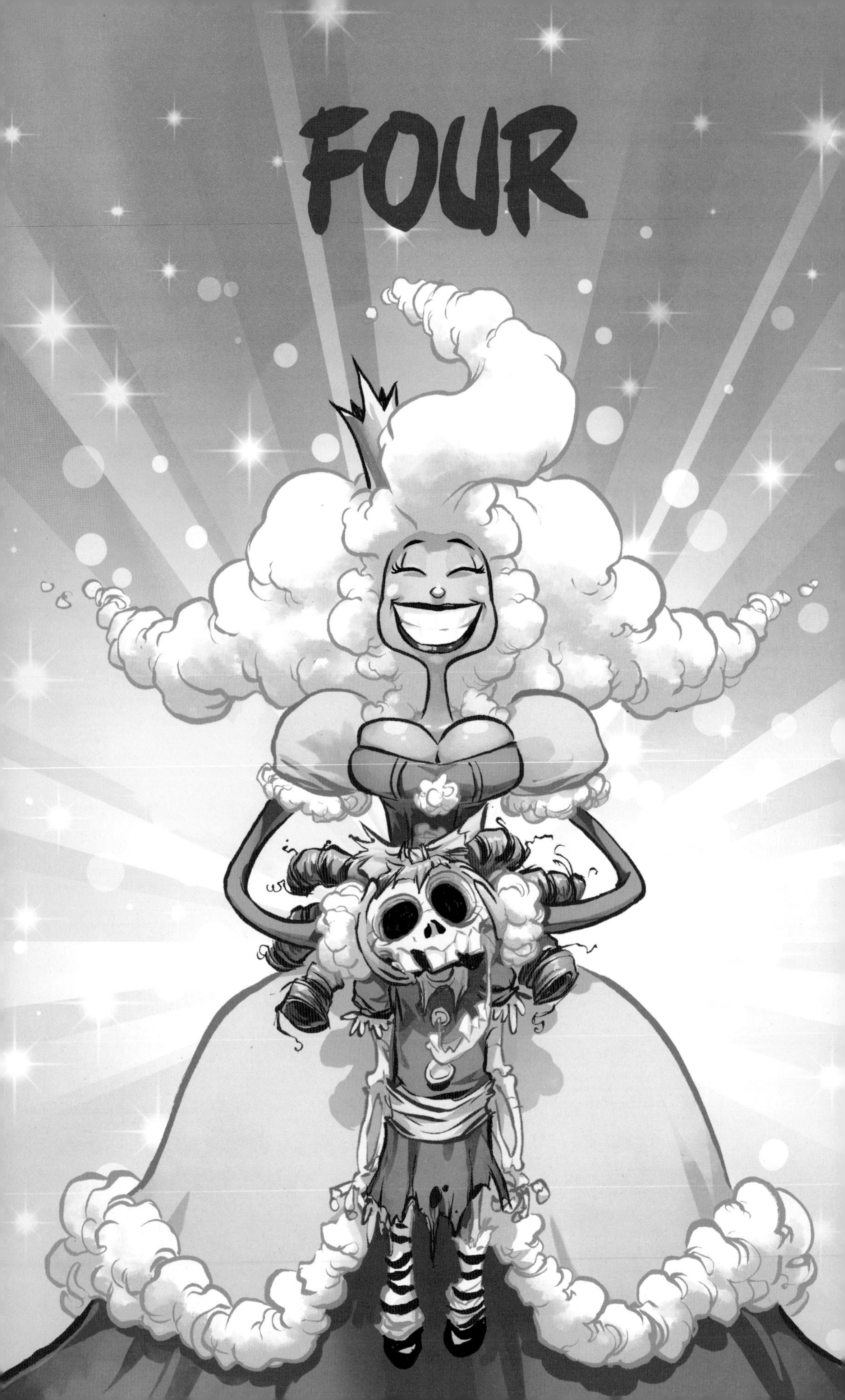
FOUR

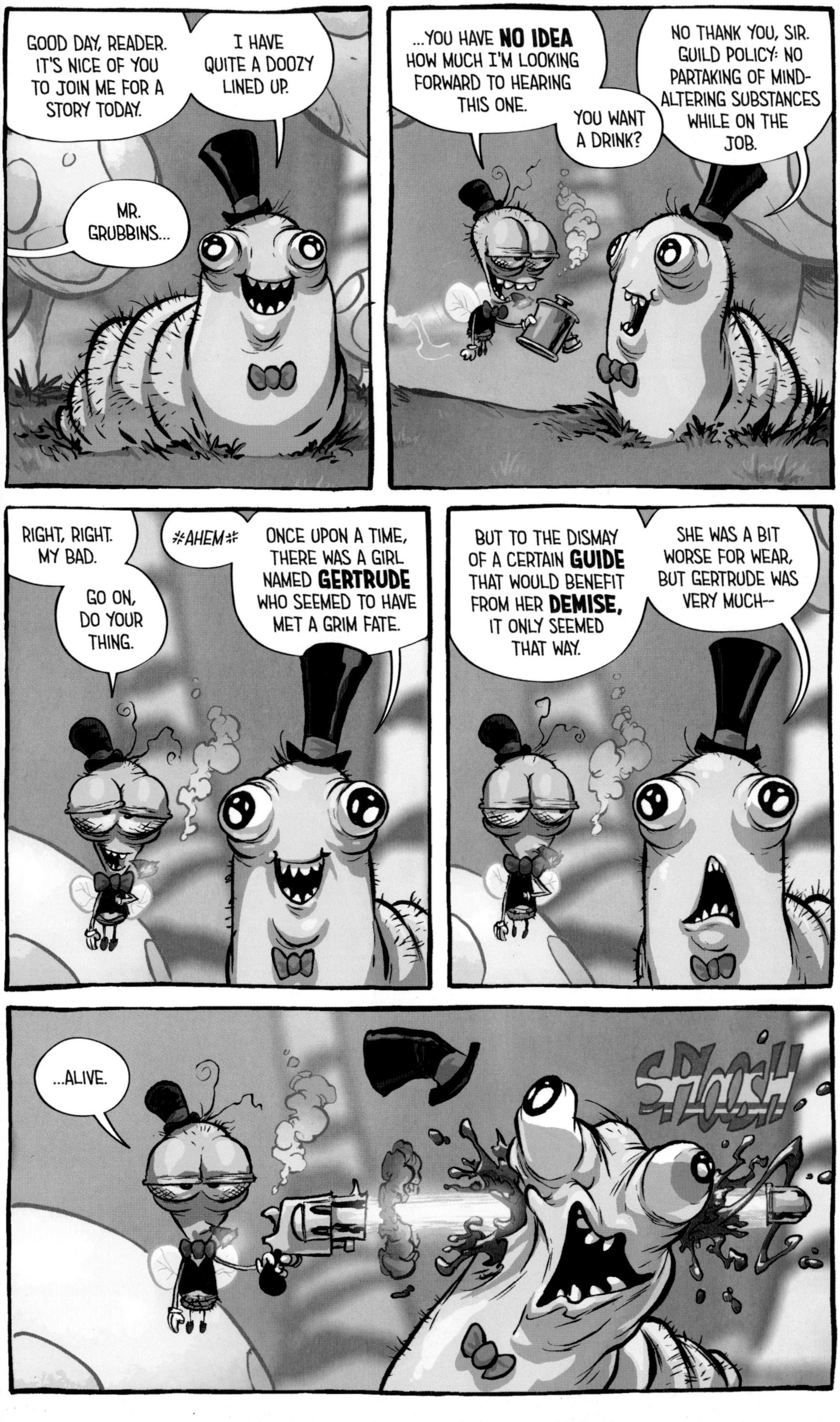
GOOD DAY, READER. IT'S NICE OF YOU TO JOIN ME FOR A STORY TODAY.
I HAVE QUITE A DOOZY LINED UP.
MR. GRUBBINS...
...YOU HAVE **NO IDEA** HOW MUCH I'M LOOKING FORWARD TO HEARING THIS ONE.
YOU WANT A DRINK?
NO THANK YOU, SIR. GUILD POLICY: NO PARTAKING OF MIND-ALTERING SUBSTANCES WHILE ON THE JOB.
RIGHT, RIGHT. MY BAD.
GO ON, DO YOUR THING.
AHEM
ONCE UPON A TIME, THERE WAS A GIRL NAMED **GERTRUDE** WHO SEEMED TO HAVE MET A GRIM FATE.
BUT TO THE DISMAY OF A CERTAIN **GUIDE** THAT WOULD BENEFIT FROM HER **DEMISE,** IT ONLY SEEMED THAT WAY.
SHE WAS A BIT WORSE FOR WEAR, BUT GERTRUDE WAS VERY MUCH--
...ALIVE.
SPLOOSH

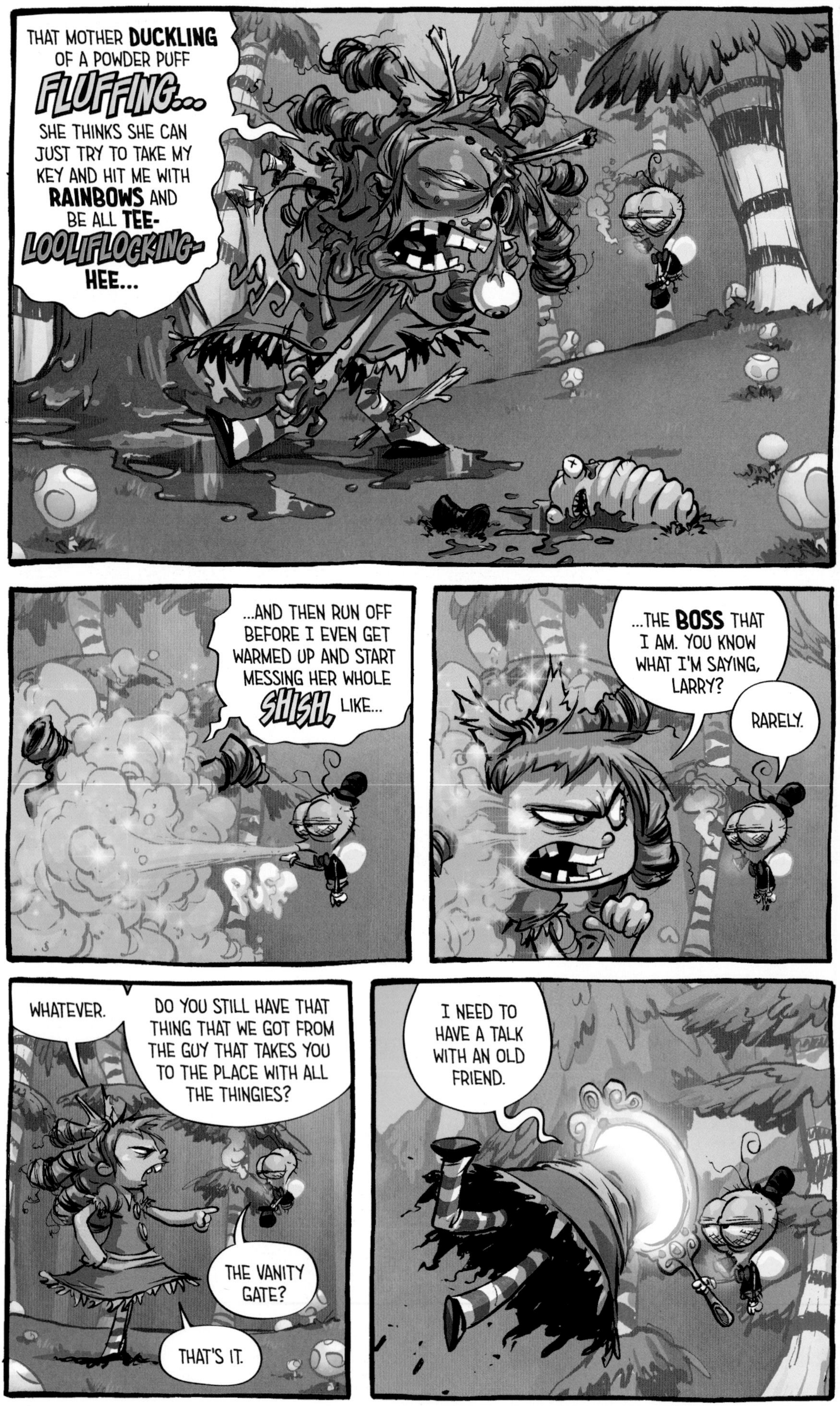

THAT MOTHER DUCKLING OF A POWDER PUFF FLUFFING... SHE THINKS SHE CAN JUST TRY TO TAKE MY KEY AND HIT ME WITH RAINBOWS AND BE ALL TEE-LOOLIFLOCKING-HEE...
...AND THEN RUN OFF BEFORE I EVEN GET WARMED UP AND START MESSING HER WHOLE SHISH, LIKE...
PUFF
...THE BOSS THAT I AM. YOU KNOW WHAT I'M SAYING, LARRY?
RARELY.
WHATEVER.
DO YOU STILL HAVE THAT THING THAT WE GOT FROM THE GUY THAT TAKES YOU TO THE PLACE WITH ALL THE THINGIES?
THE VANITY GATE?
THAT'S IT.
I NEED TO HAVE A TALK WITH AN OLD FRIEND.

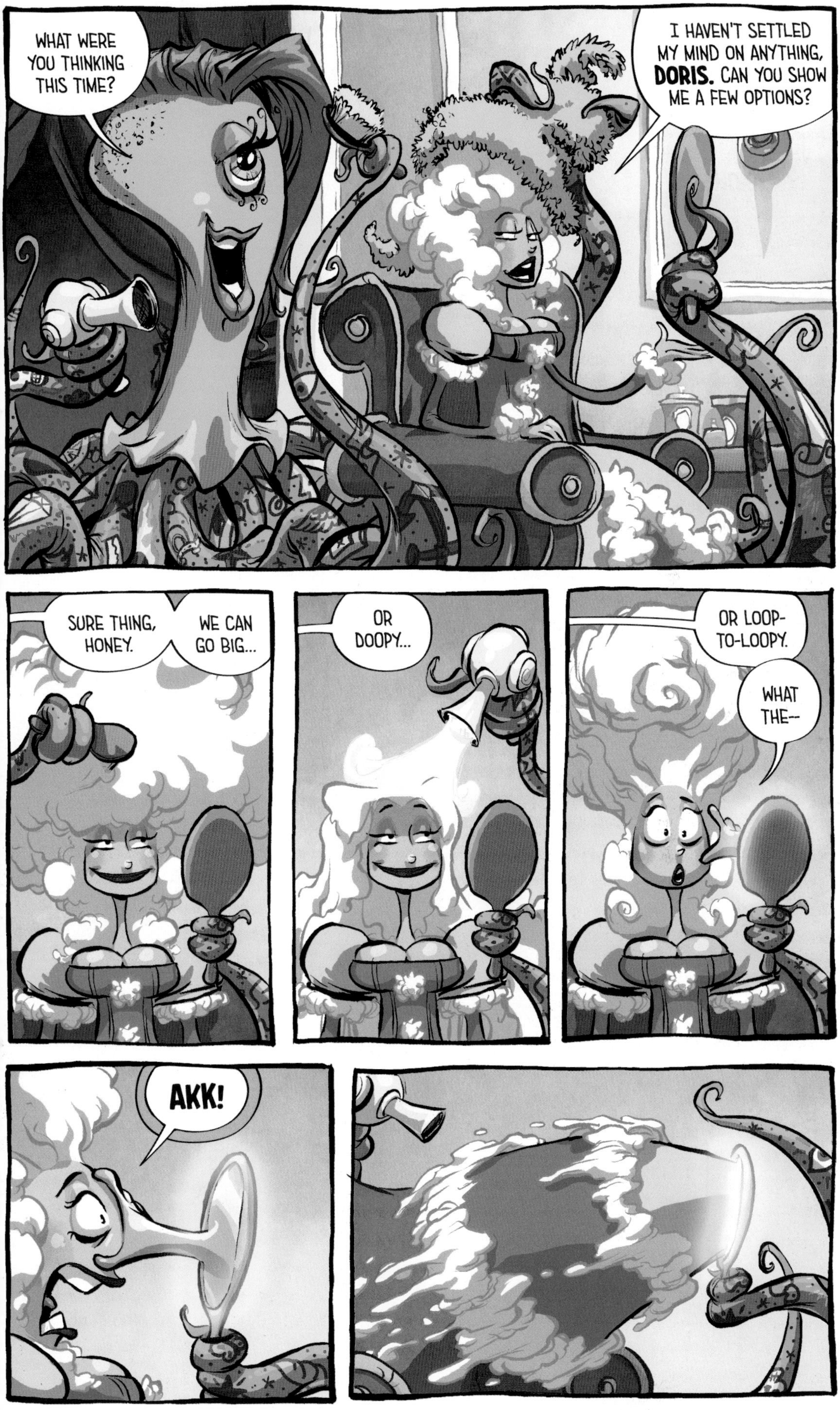

WHAT WERE YOU THINKING THIS TIME?
I HAVEN'T SETTLED MY MIND ON ANYTHING, **DORIS.** CAN YOU SHOW ME A FEW OPTIONS?
SURE THING, HONEY.
WE CAN GO BIG...
OR DOOPY...
OR LOOP-TO-LOOPY.
WHAT THE--
AKK!

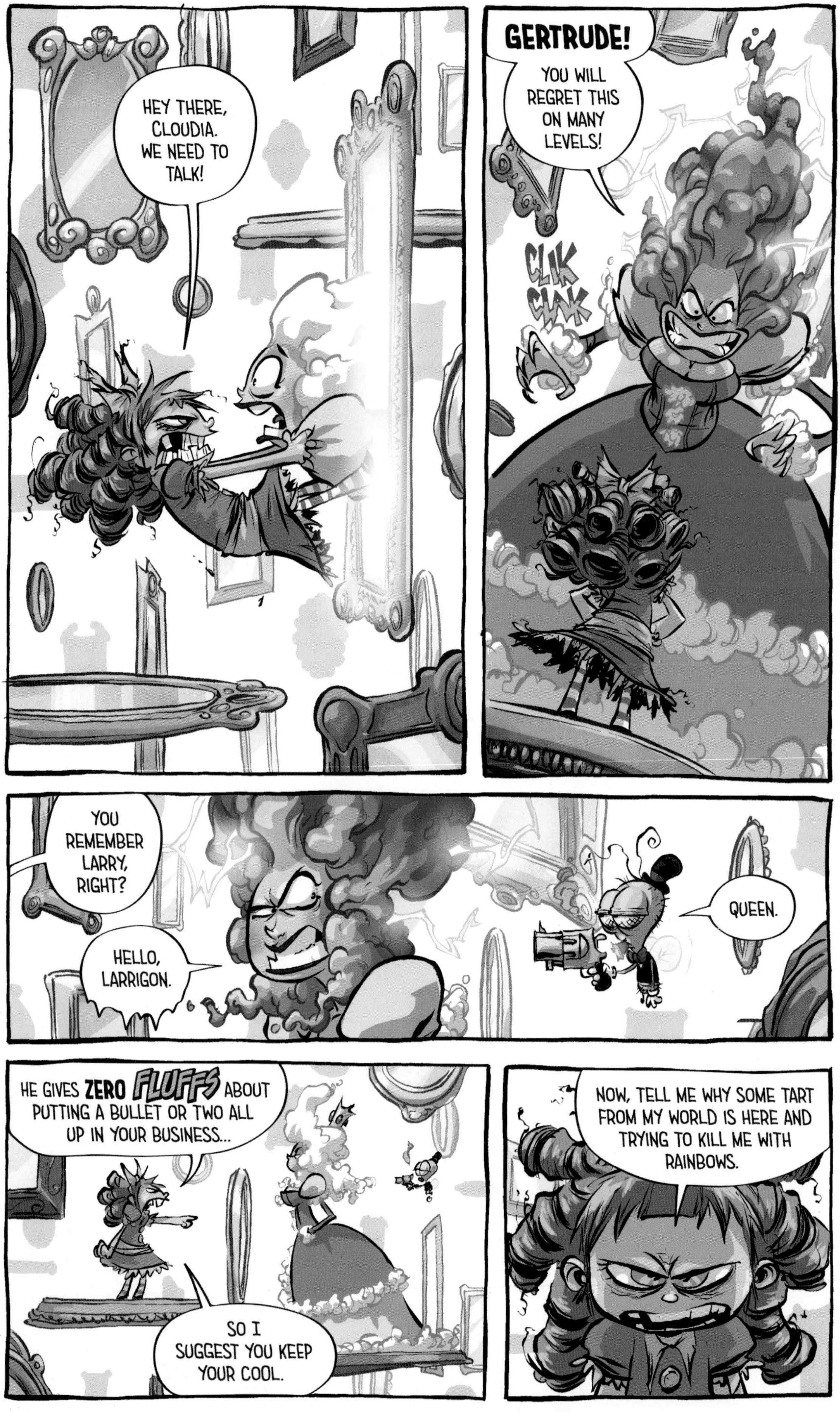
HEY THERE, CLOUDIA. WE NEED TO TALK!
GERTRUDE!
YOU WILL REGRET THIS ON MANY LEVELS!
CLIK CLAK
YOU REMEMBER LARRY, RIGHT?
HELLO, LARRIGON.
QUEEN.
HE GIVES ZERO FLUFFS ABOUT PUTTING A BULLET OR TWO ALL UP IN YOUR BUSINESS...
SO I SUGGEST YOU KEEP YOUR COOL.
NOW, TELL ME WHY SOME TART FROM MY WORLD IS HERE AND TRYING TO KILL ME WITH RAINBOWS.

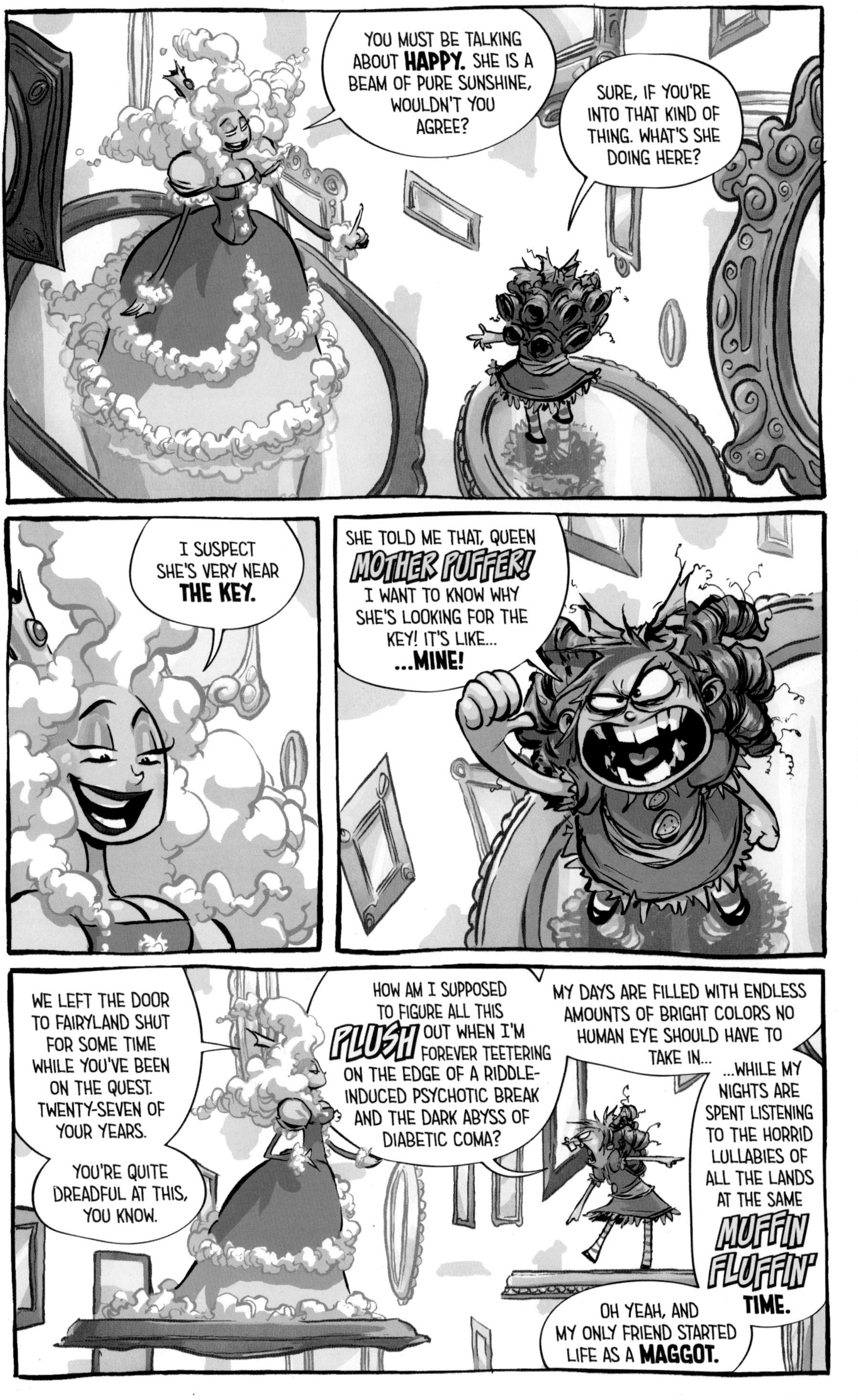
YOU MUST BE TALKING ABOUT **HAPPY.** SHE IS A BEAM OF PURE SUNSHINE, WOULDN'T YOU AGREE?
SURE, IF YOU'RE INTO THAT KIND OF THING. WHAT'S SHE DOING HERE?
I SUSPECT SHE'S VERY NEAR **THE KEY.**
SHE TOLD ME THAT, QUEEN **MOTHER PUFFER!** I WANT TO KNOW WHY SHE'S LOOKING FOR THE KEY! IT'S LIKE... **...MINE!**
WE LEFT THE DOOR TO FAIRYLAND SHUT FOR SOME TIME WHILE YOU'VE BEEN ON THE QUEST. TWENTY-SEVEN OF YOUR YEARS.
YOU'RE QUITE DREADFUL AT THIS, YOU KNOW.
HOW AM I SUPPOSED TO FIGURE ALL THIS **PLUSH** OUT WHEN I'M FOREVER TEETERING ON THE EDGE OF A RIDDLE-INDUCED PSYCHOTIC BREAK AND THE DARK ABYSS OF DIABETIC COMA?
MY DAYS ARE FILLED WITH ENDLESS AMOUNTS OF BRIGHT COLORS NO HUMAN EYE SHOULD HAVE TO TAKE IN...
...WHILE MY NIGHTS ARE SPENT LISTENING TO THE HORRID LULLABIES OF ALL THE LANDS AT THE SAME **MUFFIN FLUFFIN' TIME.**
OH YEAH, AND MY ONLY FRIEND STARTED LIFE AS A **MAGGOT.**

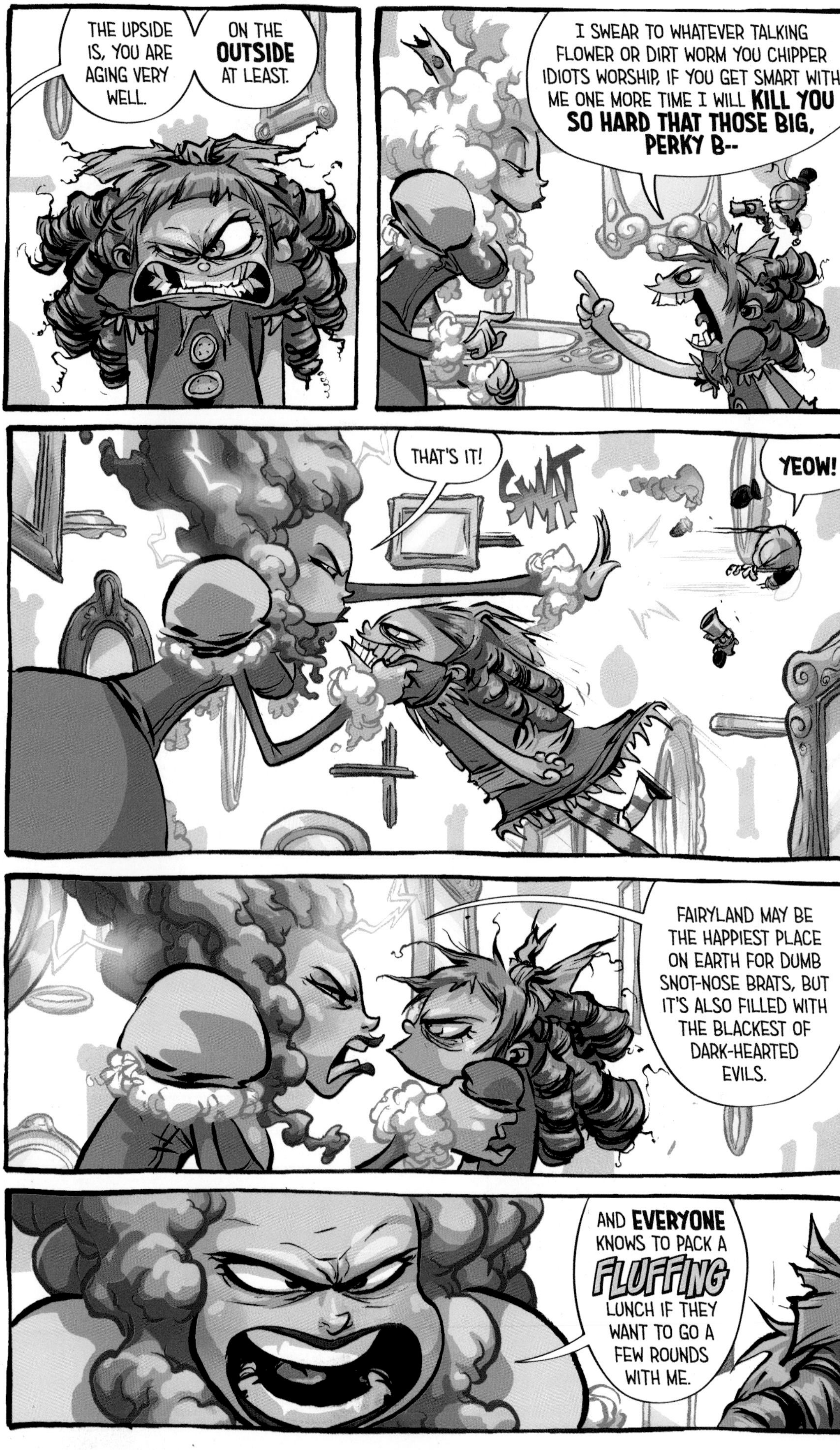

THE UPSIDE IS, YOU ARE AGING VERY WELL.
ON THE **OUTSIDE** AT LEAST.
I SWEAR TO WHATEVER TALKING FLOWER OR DIRT WORM YOU CHIPPER IDIOTS WORSHIP, IF YOU GET SMART WITH ME ONE MORE TIME I WILL **KILL YOU SO HARD THAT THOSE BIG, PERKY B--**
THAT'S IT!
SWAT
YEOW!
FAIRYLAND MAY BE THE HAPPIEST PLACE ON EARTH FOR DUMB SNOT-NOSE BRATS, BUT IT'S ALSO FILLED WITH THE BLACKEST OF DARK-HEARTED EVILS.
AND **EVERYONE** KNOWS TO PACK A **FLUFFING** LUNCH IF THEY WANT TO GO A FEW ROUNDS WITH ME.

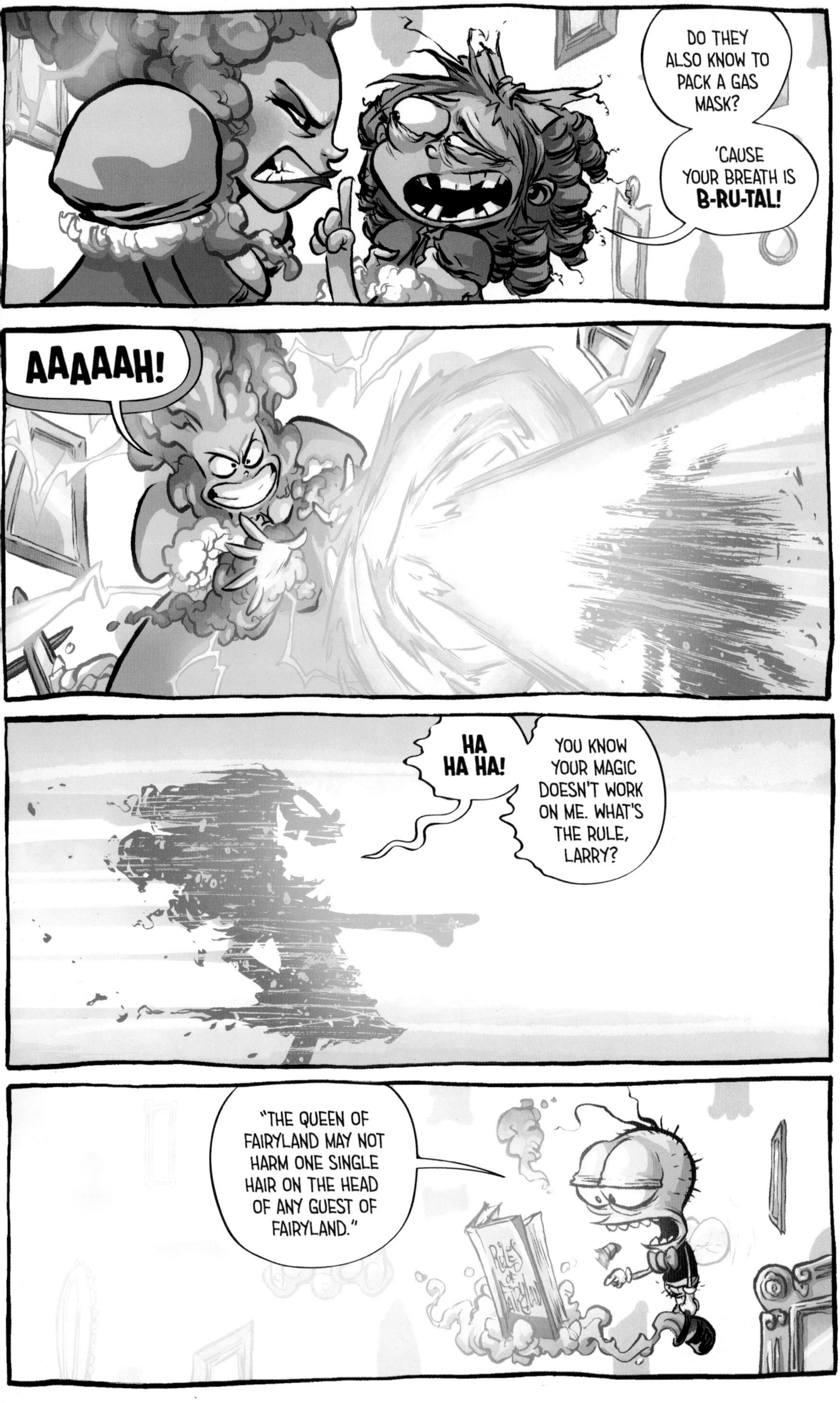
DO THEY ALSO KNOW TO PACK A GAS MASK?
'CAUSE YOUR BREATH IS **B-RU-TAL!**
AAAAAH!
HA HA HA!
YOU KNOW YOUR MAGIC DOESN'T WORK ON ME. WHAT'S THE RULE, LARRY?
"THE QUEEN OF FAIRYLAND MAY NOT HARM ONE SINGLE HAIR ON THE HEAD OF ANY GUEST OF FAIRYLAND."
RULES OF FAIRYLAND

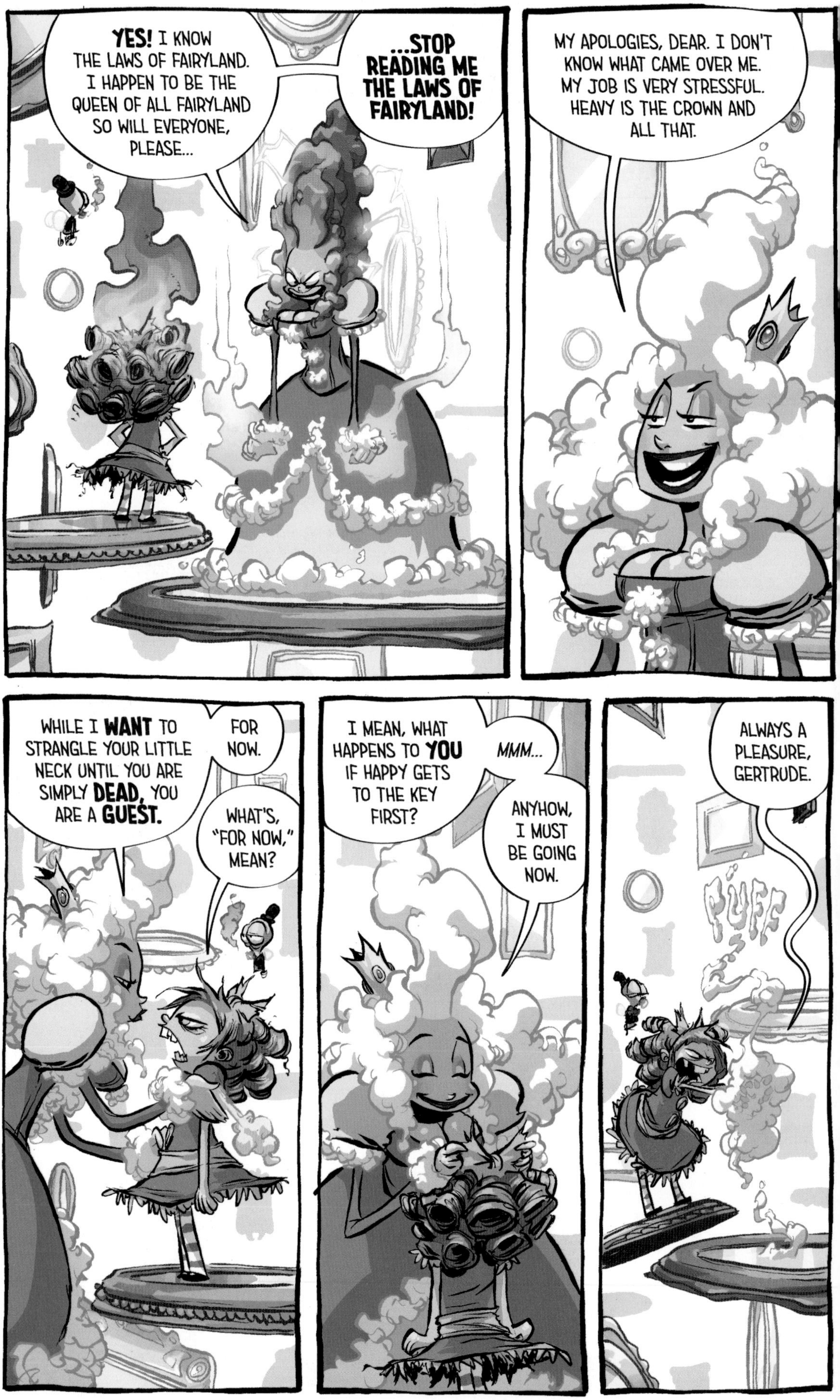

YES! I KNOW THE LAWS OF FAIRYLAND. I HAPPEN TO BE THE QUEEN OF ALL FAIRYLAND SO WILL EVERYONE, PLEASE...
...STOP READING ME THE LAWS OF FAIRYLAND!
MY APOLOGIES, DEAR. I DON'T KNOW WHAT CAME OVER ME. MY JOB IS VERY STRESSFUL. HEAVY IS THE CROWN AND ALL THAT.
WHILE I WANT TO STRANGLE YOUR LITTLE NECK UNTIL YOU ARE SIMPLY DEAD, YOU ARE A GUEST.
FOR NOW.
WHAT'S, "FOR NOW," MEAN?
I MEAN, WHAT HAPPENS TO YOU IF HAPPY GETS TO THE KEY FIRST?
MMM...
ANYHOW, I MUST BE GOING NOW.
ALWAYS A PLEASURE, GERTRUDE.
PUFF

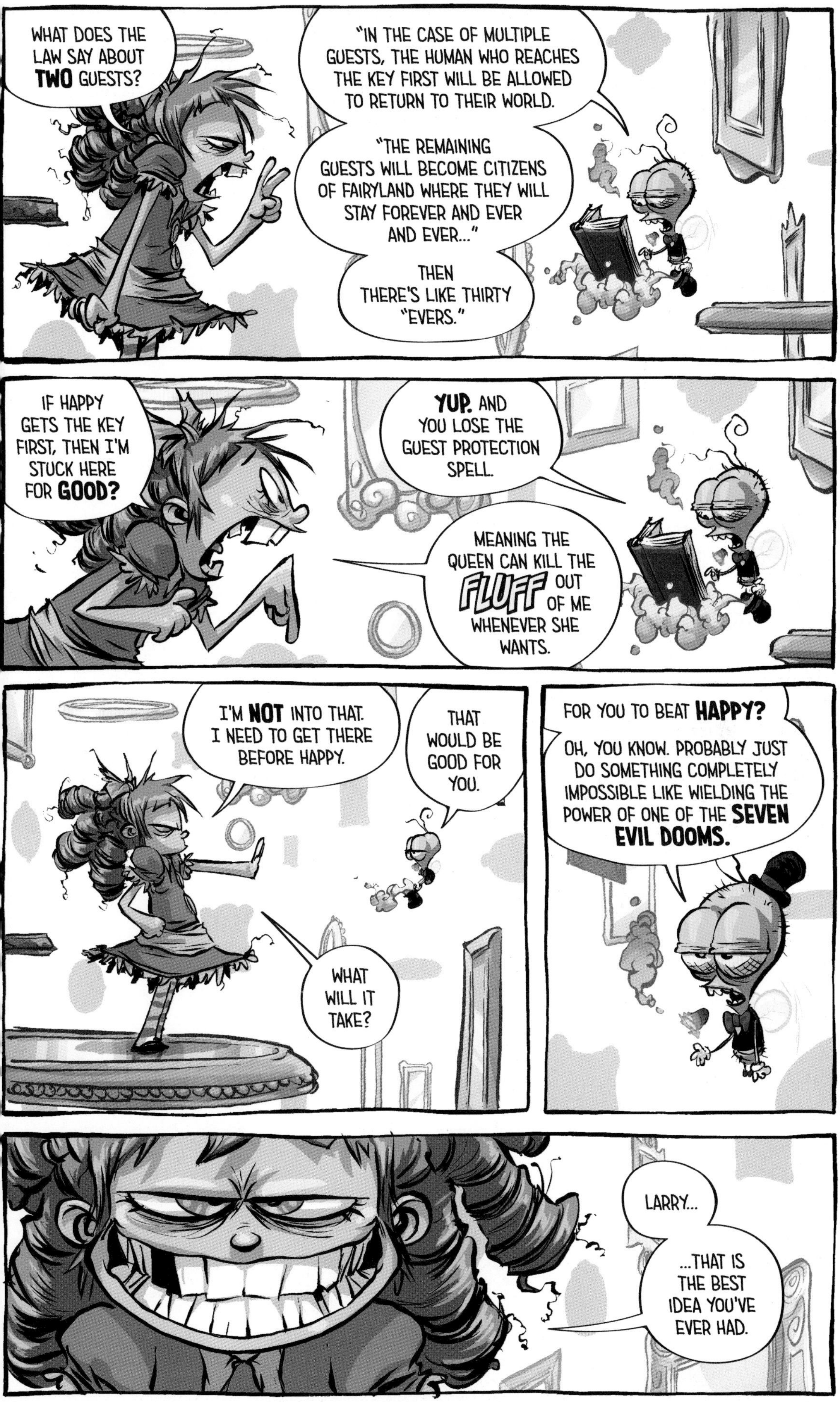
WHAT DOES THE LAW SAY ABOUT **TWO** GUESTS?
"IN THE CASE OF MULTIPLE GUESTS, THE HUMAN WHO REACHES THE KEY FIRST WILL BE ALLOWED TO RETURN TO THEIR WORLD.
"THE REMAINING GUESTS WILL BECOME CITIZENS OF FAIRYLAND WHERE THEY WILL STAY FOREVER AND EVER AND EVER..."
THEN THERE'S LIKE THIRTY "EVERS."
IF HAPPY GETS THE KEY FIRST, THEN I'M STUCK HERE FOR **GOOD?**
YUP. AND YOU LOSE THE GUEST PROTECTION SPELL.
MEANING THE QUEEN CAN KILL THE FLUFF OUT OF ME WHENEVER SHE WANTS.
I'M **NOT** INTO THAT. I NEED TO GET THERE BEFORE HAPPY.
THAT WOULD BE GOOD FOR YOU.
WHAT WILL IT TAKE?
FOR YOU TO BEAT **HAPPY?**
OH, YOU KNOW. PROBABLY JUST DO SOMETHING COMPLETELY IMPOSSIBLE LIKE WIELDING THE POWER OF ONE OF THE **SEVEN EVIL DOOMS.**
LARRY...
...THAT IS THE BEST IDEA YOU'VE EVER HAD.

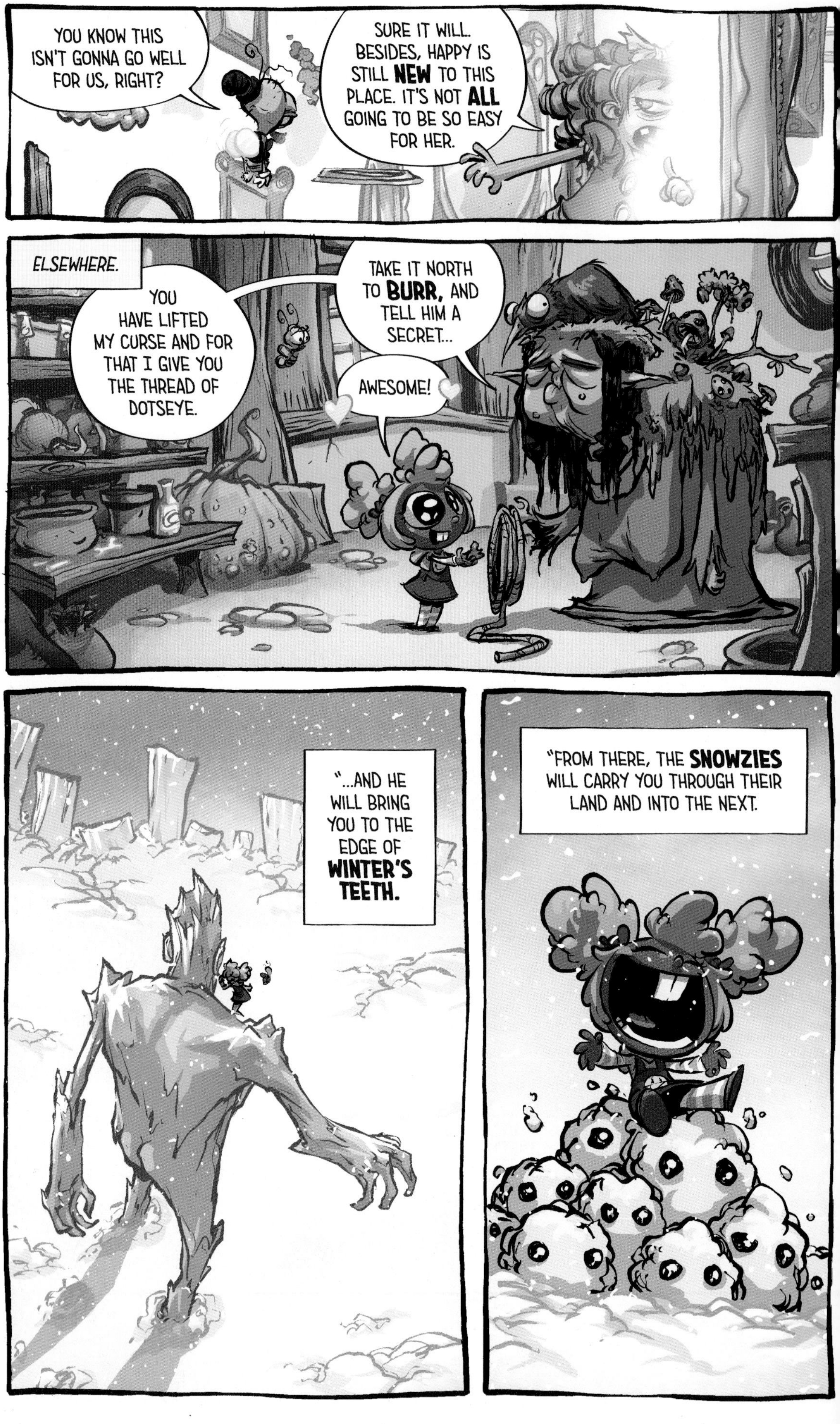
YOU KNOW THIS ISN'T GONNA GO WELL FOR US, RIGHT?
SURE IT WILL. BESIDES, HAPPY IS STILL NEW TO THIS PLACE. IT'S NOT ALL GOING TO BE SO EASY FOR HER.
ELSEWHERE.
YOU HAVE LIFTED MY CURSE AND FOR THAT I GIVE YOU THE THREAD OF DOTSEYE.
TAKE IT NORTH TO BURR, AND TELL HIM A SECRET...
AWESOME!
"...AND HE WILL BRING YOU TO THE EDGE OF WINTER'S TEETH.
"FROM THERE, THE SNOWZIES WILL CARRY YOU THROUGH THEIR LAND AND INTO THE NEXT.

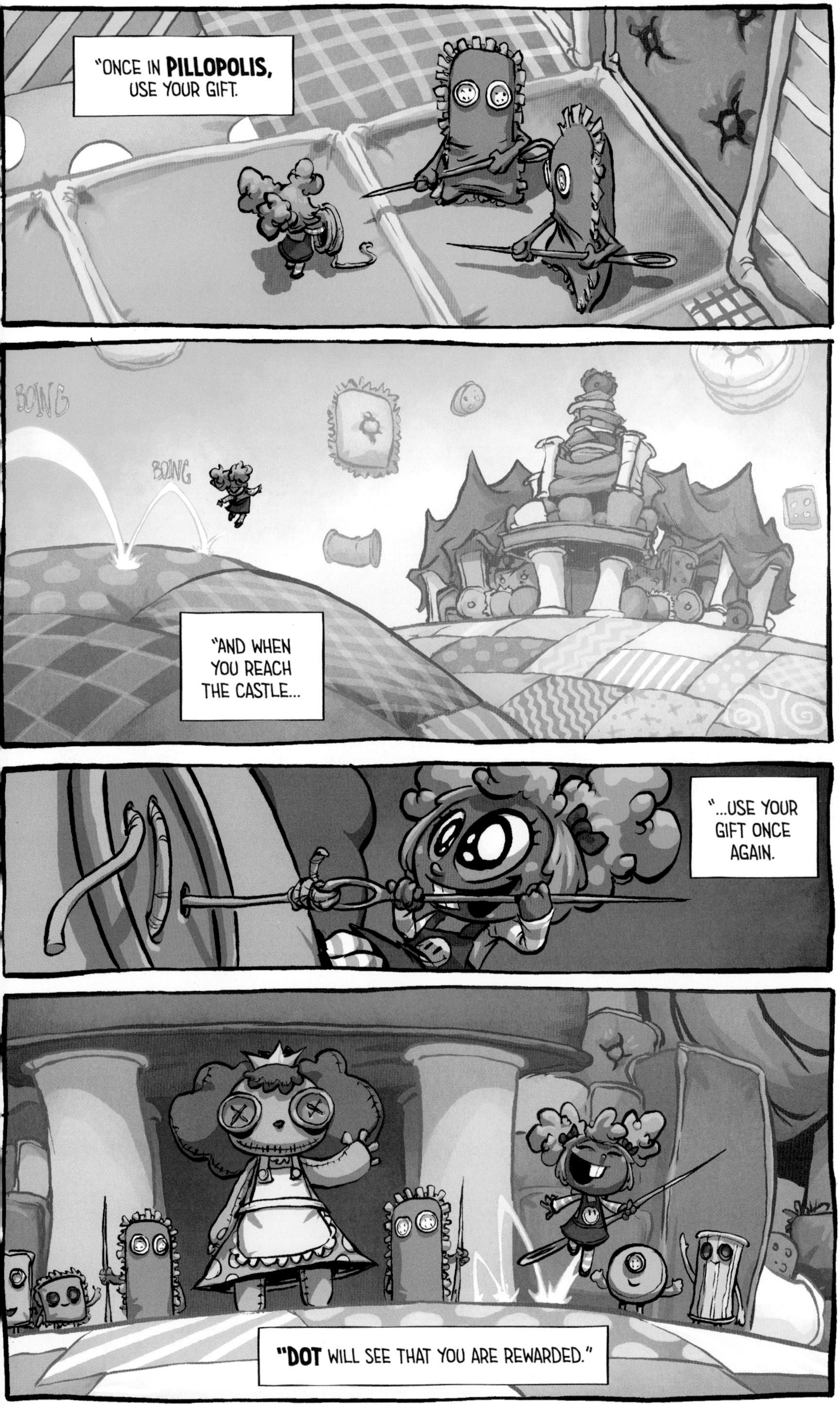
"ONCE IN **PILLOPOLIS,**
USE YOUR GIFT.
BOING
BOING
"AND WHEN YOU REACH THE CASTLE...
"...USE YOUR GIFT ONCE AGAIN.
"**DOT** WILL SEE THAT YOU ARE REWARDED."

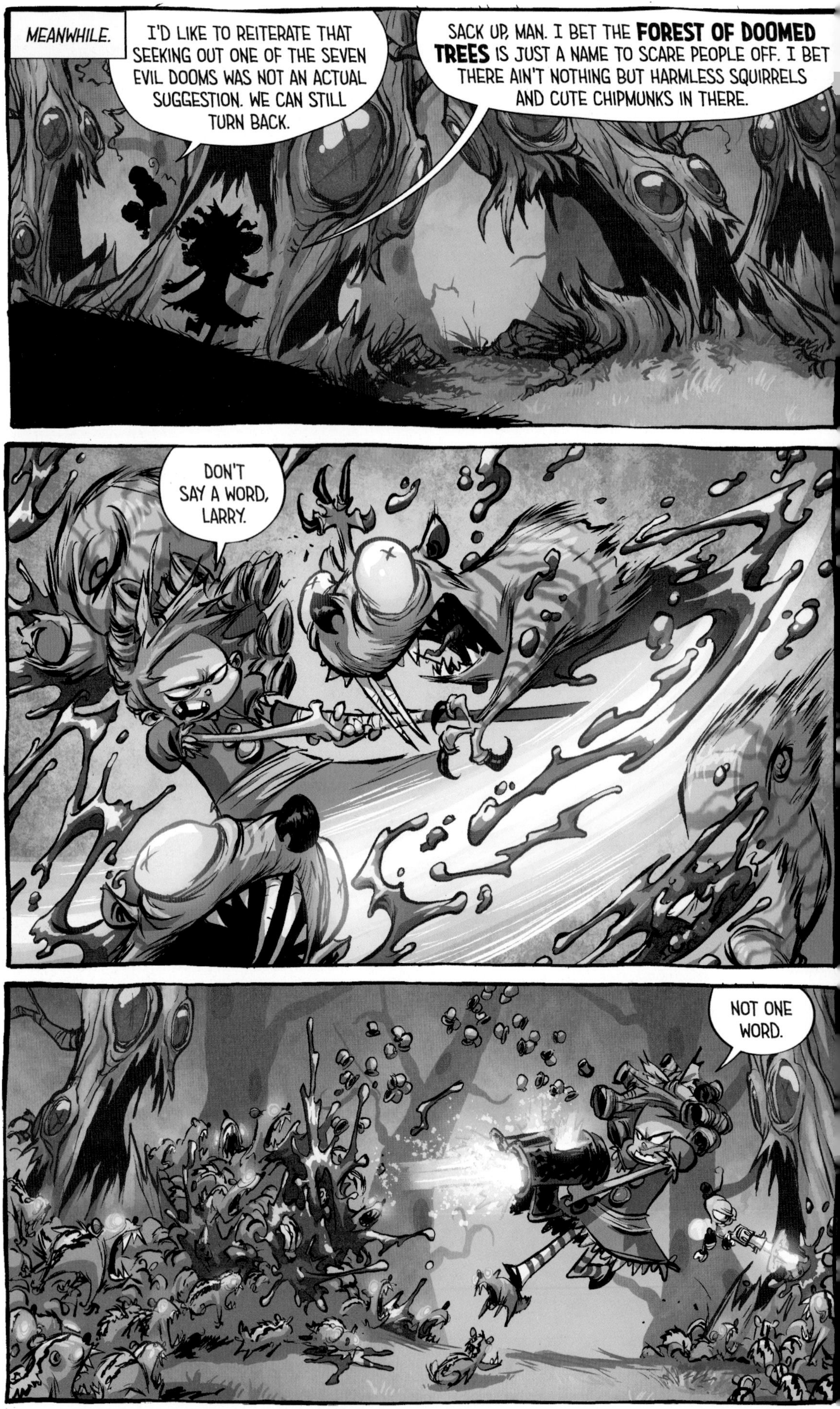
MEANWHILE.
I'D LIKE TO REITERATE THAT SEEKING OUT ONE OF THE SEVEN EVIL DOOMS WAS NOT AN ACTUAL SUGGESTION. WE CAN STILL TURN BACK.
SACK UP, MAN. I BET THE **FOREST OF DOOMED TREES** IS JUST A NAME TO SCARE PEOPLE OFF. I BET THERE AIN'T NOTHING BUT HARMLESS SQUIRRELS AND CUTE CHIPMUNKS IN THERE.
DON'T SAY A WORD, LARRY.
NOT ONE WORD.

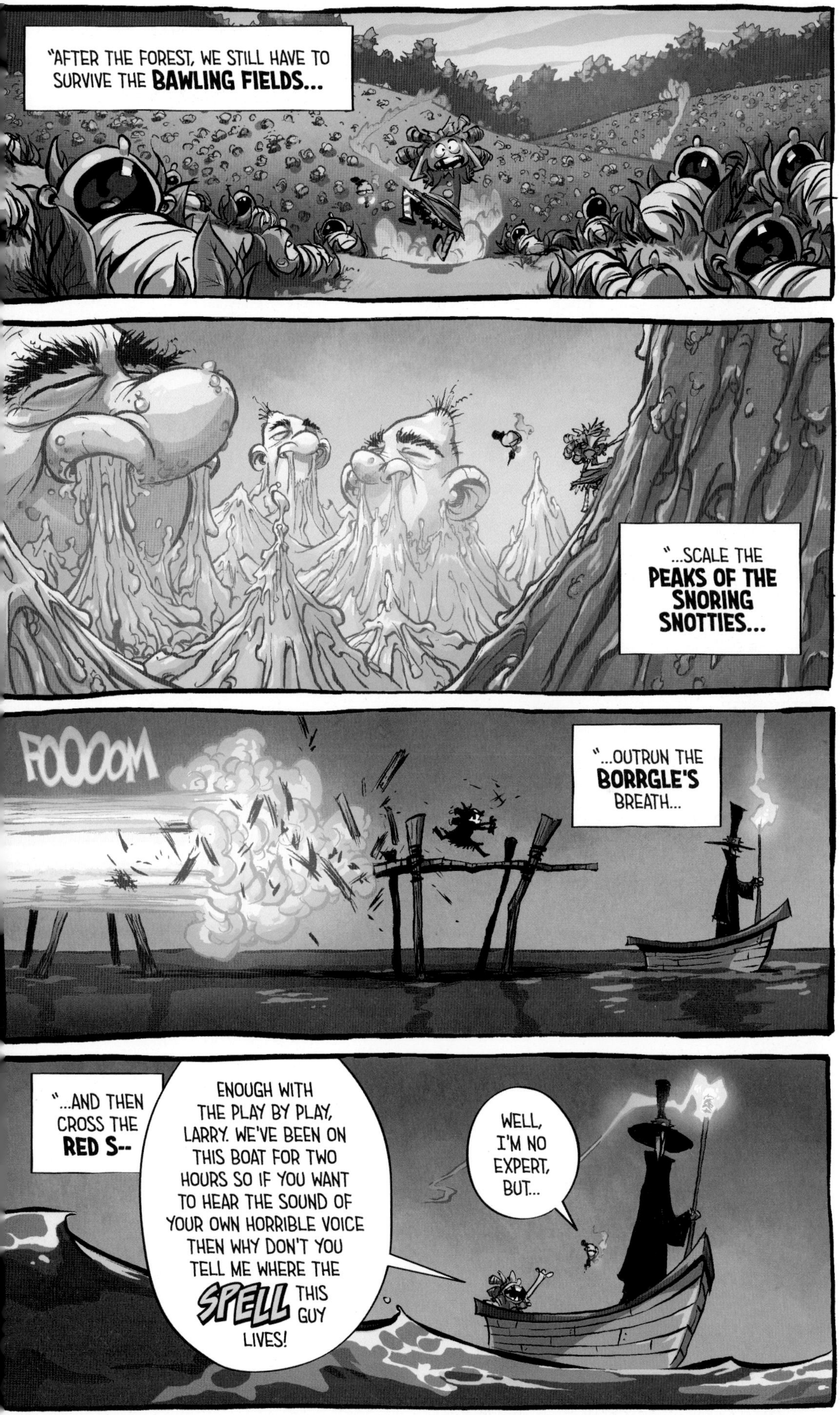
"AFTER THE FOREST, WE STILL HAVE TO SURVIVE THE **BAWLING FIELDS...**
"...SCALE THE **PEAKS OF THE SNORING SNOTTIES...**
FOOOOM
"...OUTRUN THE **BORRGLE'S** BREATH...
"...AND THEN CROSS THE **RED S--**
ENOUGH WITH THE PLAY BY PLAY, LARRY. WE'VE BEEN ON THIS BOAT FOR TWO HOURS SO IF YOU WANT TO HEAR THE SOUND OF YOUR OWN HORRIBLE VOICE THEN WHY DON'T YOU TELL ME WHERE THE SPELL THIS GUY LIVES!
WELL, I'M NO EXPERT, BUT...

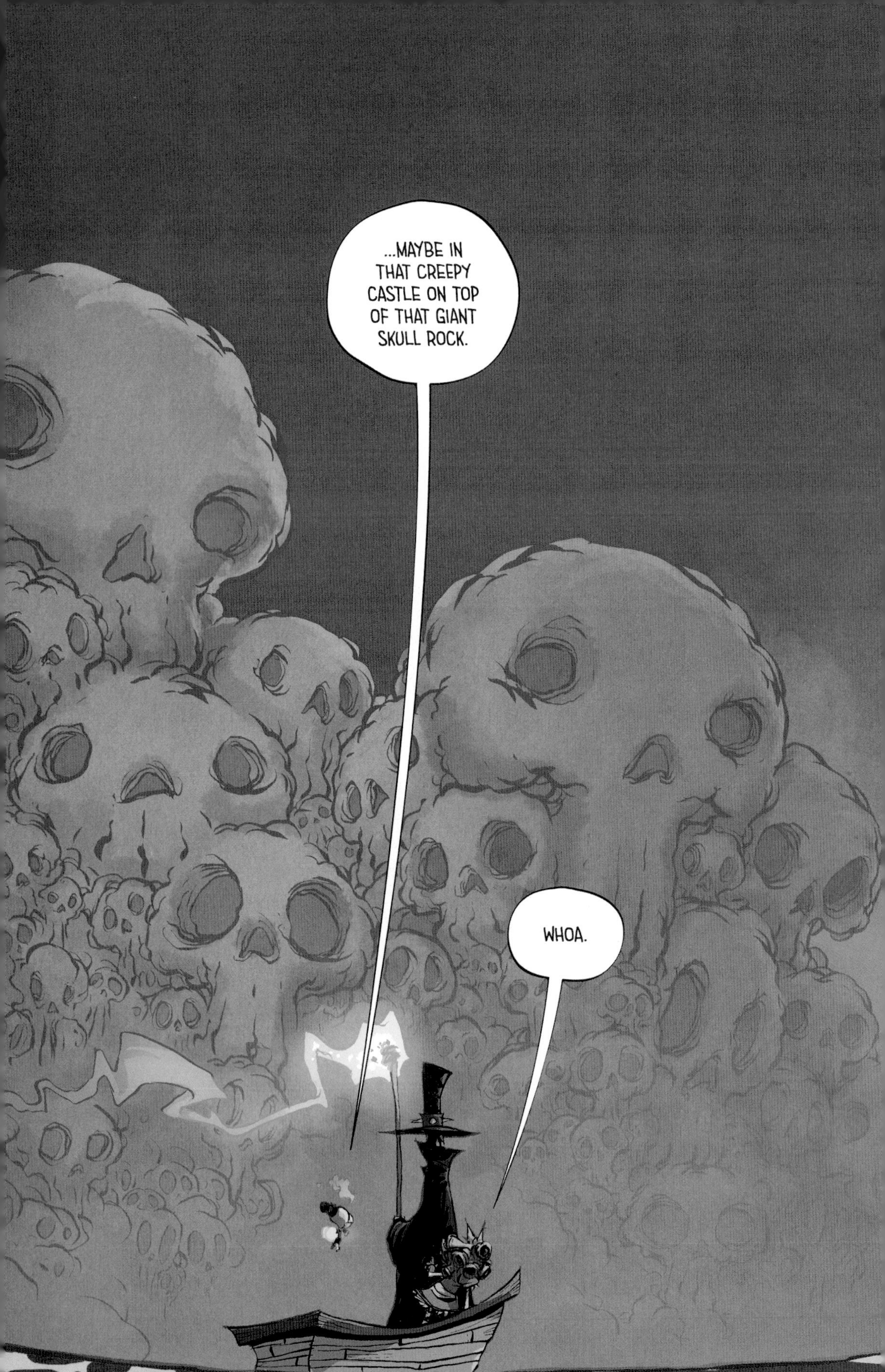
...MAYBE IN THAT CREEPY CASTLE ON TOP OF THAT GIANT SKULL ROCK.
WHOA.

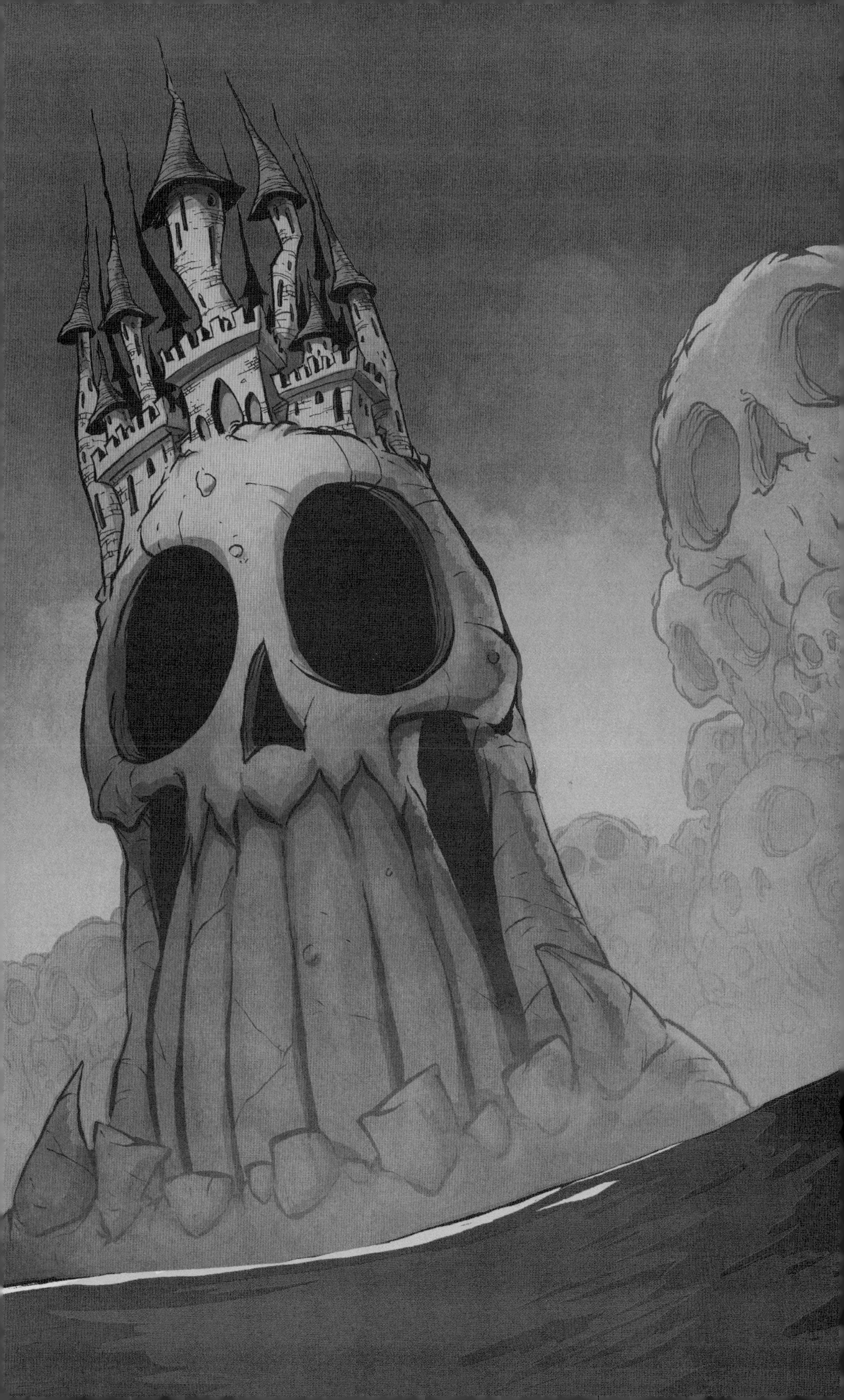

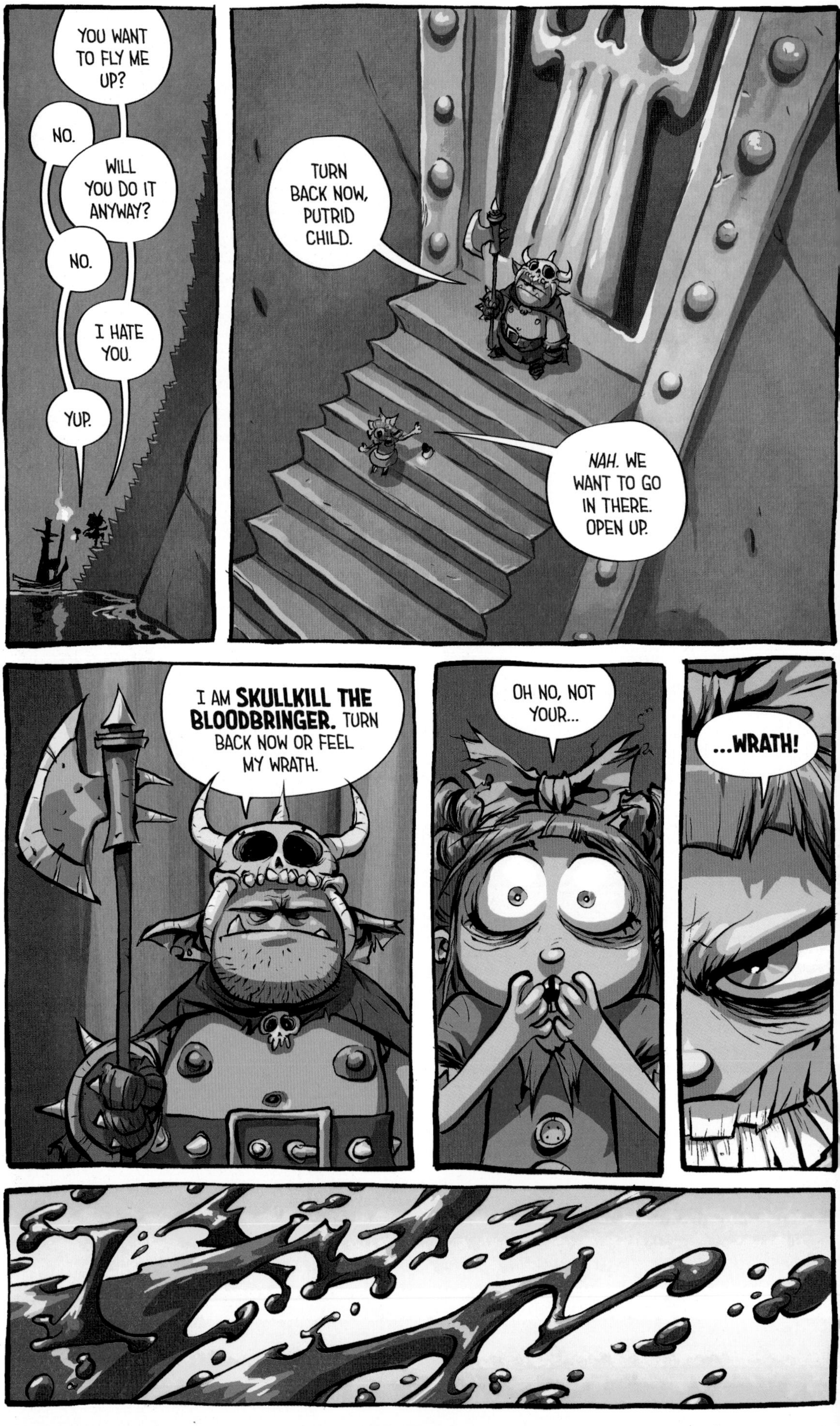
YOU WANT TO FLY ME UP?
NO.
WILL YOU DO IT ANYWAY?
NO.
I HATE YOU.
YUP.
TURN BACK NOW, PUTRID CHILD.
NAH. WE WANT TO GO IN THERE. OPEN UP.
I AM SKULLKILL THE BLOODBRINGER. TURN BACK NOW OR FEEL MY WRATH.
OH NO, NOT YOUR...
...WRATH!

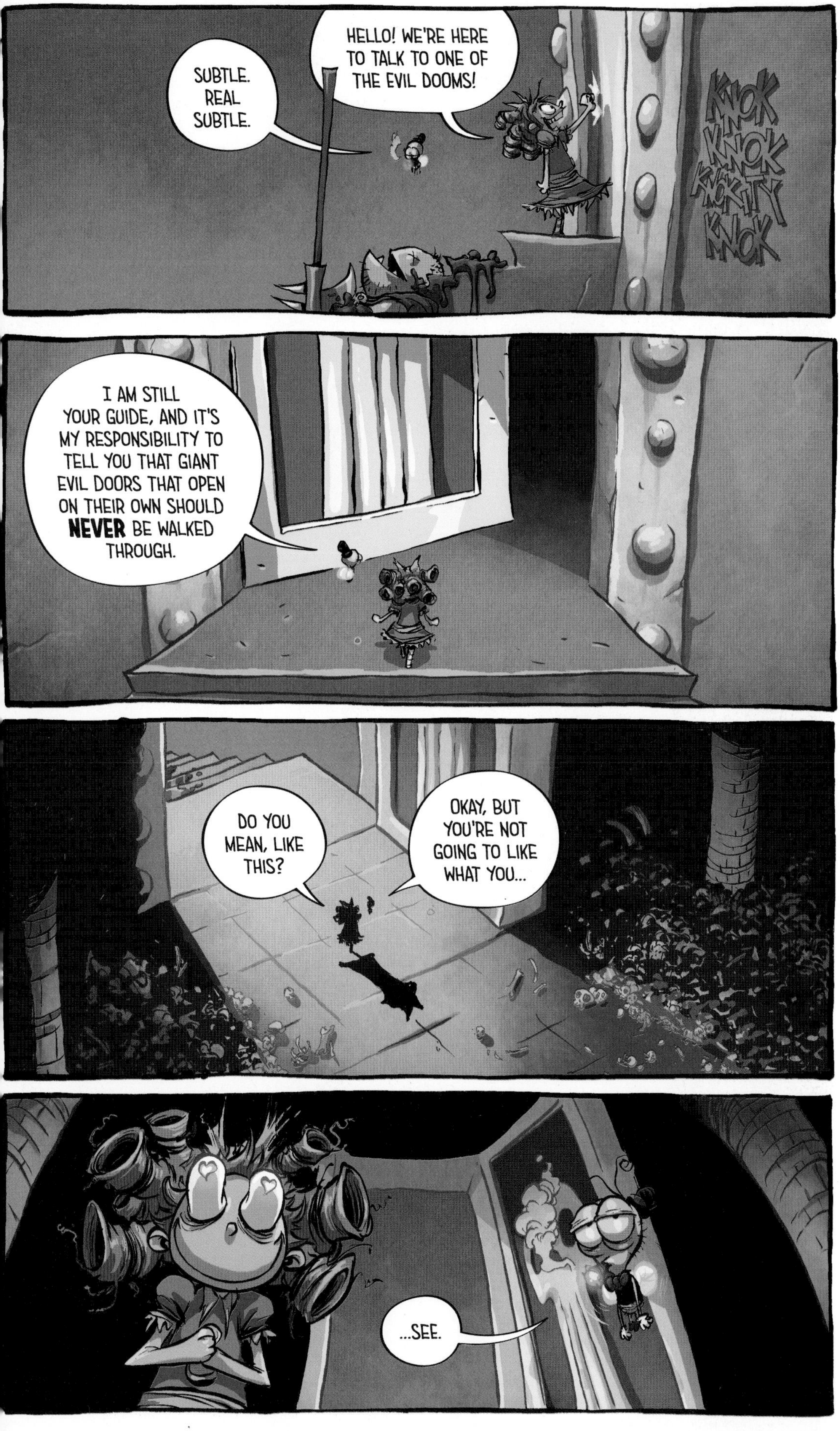
SUBTLE. REAL SUBTLE.
HELLO! WE'RE HERE TO TALK TO ONE OF THE EVIL DOOMS!
KNOCK KNOCK KNOCKITY KNOCK
I AM STILL YOUR GUIDE, AND IT'S MY RESPONSIBILITY TO TELL YOU THAT GIANT EVIL DOORS THAT OPEN ON THEIR OWN SHOULD NEVER BE WALKED THROUGH.
DO YOU MEAN, LIKE THIS?
OKAY, BUT YOU'RE NOT GOING TO LIKE WHAT YOU...
...SEE.

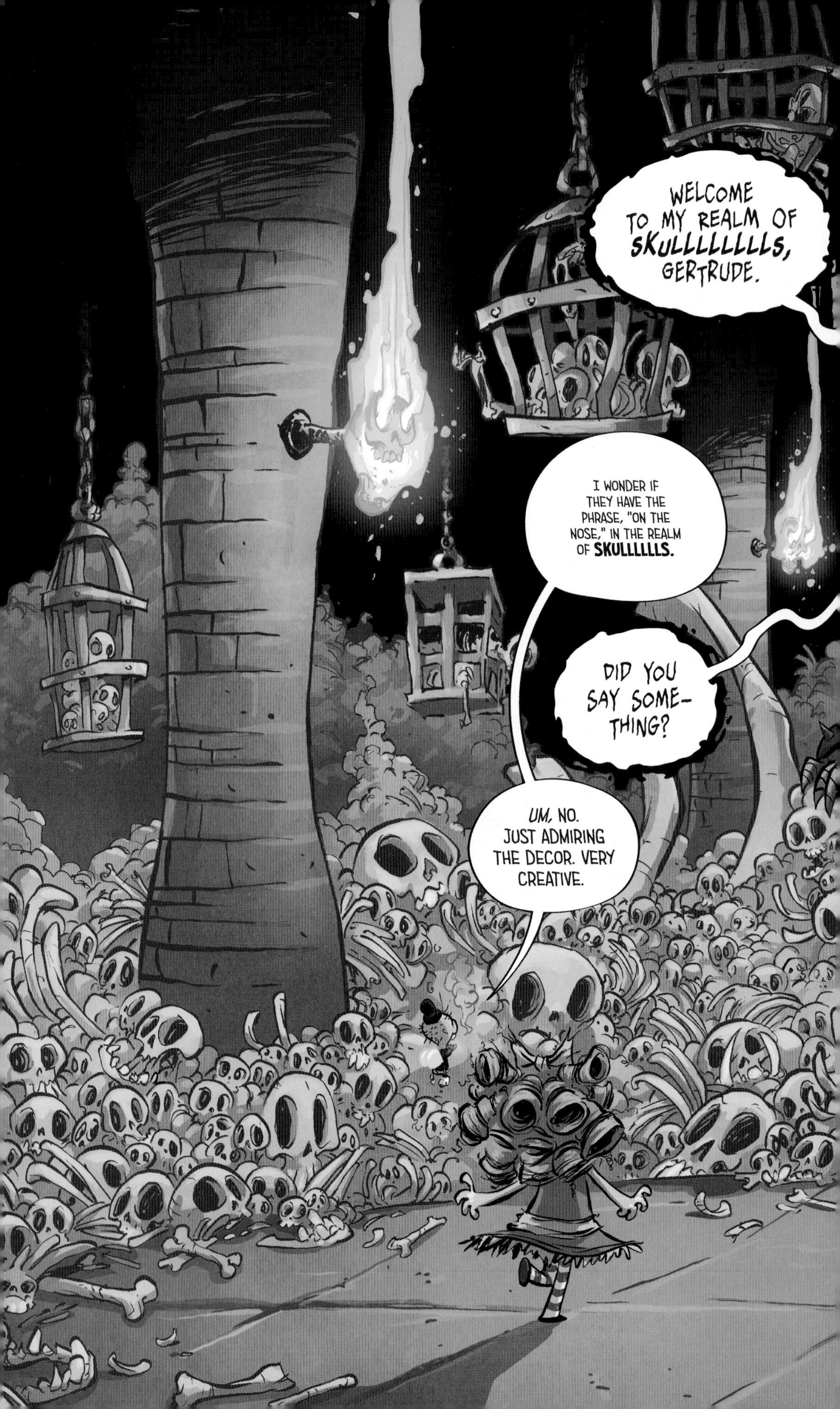
WELCOME TO MY REALM OF SKULLLLLLLLS, GERTRUDE.
I WONDER IF THEY HAVE THE PHRASE, "ON THE NOSE," IN THE REALM OF SKULLLLLLS.
DID YOU SAY SOME-THING?
UM, NO. JUST ADMIRING THE DECOR. VERY CREATIVE.

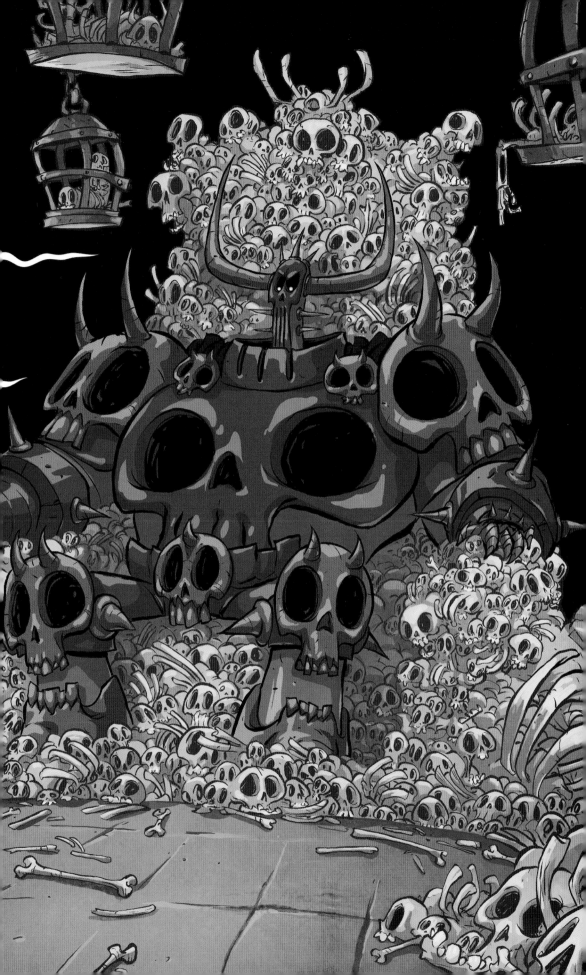

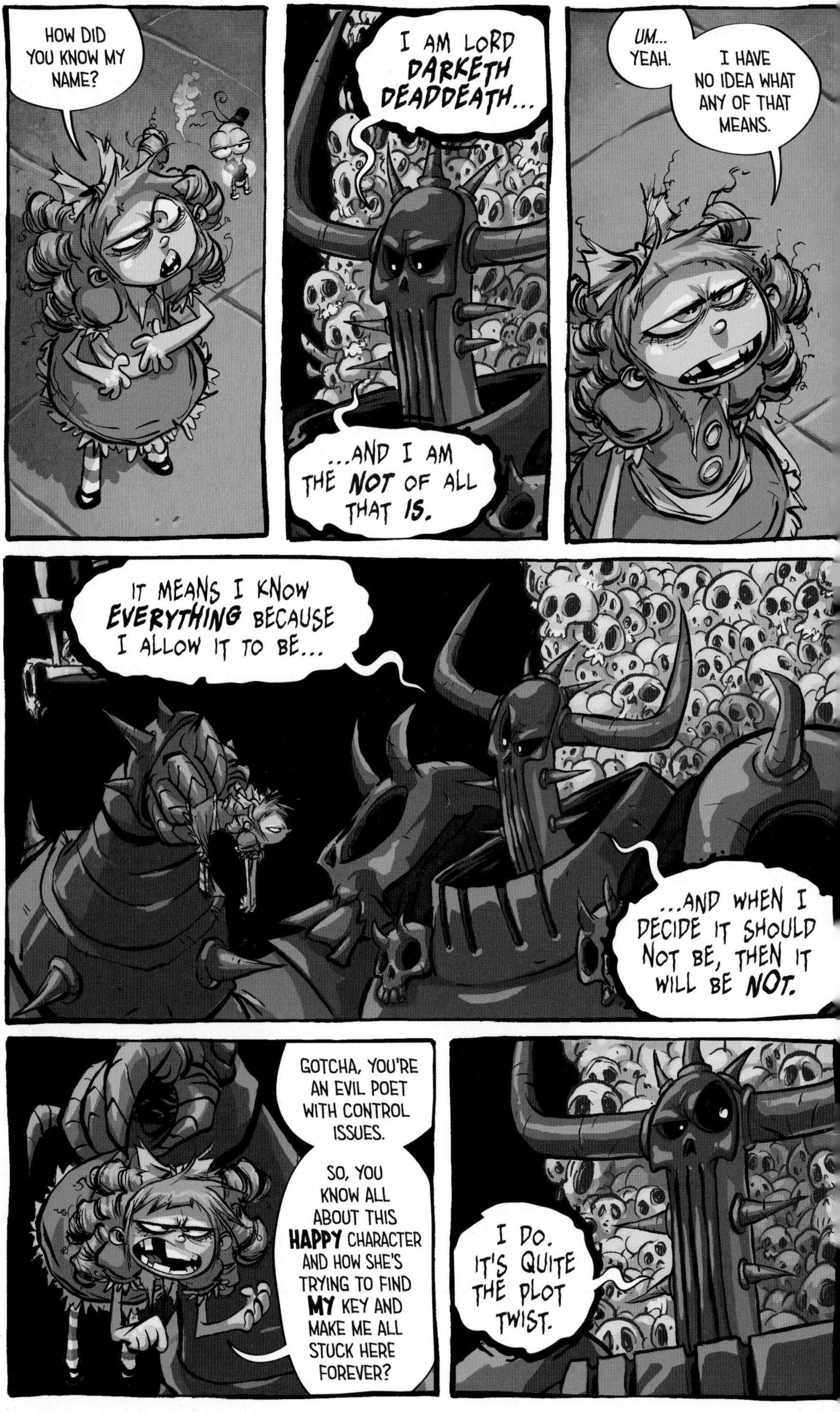
HOW DID YOU KNOW MY NAME?
I AM LORD DARKETH DEADDEATH...
...AND I AM THE NOT OF ALL THAT IS.
UM... YEAH.
I HAVE NO IDEA WHAT ANY OF THAT MEANS.
IT MEANS I KNOW EVERYTHING BECAUSE I ALLOW IT TO BE...
...AND WHEN I DECIDE IT SHOULD NOT BE, THEN IT WILL BE NOT.
GOTCHA, YOU'RE AN EVIL POET WITH CONTROL ISSUES.
SO, YOU KNOW ALL ABOUT THIS HAPPY CHARACTER AND HOW SHE'S TRYING TO FIND MY KEY AND MAKE ME ALL STUCK HERE FOREVER?
I DO. IT'S QUITE THE PLOT TWIST.

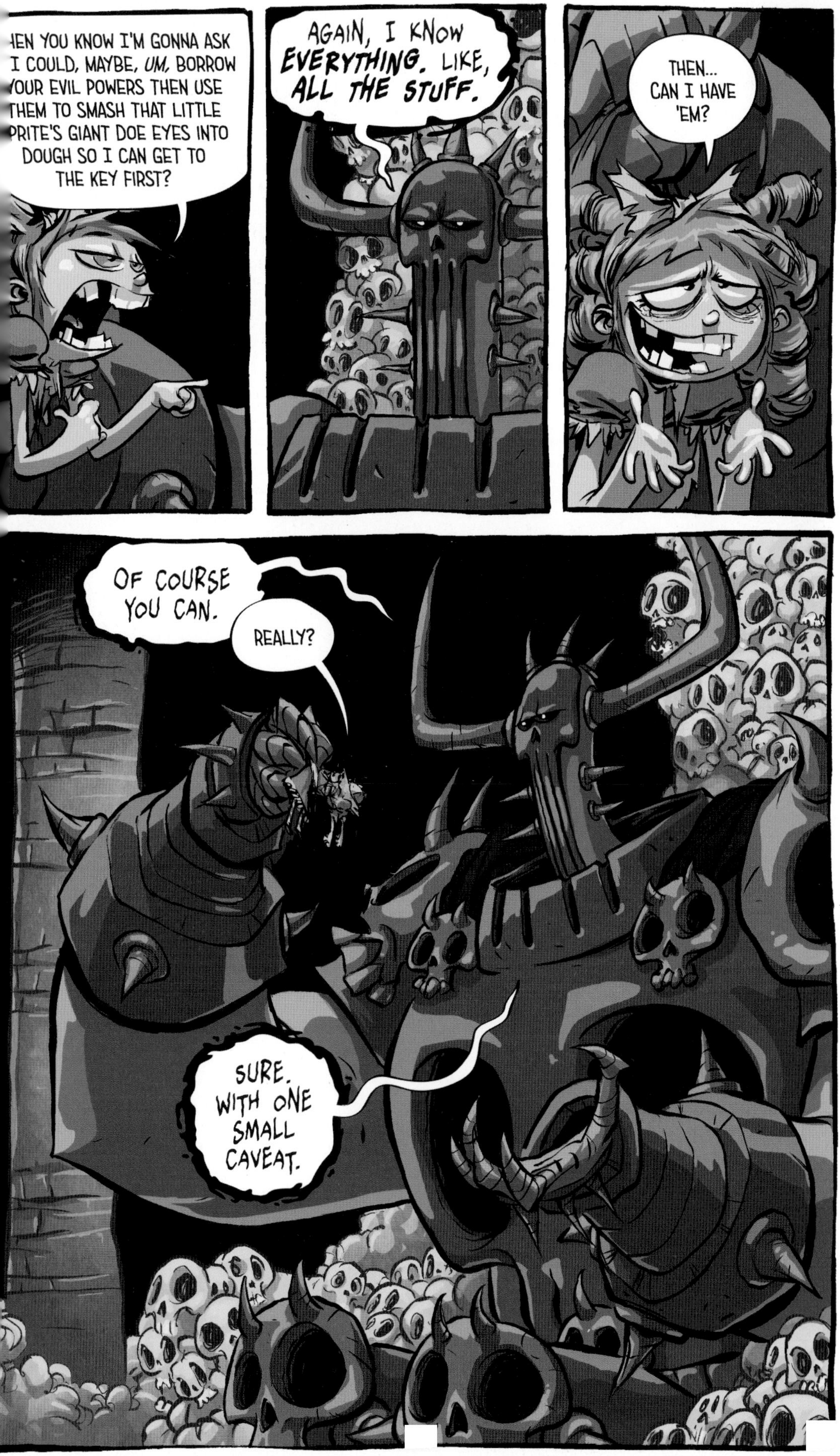
HEN YOU KNOW I'M GONNA ASK I COULD, MAYBE, UM, BORROW YOUR EVIL POWERS THEN USE THEM TO SMASH THAT LITTLE PRITE'S GIANT DOE EYES INTO DOUGH SO I CAN GET TO THE KEY FIRST?
AGAIN, I KNOW EVERYTHING. LIKE, ALL THE STUFF.
THEN... CAN I HAVE 'EM?
OF COURSE YOU CAN.
REALLY?
SURE. WITH ONE SMALL CAVEAT.

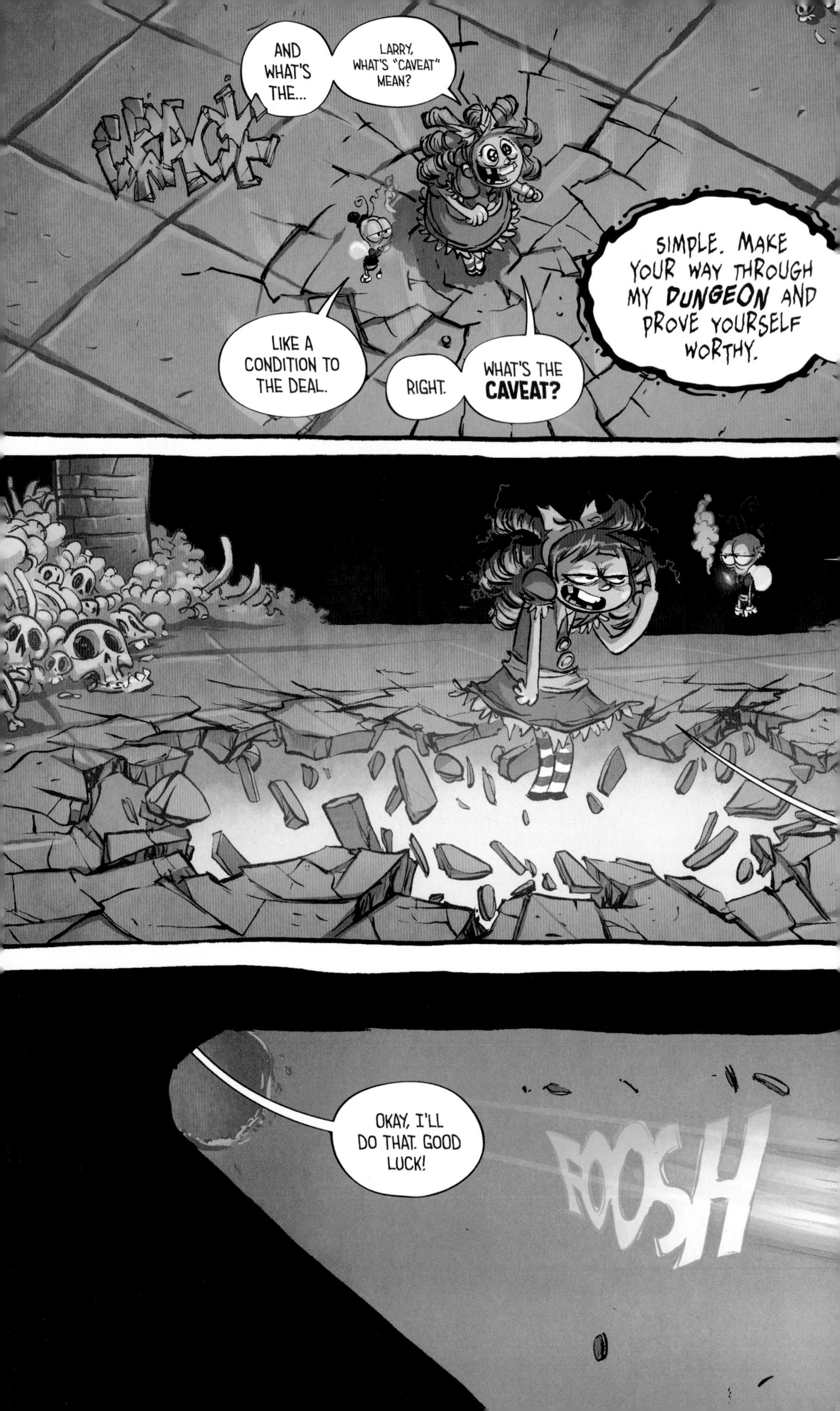
LARRY, WHAT'S "CAVEAT" MEAN?
AND WHAT'S THE...
WHACK
LIKE A CONDITION TO THE DEAL.
RIGHT.
WHAT'S THE CAVEAT?
SIMPLE. MAKE YOUR WAY THROUGH MY DUNGEON AND PROVE YOURSELF WORTHY.
OKAY, I'LL DO THAT. GOOD LUCK!
FOOSH

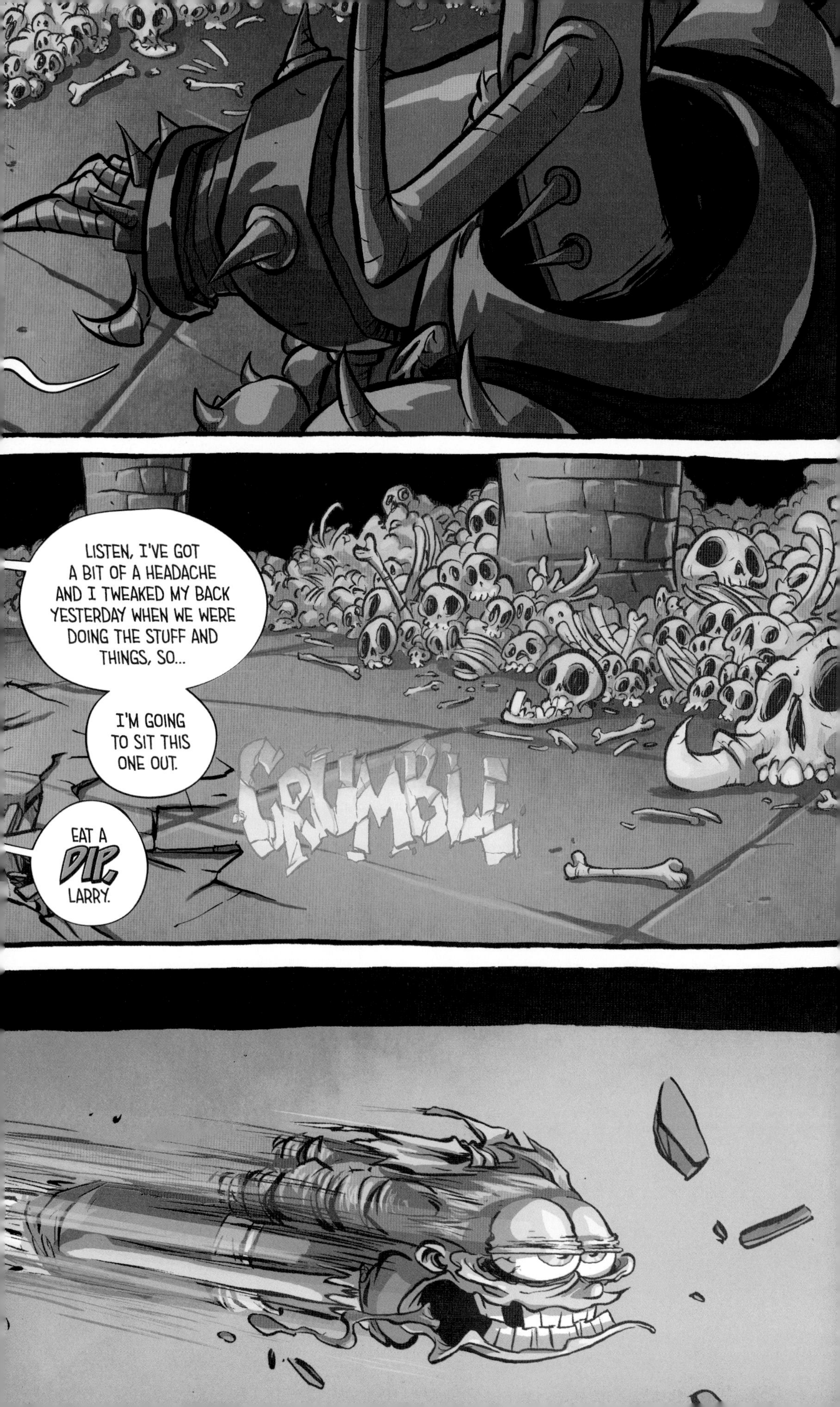

LISTEN, I'VE GOT A BIT OF A HEADACHE AND I TWEAKED MY BACK YESTERDAY WHEN WE WERE DOING THE STUFF AND THINGS, SO...
I'M GOING TO SIT THIS ONE OUT.
EAT A DIP, LARRY.
CRUMBLE

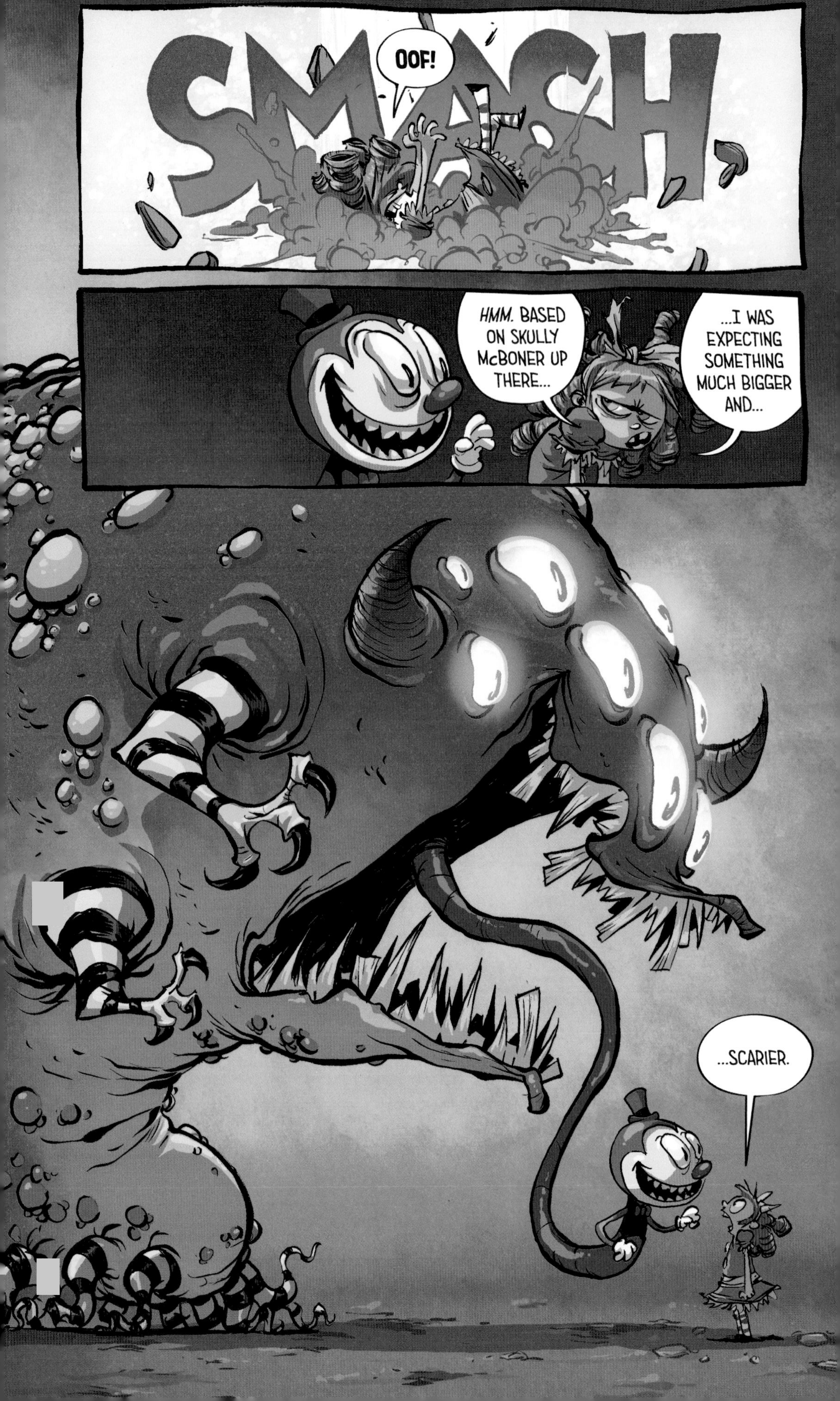
SMASH
OOF!
HMM. BASED ON SKULLY McBONER UP THERE...
...I WAS EXPECTING SOMETHING MUCH BIGGER AND...
...SCARIER.

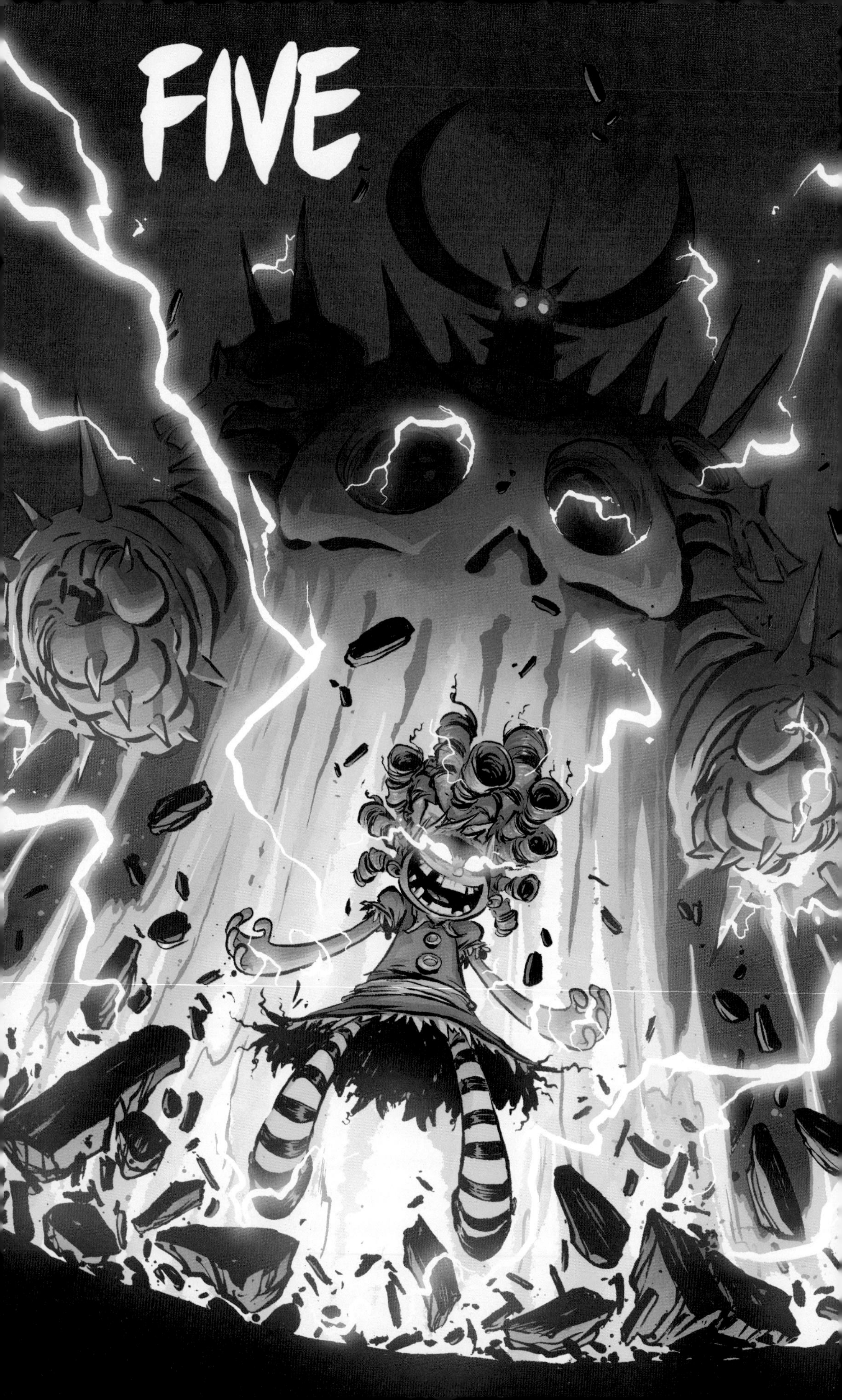
FIVE

ONCE UPON A TIME, THERE WAS A GIRL NAMED HAPPY WHO WAS ON A GRAND ADVENTURE IN THE WONDERFUL WORLD OF **FAIRYLAND.**

SHE WAS SENT ON AN EPIC QUEST ACROSS THE **PLAINS OF TIME...**

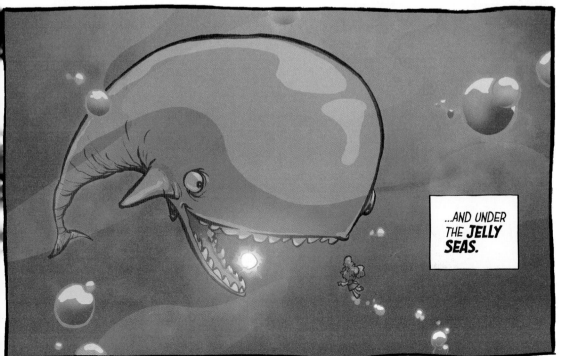

...AND UNDER THE **JELLY SEAS.**

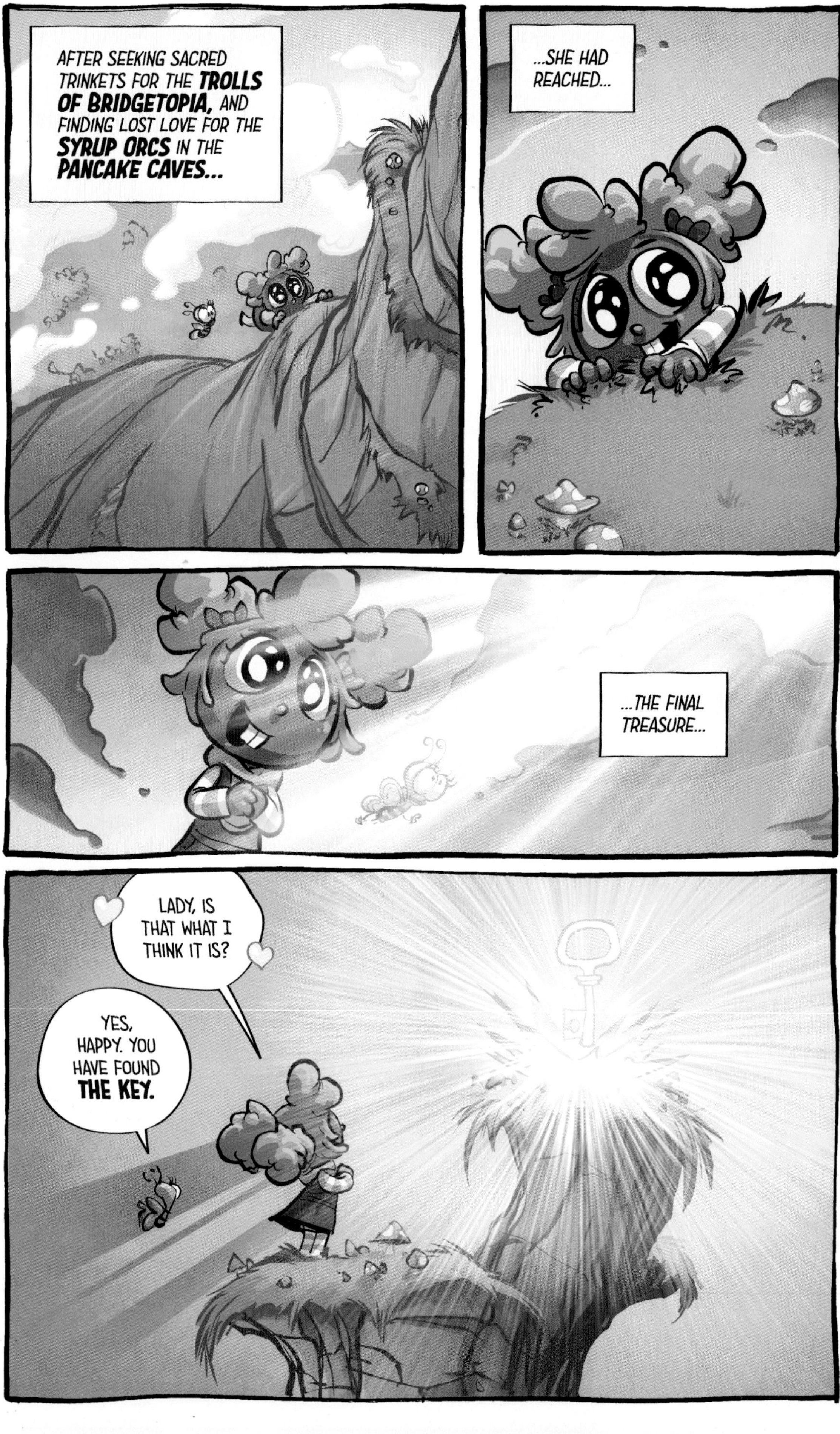
AFTER SEEKING SACRED TRINKETS FOR THE **TROLLS OF BRIDGETOPIA,** AND FINDING LOST LOVE FOR THE **SYRUP ORCS** IN THE **PANCAKE CAVES...**
...SHE HAD REACHED...
...THE FINAL TREASURE...
LADY, IS THAT WHAT I THINK IT IS?
YES, HAPPY. YOU HAVE FOUND **THE KEY.**

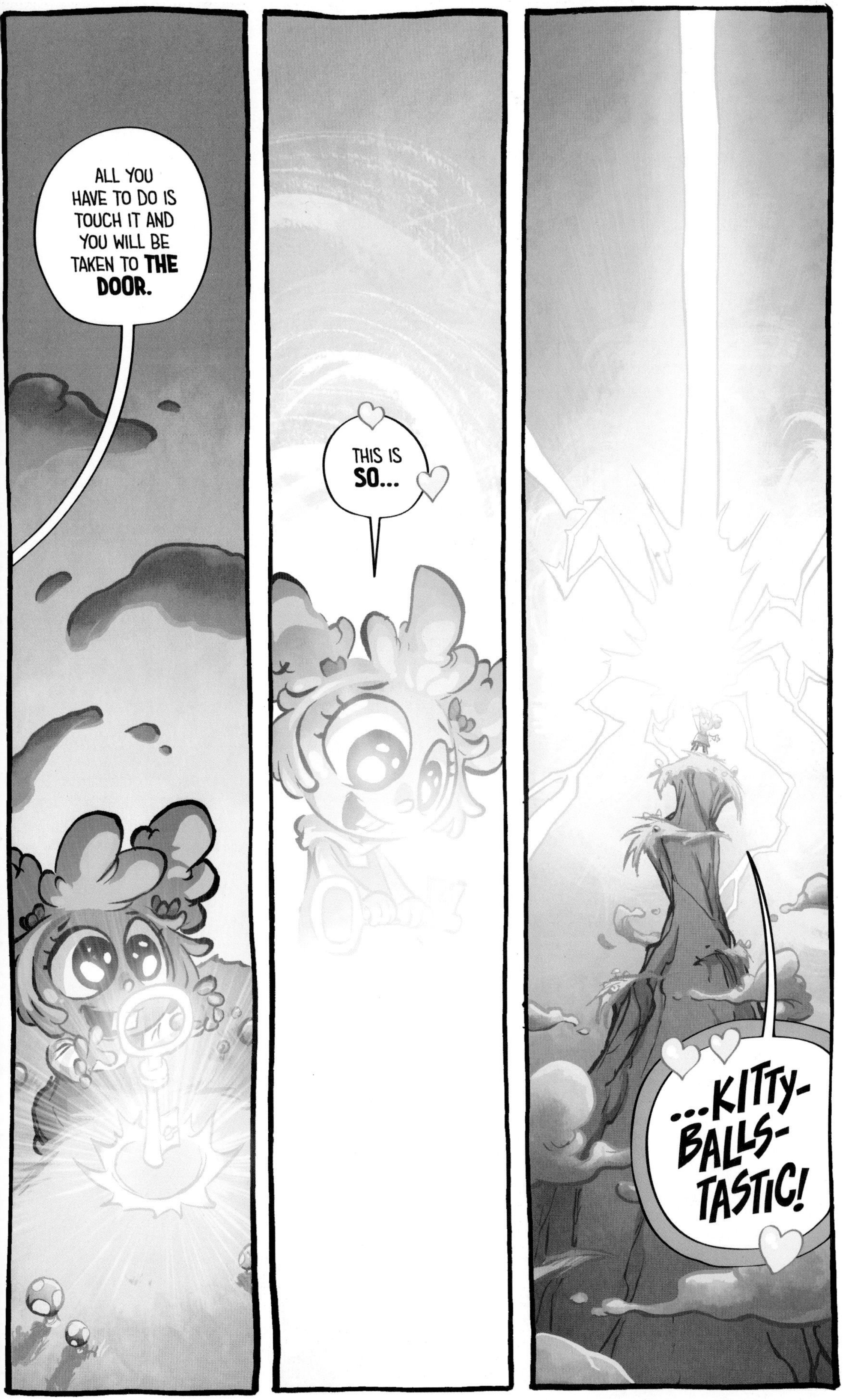
ALL YOU HAVE TO DO IS TOUCH IT AND YOU WILL BE TAKEN TO **THE DOOR.**
THIS IS **SO...**
...KITTY-BALLS-TASTIC!

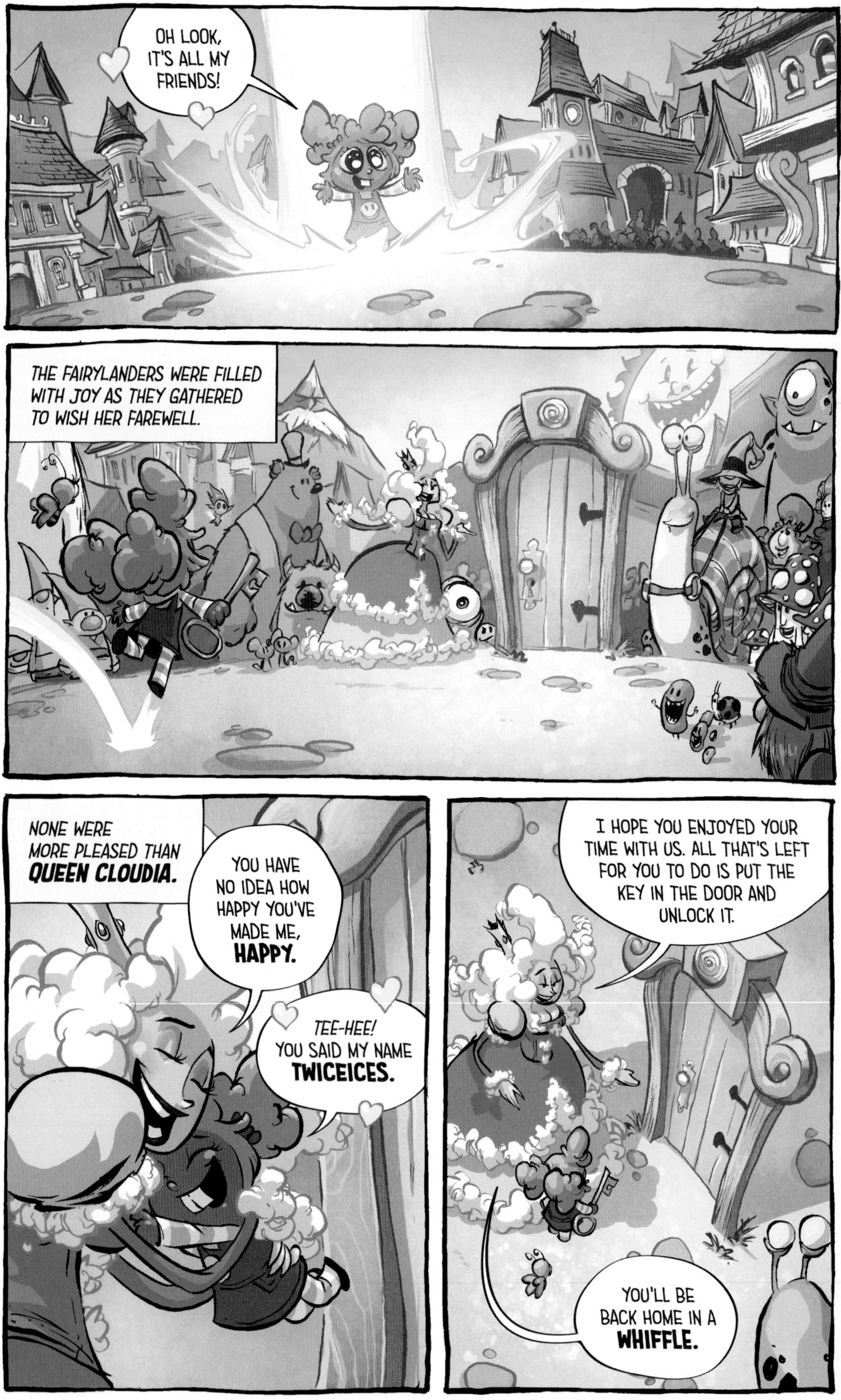
OH LOOK, IT'S ALL MY FRIENDS!
THE FAIRYLANDERS WERE FILLED WITH JOY AS THEY GATHERED TO WISH HER FAREWELL.
NONE WERE MORE PLEASED THAN QUEEN CLOUDIA.
YOU HAVE NO IDEA HOW HAPPY YOU'VE MADE ME, HAPPY.
TEE-HEE! YOU SAID MY NAME TWICEICES.
I HOPE YOU ENJOYED YOUR TIME WITH US. ALL THAT'S LEFT FOR YOU TO DO IS PUT THE KEY IN THE DOOR AND UNLOCK IT.
YOU'LL BE BACK HOME IN A WHIFFLE.

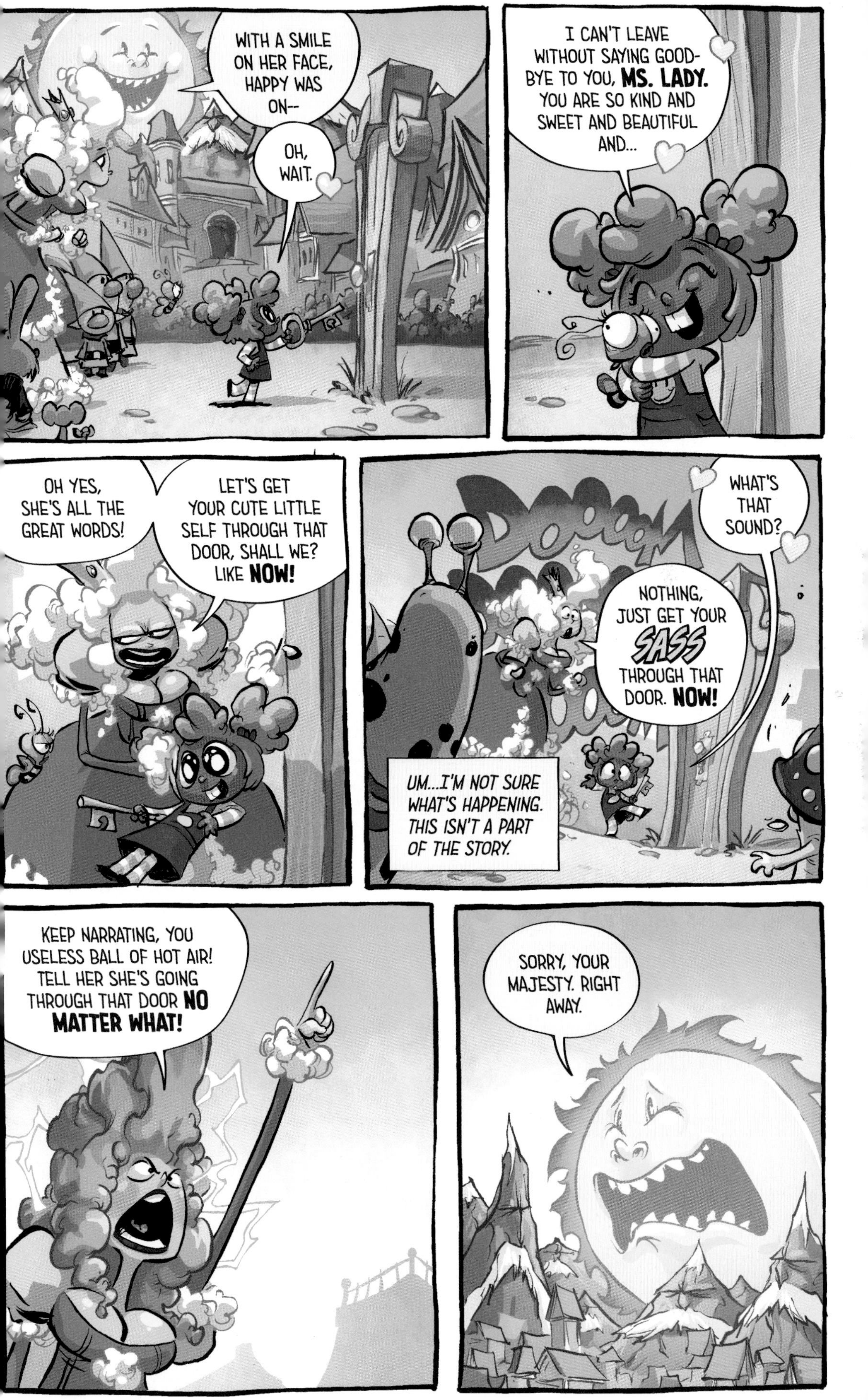
WITH A SMILE ON HER FACE, HAPPY WAS ON--
OH, WAIT.
I CAN'T LEAVE WITHOUT SAYING GOOD-BYE TO YOU, **MS. LADY.** YOU ARE SO KIND AND SWEET AND BEAUTIFUL AND...
OH YES, SHE'S ALL THE GREAT WORDS!
LET'S GET YOUR CUTE LITTLE SELF THROUGH THAT DOOR, SHALL WE? LIKE **NOW!**
DOOOM
WHAT'S THAT SOUND?
NOTHING, JUST GET YOUR SASS THROUGH THAT DOOR. **NOW!**
UM...I'M NOT SURE WHAT'S HAPPENING. THIS ISN'T A PART OF THE STORY.
KEEP NARRATING, YOU USELESS BALL OF HOT AIR! TELL HER SHE'S GOING THROUGH THAT DOOR **NO MATTER WHAT!**
SORRY, YOUR MAJESTY. RIGHT AWAY.

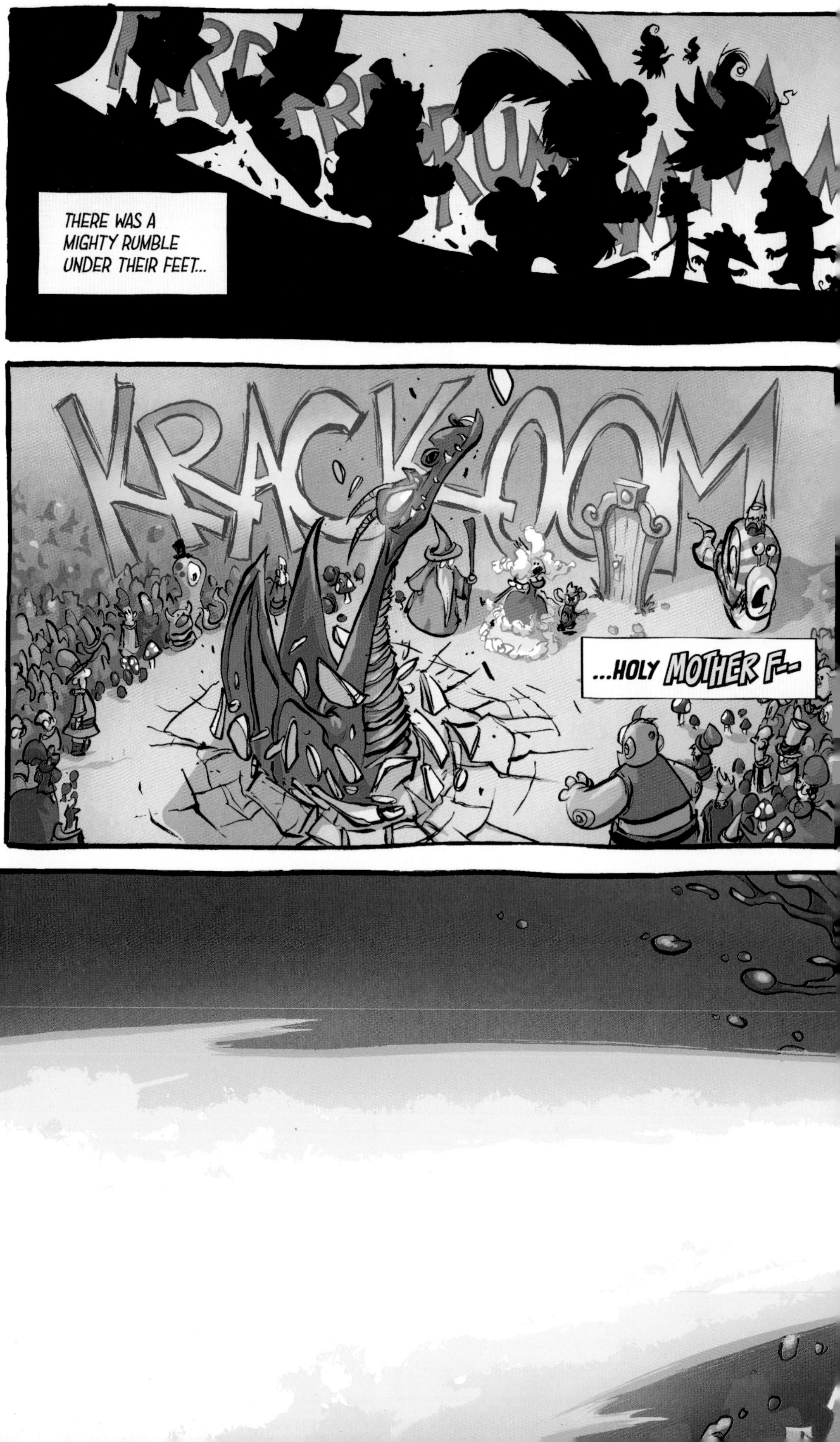
THERE WAS A MIGHTY RUMBLE UNDER THEIR FEET...
KRACKOOM
...HOLY MOTHER F--

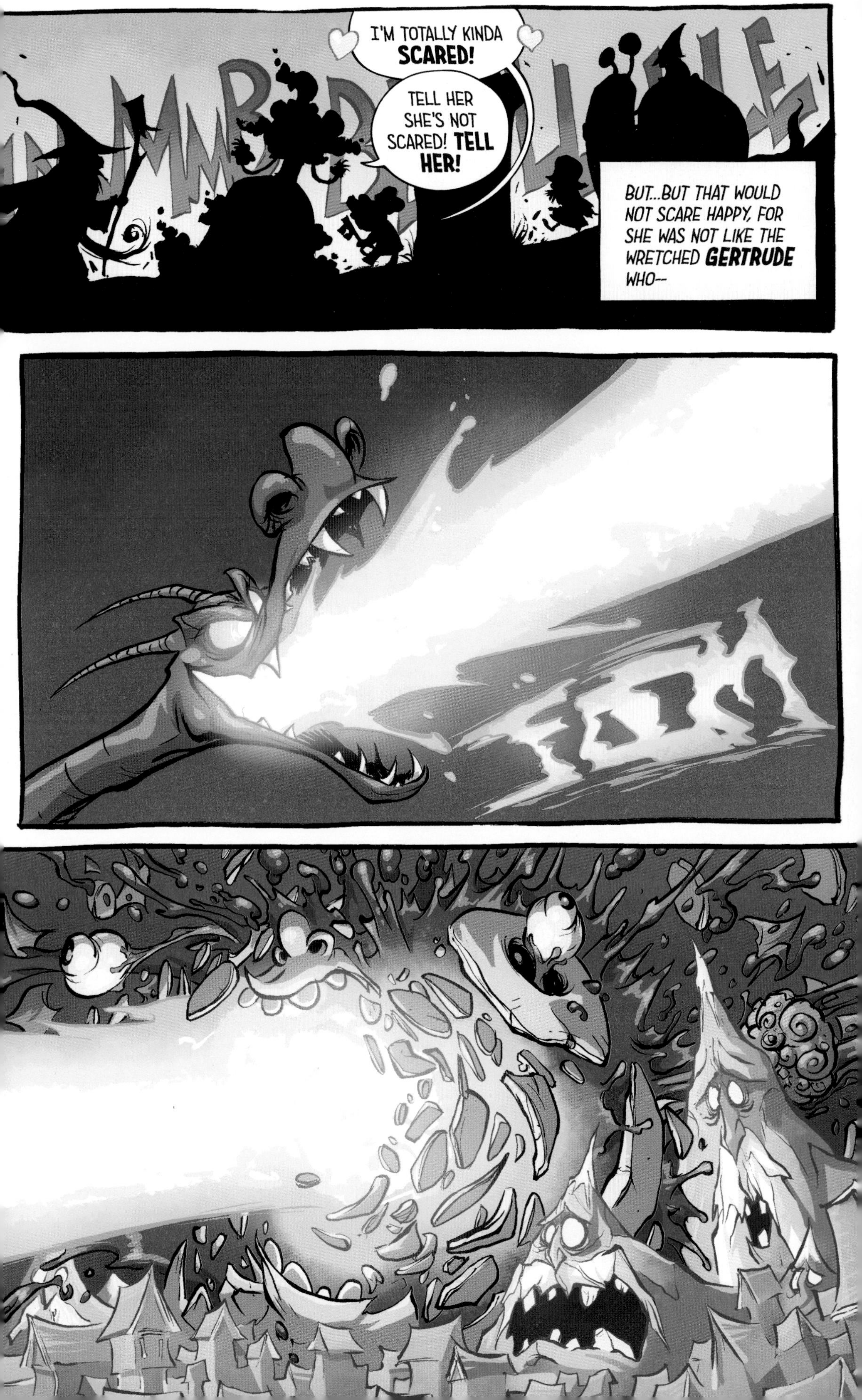
I'M TOTALLY KINDA SCARED!
TELL HER SHE'S NOT SCARED! TELL HER!
BUT...BUT THAT WOULD NOT SCARE HAPPY, FOR SHE WAS NOT LIKE THE WRETCHED GERTRUDE WHO--

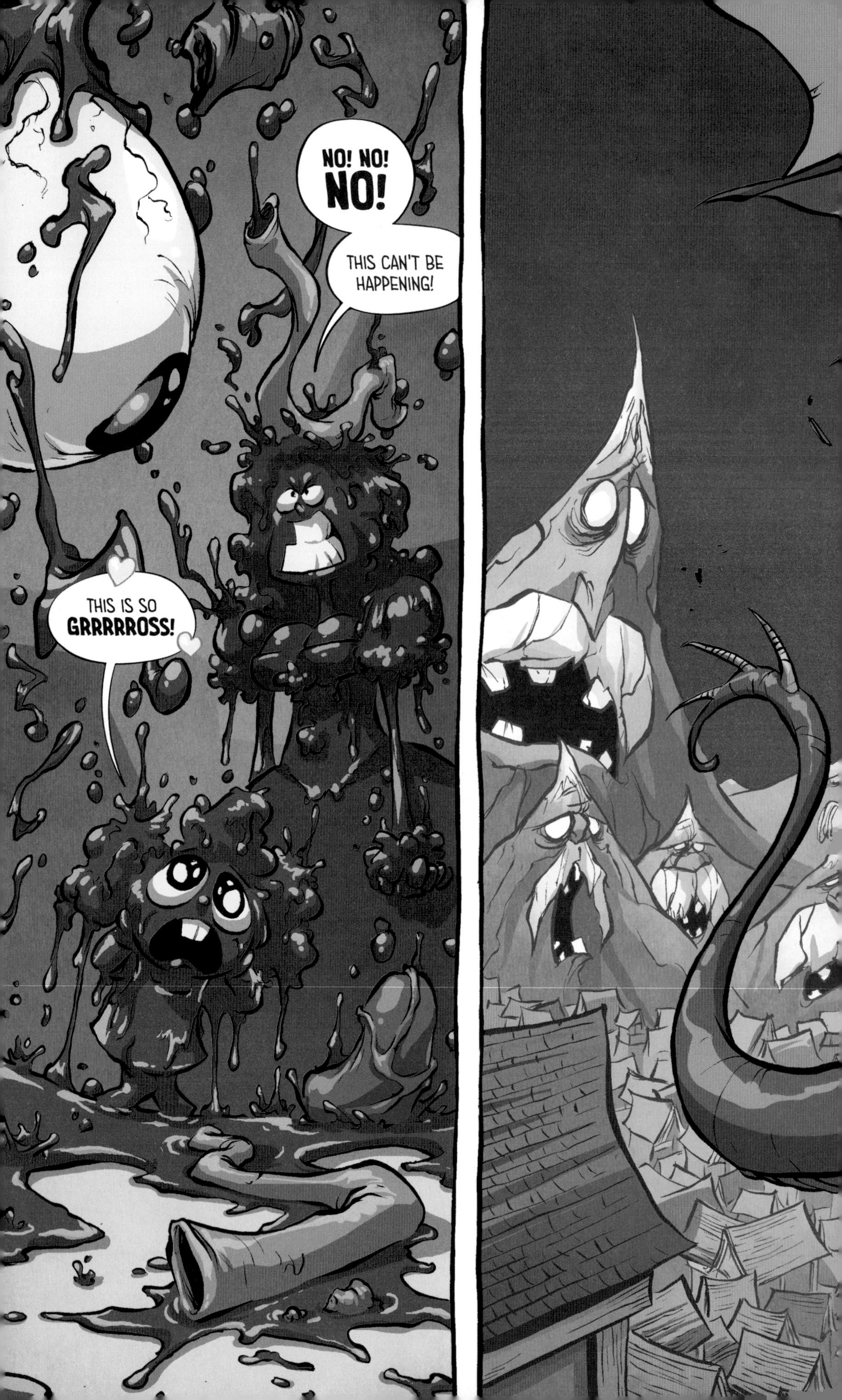
NO! NO! NO!
THIS CAN'T BE HAPPENING!
THIS IS SO GRRRRROSS!

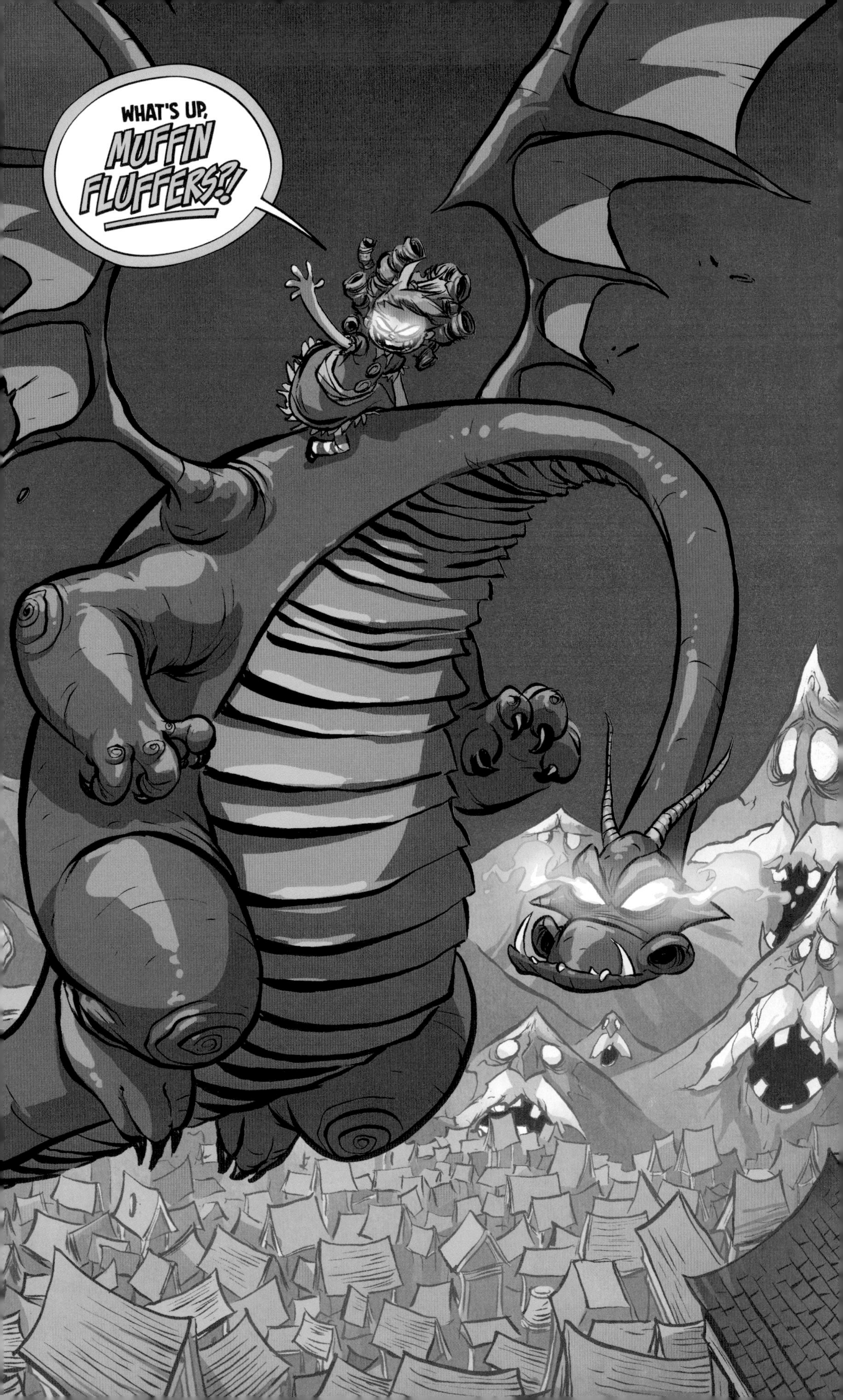
WHAT'S UP, MUFFIN FLUFFERS?!

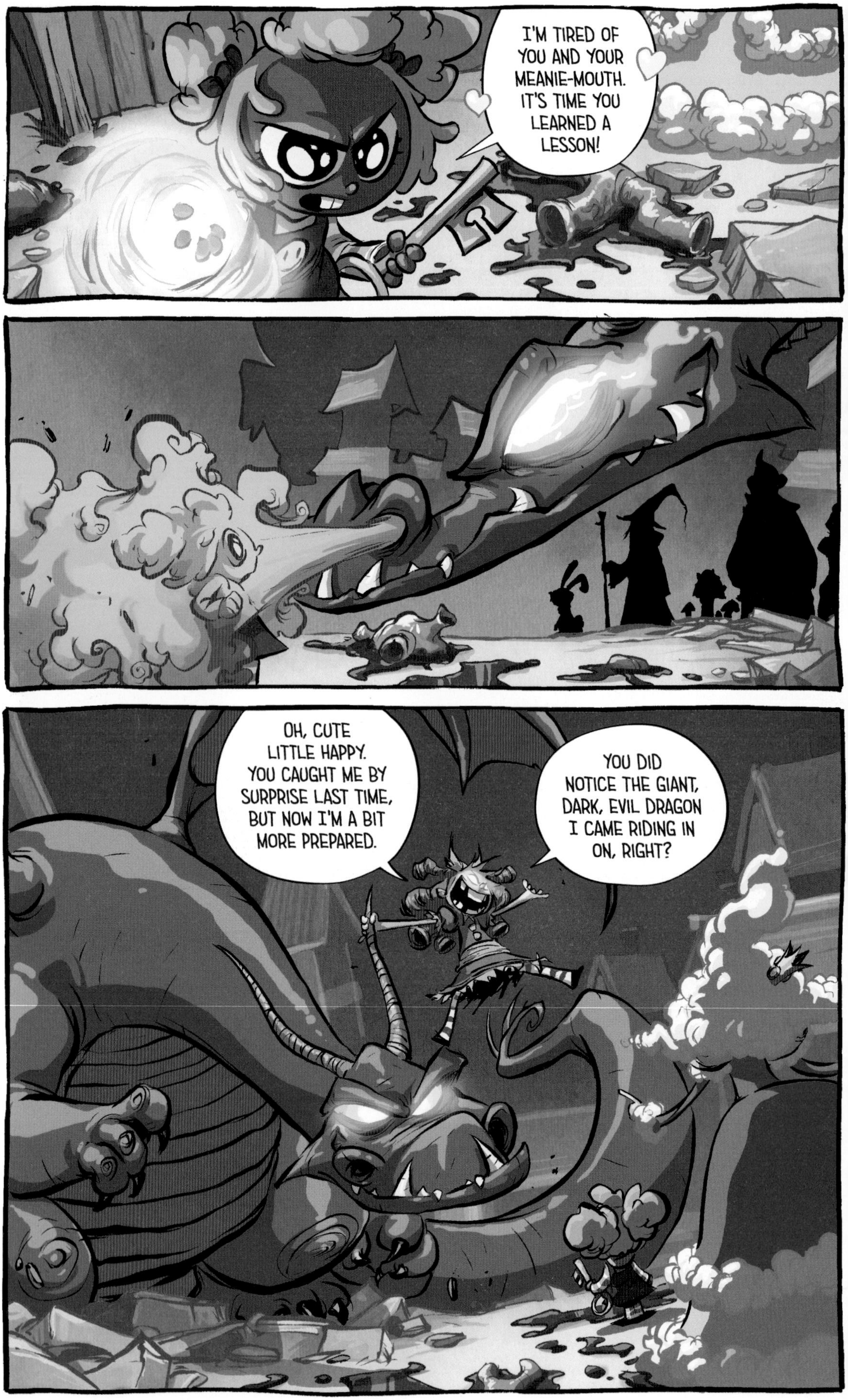
I'M TIRED OF YOU AND YOUR MEANIE-MOUTH. IT'S TIME YOU LEARNED A LESSON!
OH, CUTE LITTLE HAPPY. YOU CAUGHT ME BY SURPRISE LAST TIME, BUT NOW I'M A BIT MORE PREPARED.
YOU DID NOTICE THE GIANT, DARK, EVIL DRAGON I CAME RIDING IN ON, RIGHT?

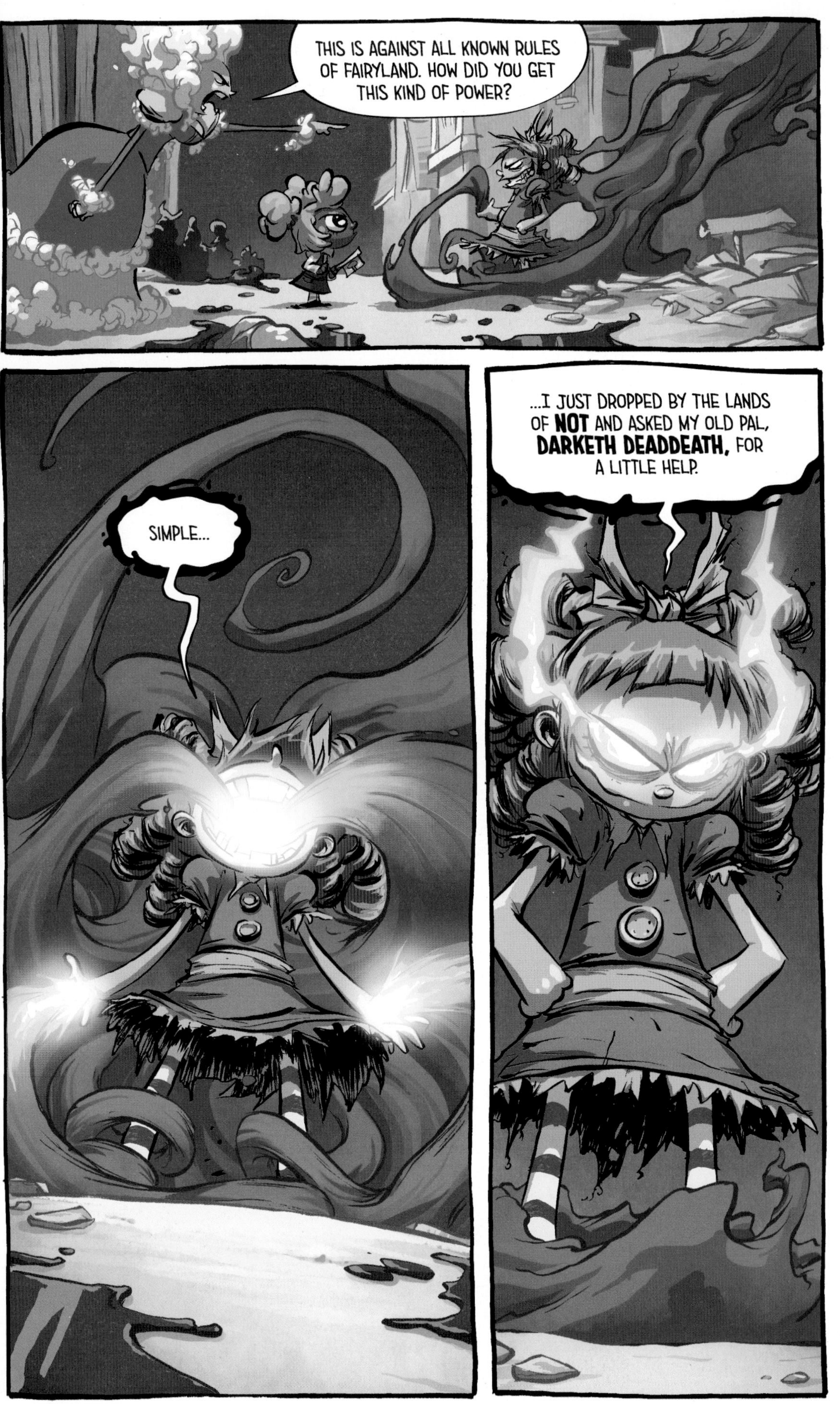
THIS IS AGAINST ALL KNOWN RULES OF FAIRYLAND. HOW DID YOU GET THIS KIND OF POWER?
SIMPLE...
...I JUST DROPPED BY THE LANDS OF **NOT** AND ASKED MY OLD PAL, **DARKETH DEADDEATH,** FOR A LITTLE HELP.

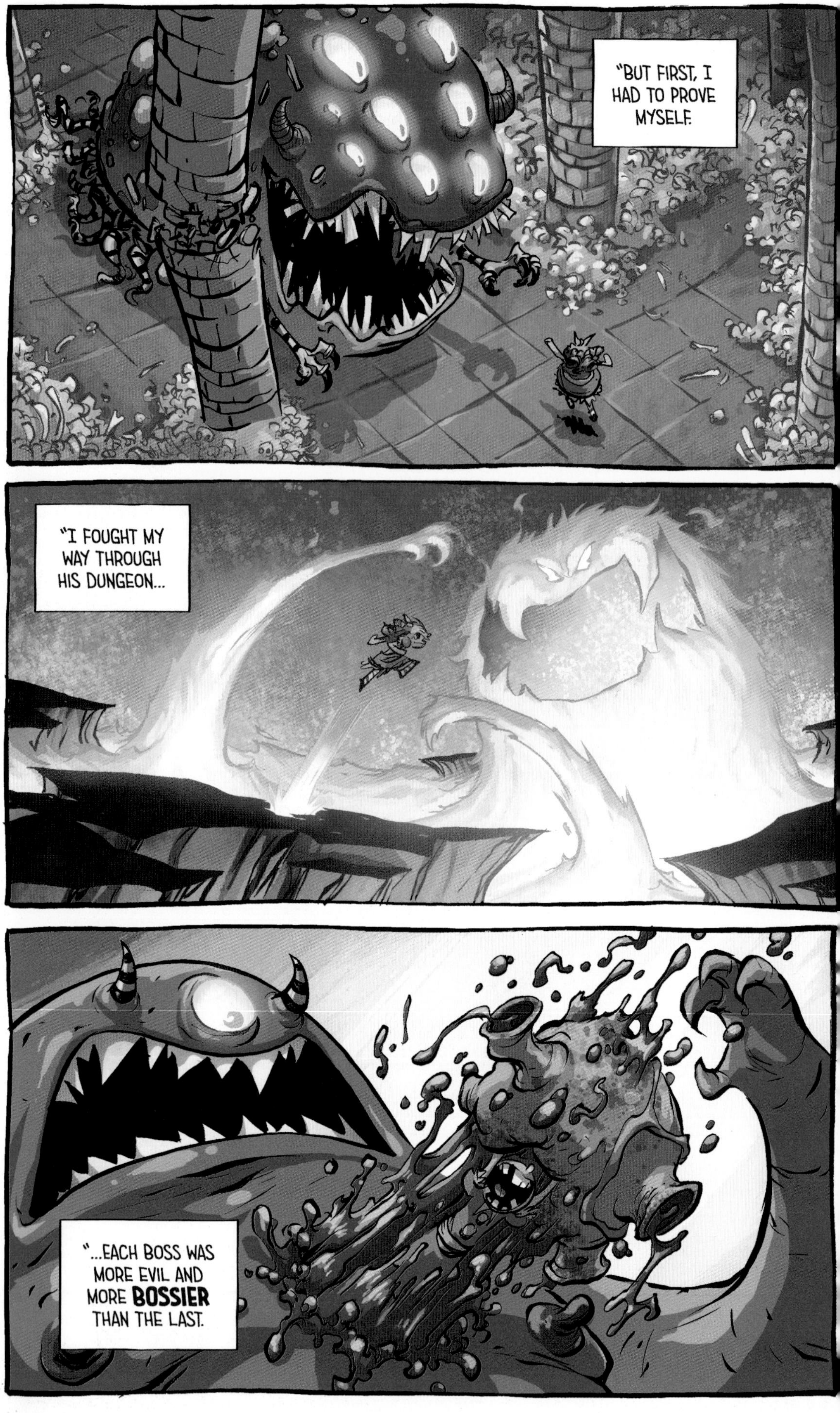
"BUT FIRST, I HAD TO PROVE MYSELF.
"I FOUGHT MY WAY THROUGH HIS DUNGEON...
"...EACH BOSS WAS MORE EVIL AND MORE **BOSSIER** THAN THE LAST.

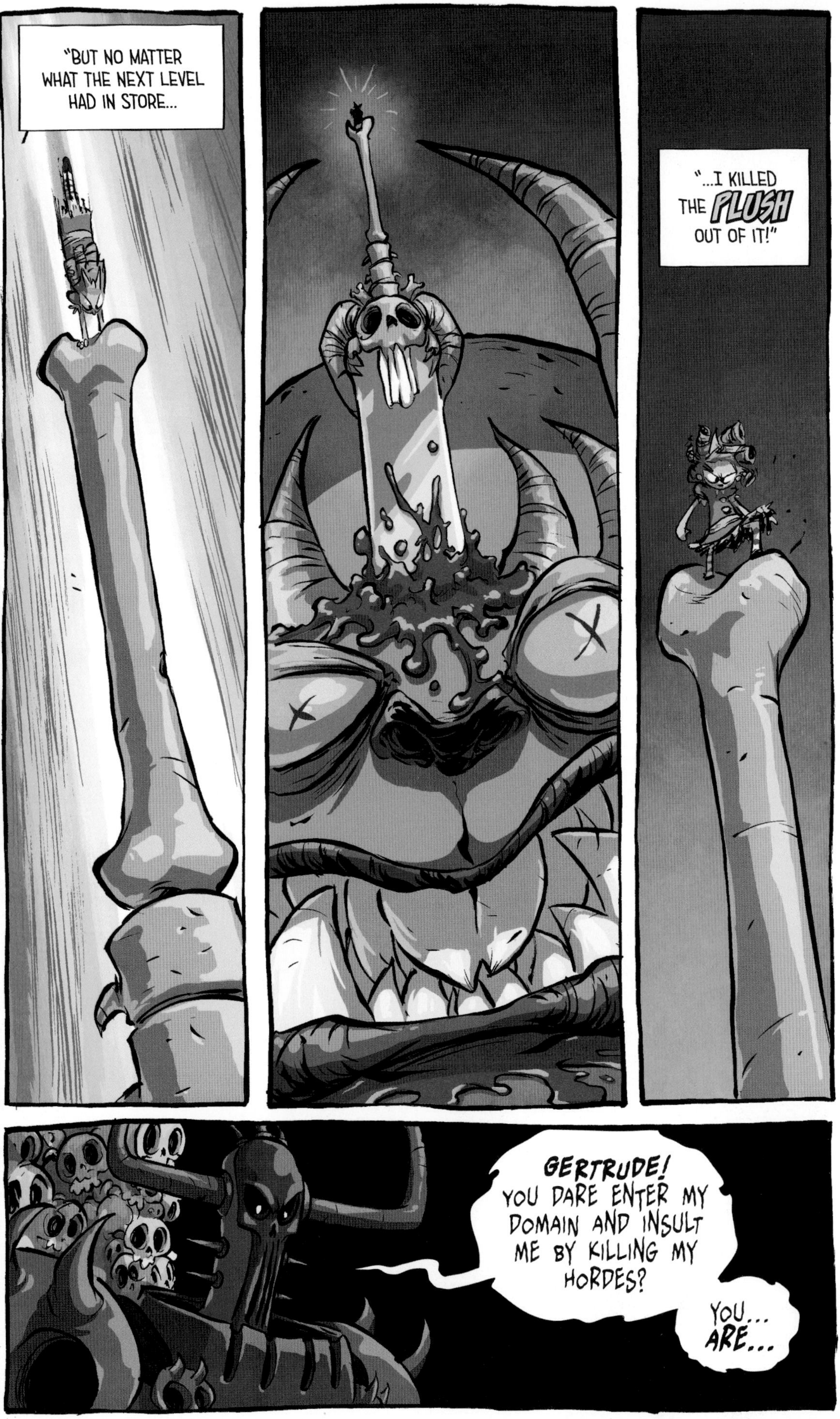
"BUT NO MATTER WHAT THE NEXT LEVEL HAD IN STORE...
"...I KILLED THE PLUSH OUT OF IT!"
GERTRUDE! YOU DARE ENTER MY DOMAIN AND INSULT ME BY KILLING MY HORDES?
YOU... ARE...

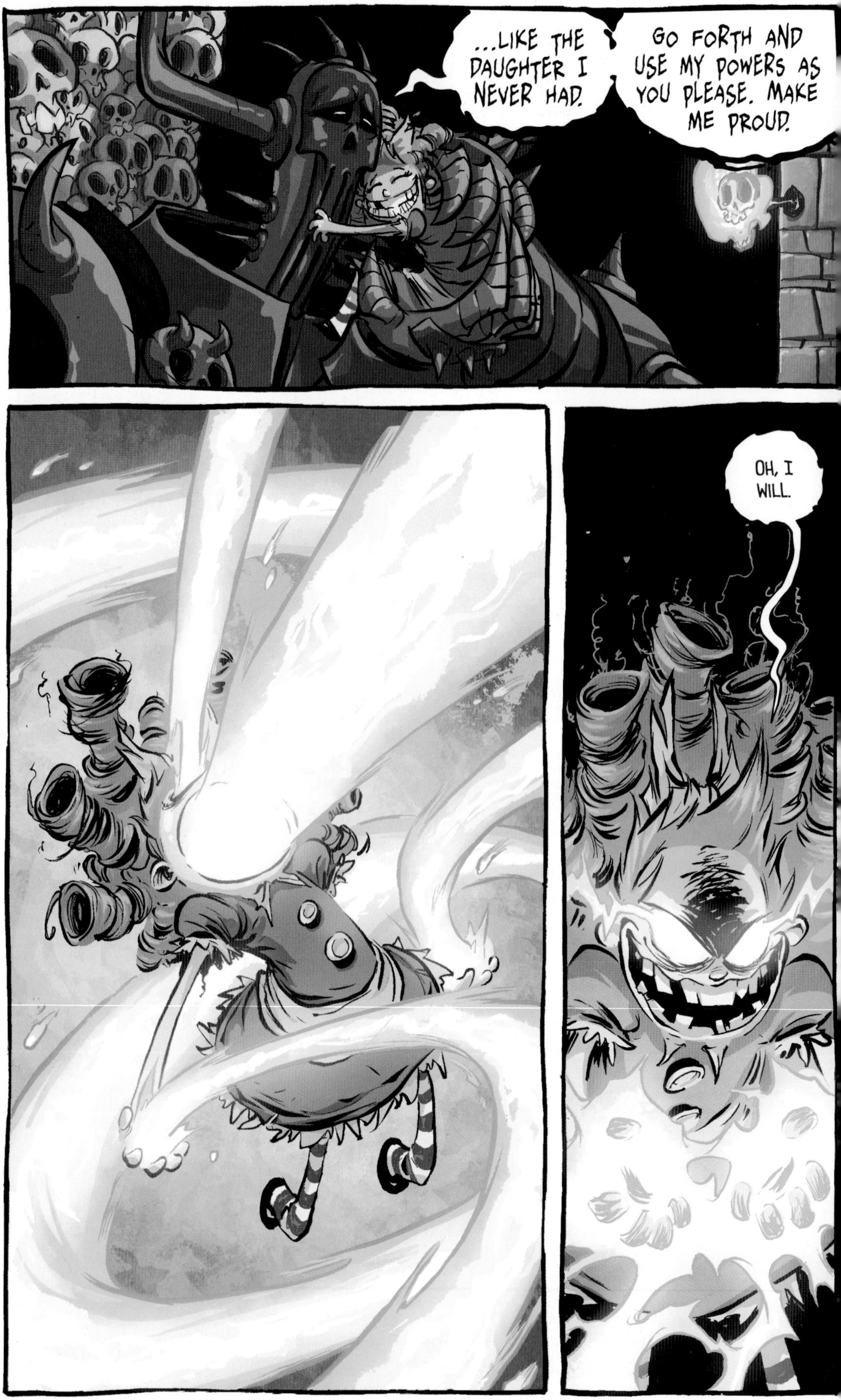
...LIKE THE DAUGHTER I NEVER HAD.
GO FORTH AND USE MY POWERS AS YOU PLEASE. MAKE ME PROUD.
OH, I WILL.

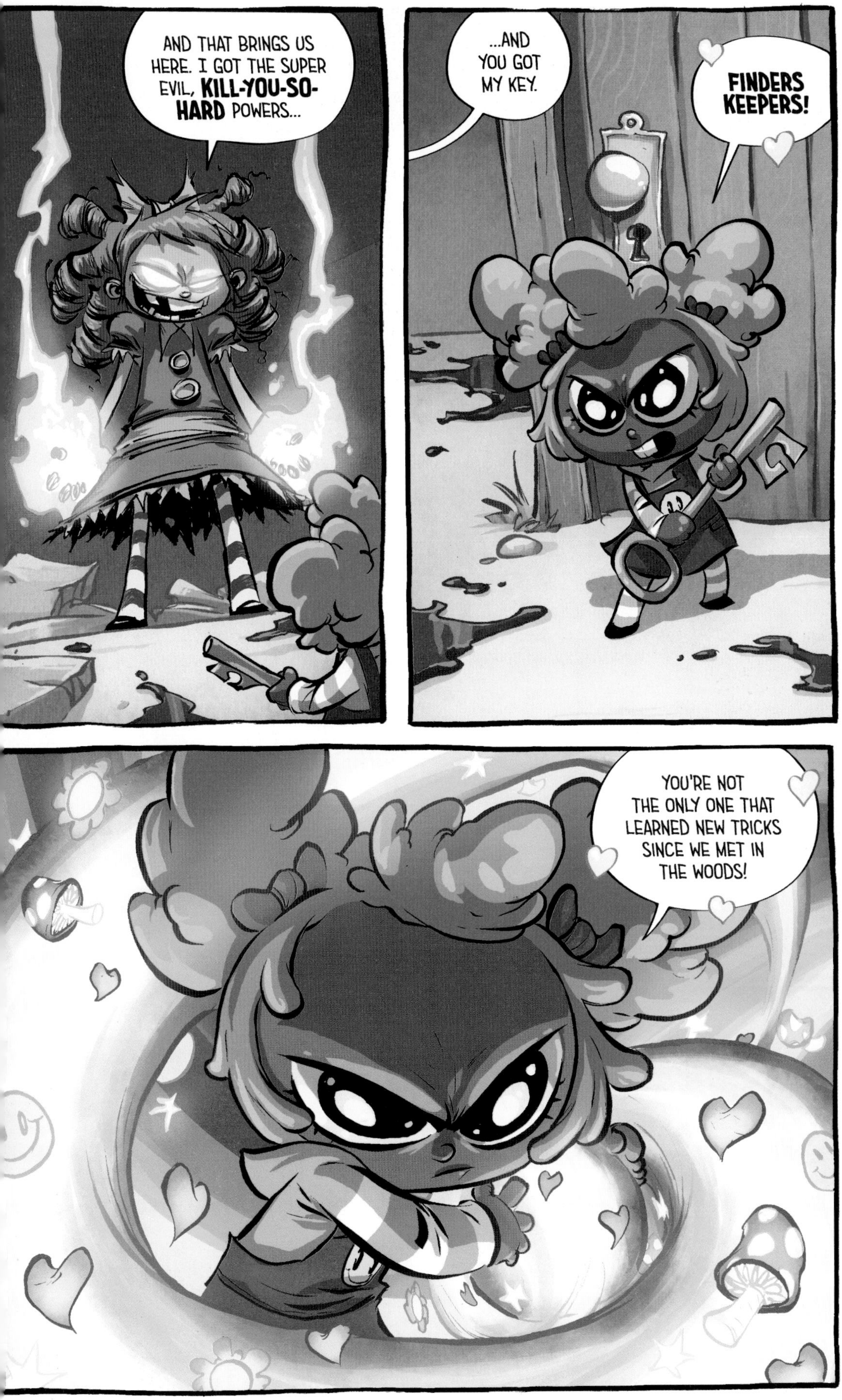
AND THAT BRINGS US HERE. I GOT THE SUPER EVIL, **KILL-YOU-SO-HARD** POWERS...
...AND YOU GOT MY KEY.
FINDERS KEEPERS!
YOU'RE NOT THE ONLY ONE THAT LEARNED NEW TRICKS SINCE WE MET IN THE WOODS!

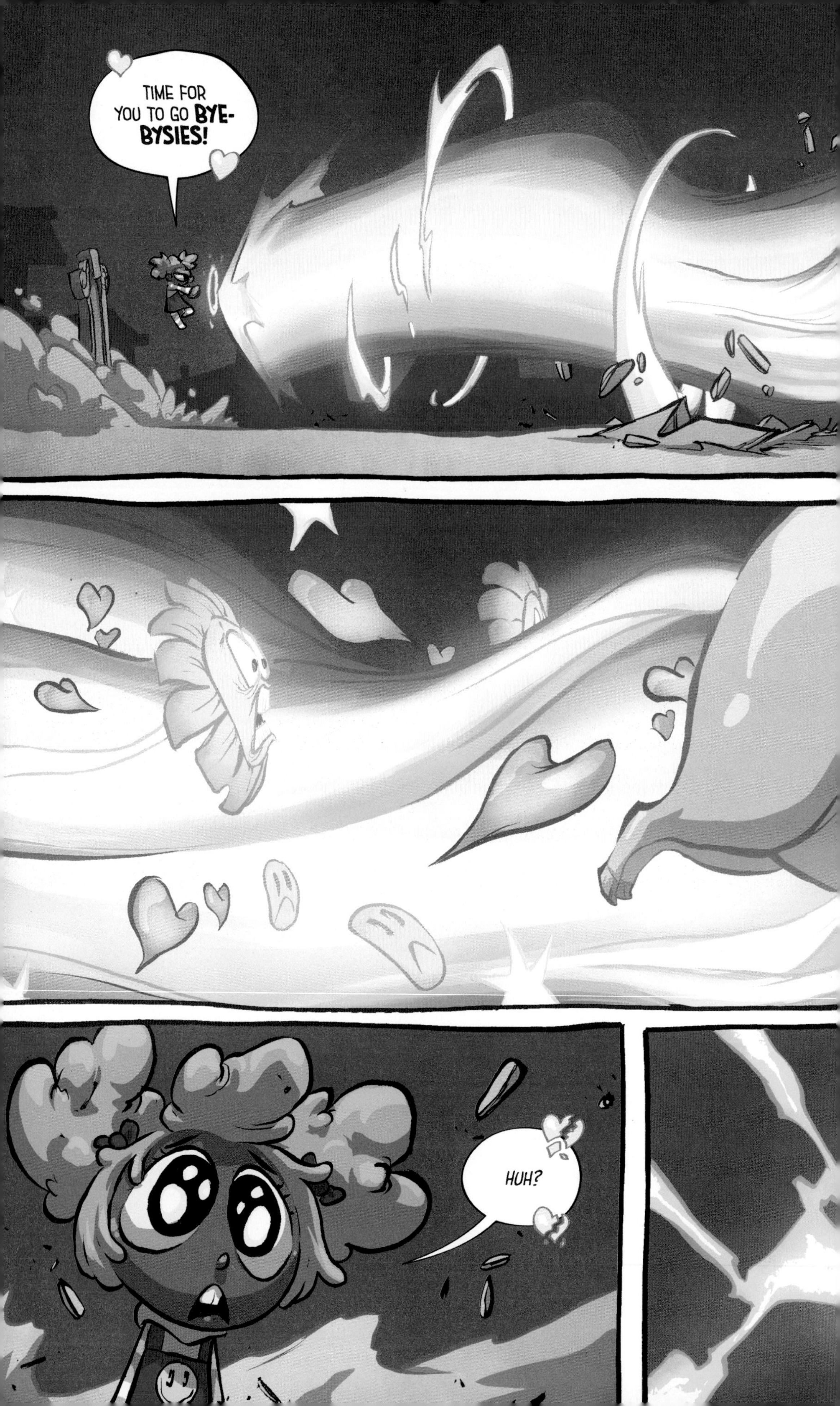
TIME FOR YOU TO GO BYE-BYSIES!
HUH?

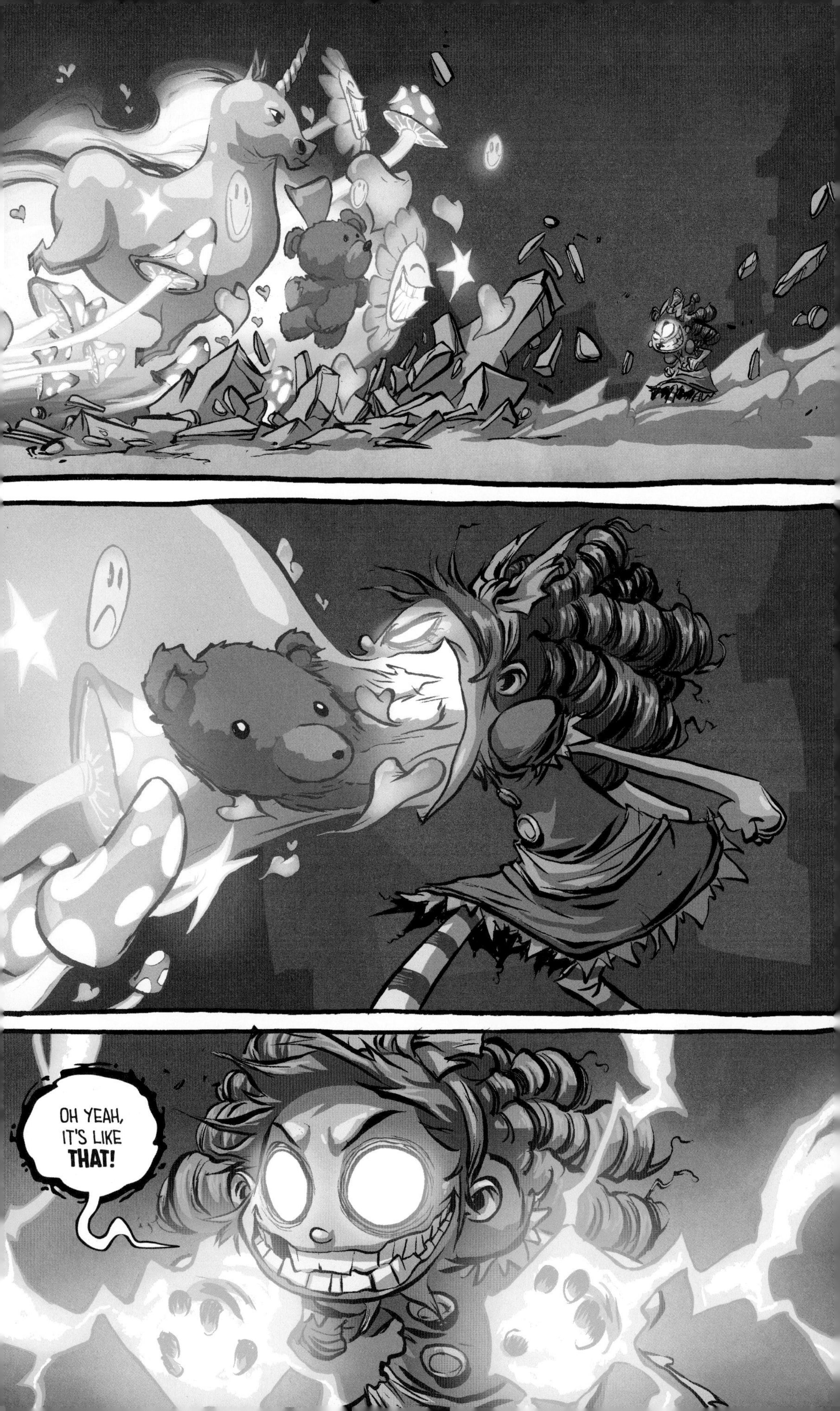
OH YEAH, IT'S LIKE THAT!

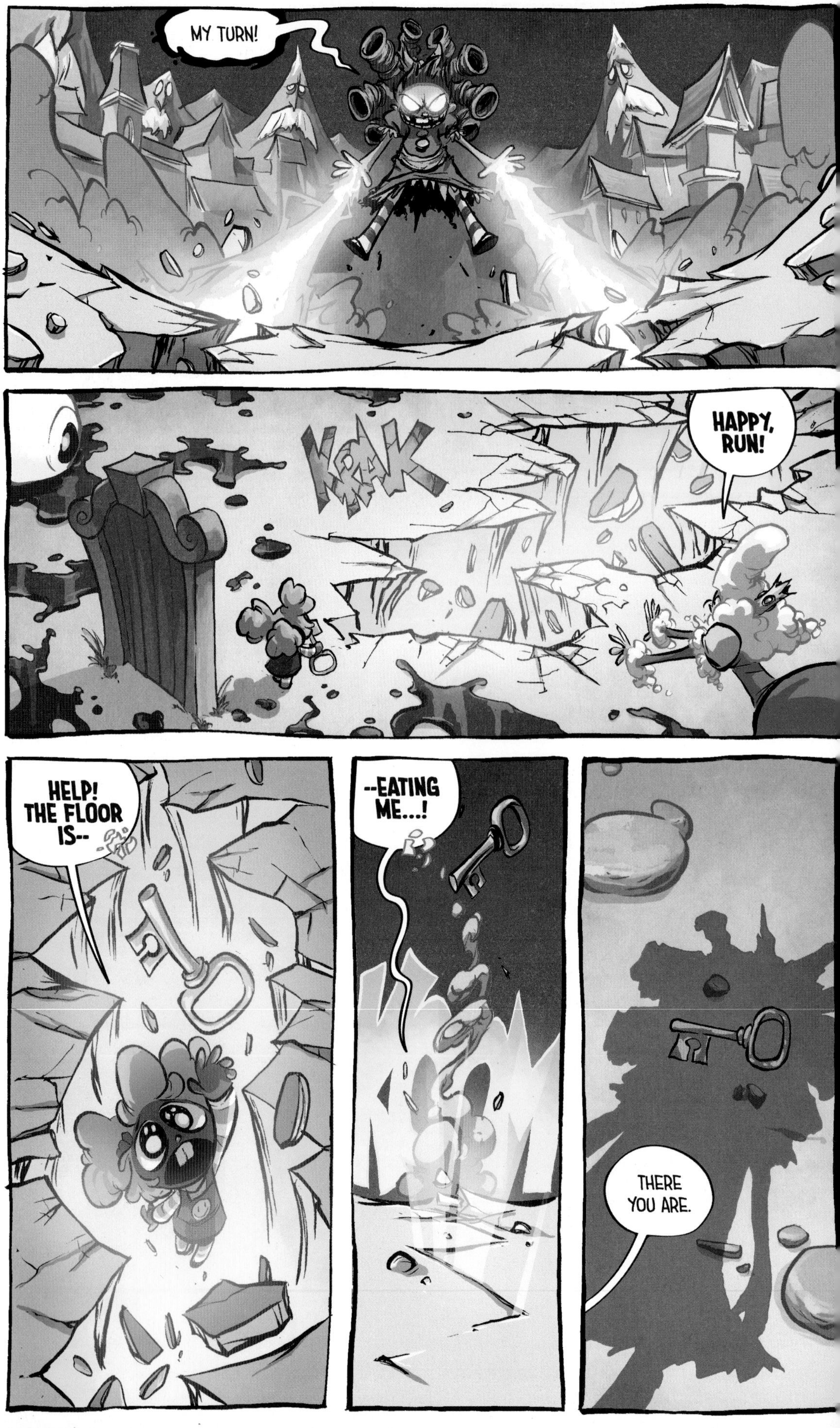
MY TURN!
KRAK
HAPPY, RUN!
HELP! THE FLOOR IS--
--EATING ME...!
THERE YOU ARE.

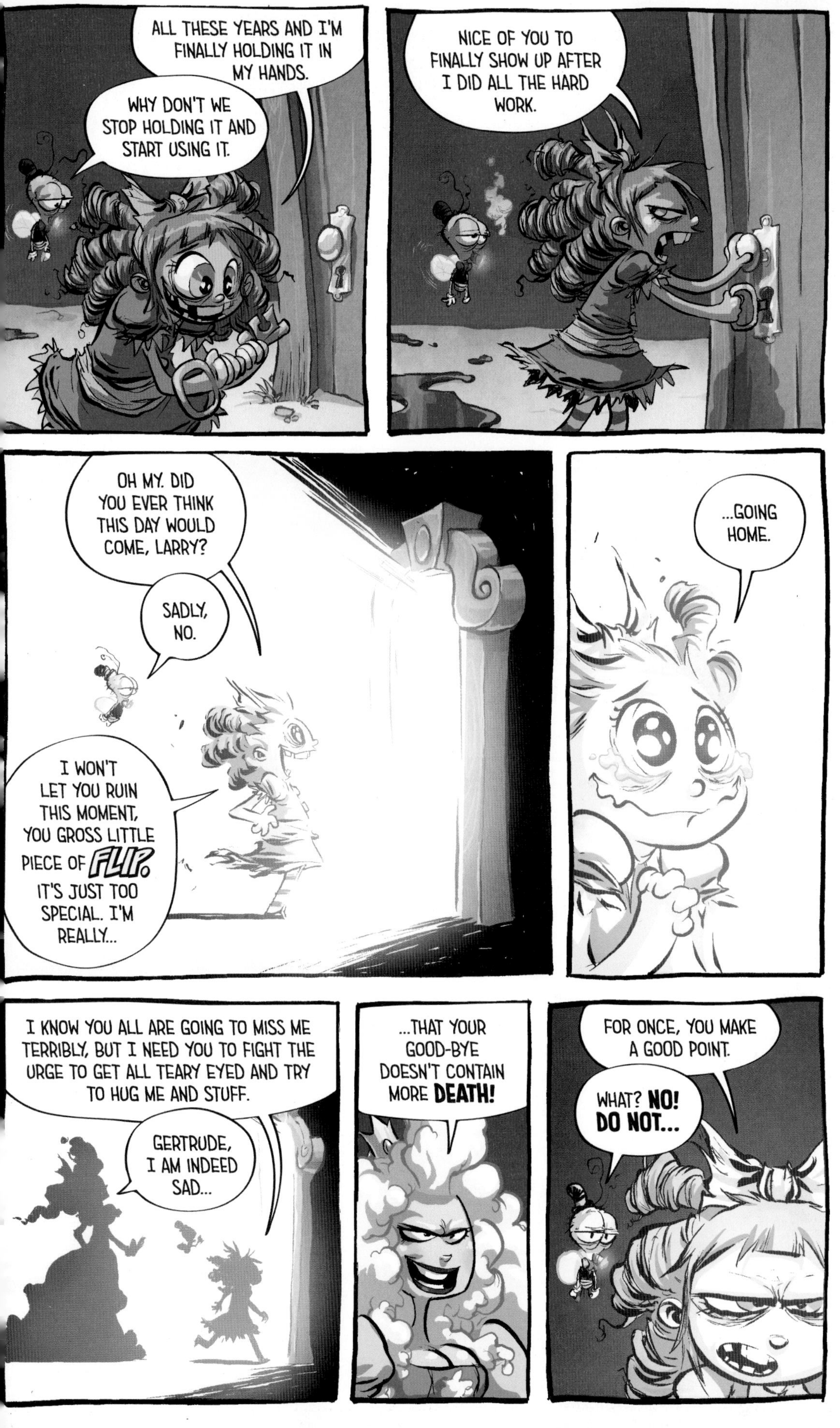
ALL THESE YEARS AND I'M FINALLY HOLDING IT IN MY HANDS.
WHY DON'T WE STOP HOLDING IT AND START USING IT.
NICE OF YOU TO FINALLY SHOW UP AFTER I DID ALL THE HARD WORK.
OH MY. DID YOU EVER THINK THIS DAY WOULD COME, LARRY?
SADLY, NO.
I WON'T LET YOU RUIN THIS MOMENT, YOU GROSS LITTLE PIECE OF FLIP. IT'S JUST TOO SPECIAL. I'M REALLY...
...GOING HOME.
I KNOW YOU ALL ARE GOING TO MISS ME TERRIBLY, BUT I NEED YOU TO FIGHT THE URGE TO GET ALL TEARY EYED AND TRY TO HUG ME AND STUFF.
GERTRUDE, I AM INDEED SAD...
...THAT YOUR GOOD-BYE DOESN'T CONTAIN MORE **DEATH!**
FOR ONCE, YOU MAKE A GOOD POINT.
WHAT? **NO! DO NOT...**

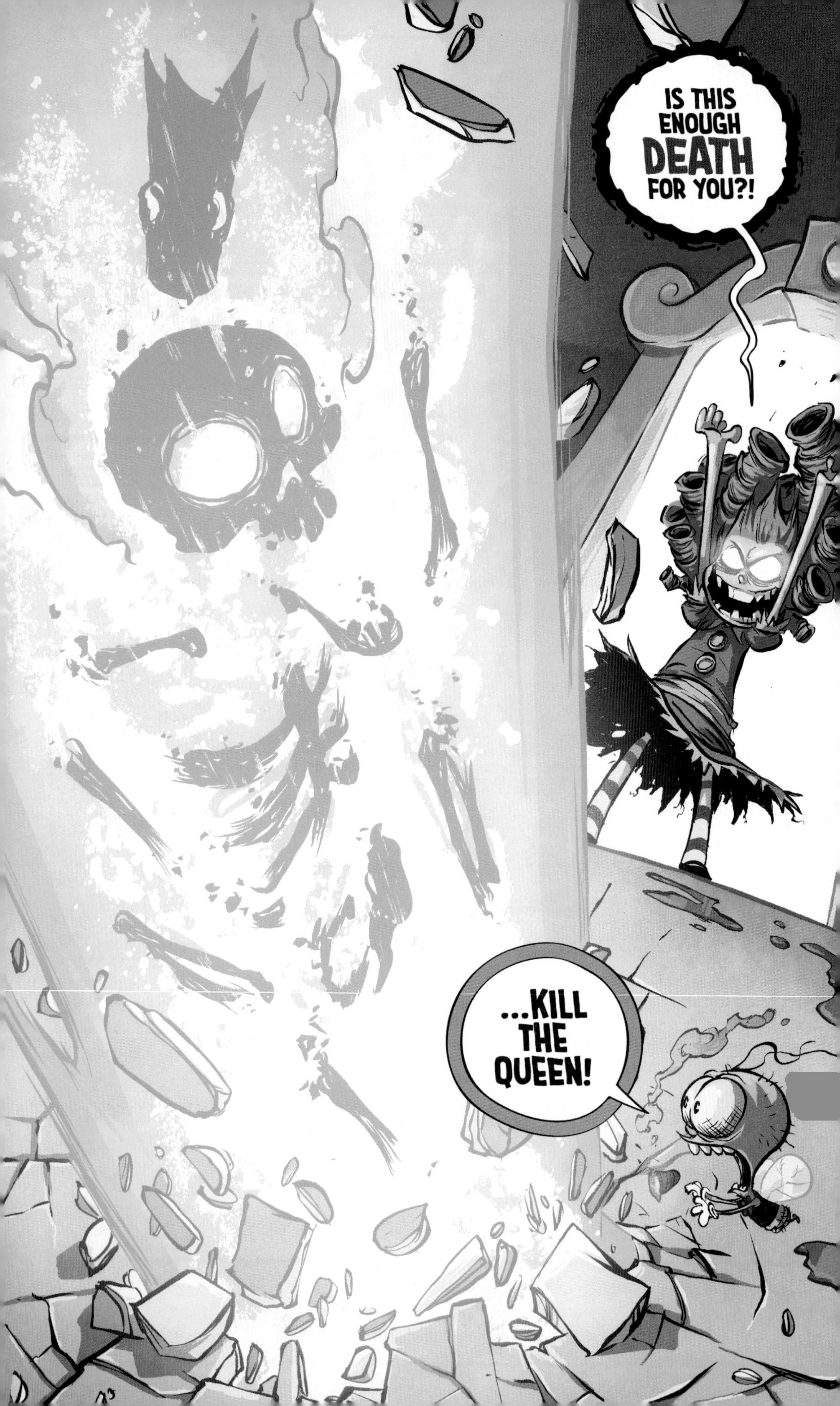
IS THIS ENOUGH DEATH FOR YOU?!
...KILL THE QUEEN!

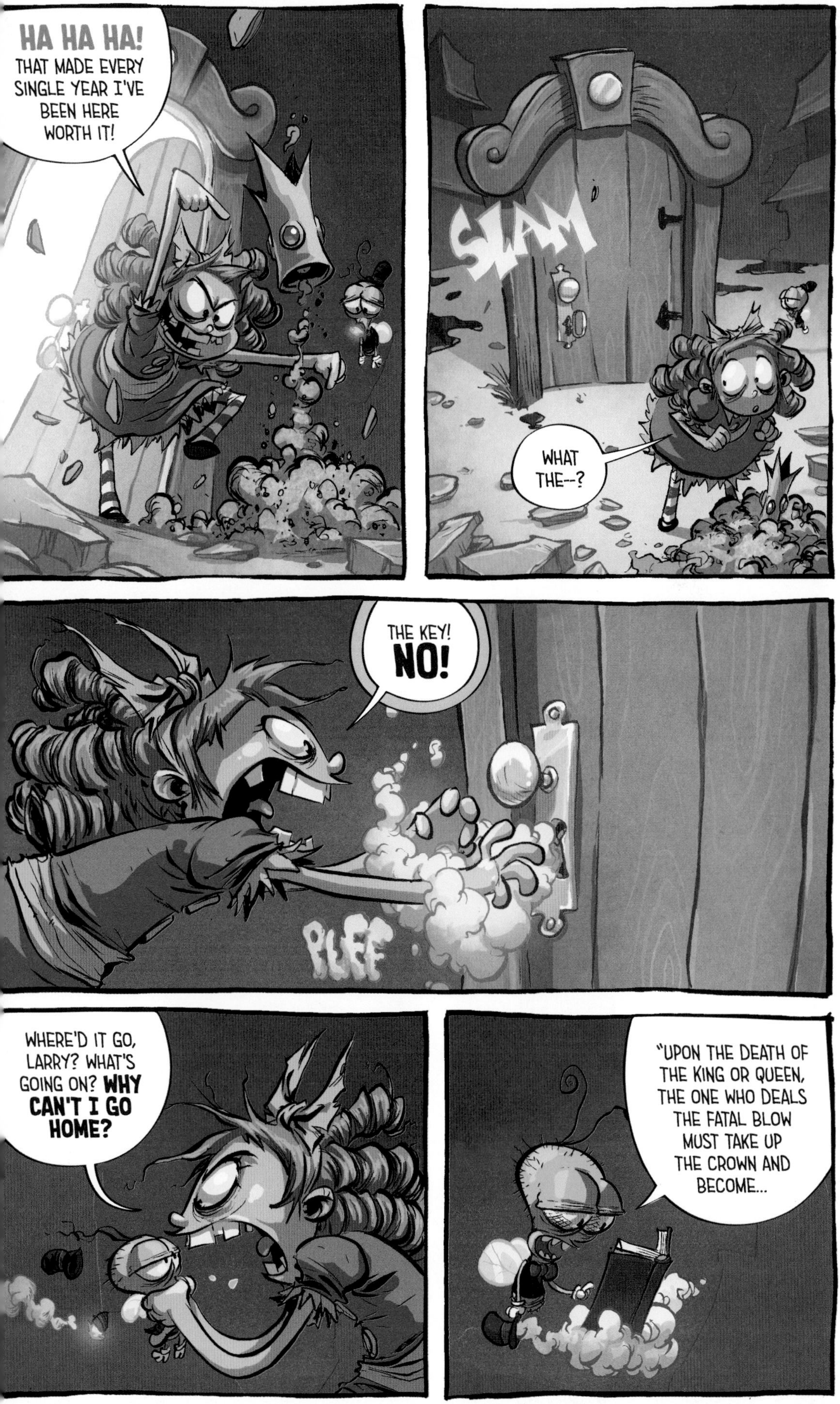
HA HA HA! THAT MADE EVERY SINGLE YEAR I'VE BEEN HERE WORTH IT!
SLAM
WHAT THE--?
THE KEY! NO!
PLEF
WHERE'D IT GO, LARRY? WHAT'S GOING ON? WHY CAN'T I GO HOME?
"UPON THE DEATH OF THE KING OR QUEEN, THE ONE WHO DEALS THE FATAL BLOW MUST TAKE UP THE CROWN AND BECOME...

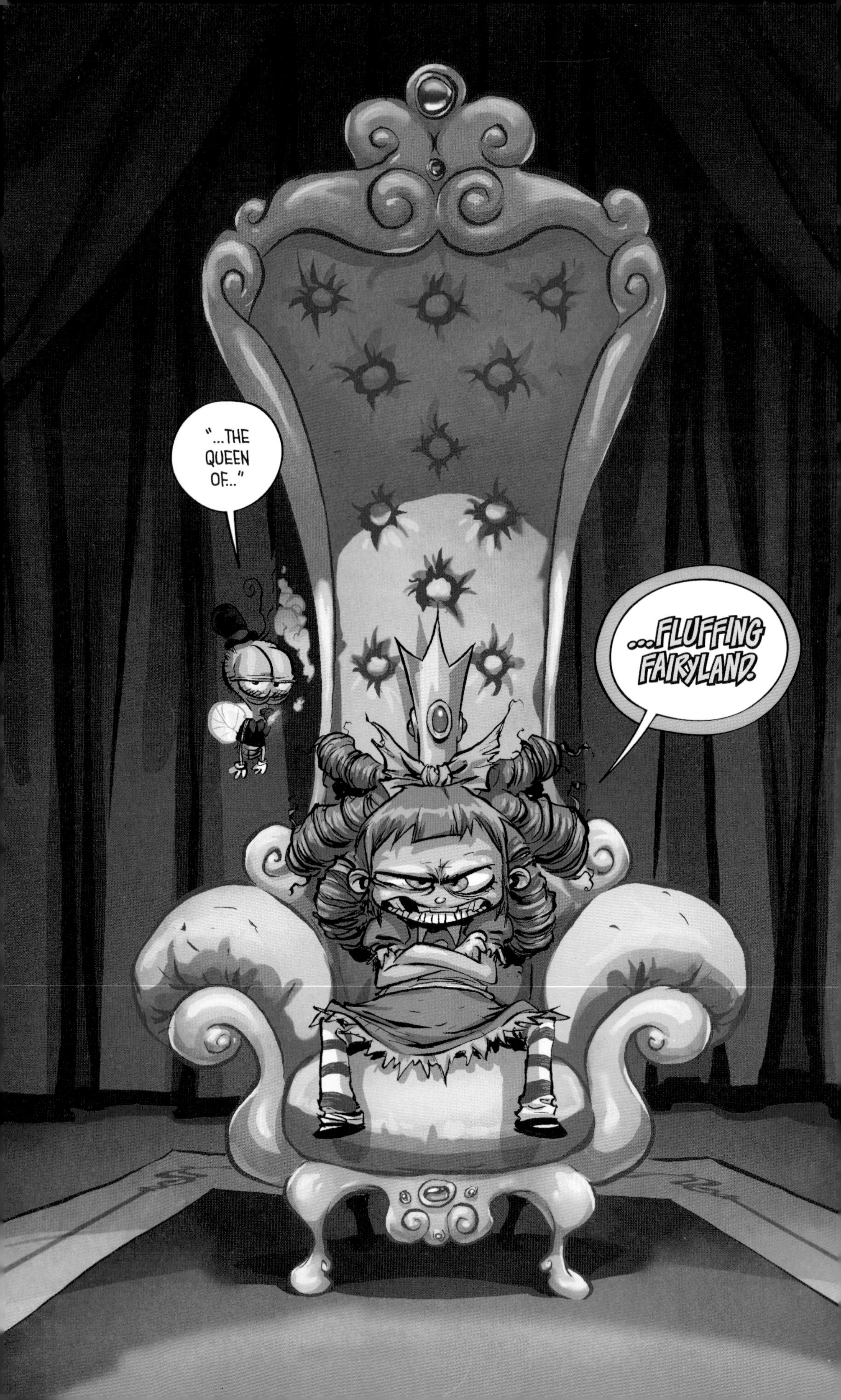
"...THE QUEEN OF..."
...FLUFFING FAIRYLAND.

SKOTTIE YOUNG

...is the New York Times Best Selling cartoonist behind Marvel's WIZARD OF OZ graphic novel adaptations, ROCKET RACCOON and GIANT-SIZE LITTLE MARVEL, as well as illustrating FORTUNATELY, THE MILK with some writer named, NEIL GAIMAN. And in case you have lived in a cave, Skottie has also produced enough Little Marvel variant covers to build a small ranch style home out of them. (Though they are not waterproof so living in said home is not advised.) He currently holds the record for most Eisner Awards won by anyone born in Fairybury, IL. Skottie lives in Central Illinois with his wife, two sons, and two dogs that drive him crazy. (The dogs, not the humans.)

JEAN-FRANCOIS BEAULIEU

...is the acclaimed colorist behind Marvel's WIZARD OF OZ Graphic Novel adaptations, ROCKET RACCOON, GIANT-SIZE LITTLE MARVEL, NEW WARRIORS, NEW X-MEN, and probably other books that Skottie Young didn't draw but since Skottie Young is writing this we'll keep it to mostly Skottie Young books. Okay, fine, INVINCIBLE. Happy? Jean and Skottie have been working together for over a decade. (Which sounds way more epic than saying ten years.) Jean is considered one of the industry's top colorists and also holds the record for most people who don't know how to pronounce his last name. He lives somewhere in the Canadian wilderness with his fiancé, three dogs, nine cats, and an unknown amount of dope robot model kits.

NATE PIEKOS

...is the founder of BLAMBOT.COM, a company with a much cooler name than any of us could probably come up with. Good job, Nate! He has created some of the industry's most popular fonts and has used them to letter comic books for Image Comics (HUCK) Marvel Comics (X-STATIX, X-MEN FIRST CLASS), DC Comics (NEW SUICIDE SQUAD), Dark Horse Comics (FIGHT CLUB 2, UMBRELLA ACADEMY) . . . and all the other companies that end with the word, "Comics". Nate has more guitars in his studio than any other letterer on the planet. (That was not fact checked, but I'm going with it.) He lives in Rhode Island with his wife and the previously mentioned guitars.

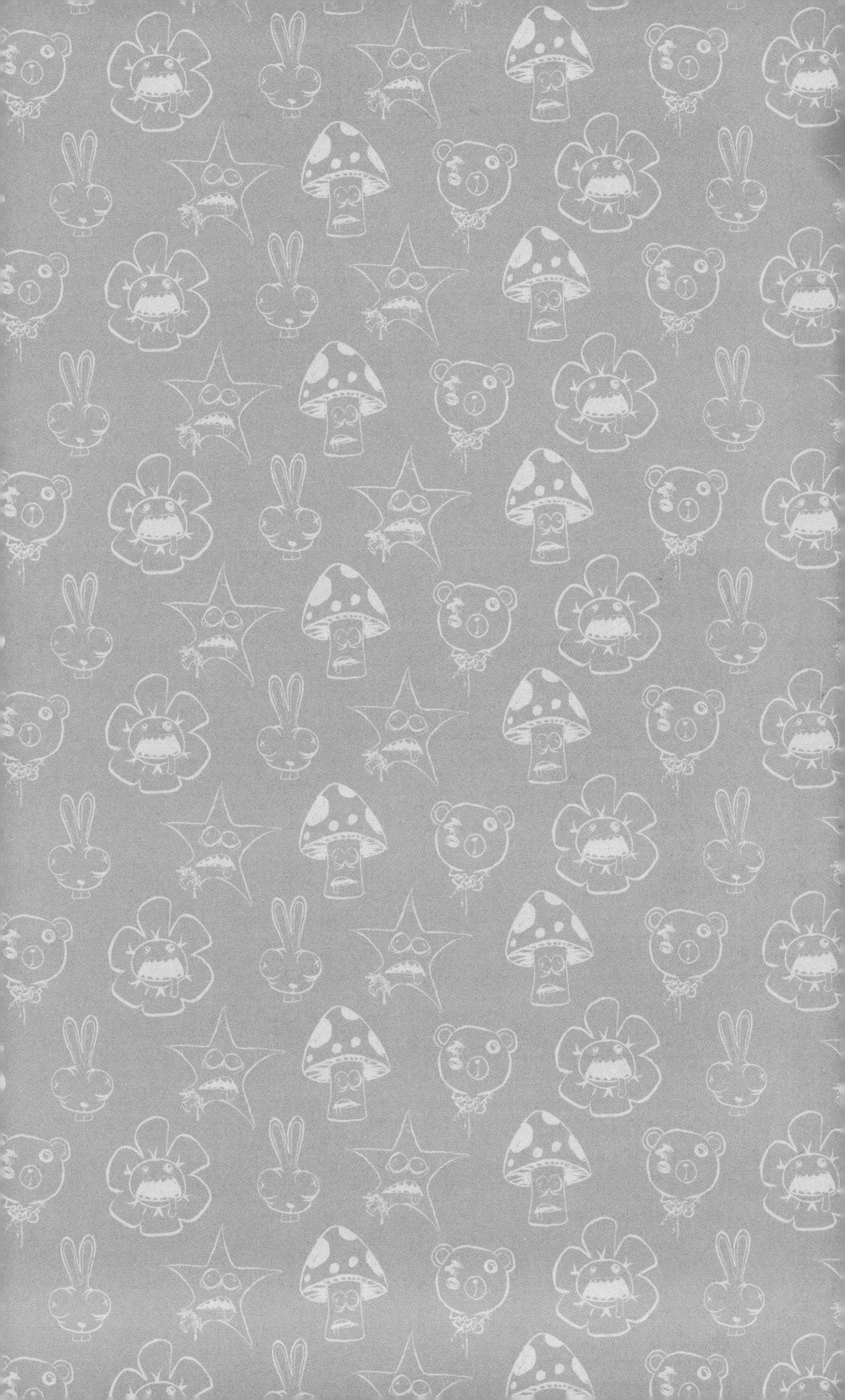